T. S. Stribling (1891—1965)

Best Dr. Poggioli Detective Stories

By
T. S. Stribling

Dover Publications, Inc.
New York

Published in Canada by General Publishing Com-
pany, Ltd., 30 Lesmill Road, Don Mills, Toronto,
Ontario.
Published in the United Kingdom by Constable
and Company, Ltd., 10 Orange Street, London
WC 2.

This Dover edition, first published in 1975, is
a new selection of detective stories by Thomas Sigismund Stribling. With the exception of "Poggioli
and the Fugitive," "The Man in the Shade" and
"The Case of the Button," which originally appeared in *The Saint Mystery Magazine,* the stories
were originally published in *Ellery Queen's Mystery
Magazine.* A new Publisher's Note has been written
especially for the present edition.

International Standard Book Number: 0-486-23227-1
Library of Congress Catalog Card Number: 75-21298

Manufactured in the United States of America
Dover Publications, Inc.
180 Varick Street
New York, N.Y. 10014

Contents

Publisher's Note

Thomas Sigismund Stribling (1891—1965) was born in Clifton, Tennessee, a small town not too far from Oak Ridge and Knoxville. He spent most of his early years here and in Florence, Alabama, both of which locales enter strongly into his fiction. He taught school and practiced law for a short time, then turned to writing as a profession.

Mr. Stribling's first literary success came in 1932 when his novel *The Store* won a Pulitzer Prize. This novel was a component in a trilogy of wide scope — *The Forge, The Store* and *Unfinished Cathedral* — which followed the fortunes of certain individuals in a Southern family through the Civil War, the later Reconstruction, and the 1920's. He also wrote other novels, mostly social in theme, often ironic, about aspects of American life, culture and politics, ending with the fantasy *These Bars of Flesh* in 1938.

Dr. Henry Poggioli, generally recognized as the most proficient of psychological detectives, is identified as a professor at Ohio State University; his chair varies slightly from Psychology to Criminology. The first of his exploits appeared in *Adventure* magazine in 1925 and 1926, at the end of which series Mr. Stribling killed Poggioli spectacularly. The Professor proved so popular, however, that Mr. Stribling resurrected him for several more stories in 1929 and the early 1930's.

The third series of stories about Dr. Poggioli appeared in various detective story magazines between 1945 and 1957, especially in *Ellery Queen's Mystery Magazine*. The fifteen best of these stories have been selected for this volume, which reveals the subtle and ingenious psychologist operating in a variety of climes — the hills of Tennessee, the cities of Florida, and Mexico — against a wide range of crimes and criminals. These stories are unique not only for enlarging the scope of the detective short story but for many penetrating touches and amusing paradoxes.

The Mystery of
the Half-painted House

Twenty-four Acacia Street is naturally across from Twenty-three, where Poggioli and I live. It was a weathered, run-down house, its only prosperous-looking adjunct a royal palm in front. One day somebody started to paint the house an unhealthy yellow, but when he got about half through he broke off work. Poggioli and I expected him, day after day, to come back and finish the job. We finally began speculating on why he had stopped. I said, considering the color of the paint, that perhaps he had bought it as a remnant at some sale, at a very cheap price, and he hadn't bought enough. The sort of house it was, and the kind of man who would live in such a house, suggested a bargain hunter who would buy too little. And certainly he would never find another remnant to match the first one he had purchased. The original mixture must have been a lot of other remnants dumped together by some wholesale house.

One morning I stood on our stoop enjoying the sunshine in the beginning of the hurricane season and I saw a man come out of Twenty-four and start toward the bus stop. He hesitated on his way, and somewhat to my surprise, came across and asked if I were Mr. Poggioli. I told him I wasn't; I was the man who wrote up Professor Poggioli's cases.

"Oh, he's a perfessor. Well, that explains it."

"Explains what?" I asked.

"Why, I heard he's a detective who would jest as soon he'p a criminal git away as he'p the police ketch him, but of course a perfessor would treat ever'body alike."

I drew breath to start a long explanation but I realized it would do no good. "How long have you lived here?" I asked with some vague notion of getting around to the puzzle of the paint.

The man drew a disappointed breath. "Not long. I come here to enjoy the advantages of a big city."

"Where did you come from?"

"Wackyjacky."

"Where is Wackyjacky?"

"Up Route Number 'leven, off State Road sixty-two, then county road thirty-four. You are right shore you ain't the perfessor?"

"You wanted to see him?"

"Well . . . no-o . . . not now."

Once more I gave up the point. As he continued simply standing there, in the fashion of folk from Wackyjacky, I had to say something else. It was one of those conversations which you had to start over again in order to bring it to a stop.

"Who you going to vote for — for the city council?" I asked.

"I'm goin' to vote for somebody who ain't on the council!" stated my neighbor belligerently.

"Sure," I agreed, "everybody does that, but the trouble is, when you vote for a man who is not on the council, and he gets elected, he becomes just a councilman like all the others. You see, it puts you back right where you started."

My visitor seemed surprised. "That is a fact, ain't it? I hadn't thought of that. There ort to be some way for us voters to express ourse'ves on that point, too."

"I don't suppose there is any way. The best we can do is to vote against all the candidates we know."

"Well, there's the bus. I gotta run."

"What do you do for a living?"

"I'm a barber." And he ran for his bus.

I mentioned the incident to Poggioli later. I said I had solved the paint problem on the house across the street. The man had bought a small amount of paint to retouch his barber pole, but it was the wrong color — so he had used it on his house.

Poggioli didn't even bother to dismiss my theory. "Why did he cross the street and speak to you?"

"He thought I was you."

"I wonder what sort of trouble he was in."

"He said he had heard you would just as soon help a criminal as help the police."

"You didn't learn what he had done?"

"I wanted to find out about the paint, but couldn't quite direct the conversation. . . ."

"The paint," caught up Poggioli, "of course, the paint! I wonder what connection that could possibly have with crime?"

"Why, none," I said, "how could paint possibly . . ."

"I don't know. That was the point I was pondering."

I told Poggioli that if he wanted to see the barber for himself, he would probably find him at the political rally that evening — he seemed to me the sort of man who attended those affairs. Of course, the criminologist and I normally never went to such meetings. We were of the intellectual aristocratic class who have nothing to do with politics, and the results are very happy indeed, because it places such interesting men in charge of our public affairs. On account of our neighbor, however, we broke our rule and went along to the rally. And we immediately regretted it.

The rally was for Bill Hinckman, candidate to succeed himself on the city council. There were free hamburgers, hot dogs and coffee, a singer from the night clubs who had a nightclub voice, and a local woman singer who had no voice at all. The price we paid for this food and entertainment was to listen to Bill Hinckman's account of how he had built up the city of Tiamara from nothing to whatever it was during his ten terms of office, and how he was going to triple the capital and population if he were elected to another term.

Nobody really listened to the speaker. Nobody expected people to listen, not even Hinckman. The crowd blinked at the stars and the moon which had risen out of the sea and said, "Doesn't look like we're going to have a hurricane, does it?" Somebody else said, "I can't figure out how a hurricane blows a hundred miles an hour but don't travel but ten miles an hour." A man who claimed to understand this riddle explained it to everybody within hearing, all the while Hinckman was making his speech.

In the midst of this mental absenteeism somebody under the flood-lights near the speaker's stand yelled out, "Hinckman, whyn't you quit throwing bouquets at yourself and give us the lowdown on the Sullivan Development Deal! Didn't Jack Spate slip you fifty grand to see it through?"

Instantly an outcry arose against the heckler. Everybody eating Hinckman's free hamburgers felt a certain loyalty towards him. Voices arose: "Kick that man out! Put Bud Simmons out of here! He ain't a Hinckman man, chase him!"

A movement stirred in the audience to do this and Mr. Simmons's voice arose in the tumult, insisting he had the right of free speech.

"Yes, but not while eatin' Bill Hinckman's chow! Simmons, you go over to Nick Howard's rally where you belong — don't come here tryin' to break up our candidate's speech!"

Why they wanted it to go on when no one was listening was obscure, but they did. At this point Bill Hinckman himself lifted a generous and statesmanlike voice from the speaker's stand.

"Let the man say his say. If I've made a mistake, I want it brought out before my constituents. The only way I can ever hope to rise to finer and higher service is to listen to public criticism!"

A great roar of applause broke out at this. Mr. Hinckman waited in gratification until it died down and then resumed his account of how he had made Tiamara what it was. The crowd was about to return to its hot dogs and hamburgers when another voice, a subdued voice, asked the speaker a question.

The orator paused and leaned over. "How's that? A little louder, my friend."

The man had one of those voices which never seem to become audible in a crowd. Finally Hinckman understood and repeated the question aloud to satisfy the curiosity of his audience. "He wants me to have the city council make it illegal for men to shave themselves at home, or for one member of a family to cut another member's hair or give another member a permanent."

An outburst of laughter greeted this. Mr. Hinckman held up a restraining hand. "Don't laugh, don't make fun. Wisdom comes from many sources, my friends. One part of the gentleman's suggestion is already a regulation in this city. Women are not allowed to give each other permanents. Of course, they still do, but it's against the city ordinances. This man evidently is a barber. He pays a license to run his shop; he pays state tax, county tax, and city tax to keep in business. So the state, county, and city owe him protection. Who's against him? Why, the plutocratic Northern safety-razor manufacturers — that's who's against him, that's who's ruining this honest man's trade! Ladies and gentlemen, I'm going to back this man's request to the limit of my ability. Who will benefit? All of us. A shave by an old-fashioned straight razor in the hands of a barber is better, smoother, and more social than any hunting of harassed hairs by a half-clad man in a bathroom. Yes, I'm all for this gentleman's suggestion — for home industry! I'll back such a measure to the limit, even if I have to lose every vote in the precinct!"

More cheering and laughter. These two interruptions were all the crowd had heard of Mr. Hinckman's speech. A little later the refreshments gave out and the rally ended. A few local bigwigs came up to congratulate the speaker on his "effort." There is always that unconscious touch of realism in the praise of local men for their local politicians. They never congratulate their bellwether on his oration, but on his "effort."

On our way back to the apartment I sympathized with Hinckman for being heckled by Bud Simmons about the Sullivan property deal. What made it particularly shameful was that every man at the rally knew that it was true. Hinckman had been in on that deal.

Poggioli said, "Do you think that Simmons really heckled Hinckman?"

I was amazed. "Why, I heard and saw him do it."

"But didn't you also hear Hinckman's answer?"

"Yes, very smooth — very urbane and statesmanlike."

"And what influence will that have on the voters?"

"Well . . . they thought Hinckman was a . . . a generous and tolerant man, passing over an insult like that."

"Let me analyze exactly what it will do. They all knew that Hinckman was in on the Sullivan deal and they all held it against him. But when they think of the Sullivan deal now, they will also think how generous and tolerant Hinckman is, for he has now attached those riders to the accusation against him."

"Just what are you getting at, Poggioli? The first thing I know, you'll be claiming Hinckman *asked* Simmons to heckle him."

"Surely you wouldn't think that."

I didn't know whether Poggioli was being sarcastic or not. I never know.

We got out of our jitney about two blocks from home and walked the rest of the way. The night was balmy, but the stars were faintly dim. A slight breeze set from the North. The hurricane, when it finally came, would approach from the South or Southwest. Always there is a faint wind against a coming hurricane, as if it were trying to push the terror back.

At some distance ahead of us in the street moved a solitary man. He turned into Twenty-four, across from our house. Suddenly I spoke up: "That was our barber — he must have been the man who asked Hinckman to pass a law against home barbering."

"I wonder why he painted half his house, then quit," said Poggioli.

The coming of a hurricane is an interesting feature of Tiamara life. The newspapers print maps of its whereabouts and of its direction of travel for days before it arrives. All windows are boarded up. Everybody buys food that needs no cooking, because all during the storm the electricity will be shut off. The newspapers also print detailed directions of what to do: everyone must leave a window open on the lee side of your home so that your house will not explode when the low-pressure center of the hurricane arrives.

There is little use giving here a description of the storm that passed over us at last. It looked like a gray hurtling wall of wind which you could actually see, and it sounded like a banshee. You knew when night came, but not when it was day. The most sinister thing about it was the eye of the storm: its center — a dead calm which crept along at about ten miles an hour. All the rest was a dizzy dance around this slowly moving calm. It was fatal to get into the eye of the storm, because the other arc of the hurricane, blowing in the opposite direction, would sweep you away. In the eye of one storm hundreds of motorists thought the hurricane was over and tried to get back to the city along the causeway from the strand; they were all blown into the sea. . . .

When this menacing calm surrounded us, Poggioli and I remained indoors. But a strange thing happened. Somewhere on the outside we heard a noise like the backfiring of a motor, and we wondered what insane man was driving a car in the eye of the storm. Sometime later, the eye passed over and the wind leaped at once to hurricane velocity, in the reverse direction from which it had just been blowing.

The next morning everything was over and the sun was shining. Sand drifts, blown from the beaches, choked the streets. Drifts of splintered glass lay in the business districts where shop windows had been shivered. Only one constructive thing had happened during the storm and that was a very odd one: Twenty-four Acacia Street, across from our apartment, had been completely painted!

Poggioli and I looked at it and decided that it must have been finished before the storm began, and that we simply had not noticed it before. That was all we could think.

After a big hurricane I, personally, have rather lean pickings. I mean in the matter of crimes. Of course, there is looting in the wrecked stores and houses, but there are no great and impressive crimes. It is as if the violence of nature had abashed the violence of men. It was therefore with professional relief that I saw in our morning paper, on the third day after the storm, the headlines of a murder.

I unfolded my *Times,* then stopped dead. William J. Hinckman had been assassinated. The veteran councilman had been shot last night, on the way home from his office. He had died of three bullets from a Luger pistol. No clue. The paper said Bill Hinckman had many political and professional opponents, but never, so far as anyone knew, a personal enemy. All the municipal organizations would attend Hinckman's funeral. Services would be held at the First Church of Tiamara. Five councilmen and the Mayor would be pallbearers. The city police would furnish a guard of honor.

I took the paper in to Poggioli. I had seen Hinckman only once — at the political rally; but I felt as if I had lost a friend — someone who, if I were in trouble, would promise me anything.

I told Poggioli what I thought had happened: Hinckman had been shot by one of his political opponents.

"Not his personal enemy?"

"No, he had none."

"Then it ought to be easy to find the murderer."

"Why?"

"Because you have a complete list of his opponents. Just look over the list, pick out the one who is interested in collecting guns, and arrest him for shooting Hinckman with his Luger."

"You are joking, Poggioli!" — for I never was sure when he was or wasn't.

"No, a prominent man who would shoot another prominent man with an old Luger pistol, a readily identifiable weapon, evidently expects to be found out and plans to clear himself with a shrewd lawyer. No, I would say some very wealthy man committed that murder — someone who can give his name and address to the police and laugh at the law."

That was an astonishing deduction just to come from a Luger. . . .

I expected Gebhardt of the *Times* to visit us and have a powwow with Poggioli over something or other he had discovered, but Gebhardt did not come. I mentioned the fact to Poggioli, saying, "You were right about a rich man committing the murder — the papers are going to hush it up."

"How do you figure that?" he asked, because Poggioli often shifts to the opposite view just as soon as I agree with him.

"Because Gebhardt hasn't come to see you. The papers don't want to know who killed Hinckman."

"That is something I hadn't thought of. . . . So it was a very wealthy man, a political opponent."

A moment later our doorbell rang.

Under the circumstances it gave me quite a start. "Gebhardt!" I said. "Now we'll get the undercover story" — and I hurried to the door.

I opened the shutter with a question on my lips, then came to a stop. On the stoop was a man I had seen before but whose name slipped my memory. I shook his hand, invited him in, and told him I had just been thinking about him — I find that the best thing to say to anyone whose name I can't remember.

Our caller looked at me antagonistically. "So you believe I did it?"

"Why should I think that?" I said, groping for his identity.

"Because you were thinking about me."

Then I knew he was speaking of Hinckman's murder and must be the murderer — "a guilty conscience needs no accuser." At the same moment I suddenly remembered him. "No, no, I don't think that at all, Mr. Simmons. If you were the murderer you would never come to see Professor Poggioli."

"Why not?"

"Because he would prove you guilty. No, you would stay just as far away from Poggioli as you possibly could."

"Yes, I get your point. Now, could I see Mr. Poggioli?"

"Sure, come on in."

I went in with him and would have introduced him to Poggioli, but naturally Poggioli remembered him at once.

"You are the Mr. Simmons who made a few remarks at the political rally, and you have come to see me about the murder of your friend."

"Friend? Bill really was my friend, but why do you say he was my friend?"

"Because you heckled him the night of his rally."

Simmons drew a breath of great relief. "Well, I declare . . . so you saw through that. . . . Yes, we really were friends. Bill was worried about the Sullivan scandal. I said to him, I said, 'Bill, if you'll let me bring it up at one of your meetings and if you pass over it like the gentleman you are, it'll create a mighty good impression among the voters.'"

"So you've come to me to help find his murderer?"

"No, not that at all. You see, nobody else understands that my heckling at the rally was a friendly act. The people think Bill and I were enemies. So they've picked me to hang the murder on — I'm now out on bail. So I came here to ask you not to find Bill's murderer, but to prove I didn't do it."

Poggioli looked at our visitor. "Of all the ridiculous accusations . . ."

"Look here, why don't you go to the Chief of Police and tell him that my heckling was a favor to Bill?"

"No, if he didn't see that at once he never will. Do you have any other evidence of your friendship with Hinckman?"

"Well, ye-e-es, as a matter of fact I have."

"But you don't want to show it?"

"I'd rather not. . . . In fact, I won't show it no matter what they do to me."

"Then it involves others?"

"How did you know that?"

"Because you value this thing, whatever it is, more than you do your own life. That's bound to involve other men . . . or women."

"Men," said Simmons.

"We'll drop the point," said Poggioli.

"I don't mind telling you personally," said Mr. Simmons, "but I don't want it brought up before any court."

Poggioli lifted an agreeable hand and Mr. Simmons reached in his pocket and drew out a sheaf of papers. He riffled through them, selected one, and handed it to the criminologist. I moved about and looked over Poggioli's shoulder. It was a cancelled check marked *Paid,* made out to William J. Hinckman in the sum of $56,784.16.

Poggioli studied the check. "You paid him this for his influence on the City Council. You made it this uneven amount to give it the appearance of some sort of ordinary business deal."

"Sure."

"But I understood at the political rally that you were backing Nick Howard?"

"I was and am, Mr. Poggioli. Here's my check to Nick." He flipped through and produced another cancelled check. "I always back all of 'em — all of 'em who can win. It's a fair and square deal — all the boys know about it. I tell 'em somebody's got to foot you boys' bills — might as well be me. If each one of you goes out an' gets a different backer, most of the backers will have to lose; then the whole bunch of you will finally run out of angels. But if you all come to me, no matter who wins, I'll make it back. Next election, come to me and I'll back you all again."

"It sounds logical," said Poggioli.

"Sure, it's politics."

"Look here, putting these tokens of friendship aside, couldn't you prove an alibi for the night your friend was killed?"

"Oh, sure — easy."

"Then let's do that."

Mr. Simmons shook his head. "No, if I'd been willing to establish an alibi, my lawyer could have done that for me."

"Why do you object to an alibi?"

"Why, Mr. Poggioli, if I should bring into court the men I was with and prove where we were and what we were doing on the night of the murder, it would raise twice as much stink as the murder itself."

Poggioli nodded. "I see. I should have thought of that." He relapsed into reflection again. "Mr. Simmons, I see one slight chance of clearing you — if the court would accept it."

"What's that?"

"The Luger pistol the deceased was killed with. No man in your position, associating with men who use only tommyguns and the newest automatics, would use an old-fashioned Luger to . . ."

"Mr. Poggioli, I'm sorry, but I do own some Luger pistols."

"You do!"

"Yes, I'm a collector of guns. I have a few Lugers in my collection."

Poggioli thought this over. "All right," he said, "Hinckman was shot with a Luger and you own a few Lugers. We will simply exonerate you on those grounds."

"How're you going to do it?"

"Let's ride over to the police station and you'll see."

We walked outside, got into Simmons's car, and he directed his chauffeur to the police station. When we reached the place, Poggioli explained to Lieutenant Briggs of the homicide squad what he wanted. He wanted Briggs to go with us to the Simmons home, take all the Lugers in the Simmons collection, bring them back to headquarters, and test them ballistically against the bullets that killed Hinckman. If the test was negative, it would prove Simmons was not the murderer.

"He might have had still another Luger," protested Briggs.

"I keep a record of every Luger I buy," said Simmons.

"It's flimsy," said Briggs; "it's a negative proof."

"So's an alibi. Lieutenant, I thought of this plan and came straight to you with it from my own residence on Acacia Street. Simmons has had no chance to arrange or hide or change anything in his collection. If he had suggested the idea, I would agree it smelled of trickery. But it's my plan."

This impressed Briggs sufficiently to get him into our car and go to Simmons's home. I won't pause to describe Simmons's collection of antique guns. Some of them had interesting histories. He had, for example, the gun that killed President McKinley, the old-fashioned forty-one caliber weapon that shot Theodore Roosevelt while he was making a speech — the time when, even with a bullet wound in him, he would not stop speaking.

He had three World War I Lugers in his collection, and these Briggs took back to headquarters to test ballistically. The Lieutenant was quite skeptical. As he loaded and fired the three guns, he said to Poggioli, "I'm doing this purely out of respect for you, Professor Poggioli. It won't serve any purpose at all." He took the three bullets and compared them with one of the missiles that killed Hinckman. "No purpose at all, Poggioli. No sane murderer is going to . . ." Here he stopped, looked up from his microscope at Poggioli and then at Simmons. "This gun did it," he said, touching the middle Luger.

Simmons stared at his own pistol. "This is one heck of a note!"

Poggioli, on the contrary, was delighted. For once in his life he showed enthusiasm. "This is magnificent! It's extraordinary luck. I don't believe in luck, I believe in logic, but do you generally have this kind of luck, Mr. Simmons?"

"Yes, it seems like I do," growled Simmons, looking at his gun.

Briggs interrupted. "Professor Poggioli, would you mind explaining to me, just as a friend, what the applause is all about?"

"Why, it's simple, Lieutenant. It establishes Simmons's innocence beyond question. Would any sane murderer bring his weapon to the police for examination?"

"But that's his pistol and it came out of his own collection!"

"Certainly it's his pistol, but if he had known it was the one that killed Hinckman, he wouldn't have brought it to you. It's a psychological proof, Lieutenant Briggs, and a very clear and simple one."

"Well . . . what happened?"

"The murderer, whoever he was, was a very clever man. He shot Hinckman and then wanted to hide his weapon. He knew that Simmons collected guns. So he simply sold it to Mr. Simmons! Of course, he did not foresee that Simmons would be suspected and that his guns would be tested ballistically. Nobody could have foreseen that. He thought he had buried his gun where it would never be suspected — in a rich man's gun collection. Only a very bad break in luck spoiled his scheme. Simmons himself was suspected of the murder. That's why I inquired of Simmons if he is habitually lucky. You see, luck has never been scientifically investigated. I thought I would take the lives of a hundred lucky men . . ."

"Wait just a moment, Professor Poggioli! Mr. Simmons here isn't completely out of danger because he owns the gun that killed Hinckman."

"Practically, Lieutenant. Mr. Simmons, when did you buy this Luger?"

The politician referred to a list he had with him. "Why, only three days ago. That does confirm —"

"Wait a moment, gentlemen!" interrupted Briggs. "That's evidence for the jury — you needn't practice it before me. Now, Poggioli, no one could possibly have *made up* a defense like this . . . could they, Poggioli?"

"You have known me for a long time, Briggs. Have I ever made up anything?"

"No, you haven't, but Simmons is the wealthiest man you ever worked for, Poggioli. I'm speaking frankly, as a police officer."

The great criminologist was offended, as he had a right to be. His voice took on a different tone.

"Simmons, whom did you buy this Luger from?"

"I don't know the man."

"Complete stranger?"

"Not quite . . . I . . . I'm trying to think now. . . . I had seen him somewhere before, but I had never heard his name."

"You didn't ask his name?" suggested Briggs skeptically.

"Lieutenant Briggs, I never ask the name of anybody who is doing business with me."

"But you would have remembered his name if you had ever heard it?"

"Oh, yes, I never forget a name or a face."

"This man's face — you say you had seen it before?" probed Poggioli.

"Yes, I'm sure I did."

"In one of your night clubs, possibly?"

"Mm — mm . . . no-o . . . no."

"Doesn't the face associate itself with anything at all in your mind?"

Mr. Simmons gave a single dry click of laughter. "Yes, it does, Mr. Poggioli."

"With what?"

"With Hinckman."

Poggioli thought that over, then said, "That is remembering in a kind of circle. You are in trouble over Hinckman; the man's face reminds you of Hinckman. That's what I would call a memory induced after the fact."

"Maybe so," agreed Simmons emptily, "but it's all I can think of about this man."

"Well, the thing for me to do is to find that man," said Poggioli. "With your luck, Mr. Simmons — and I really must investigate this matter of luck — with your luck it won't be too hard to find him."

We were about to leave the police station when Briggs interrupted. "I'll just keep this middle Luger as evidence, Mr. Simmons."

"Certainly, certainly."

"And just wait a moment here until I can get in touch with Judge Abbott, to see if he wants to make your bail bond larger."

This meant that Simmons would not be able to leave police headquarters with us. He said, "Look here, Mr. Poggioli, I know you can find that man."

"Certainly. In a pinch we can trace the ownership of the gun — it only goes back to the first World War." That, I thought, was whistling in the dark.

"Well, I have here another check, Mr. Poggioli. I know you don't usually accept fees for your services. You do it for . . . shall we say, for the sake of art? I, too, admire art and artists. So I want you to take this check, and if you have any pet art charity you'd like to help — say, the Metropolitan Opera Company in New York or the Boston Symphony Orchestra — they are all deserving charities and always in the red — you can give it to one of them."

We left Poggioli's wealthy client at the police station and his chauffeur drove us home. The chauffeur was blasé. He said, "Bud'll get out. He'll luck out somehow. If you need anything from me, Mr. Poggioli, ring up Pineapple 23001."

Mr. Simmons's man drove away. We stood looking at our drab thoroughfare. The only flourishing thing on it was the royal palm across the street. Then I noticed something else. "Look," I said, "the man who finished painting his house has moved out and left it."

Poggioli asked me how I knew. I pointed out that the window blinds were gone and the door looked permanently shut.

Poggioli began to make fun of me, as usual — a door looking permanently shut! — but somehow it did look that way.

"You've got a better proof than that," said my friend. "That sign stuck on the palm — I imagine it's a *For Rent* card. So that's the answer: the man finished painting in order to rent his house."

"He was the owner," I said.

"No, he was only the tenant. The owner would have had to paint it all over at once to attract an occupant, but a tenant could have painted part of it, and lived in it; then when he wanted to sublease, he would be forced to finish the job."

I started walking over to see if Poggioli was right. "Why didn't he finish it in the first place?"

"That's the real mystery of this whole situation — the only mystery. A murder is never a mystery. It is committed because somebody hates somebody, or wants somebody out of the way. Exactly who did it is a problem, but it's no mystery. But this house — half-painted, then painted and deserted — that's a real mystery."

By this time we were across the street. Sure enough, the card on the palm was a *For Rent* sign. It was home-made, and read:

Anybody wanting to sublease this property inquare of B. Beshears, War Veterans Building, Wackyjacky. Directions how to git there. Take Number eleven to State road 62. Go west 34 mi. Take LaRue County Road 5. North ten and a half miles to Wackyjacky. First come first served.

Poggioli stood reading the sign slowly, pulling at his bluish chin. "That's clearly our man," he said at length, "but I still don't see why he didn't finish painting his house in the first place."

I recovered from my shock. "Our man!" I cried. "What do you mean . . . our man!"

"The man who murdered Hinckman, of course."

"Why do you think he is . . ."

"Because he is a war veteran. He'd have a Luger that he brought back from Germany as a souvenir. . . . But why should he finish painting his house and then run off and leave it . . . and why did he first paint it halfway and then stop?"

"If he really is the murderer, he ran off because he committed the murder," I said.

"Very silly of him. If he had stayed here and had not written his Veterans Building address, I would never have suspected him."

"He didn't know . . ."

"No, certainly not . . . it's just a stroke of luck. Well, we've got to run over to Wackyjacky, look up Mr. Beshears, and find out why he painted half of his house and quit, then painted the other half and went away."

"Aren't you going to find out why he killed Hinckman?"

"I imagine that will come out, but it is not the important part of the mystery."

I could but admire the strict logic of Poggioli's brain. We called up Simmons's chauffeur at Pineapple 23001, and had him come and take us over to Wackyjacky, in LaRue County. Wackyjacky has two stores, a post office, a pool room, and the War Veterans Building. On the building was a home-made sign: *Temporary Barber Shop of B. Beshears.* Inside was another notice: *Shaves — 15 cts. Haircuts — 25 cts. Scalp treatment for falling hair, not guaranteed — 20 cts.*

Mr. Beshears was cutting a small boy's hair as we went in.

The boy twisted around and looked at us out of the corner of his eyes, but Mr. Beshears paid no attention to us. We sat down to wait. As I looked at his price list again, the thought came to me: if we were wise, we would get haircuts, not mention the murder, then turn around and go back to Tiamara. It seemed against the public welfare to arrest a barber who gave twenty-five cent haircuts for murdering a politician.

After a space Beshears noticed us and recognized me. "So you seen my notice on the palm!" he exclaimed.

"Yes, I did. Those prices up there — are they your regular prices?"

"They are here. Of course they wasn't in Tiamara. You ain't allowed to charge low prices in Tiamara. You got to charge the standard high prices even if you kain't git no work at the high prices. I could 'a' done a big business in Tiamara at reasonable prices . . . but you-all come here to see about rentin' my house, you all are interested in that?"

"Yes, we are," said Poggioli. "Were you the one who painted it?"

The barber gave a snort of sardonic laughter. "An' did I have a time paintin' it. Got it half-done and they come up an' stopped me."

"Who?"

"Officers with city regulations. Said I couldn't use no blowgun paint bresh, hit painted too quick. I told him I had to paint quick, I had no time for a reg'lar bresh. I was a barber by trade. 'Then,' says he, 'you kain't paint atall.' 'Why kain't I paint atall?' says I. 'Because you ain't a painter by trade, says he, 'it's aginst regulations.' 'Then what am I goin' to do about this job?' I ast. 'I haff to finish hit.' 'No, you don't,' says he, 'you haff to quit.' So I quit. But when I wanted to leave the city I knowed I'd never be able to sublease hit half-painted.

"I didn't have no money to har nobody, so I fin'ly painted her up myse'f, stuck up my sign an' come home."

"But when did you finish painting without anybody stopping you?" asked Poggioli.

"You'd never guess, gen'men, you'd never guess." Mr. Beshears made a pleased gesture with his scissors, "It was durin' the eye of the storm. Quiet as a lamb, not a soul stirrin', moon shinin'. I was born and brought up in this state. I knowed I had enough time in the eye of the storm to finish paintin'. I been in dozens of hurricanes. So I finished it up, stuck up my sign when the blow was over an' come home."

So that was the mystery of the half-painted house. The whole thing was solved. I said, "Well, Poggioli, let's get twenty-five cent haircuts and go home."

But Poggioli said, "Why did you sell your Luger to Simmons?"

"Well, I had to have money to git home on. I inquared aroun' and found out he paid the best prices. I was broke. Y'see, they charge two dollars for a haircut in Tiamara but I didn't git many customers. They wasn't enough for all of us. It seemed to me the city needed another reguhlation; instead of stoppin' private paintin', stop private shavin'. Make it illegal for a man to shave hise'f. Make him patronize his barber. . . ."

Poggioli suddenly remembered. "Oh, yes, you are the man who advocated such a law at Hinckman's rally?"

"Yeh, an' he promised he'd pass it for me. . . ."

"Then why did you take your Luger and kill him?"

Mr. Beshears stopped clipping the boy's head.

"You ast me that?"

"Yes, I ask you that. Why?"

"I'll tell you. I thought Hinckman was goin' to pass that reguhlation for me. I mentioned it to some of my barber frien's. They laughed at me just like the crowd laughed at me. Then I knowed he was one of them politicians that wasn't goin' to do nothin' he promised and do ever'thing he didn't promise. It made me mad. He had made all kinds of reguhlations aginst me and none for me. I couldn't paint my house. I couldn't reduce my prices on haircuts and shaves in Tiamara low enough to git no work, reducin' wasn't allowed. I had to starve on two-dollar haircuts where I could have lived on fifty-cent uns. I decided to sell my Luger — it was all I had left — and go home, but I decided to use it first jest as an American citizen's protest aginst city politicians." He came to a close, resumed his clipping on the small boy's head. "What are you-all goin' to do about it?"

"Well, as for me, Mr. Beshears," said Poggioli, "I'm going to mail a certain check to the Metropolitan Opera Company of New York City . . . but first I'll take a haircut."

The Mystery of
the Chief of Police

In his room on the seventh floor of the St. Regis Hotel, my friend, Dr. Henry Poggioli, Professor of Criminology in Ohio State University, laid out on his bed files of the recent Tiamara newspapers. A number of stories he had circled in red, others in black, and had checked cross references here and there.

The leading headlines in all these papers naturally had to do with the current ouster proceedings brought by the Municipal Board against the Tiamara Chief of Police. The general charge against Chief Toppertoe was inefficiency in office; sub-heads brought out the particular count that his department never arrested or convicted a criminal . . . quite a journalistic scandal for the Spring months when the tourists were all going North and there wasn't much news to print. Dr. Poggioli had brought the file with him from Ohio and had studied them on the train as he came South.

"And this is the amazing fact that I have dug out of these papers," the criminologist pointed to the red-circled articles, "While the Tiamara police seem never to catch a thief, they invariably recover and return to the owner any money he has lost . . . money, mind you, never stocks, bonds, jewels — just money."

Here I drew breath to express surprise, but my friend ran on as if lecturing his class in criminology.

"Take this story, for example, in the Tiamara *Telegram* of May 29: 'Movie Star's Ocean Villa Robbed; Cash, Jewels, Bonds Missing.'" Here Poggioli referred to a cross check, turned to another paper, and continued, "This is from the *Afternoon Sun*, same date, page 2: 'Cash Lost by Elise Eliot, Movie Star, Recovered by Police; Jewels, Bonds Still Missing; Thieves Escape.' What do you think of that? But one instance means nothing. One instance could happen. Take another from the *Sun*: 'Pennsylvania Couple Lose Twelve Thousand Dollars to Confidence Men; Police Recoup Money.'" He waved his hand at the papers, "All the rest are just the same except in one instance, just one, where the police did not get the money back."

I sat looking at Poggioli wondering what solution of this queer one-sided set of recoveries he would reach; for I had never known him to quit cold on any criminological riddle. I asked him what was the one exception he had found.

"Oh, that . . . the thirty thousand dollar race-track robbery and murder. Here it is, *Telegram*, May 9: 'Unidentified man who was known to have won thirty thousand dollars on the daily double was murdered and robbed on highway between Poinciana Race Track and City. Nothing left on body to identify him.' That's the only instance recorded in the papers in which the Tiamara police failed to return stolen money."

"Had nobody to return it to," I pointed out by way of a joke. "The man's dead and they don't know who his heirs are."

Poggioli doesn't care for jokes. Lecturers before classes of youth-happy young collegians seldom do. He said "Mm-huh." To recoup my momentary fall from grace I asked seriously why he had circled some stories in black.

"They are fatal traffic accidents, suicides, deaths from unknown causes. Tiamara has thirty-one percent more such incidents than is normal for a city of its size. I was just wondering if there were a possible lead here. . . ."

"You're not trying to link up that fact with the police recovering all stolen money?"

"No, I'm not *trying*; I'm simply holding it in mind. I have found many times, and you know this as well as I do, that when there are two abnormalities in the same community they are likely to be cognates and help explain one another."

"Did you come down from Ohio just to see why the Tiamara police return stolen money and to look into the traffic accident rate?"

"No, no. I'm down here on a commission." He looked at his watch as if his commission were close upon him. "When I travel anywhere I always take a file of the local papers and read them on the train — to see if there is anything in my professional field I want to investigate."

"And just how are you going to start in this case?" I asked.

The criminologist glanced at his watch again. "I'd like to run over to the County Court House and see Bundley, if I have time."

"Bundley," I repeated. "You mean the detective the Municipal Board is afraid to call to the witness stand?"

"Now, now, really," protested Poggioli, "when you say 'afraid' that's your own deduction. The Board explained that they declined to put Bundley on the witness stand for the best public welfare."

I was shocked at my friend's naiveté. I said, "Why, Poggioli, don't you know that's just their excuse for not putting Bundley on the stand. Best public welfare — piffle! They keep him off to cover up their own rottenness and graft! What other reason could an American Municipal Board have for hushing up a witness?"

Here Poggioli began a theoretic and rather foolish argument that because the Municipal Board was trying to clean house by ousting an inefficient police head, they were honest themselves. Corrupt municipal gangs never invited the scrutiny of the law by instituting formal legal action in their own department.

"Well, Poggioli," I said, "I don't agree with you at all. A thing may appear unreasonable but when I see it going on before my eyes, I admit it's there. Now let's go to the Court House and talk to Bundley — you'll see I'm right."

My friend consulted his watch again. "I have an appointment here at the St. Regis at 10:14 A.M. It's 10:03 now."

"That's a queer time . . . ten-*fourteen!*"

"Yes, it's evidently something very vital and intimate to my employer."

"Who is he?"

"A Mr. Claymore from Chicago."

"Why should he pick out a time like 10:14?"

"I'm to meet him here in the lobby. At that hour the lobby will be almost empty and he will be able to get a view of me before I see him. In other words, he wanted to size me up first — obviously because he is going to take a risk with me, if he employs me at all, with something that is very touchy. But you'll see him for yourself, and I want you to notice him carefully and tell me what you think."

"I'm to see him?"

"Naturally, you know very well the important thing about my work is that you get stories out of it." Here Poggioli gave the faint half-smile with which college professors discipline their classes.

"How am I going to see him? Am I going down with you?"

"No, you go down in the lobby now. Get a paper and sit down in some corner where you can see the doors. I want you to note the precise minute when he comes in just as a check on my forecast of the sort of work he wants done. And I don't have to tell you, unless I call you over, you will not recognize me. I hope to get through in an hour and I'll meet you at the County Court House around eleven and we'll see Bundley."

There was something pleasantly exciting about the prospective Mr. Claymore although I really hoped that Poggioli had got him completely wrong so that I too could use a faint academic half-smile. I hoped Claymore would prove a big fat blustery fellow who chose 10:14 because his watch hands hung at 10:15 and he never was sure of the time after that.

In the St. Regis lobby I bought a paper and sat down by a window. But I couldn't read much. I kept wondering about Claymore. His business with Poggioli naturally had something to do with crime, most probably he wanted some mystery unravelled. Then why didn't he go to a regular detective agency?

Poggioli entered the lobby at 10:13. At 10:14½ a trim smallish gentleman entered from an interior door, walked across to my friend.

"This is Mr. Poggioli?" "And this would be Mr. Claymore, I believe?" The smallish gentleman agreed, then nodded across the lobby at me, "And if I am correct, there sits the gentleman who writes the stories about your criminological work, Dr. Poggioli?"

I was completely taken aback but Poggioli must have been prepared for something of the sort for he replied very easily, "We weren't sure, Mr. Claymore, whether you could use my associate or not; so I suggested that he sit where he would be handy."

Mr. Claymore beckoned me over to them, gave me a thoughtful look. "That's perfectly all right. I know you two work together." Then he added this rather odd remark, "However, don't give this matter any publicity as long as I'm alive."

We agreed to this. Then I asked Mr. Claymore how he had known instantly I was with Dr. Poggioli. The newcomer gave me a compressed but very friendly smile. "You glanced at your watch as I entered the door. You were not reading because you held your paper to one side so you could watch the entrances. Then I knew that somebody wrote Dr. Poggioli's adventures and you looked like a man who might write something."

This last remark made a sort of joke out of writers at which both Claymore and Poggioli smiled. I said, "I don't see why you want to hire somebody to help you find out anything when you are such an acute observer yourself."

"You think I want to find out something?" inquired the small man, moving us toward chairs.

"Naturally, if you engage Dr. Poggioli, you want to find out something; usually about a crime."

"God forbid!" ejaculated Mr. Claymore earnestly. "But I do want to find out something. I have a brother — rather I had a brother — here in Tiamara during the early part of May. But I've lost trace of him and I wanted Dr. Poggioli to help me find him."

"What was the last certain news you had from your brother?" asked Poggioli.

"This airmail letter." He handed it over to the psychologist. "I received it soon after he reached Tiamara and I haven't heard anything from him since."

Poggioli read it, knit his brows, then asked if he could show it to me. "Certainly. From now on I consider you two as one man."

The letter which Poggioli handed me simply said, "Dear Cy: Won daily double, will spend week here, another in New Orleans, then expect me home. Luck, James Barocher."

The phrase "daily double" held my eye, then I looked at the date. It was May ninth. A slightly unsure but shocking recollection entered my head. My heart began to beat. Was it possible that the very murder and robbery which Poggioli and I had just been discussing. . . . But my friend, Poggioli, was quite calm and I decided he hadn't observed the amazing coincidence. He was saying, "If your brother's name was James Barocher, Mr. Claymore, then he was your half-brother?" The smallish man assented. Poggioli went on, "And he didn't come home after his week in New Orleans?"

"I telegraphed him here and at all the larger hotels in New Orleans, but have heard nothing more from him."

At this point I could no longer contain myself. I said in a significant tone, "Poggioli . . . May ninth . . . daily double . . . haven't we heard something about a man winning . . . the daily double . . . on May the ninth?"

The psychologist assented in a tone so casual I was not sure whether or not he recalled the celebrated race-track murder.

"Yes, I believe we have." He pondered a moment, then asked, "Mr. Claymore, was your half-brother a heavy gambler, a plunger?"

"Yes, he lost considerable amounts of money on the horses."

Poggioli beckoned a bell-boy, gave him his room key, and directed him to go to room 719, look on his bed, and bring down the May 9th issue of the Tiamara *Telegram.* Then he said to Mr. Claymore, "You say you telegraphed your brother here at this hotel?"

"Twice. But listen, what is there about Jim that you . . ."

"Just a moment, Mr. Claymore. I want to pick up the telegrams you sent to this hotel."

He crossed the lobby to the mail desk and presently returned with two Western Union envelopes addressed to James Barocher. The first, of May 14, was from Mr. Claymore asking his brother to telegraph his plans; the second, of the 17th, urged his brother to quit drinking and come home. The smallish gentleman hastened to explain the latter.

"Jim didn't drink often, but I knew if he started he would go for a week or two at a time. And when he wrote me he had won a daily double, I knew he must have won a good deal, because, as I say, he was a strong bettor. And if he had won a lot of money he was likely to celebrate. That's why I sent him that second telegram."

All this was said in the anxious hurried tone of a man who realized some unknown evil was impending. I felt achingly sorry for the little man. I was almost sorry to see the bell-boy come out of the elevator with Poggioli's newspaper. All three of us stopped talking at the boy's approach. Poggioli glanced at the headlines, then said to Mr. Claymore in the slightly elevated monotone men use to break shocking news. "Now, Mr. Claymore, this *may* not be your half-brother. There undoubtedly were other men who won the daily double on May 9th."

Poggioli turned the paper so we could both read the headlines.

The small gentleman's shoulders sagged; he seemed to collapse physically. "I . . . I had no idea you would . . . answer my question so . . . quickly."

"But wait, wait, Mr. Claymore. This is by no means a certain answer. As I say, two persons could have won a daily double — it happens every day. Now you write out a description of your half-brother, a physical description, his dress, jewelry, watch — everything about him. I'll take it over to the Police Department and check it."

"But if he hadn't been . . . been murdered, Mr. Poggioli, he would have . . . come home."

"Mr. Claymore, please . . . write out the description."

The three of us got up together and went to the writing room. As Mr. Claymore pondered and wrote, and pondered and wrote again, Poggioli said comfortingly, "Now it may not be your half-brother, but if it should be, I suppose you will want the body exhumed and sent back to Chicago?" Mr. Claymore said he would.

Poggioli took the description Mr. Claymore had written, together with the two telegrams and we set out for the Tiamara Police Department.

In the taxicab I expressed my astonishment, my amazement, that the very murder and robbery which my friend and I had been discussing had floated out of the blue into our very hands. Poggioli pulled at his nether lip in his reflective fashion. "What I don't understand is why he made his appointment to meet me at 10:14."

I looked at the criminologist. "That's a queer point to bring up."

"Yes, but why should he want to take a look at me before I saw him? Why should he test my precision to an exact minute? How could my personality mean something vital to him if he were simply trying to locate a lost half-brother?"

"But Poggioli," I argued, "Claymore is simply one of these finical little men. He dresses like one, talks like one, is one."

"Mm-mm, you may be right, but an ordinary man would never have set such an odd hour and minute unless he had some extremely cogent reason for doing so."

At the Police Department we inquired for the homicide records and were referred to Chief Toppertoe in person. We went to his office and learned that he was before the Municipal Board defending his ouster suit. We therefore had some time to use and Poggioli asked where we would find detective Bundley. We were directed to the City Court on the 16th floor of the Glades County Court House.

The City Court in Tiamara is not so much a court as it is a procession. In the City Court cases are decided so swiftly and so informally that while one defendant is retiring to freedom or to jail, another talks hurriedly before the court while a third flanked by witnesses and lawyer pushes earnestly forward in the fear that his case will be decided before he ever reaches the bar at all.

As Poggioli and I entered the City Court a little dried-up Negro stood before the bench while his fat comfortable lawyer made his argument to the judge. The lawyer contended that detective Bundley had entered the home of his client, Stogie, and illegally searched said premises. The facts were as follows: Bundley executed a search warrant which called for 70 Joob Street, whereas Stogie's domicile was 70½

Joob Street. It seemed that the evidence found against Stogie really came from 70 Joob Street. The fat attorney argued that owing to this flaw in the writ his client should be released and the confiscated evidence returned to him.

Detective Bundley stood at the end of the bar glowering at the undisturbed little Negro and holding the evidence which seemed to be a cigar-box full of bits of paper. Poggioli and I worked our way against the current of litigation and I asked Bundley what sort of evidence he had in his box. He growled out, "Number-racket tickets." I asked him what was the numbers racket. He looked to see what sort of man I was who hadn't heard of the numbers racket, then explained briefly in both words and temper that they were Cuban lottery numbers. I observed that they were not Cuban lottery tickets because I had bought some of them.

"Naw, they print these things theirse'ves," Bundley shook his box, "but they pay off accordin' to the Cuban lottery prizes."

It required a moment for me to comprehend the detective's implication, then I ejaculated, "You mean that little Negro will pay off thousands of dollars if one of his tickets happens to call for such an amount?"

"Naw, he's jest a front, but the gang he works for pays off."

At this moment the judge rendered his decision. "Prisoner guilty as charged. I fine him fifty dollars and costs. Next case."

Bundley seemed peeved despite the verdict. I said, "Well, your prisoner was convicted, anyway."

Bundley spat. "Call that a conviction? It's jest an ad. He'll sell fifty dollars' worth of tickets before he leaves Court House Square count o' the publicity he jest got here."

The little black man evidently did a prosperous business, because when he paid his fine he drew out of his trouser's pocket a roll of bills as large as his arm, peeled off a fifty, then stuffed the money back into his bulging pocket.

Poggioli leaned toward the disgusted detective. "This numbers racket — is that what you meant to tell, Mr. Bundley, if the Municipal Board had called you before them as a witness?"

"Sure it is."

"But the Board kept you off the stand in the public welfare?"

"Public welfare or . . . somebody's pocketbook," said Bundley.

This started again the argument between me and Poggioli. Bundley's remark proved to me the complete corruption of the Municipal Board and Poggioli fell back on his former contention if the Board had instituted an ouster suit against Chief Toppertoe, it was a sound patriotic organization.

"Even," I said, "if they take graft from the little Negro, Stogie?"

"You have no proof that anybody in the Court House takes graft from Stogie except the word of one disgruntled detective."

Outside on the great granite steps of the skyscraper I caught sight of

Stogie. The first thing I noticed was that his trouser's pocket was empty; it was quite flat. It amused me, my proof coming so quickly. I called Stogie over and asked him if he sold Cuban lottery tickets. He said he did and I bought one. He produced a bit of evilly printed paper as indifferent to the publicity of Court House Square as if he had been selling popcorn. I offered him a ten-dollar bill. He took the bill, hesitated a moment, then said, "Scuse me, Boss, I'll haff to run git this broke. You want to hol' my watch while I'm gone? I ain't got no change rat now."

This was such a complete and final proof of what I had been contending that I broke out laughing, but when the Negro had gone for the change, Poggioli stood shaking his head slowly and repeating, "It isn't logical. Simple municipal crooks don't start an investigation of themselves. If the Board stated they quashed Bundley's evidence for the public welfare, I'm still inclined to think they did."

"There are none so blind as they etc., etc." I quoted in excellent spirits because I am sorry to say I am the sort of man who would have the whole municipal structure collapse into anarchy if it would support a point in one of my arguments.

We returned to the Police Department and found Chief Toppertoe in his office. The Chief was a tall thin man who talked with a southern hill twang and with an occasional slip in grammar such as often plague self-educated men. When Poggioli asked for an appointment Mr. Toppertoe said, "If you want to see me while I'm Chief of Police, better see me now."

The criminologist introduced himself and the Chief reached out a warm hand, "I've heard of you-all, Mr. Poggioli. I've read your stories and often wished I could meet you two. Walk in my office, gen'lmen, and set down. What do you drink, rye or bourbon?"

Such a pleasant start placed us on a confidential footing at once. Poggioli spoke of the newspaper fight against the Chief which had resulted in the present ouster suit against him. "Now I am a criminologist, Mr. Toppertoe, and unless we can be frank I will waste not only my time but yours. The general charge the Board brings against you is inefficiency, but the specific count is the small percentage of criminals in Tiamara who are brought to trial and punished."

The Chief sat looking at Poggioli for several moments, then said drily, "Well, a small percent *is* brought to trial . . . purty near none."

The criminologist nodded very faintly at this and I knew that his whole extraordinary analytical power was focussed on every word, every nuance in the Chief of Police's speech.

"Mr. Toppertoe, the fewness of your arrests and trials, is that a mere accident of chance or is it a departmental policy?"

A different expression came into the Chief's face. "You know, Mr. Poggioli, you are the first man who has ever thought to ast me that question."

"So it is a departmental policy?"

"Why, nachelly, Mr. Poggioli, I could have caught some of them men and brought 'em to trial . . . anybody could."

"But you didn't?"

"No, what's the use. . . . " Here he suddenly put down his jigger and burst into a long tirade. "What's the use when legal technicalities are meshes through which the guiltiest criminals escape? And if they don't git out on a technicality they get let off through the sentimentalism of the jury, or the fixin' of the jury. And if I send 'em to prison, what happens? The jails are high schools and our penitentiaries universities of crime. They come out better equipped than when I put 'em in. So why put 'em in?"

"But Mr. Toppertoe," I exclaimed, "you can't by deliberate policy just let all criminals go!"

The Chief paused again. "Now there's another pint to my administration and nobody seems to have noticed that either. . . . Not many of the crooks git away with the money. I figger if I can make the criminal element of my city understand that crime don't pay money dividends, they'll quit. And think of what the City saves in prosecution fees. Why, to send a criminal to the penitentiary is a ridiculously expensive proposition, what with the trials and rehearings and appeals, and changes of venue, and it all costs loads and loads of money, and the people have to pay for it. I'm against that, Mr. Poggioli, I run an economical administration."

Here Poggioli brought up the subject of Bundley whose evidence the Municipal Board excluded on the grounds of public welfare. "From what I gathered in an interview with Bundley, his testimony would have centered about the numbers racket, so I deduce the Board feels that the numbers racket is somehow connected with the public welfare."

The Chief looked at my friend in astonishment. "Well, you really are some guesser, Mr. Poggioli. Yes, the Board knows about the numbers racket and they approve that."

"You mean you deliberately tolerate the numbers racket?" I inquired.

"Oh no, not at all," smiled the Chief drily, "I mean my department runs the numbers racket. We *own* it. When I entered office thirteen years ago the numbers racket was in irresponsible hands. Tickets wasn't paid off. They caused fights and murders. Today a winnin' ticket is the same as a check on the bank. I regularized it. I use the proceeds for departmental purposes jest the same as the state uses the proceeds of the race tracks and dawg tracks and *jai alai* for education. Yes, the Board approves of that much of my policy."

"But your own men arrest the ticket sellers," I pointed out. "Look at Bundley."

"Oh, I have that done for the benefit of the clergy," laughed the Chief.

"Just what do you mean when you say benefit of. . . ."

"Well, the ministers all think a police department ort to be run jest the same as the church. They don't realize that they are tryin' to get sinners into heaven, but we are jest tryin' to keep 'em out of jail. Our ambition ain't as towerin' as theirs."

Somewhat later, almost incidentally, Poggioli mentioned the murder and robbery of Mr. Claymore's half-brother, James Barocher. Toppertoe inquired how much money Barocher had lost in the robbery.

"It happened on May 9th," specified Poggioli. "The papers of that date published the story of an unidentified man who was murdered and robbed of thirty thousand dollars which he had just won at the race track. That man probably was James Barocher."

This recalled the whole affair to the Chief. "Sure, I remember that case. What does your Mr. Claymore want done in the matter?"

"He wants to take his brother's body to Chicago for burial. He gave me this description to give to you." Poggioli handed over the written sheet.

"O.K. I'll look into this case, Mr. Poggioli, and make you a personal report on it . . . if I am still Chief."

That ended our interview. Instead of returning to the St. Regis I took Poggioli home with me for lunch. On the way over I remarked how pleased I was with Chief Toppertoe. Poggioli came out of a deep study to say that Toppertoe was one of the most dangerous men he had ever met. I was amazed and asked how he had reached such a conclusion. He said Toppertoe was a radical, unscrupulous and perfectly *honest* individualist in power and out of such stuff dictators were fashioned and democracies overthrown.

Here I had to protest. I said, "Poggioli, would you rather the Chief be crooked than honest?"

My friend mounted his theoretic Pegasus again. "Certainly not. Today America owes her liberty to the fact that she has been ruled in the main by crooks who have no moral standing and can be tossed out of office like so much trash. But an honest brainy individualist can't be handled like that. He really sees what is best for a country long before the country itself perceives it. And he gathers about him a strong enough minority to force his measures. That creates a self-perpetuating dictatorship. No, I always thank God that America elects to public office numbskulls, clowns and thieves. If we ever should put our finest brains in power, on that day we cease to be a democracy."

Of course that was ridiculous, but I let it go. There's never any arguing with Poggioli. We had hardly arrived at my home and sat down to lunch when my telephone rang. When I answered it the hillman's drawl of Chief Toppertoe asked for Poggioli. I inquired lightly how he knew Dr. Poggioli came home with me. He said he had found it out from our taxi driver when he got back to his stand. I laughed and asked if all detection was as simple as that. He said it was — if you knew what to do.

Poggioli took the receiver, made a remark or two, listened for several minutes, then broke out in amazement.

"You say your men recovered the thirty thousand dollars!" After another interval, "I see, you seized it immediately after the robbery, but the owner was murdered and you didn't know whom to return it to. . . . No, I'm not acquainted with Mr. Claymore personally. . . . He telephoned me from Chicago to meet him here in Tiamara. First time I had ever heard of him. . . . No, I have no opinion about the correctness of returning the half-brother's money to Mr. Claymore. . . . You say the description Claymore wrote out fits the body, clothes and all? . . . So he seems genuine to you? . . . Yes, yes, Chief, I could do something. . . . I could interview Claymore and telephone you the impression I receive from him. . . . What's that? You will deliver the money to him while I am with him so I can observe his immediate reactions. . . . Won't you be taking a great risk? . . . You are willing to accept the risk. . . . Very well, we will do that. Good-bye."

The criminologist turned blankly from the telephone. "Isn't that the most amazing. . . ."

"You mean he wants you to find out if Mr. Claymore is the proper person to receive the thirty thousand. . . ."

Poggioli made a gesture. "That's no problem, that will be easy to determine. The riddle is where did Chief Toppertoe get that thirty thousand dollars!"

"Why, he just told you his men recovered it."

"Listen, if his men actually had recovered that thirty thousand dollars, wouldn't that fact have been engraved on the Chief's mind? Wouldn't he have mentioned it as soon as we spoke of the race-track robbery? Certainly! That's human nature. But when he spoke of the money just then, he had no pride of accomplishment in his voice, no particular interest in the matter. It was just office routine. He said he had the money and would pay it to its owner if I could ascertain Claymore was the proper owner. Now what does that mean?"

Dr. Poggioli has the trick of turning simple matters into riddles and riddles into very simple matters. I couldn't answer and he continued his monologue. "Let me think. . . . Do you remember that moving picture actress who lost her cash and jewels and the police recovered her cash? Try to get her on the telephone."

I began looking for Elise Eliot's name in the directory, when Poggioli snapped nervously, "She won't be in that. Movie stars use blind numbers. Call up some War Bond sales agency, they'll know her number." I did this and was fortunate enough to find Miss Eliot there. Dr. Poggioli introduced himself, said he was a great admirer of her pictures and finally got around to his point.

"Miss Eliot, when the Tiamara police returned the cash that was stolen from you, did they send back the same currency you lost, or a check, or did they substitute other bills? . . . I see, sent you some filthy bills you couldn't use. . . . You sent your maid with them to the bank and had them exchanged for clean ones. . . . That's all, Miss Eliot, thank you very much. Goodbye." He turned to me and nodded, "That proves my theory."

"What in heaven's name are you talking about, Poggioli?"

"Why, I've solved the mystery of the Chief of Police."

"Will you please explain it to me?"

"Listen and see if you don't get it yourself. Miss Eliot lost new fresh bills. The police department returned dirty bills. What caused that?"

"Mm — mm . . . well . . . the thief got her bills dirty."

Poggioli was disgusted. "Don't you know it takes from six to eight months of ordinary wear to soil a piece of currency! What class of men habitually use dirty bills?"

"The poor class," I answered hoping this would not increase his contempt for my thinking.

"Correct, the poor class. Now where did the Police Department get the dirty bills it sent to Miss Eliot?"

A light broke on me. "From the numbers racket!" I cried.

"Fine! Simplicity itself! The numbers racket. The Police Department evidently doesn't trust any bank with its secret or its money. Chief Toppertoe uses the same bills he collects from his numbers racket to pay off all losses from theft in Tiamara. In brief, *he runs a theft insurance bureau for the public benefit of Tiamara!* That is why he never recovers bonds or jewels that are lost, only cash. The Municipal Board evidently knows of this arrangement and approves it because they declined to allow detective Bundley to air the matter in open court. So you see Bundley's testimony really would have been against the best public welfare."

I was bewildered at such a turn. The Board's thesis, "against the best public welfare," had appeared so impossible to sustain.

"But the point that puzzles me," went on Poggioli, "is why Toppertoe is willing to hand thirty thousand to Claymore before my eyes for me to decide whether Claymore is the correct payee or not. Won't it be too late to decide after Claymore has the money?"

"Don't climb mountains till you get to 'em. Come on, let's go see Claymore."

Frankly, I was delighted. I was charmed. I believe that was the first time in our association together that Poggioli had ever worked out a mystery to anybody's credit and honor. And I had liked Chief Toppertoe from my very first word with him. I twitted Poggioli about being a Northern man by saying, "Uh, huh, you see you had to come South before you ever found an honorable mystery to solve."

At the St. Regis Mr. Claymore received us in his suite on the twenty-first floor with elaborate but melancholy politeness. He said he had contacted the police over the phone (that was his word, "contacted")

and had made arrangements to ship his half-brother's body to Chicago. Poggioli approached his own point very carefully by saying that he had learned an important fact about James Barocher's death and robbery. Mr. Claymore asked unhappily what it was.

"Chief Toppertoe's men recovered the thirty thousand dollars your half-brother lost," said the psychologist.

The smallish man did not change his unhappy mien. "I am more interested in my brother himself. Did my description fit?"

"Naturally the description did fit," said Poggioli, "or the Chief wouldn't have gone into the matter of the money. He is sending it to you by messenger at once. He said you could express it to your brother's executor in Chicago, or could receive it here yourself as agent of the executor."

"I happen to be Jim's executor," said Mr. Claymore in his grieved voice.

"Then you might as well sign for it and receive it here."

"Whatever you think best, Dr. Poggioli. It's as broad as it's long."

"It would simplify matters for you to receive it here. I sympathize with you in your loss, Mr. Claymore. Race-track followers win no particular honor from their hobby but they are usually the frankest, most generous, big hearted men in the world."

"That was true of Jim, Dr. Poggioli."

"I suppose he was like other racing devotees, bet according to systems, believed in luck, wore striking clothes, and so on?"

"Oh, yes, Jim had worked out ways of betting and he was a great dresser. Well . . . he's gone now."

The messenger arrived with the package of bills. Mr. Claymore signed for them and Poggioli and I left.

At the curb in front of the hotel we chose a taxicab but the driver, a little dried-up Negro, touched his cap and excused himself. He said his taxi was on call. We took another and drove a short distance to a corner drugstore where Poggioli got out to telephone his report to the Chief.

Enormously curious I went into the booth with him. By good luck the telephone was one of those squeaky contraptions which spoke loud enough for a third person to overhear what was said.

The Chief asked Poggioli how Mr. Claymore had taken the announcement of the money being recovered. The psychologist replied that Claymore had shown more interest in his identification of the dead man than in the money. "His first question was 'Did my description fit?'"

"And what do you make of that, Dr. Poggioli?" inquired the Chief's squeak.

"That's simple, Chief; he was not surprised to learn of the money. In some way he had already found out that the police refunded all monies lost by theft in Tiamara. His interest therefore lay in identifying the dead

man and obtaining the money. If you have his description beside you, look at it and you will see he made the great mistake of correctly identifying the dead man's clothes."

Came a pause as the Chief evidently consulted the paper, then he asked, "Why was that a mistake, Dr. Poggioli?"

"Because just a moment ago in our interview, Claymore told me his brother was a great dresser, the usual sporting type. Now if Claymore had really been in Chicago when Barocher was murdered, it would never have occurred to him to try to identify the victim *by describing his clothes*. He could not possibly have guessed *what suit Barocher had worn on the day of his death.* But his description says . . . a checked suit. I was with him when he wrote it. He thought and thought, but finally wrote down, a checked suit. He was obsessed by Barocher's checked suit, couldn't get it out of his mind. There can be only one explanation for that, Chief."

"And what is that, Dr. Poggioli?"

"He was *with* Barocher on the day and hour his pretended brother was murdered."

Came another pause, then, "I see, I see. Claymore is the murderer. He robbed the dead man of thirty thousand dollars, then tried to come back and swindle my department out of another thirty thousand dollars."

"Exactly. Claymore is one of the most daring criminals I have ever known. And before closing my opinion I have a tag of corroborative evidence."

"And that is . . . ?"

"A phrase Claymore used in our interview. When I offered him his choice between receiving the money here or having it expressed to Chicago he said it made no difference to him, it was as broad as it was long. Now the phrase 'as broad as it is long' is the positive index of a complacent and gratified mind. If he had felt any grief for the dead man, he would have said it made no difference to him but he never would have added, 'as broad as it is long'. That stamped him as completely heartless toward his victim, as naturally a murderer would be."

Under such unexpected revelations the telephone booth in which I stood seemed to sway. I don't know how the Chief at the other end of the line was affected, but his squeak came in very normally. "Thank you for your analysis, Dr. Poggioli, and for delivering the money. You may be interested to know that Mr. Claymore wrote to this department several weeks ago in his pretended search for his brother, and I gave him your name as a man who might assist him. That was one, out of many reasons, I was so delighted to see you when you called at my office." The Chief gave his brief nasal hillman's laugh. "I thank you again, most sincerely. Good-bye."

Poggioli stepped out of the booth with the most dazed expression. He looked at me and breathed, "Merciful Lord, what have I done?"

"You mean because the Chief recommended you?" I asked.

"No, no, that's nothing, a mere detail. . . . But the Chief's laugh — his perfectly careless laugh when I tell him he has delivered thirty thousand dollars to a murderer!" Suddenly he rushed out of the drugstore to the waiting taxicab. I followed. We leaped in. Poggioli snapped out, "Driver, back to the St. Regis, fast as you can make it! Then take the nearest route to the T.W.A. airfield!"

As we shot away I said, "Poggioli, are you following Claymore to get the money back?"

"No, no, I'm trying to save the little devil's life for a lawful trial!"

I was bewildered. "Save his life . . . why do you imagine his life is in . . ."

"Heavens, man, can't you interpret anything! Didn't you hear the Chief *laugh?* Laugh in complete indifference when I told him Claymore had got away with a fortune! Don't you realize he is sure he will get the money back?"

"But how will he get it back? It's gone now."

Poggioli explained rapidly and tensely, staring ahead as we sped from the hotel to the air depot. "How? By assassinating him! Chief Toppertoe sidesteps legal processes. *That explains why there are three times as many traffic accidents in Tiamara as any other city of its size in America!* You heard him rave against juries releasing guilty men. Well, they don't here in Tiamara. Juries never get a chance at guilty men in Tiamara. . . ." Poggioli's half-frantic explanation was brought to an abrupt halt by the sight of a taxicab wrecked on the slope of an embankment. "Stop here!" yelled the criminologist.

Our cab drew up but we were too late. The tragedy was over. Mr. Claymore lay amidst the wreck looking even smaller than when alive. The little dried-up Negro chauffeur was working apparently trying to get the body out. The package of currency had vanished.

Poggioli and I stood looking at the wreck. I mentioned the money. I asked if he supposed the Chief would ever get his money back.

"Of course," said the criminologist. "That chauffeur is Stogie, the little Negro who delivers the racket money to the Chief's department. Now he is delivering it again. Evidently the Chief hires Stogie to create these accidents. They are relatively inexpensive and don't depend upon the sentimentality of a jury."

"Yes, but you know, Poggioli," I said with a kind of sick thoughtfulness, "if Stogie hadn't murdered him like this, Claymore would have gone free. No jury in the world would have accepted your findings as legal evidence. . . ."

Here I was interrupted by a newsboy shouting, "Extry! Extry! Trial's Ended! Municipal Board Ousts Police Chief Toppertoe for Inefficiency!"

A Daylight Adventure

The following notes concerning Mrs. Cordy Cancy were not made at the time of her alleged murder of her husband, James Cancy. Worse than that, they were not taken even at the time of her trial, but seven or eight months later at the perfectly hopeless date when Sheriff Matheny of Lanesburg, Tennessee, was in the act of removing his prisoner from the county jail to the state penitentiary in Nashville.

Such a lapse of time naturally gave neither Professor Henry Poggioli nor the writer opportunity to develop those clues, fingerprints, bullet wounds, and psychological analyses which usually enliven the story of any crime.

Our misfortune was that we motored into Lanesburg only a few minutes before Sheriff Matheny was due to motor out of the village with his prisoner. And even then we knew nothing whatever of the affair. We simply had stopped for lunch at the Monarch café in Courthouse Square, and we had to wait a few minutes to get stools at the counter. Finally, two men vacated their places. As Poggioli sat down, he found a copy of an old local newspaper stuck between the paper-napkin case and a ketchup bottle. He unfolded it and began reading. As he became absorbed almost at once in its contents, I was sure he had found a murder story, because that is about all the professor ever reads.

I myself take no interest in murders. I have always personally considered them deplorable rather than entertaining. The fact that I make my living writing accounts of Professor Poggioli's criminological investigations, I consider simply as an occupational hazard and hardship.

The square outside of our café was crowded with people and filled with movement and noise. In the midst of this general racket I heard the voice of some revivalist preacher booming out through a loudspeaker, asking the Lord to save Sister Cordy Cancy from a sinner's doom, and then he added the rather unconventional phrase that Sister Cordy was not the "right" sinner but was an innocent woman, or nearly so.

That of course was faintly puzzling — why a minister should broadcast such a remark about one of his penitents. Usually the Tennessee hill preacher makes his converts out to be very bad persons indeed, and strongly in need of grace, which I suppose most of us really are. Now to hear one woman mentioned in a prayer as "nearly innocent" was a sharp break from the usual.

I suppose Poggioli also caught the name subconsciously, for he looked up suddenly and asked me if the name "Cancy" had been called. I told him yes, and repeated what I had just heard over the megaphone.

The criminologist made some sort of silent calculation, then said, "Evidently Mrs. Cancy has had her baby and the sheriff is starting with her to the penitentiary in Nashville."

I inquired into the matter. Poggioli tapped his paper. "Just been reading a stenographic account of the woman's trial which took place here in Lanesburg a little over seven months ago. She was sentenced to life imprisonment, but she was pregnant at the time, so the judge ruled that she should remain here in Lanesburg jail until the baby was born and then be transferred to the state penitentiary in Nashville. So I suppose by this noise that the baby has arrived and the mother is on her way to prison."

Just as my companion explained this the preacher's voice boomed out, "Oh, Lord, do something to save Sister Cordy! Sheriff Matheny's fixin' to start with her to Nashville. Work a miracle, Oh, Lord, and convince him she is innocent. You kain't desert her, Lord, when she put all her faith an' trust in You. She done a small crime as You well know, but done it with a pyure heart and for Yore sake. So come down in Yore power an' stop the sheriff and save an innocent woman from an unjust sentence. Amen." Then in an aside which was still audible over the megaphone, "Sheriff Matheny, give us five minutes more. He's bound to send Sister Cordy aid in the next five minutes."

Now I myself am a Tennessean, and I knew how natural it was for a hill-country revivalist to want some special favor from the Lord, and to want it at once; but I had never before heard one ask the rescue of a prisoner on her way to Nashville. I turned to Poggioli and said, "The minister admits the woman has committed some smaller crime. What was that?"

"Forgery," he replied. "She forged her husband's will in favor of herself, then applied the proceeds to build a new roof on the Leatherwood church. That's part of the court record."

"And what's the other crime — the one she claims to be innocent of?"

"The murder of her husband, Jim Cancy. She not only claims to be innocent, she really is. The testimony in the trial proved that beyond a doubt."

I was shocked. "Then why did the judge condemn . . ."

The criminologist drew down his lips. "Because the proof of her innocence is psychological. Naturally, that lay beyond the comprehension of the jury, and the judge too, as far as that goes."

I stared at my companion. "Can you prove her innocence, now, at this late date?"

"Certainly, if this paper has printed the court reporter's notes correctly, and I'm sure it has."

"Why, this is the most amazing thing I ever heard of — hitting in like this!"

"What do you mean 'hitting in like this'?"

"Good heavens, don't you see? Just as the sheriff is starting off with an innocent woman, just as the preacher is asking the Lord to send down some power to save her, here you come along at exactly the right moment. You know she is innocent and can prove it!"

Poggioli gave the dry smile of a scientific man. "Oh, I see. You think my coming here is providential."

"Certainly. What else is there to think?"

"I regret to disillusion you, but it is not. It couldn't be. It is nothing more than an extraordinary coincidence — and I can prove that, too." With this my friend returned to his paper.

This left me frankly in a nervous state. It seemed to me we ought to do something for the woman outside. I looked at the man sitting next to us at the counter. He nodded his head sidewise at Poggioli. "He don't live around here, does he?"

I said he didn't.

"If he don't live here, how does he know what's happened in these parts?"

"You heard him say he read it in the paper."

"He didn't do no such thing. I watched him. He didn't read that paper a tall, he jest turned through it, like I would a picture book."

I told him that was Poggioli's way of reading. It is called sight-reading — just a look and he knew it.

The hill man shook his head, "Naw, Mister, I know better'n that. I've watched hunders of men read that paper sence it's laid thar on the counter, and the fassest one tuk a hour an twelve minutes to git through."

I nodded. I was not interested, so I said, "I daresay that's true."

"Of course hit's so," he drawled truculently, "ever'thing I say is so."

"I'm not doubting your word," I placated, "it is you who are doubting mine. You see I know my friend's ability at sight-reading."

This silenced him for a few moments, then he said shrewdly, "Looky here, if he gits what he knows out'n that paper, how come him to say Cordy Cancy is innocent when the paper says she's guilty?"

"Because the judgment in the paper doesn't agree with the evidence it presents. My friend has gone over the evidence and has judged for himself that the woman is guilty of forgery but innocent of murder."

This gave the hill man pause. A certain expression came into his leathery face. "He's a detectif, ain't he?"

"Well, not exactly. He used to be a teacher in the Ohio State University, and he taught detectives how to detect."

"Mm — mm. Who hard [hired] him to come hyar?"

"Nobody," I said, "he just dropped in by chance."

"Chanst, huh? You expeck me to b'leve that?"

"Yes, I must say I do."

"Well, jest look at it from my stan'point — him comin' hyar the very minnit the preacher is prayin' fer he'p and the shurrf startin' with her to the penitentiary — a great detectif like him jest drap in by chanst. Do you expeck me to b'leve that?"

All this was delivered with the greatest heat and my seat-mate seemed to hold me personally responsible for the situation.

"Well, what do you believe?" I asked in an amiable tone which gave him permission to believe anything he wanted to and no hard feelings.

"Why, jess what I said. I b'leve he wuz hard."

His suspicion of Poggioli, who would never accept a penny for his criminological researches, amused me. "Well, that's your privilege, but if it would strengthen your faith in me I will say that to the best of my knowledge and belief Professor Henry Poggioli's arrival in Lanesburg, Tennessee, on the eve of Mrs. Cordy Cancy's committal to the Nashville penitentiary, was a coincidence, a whole coincidence, and nothing but a coincidence, so help me, John Doe."

I had hoped to lighten my companion's dour mood, but he arose gloomily from his stool.

"I hope the Lord forgives you fer mawkin' His holy words."

"They are not the Lord's holy words," I reminded him, "they're the sheriff's words when he swears in a witness."

"Anyway, you tuk His name in vain when you said 'em."

"Didn't mention His name, sir. I said 'John Doe.'"

"Anyway, Brother," he continued in his menacing drawl, "you shore spoke with lightness. The Bible warns you aginst speakin' with lightness — you kain't git aroun' that." With this he took himself out of the café, scraping his feet in the doorway as a symbol of shaking my dust from his shoes.

As I watched the saturnine fellow go, Poggioli turned from his paper.

"Poses quite a riddle, doesn't he?"

"Not for me," I said. "I was born here in the hills."

"You understand him?"

"I think so."

"You didn't observe any more precise and concrete contradiction about him?"

I tried to think of some simple contradiction in the man, something plain. I knew when Poggioli pointed it out it would be very obvious, but nothing came to my mind. I asked him what he saw.

"Two quite contradictory reactions: he was disturbed about my being a detective and about your near profanity."

"I am afraid I don't quite see what you mean."

"I'll make it simpler. He evidently was a deacon in some church."

"Why do you say that?"

"Because he reproved the 'lightness' of your language. The scriptures instruct deacons to reprove the faults of the brethren, and lightness of language is one of them. So he was probably a deacon."

"All right, say he was. What does that contradict?"

"His disturbance over my being a detective. Deacons are supposed to ally themselves with law and order."

I laughed. "You don't know your Tennessee hill deacons. That contradiction in them is historical. Their ancestors came here before the Revolution to worship God as they pleased and escape the excise tax. They have been for the Lord and against the law ever since."

At this point another man hurried from the square into the Monarch café. I noted the hurry because under ordinary circumstances hill men never hurry, not even in the rain. He glanced up and down the counter, immediately came to my companion, and lifted a hand. "Excuse me, Brother, but you're not a preacher?"

"No, I'm not," said my companion.

"Then you are the detective that was sent. Will you come with me?"

"Just what do you mean by 'sent'?" asked the criminologist.

"Why the Lord sent you," explained the man hurriedly but earnestly. "Brother Johnson was jest prayin' to the Lord to send somebody to prove Sister Cordy Cancy innocent and keep her from going to the pen. Jim Phipps heard you-all talkin' an' hurried out an' told us there was a detectif in here. So He's bound to have sent ye."

Poggioli reflected. "I am sure I can prove the woman innocent — from the evidence printed in this paper. But what good will that do, when the trial is over and the woman already sentenced?"

"Brother," said the countryman, "if the Lord started this work, don't you reckon He can go on an' finish it?"

"Look here, Poggioli," I put in, "we're here for some reason or other."

"Yes, by pure chance, by accident," snapped the psychologist. "Our presence has no more relation to this woman than . . ."

He was looking for a simile when I interrupted, "If you know she is innocent don't you think it your duty to —"

The psychologist stopped me with his hand and his expression. "I believe I do owe a duty . . . yes . . . yes, I owe a duty. I'll go do what I can."

The man who came for him was most grateful; so were all the people in the café, for they had overheard the conversation. Everybody was delighted except me. I didn't like Poggioli's tone, or the expression on his face. I wondered what he really was going to do.

Well, by the time we got out of the restaurant everybody in the square seemed to know who we were. There was a great commotion. The preacher's prayer for help had been answered instantly. It was a miracle.

The sound-truck which had been booming stood in front of the county jail on the south side of the square. Beside the truck was the sheriff's car with the woman prisoner handcuffed in the back seat. Near the car stood another woman holding a young baby in her arms. This infant, I gathered, was the prisoner's child, and would be left behind in the Lanesburg jail while its mother went on to the penitentiary in Nashville. The crowd naturally was in sympathy with the woman and expected us immediately to deliver her from her troubles. I heard one of the men say as we pushed forward, "That heavy man's the detective and that slim 'un's his stooge; he writes down what the big 'un does."

Frankly, I was moved by the situation, and I was most uneasy about the outcome. I asked Poggioli just what he meant to do.

He glanced at me as we walked. "Cure them of an illusion."

"Just what do you mean — cure them of an . . ."

He nodded at the crowd around us. "I will prove to these people the woman is innocent, but at the same time show that my proof can be of no benefit to the prisoner. This ought to convince the crowd that providence had nothing to do with the matter, and it ought to make them, as a group, a little more rationalistic and matter-of-fact. That is what I consider it my duty to do."

His whole plan appeared cruel to me. I said, "Well, thank goodness, you won't be able to do that in five minutes, and the sheriff gave them only that much more time before he starts out."

My hope to avoid Poggioli's demonstration was quashed almost at once. I saw the sheriff, a little man, climb out of his car, walk across to the sound-truck, and take the microphone from the minister. Then I heard the sheriff's voice boom out.

"Ladies and gentlemen, I understand there really is help on the way for Mrs. Cancy. Whether it is miraculous help or jest human help, I don't know. But anyway I'm extendin' Mrs. Cancy's time to prove her innocence one more hour before we start to Nashville."

A roar of approval arose at this. The minister in the truck then took over the loudspeaker, "Brothers and Sisters," he began in his more solemn drawl, "they ain't one ounce of doubt in my soul as to who sent this good man. I'll introduce him to you. He is Dr. Henry Poggioli the great detective some of you have read about in the magazines. The Lord has miraculously sent Dr. Poggioli to clear Sister Cordy Cancy from her troubles. And now I'll introduce Sister Cordy to Dr. Poggioli. Doctor, Sister Cordy don't claim complete innocence, but she's a mighty good woman. She did, however, forge her husban's will by takin' a carbon paper and some of his old love letters and tracin' out a will, letter by letter. She sees now that was wrong, but she was workin' for the glory of the Lord when she done it."

Shouts of approval here — "Glory be!" "Save her, Lord!" and so forth. The divine continued, "Jim Cancy, her husban', was a mawker and a scoffer. He wouldn't contribute a cent to the Lord's cause nor bend his knee in prayer. So Sister Cordy forged his will for religious ends.

Now I guess the Lord knew Jim was goin' to git killed. But Sister Cordy didn't have a thing in the world to do with that. He jest got killed. And you all know what she done with his money — put a new roof on the Leatherwood churchhouse. Save her, Oh, Lord, from the penitentiary!" (Another uproar of hope and sympathy here.) "And Brothers and Sisters, look how she acted in the trial, when suspicion fell on her for Jim's murder. She didn't spend one cent o' that money for a lawyer. She said it wasn't hers to spend, it was the Lord's and He would save her. She said she didn't need no lawyer on earth when she had one in Heaven. She said He would send her aid. And now, praise His name, He has sent it here at this eleventh hour." Again he was interrupted by shouts and applause. When a semi-silence was restored, he said, "Dr. Poggioli, you can now prove Sister Cordy innocent of her husband's murder and set her free."

In the renewed uproar the minister solemnly handed the microphone down to Poggioli on the ground. I have seldom been more nervous about any event in Poggioli's eventful career. I didn't suppose he would be in any actual danger from the irate hill people when they found out what he was trying to do, but on the other hand a mob can be formed in the South in about three minutes. And they are likely to do anything — ride a man out of town on a rail, tar and feather him, give him a switching, depending on how annoyed they are. Poggioli never lived in the South, he had no idea what he was tampering with.

He began, "Ladies and gentlemen, I have little to say. I have just read the report of Mrs. Cancy's trial in your county paper. From it I have drawn absolute proof of her innocence of her husband's murder, but unfortunately that proof can be of no benefit to her."

Cries of "Why won't it?" "What's the matter with it?" "What makes you talk like that?"

"Because, my friends, of a legal technicality. If I could produce new evidence the trial judge could reopen her case and acquit Mrs. Cancy. But a reinterpretation of old evidence is not a legal ground for a rehearing. All I can do now is to demonstrate to you from the evidence printed in your county paper that Mrs. Cancy is innocent of murder, but still she must go on with the Sheriff to the penitentiary in Nashville."

Despair filled the square; there arose outcries, pleas, oaths. The revivalist quashed this. He caught up his microphone and thundered, "Oh, ye of little faith, don't you see Sister Cordy's salvation is at hand? Do you think the Lord would send a detectif here when it wouldn't do no good? I'm as shore of victory as I'm standin' here. Brother Poggioli, go on talkin' with a good heart!"

The irony of the situation stabbed me: for Poggioli to intend a purely materialistic solution to the situation, and the minister who had besought his aid to hope for a miracle. It really was ironic. Fortunately, no one knew of this inner conflict except me or there would have been a swift outbreak of public indignation. The scientist began his proof:

"Ladies and gentlemen, your minister has recalled to your memory how Mrs. Cordy Cancy forged her husband's will by tracing each letter of it with a carbon paper from a package of her husband's old love letters. But he did not mention the fact that after she did this — after she had underscored and overscored these letters and made them the plainest and most conclusive proof of her forgery — she still kept those love letters! She did not destroy them. She put them in a trunk whose key was lost, and kept them in the family living room. Now every man, woman, and I might almost say child, sees clearly what this proves!"

Of course in this he was wrong. He overestimated the intelligence of his audience. Those nearer to him, who could make themselves heard, yelled for him to go on and explain.

"Further explanation is unnecessary," assured the psychologist. "If she felt sufficiently sentimental about her husband to preserve his love letters, obviously she did not mean to murder him. Moreover, she must have realized her marked-over letters would constitute absolute proof of the minor crime of forgery. She must have known that if her husband were murdered, her home would be searched and the tell-tale letters would be found. Therefore, she not only did not murder her husband herself but she had no suspicion that he would be murdered. Those letters in her unlocked trunk make it impossible that she should be either the principal or an accessory to his assassination."

A breath of astonishment went over the crowd at the simplicity of Poggioli's deduction. Everyone felt that he should have thought of that for himself.

Poggioli made a motion for quiet and indicated that his proof was not concluded. Quiet returned and the psychologist continued.

"Your minister tells us, and I also read it in the evidence printed in your county paper, that Mrs. Cancy did not hire an attorney to defend her in her trial. She used the entire money to place a new roof on the old Leatherwood church, and she told the court the reason she did this was because God would defend her."

Here shouts arose. "He did! He's doin' it now! He's sent you here to save her!"

Poggioli held up a hand and shook his head grimly. This was the point of his whole appearance in the square — the materialistic point by which he hoped to rid these hill people of too great a reliance on providential happenings and place them on the more scientific basis of self-help. He intoned slowly:

"I regret to say, ladies and gentlemen, that my appearance here is pure accident. Why? Because I have come too late. If a supernal power had sent me here to save an innocent woman — and she is an innocent woman — if a supernal power had sent me, it would certainly have sent me in time. But I am not in time. The trial is over. All the proof is in. We cannot possibly ask a new trial on the ground of a reinterpretation of old proof, which is what I am giving you. That is no ground for a new trial.

So this innocent woman who is on her way to the penitentiary must go on and serve out her unjust term. My appearance here today, therefore, can be of no service to anyone and can be attributed to nothing but pure chance."

At this pitiful negation an uproar arose in the square. Men surged toward the sheriff, yelling for him to turn the woman free or they would do it for him. Cooler heads held back the insurgents and voices shouted out:

"Dr. Poggioli, who did do the murder? You know ever'thing — who done it!"

The criminologist wagged a negative hand. "I have no idea."

"The devil!" cried a thick-set fellow. "Go ahead an' reason out who killed Jim Cancy — jest like you reasoned out his wife was innocent!"

"I can't do that. It's impossible. I haven't studied the evidence of the murder, merely the evidence that proves non-murder — a completely different thing."

"Go ahead! Go ahead!" yelled half a dozen voices. "The Lord has he'ped you so fur — He'll stan by you!"

It was amusing, in a grim fashion, for the crowd to twist the very materialistic point Poggioli was making into a logical basis for a spiritualistic interpretation. However, I do not think Poggioli was amused. He held up his hands.

"Friends, how could I know anything about this when I stopped over for lunch in this village only one hour ago?"

A dried-up old farmer, whose face had about the color and texture of one of his own corn shucks, called out, "Somebody shot Jim, didn't they Dr. Poggioli?"

"Oh, yes, somebody shot him."

"Well, have you got any idyah of the kind of man who shot Jim Cancy?"

"Oh, certainly. I have a fairly clear idea of the kind of man who murdered Cancy."

"I allowed you had, Brother, I allowed you had," nodded the old fellow with satisfaction. "The Lord put it into my heart to ast you exactly that question." The old fellow turned to the officer, "Shurrf Matheny, has he got time to tell what kind of a fellow murdered Jim before you start with Sister Cordy to the pen?"

The officer held up his hand. "I am extendin' Sister Cordy's startin' time two more hours — so we can find out who murdered her husban' instid of her."

"O.K." called a woman's voice, "go ahead and tell us the kind of skunk that done that!"

"Well, Madam, I would say it was a man who shot Jim Cancy."

"Oh, yes, we all know that," shouted several listeners. "Women don't shoot nobody, they pisen 'em . . . as a rule." "Go on, tell us somp'm else."

"Well, let me see," pondered Poggioli aloud. "Let us begin back with the forgery itself. Mrs. Cancy did this. She admits it. But she did not originate the idea, because that is a highly criminal idea and she does not have a highly criminal psychology. She has, in fact, a very religious and dutiful psychology. I also know that if she had been bright enough to think of tracing the will from her old love letters, she would have realized how dangerous they were to keep in her unlocked trunk and would have destroyed them immediately. Therefore, I know somebody suggested to her how she could forge the will."

More angry shouts interrupted here, as if the crowd were reaching for the real criminal. Some voices tried to hush the others so the psychologist could proceed. Eventually Poggioli went on.

"All right, Mrs. Cancy did not originate the idea of forgery. Then she was used as a tool. But she is not a hard, resolute woman. Just look at her there in the sheriff's car and you can see that. She is a soft, yielding woman and would not carry any plan through to its bitter end. But in her trial she did carry a plan through to its bitter end, and this end, odd to say, was to put a new roof on the Leatherwood church. Ladies and gentlemen, a new roof on Leatherwood church was the basic motive for Cancy's murder. It is fantastic, but it is the truth. Mrs. Cancy refused to hire a lawyer when she came to trial. Why? To save the money to put a roof on Leatherwood church. So the person who persuaded her to commit the forgery must also have persuaded her to withhold the money for the church roof, and that God would come down and set her free from the charge of murder."

At this the enthusiasm of the crowd knew no bounds. They flung up their hats, they yelled, they cried out that now the Lord had come to help Sister Cordy just like He had promised. The sheriff arose in his car and shouted that he extended Sister Cordy's leaving time for the rest of the day. He yelled that they were hot on the trail of the man who done it and he would remain in town to make the arrest.

I could see Poggioli was unnerved. It would take a cleverer psychologist than I am to explain why he should be. Of course, his demonstration was going awry. He was not getting where he had intended to go. He lifted up his hands and begged the crowd.

"My friends, please remember this. I do not know the man. I have no idea who he is. I can only give you his type."

"All right," shouted many voices, "go on and give us his type, so Sheriff Matheny can arrest him!"

The criminologist collected himself. "As to his type: I ate lunch in the Monarch café a little while ago and was reading an account of Mrs. Cancy's trial in your county paper. As I read, a gentleman beside me said that he had been watching strangers read the story of that trial for months, as it lay there on the lunch counter. It is possible such a man might have some connection with the murder; or he may have been morbidly curious about crime in general —"

Shouts of satisfaction here — "Go ahead, now you're gittin' somewhere!"

Poggioli stopped them. "Wait! Wait! I by no means incriminate this gentleman. I am trying to show you the various hypotheses which a criminologist must apply to every clue or piece of evidence."

"All right, Doctor, if he didn't kill Jim Cancy, who did?"

Poggioli mopped his face. "That I do not know, nor do I know anything whatever about the man in the café. I am simply trying to give you a possible psychological description of the murderer. Now, this man at my table also reprimanded my friend here for what he considered to be an infraction of a religious formality. In fact, he became quite angry about it. That would link up with the fact that Jim Cancy was reported to be a free-thinker. A free-thinker would have irritated such a man very deeply. If Cancy had jibed at this man's faith, the fellow would have felt that any punishment he could inflict on the mocker would be justified, even unto death. Also, he could have persuaded himself that any money he might receive from Cancy's death should be devoted to the welfare of the church — as for example, to put a new roof on the Leatherwood church. Following these plans, he could have easily influenced Mrs. Cancy to forge Cancy's will, with the understanding that the money would go to the church. Then he could have waylaid and shot Cancy, and made the will collectible. This would have accomplished two things; gratify his private revenge and make a contribution to the church. . . . The murderer could be of that type or he could be of a completely different type which I shall now try to analyze. . . ."

How many more types Poggioli would have described nobody knew, for at this juncture the sheriff discovered that his prisoner had fainted. This created a tremendous commotion. For a hill woman to faint was almost as unparalleled as for a horse to faint. Sheriff Matheny arose in his car and hallooed that he would carry no sick woman to the Nashville pen, and that Mrs. Cancy should remain here with her baby until she was completely recovered, even if it took a week. After making this announcement, the officer climbed out of his car and disappeared in the throng.

Everybody was gratified. They came pouring around Poggioli to congratulate him on his speech. A fat man elbowed up, seized Poggioli by the arm, motioned at me, too, and shouted at us to come to dinner in his hotel. Poggioli said we had just eaten at the Monarch café.

"Then you-all are bound to be hungry. Come on, my wife sent me over here to bring ye. She feeds all the revivalists and their singers who come to preach in the square."

The criminologist repeated that we were not hungry, but the fat man came close to him and said in what was meant for an undertone:

"Don't make no diff'runce whether you are hungry or not — my wife wants you to come inside while you and your buddy are alive!"

"Alive!" said my friend.

"Shore, alive. Do you think Deacon Sam Hawley will let any man stand up in the public square and accuse him of waylayin' Jim Cancy, and then not kill the man who does the accusin'?"

My friend was shocked. "Why, I never heard of Deacon Sam Hawley!"

"He's the man you et by, and he knows you. Come on, both of you!"

"But I was simply describing a type —"

"Brother, when you go to a city you find men in types — all dentists look alike, all bankers look alike, all lawyers look alike, and so on; but out here in these Tennessee hills we ain't got but one man to a type. And when you describe a man's type, you've described the man. Come on in to my hotel before you git shot. We're trying to make Lanesburg a summer resort and we don't want it to git a bad name for murderin' tourists."

We could see how a hotel owner would feel that way and we too were anxious to help preserve Lanesburg's reputation for peace and friendliness. We followed our host rather nervously to his hotel across the square and sat down to another lunch.

There was a big crowd in the hotel and they were all talking about the strange way the Lord had brought about the conviction of Deacon Sam Hawley, and rescued a comparatively innocent woman from an unjust sentence. Poggioli pointed out once or twice that the woman was not out of danger yet, but all the diners around us were quite sure that she soon would be.

The whole incident seemed about to end on a kind of unresolved anticlimax. The diners finally finished their meal and started out of the hotel. We asked some of the men if they thought it would be safe for us to go to our car. They said they didn't know, we would have to try it and see. Poggioli and I waited until quite a number of men and women were going out of the hotel and joined them. We were just well out on the sidewalk when a brisk gunfire broke out from behind the office of the *Lane County Weekly Herald*, which was just across the street from the hotel. It was not entirely unexpected. Besides, that sort of thing seemed to happen often enough in Lanesburg to create a pattern for public action. Everybody jumped behind everybody else, and holding that formation made for the nearest doors and alleys. At this point Sheriff Matheny began his counterattack. It was from a butcher's shop close to the hotel. How he knew what point to pick out, I don't know; whether or not he was using us for bait, I still don't know.

At any rate, the sheriff's fourth or fifth shot ended the battle. Our assailant, quite naturally, turned out to be Deacon Sam Hawley. He was dead when the crowd identified him. In the skirmish the sheriff was shot in the arm, and everybody agreed that now he would not be able to take Mrs. Cancy to the penitentiary for a good three months to come. She was reprieved at least for that long.

As we got into our car and drove out of Lanesburg, the crowd was circulating a petition to the Governor to pardon Mrs. Cordelia Cancy of the minor crime of forgery. The petition set forth Mrs. Cancy's charity, her purity of heart, her generosity in using the proceeds of her crime for the church, and a number of her other neighborly virtues. The village lawyer put in a note that a wife cannot forge her husband's signature. He argued that if she cannot steal from him, then she cannot forge his name, which is a form of theft. She simply signs his name for him, she does not forge it.

The petition was signed by two hundred and forty-three registered Democratic voters. The Governor of Tennessee is a Democrat.

At this point we drove out of Lanesburg . . .

Count Jalacki Goes Fishing

By a trivial coincidence, Professor Poggioli and I were discussing the extraordinary harmony that reigned in American families of great wealth when my telephone buzzed. As my friend reached for it he was saying that beyond the usual divorces which appeared to be the concomitants of great fortunes, our leading financial families lived together in extraordinary peace, never a lawsuit, never a rumor of ill usage, never a . . . here he turned from me to the telephone: "Poggioli speaking. . . . Yes, I am a criminologist, I would hardly say *the* criminologist. . . . What? . . . Are you suggesting that I accept a . . . Who is this speaking?"

A moment later he placed his palm over the transmitter and said to me in surprised *sotto voce*, "She says she is the Countess Everhard-Jalacki!"

I was even more surprised than Poggioli. I asked what she wanted.

"She wants me to apply for the position of private secretary to her father, John Everhard I, at the penthouse of the Ritz-Carlton Hotel."

"Didn't know there were any Everhards at the Ritz-Carlton — thought they all lived on Ocean Drive."

"She does live on Ocean Drive."

"I can't quite figure it," I said. "Why does a daughter who lives in one place engage a private secretary for a great financier who lives in another place? And especially why should she want a criminologist?"

Poggioli lifted a finger to indicate that he would ask the reason. After listening for a half-minute, he said: "She wants her father to have a companion who is highly intelligent and can amuse him. He is old and sick in the Ritz penthouse and needs entertainment. She said my honorarium would be any figure I cared to name."

"Just who is going to pay this honorarium?" I inquired, "the daughter on Ocean Drive, or the father in the penthouse?"

Poggioli made this inquiry with delicacy. He listened another moment, then said the Countess wanted him to call on her at 7525 Ocean Drive before settling the point.

That really amazed me. It settled the point that there was an actual Everhard on the wire telephoning us. Up till now I had vaguely suspected an impostor.

"Well, are you going to take it?" I asked.

"Don't have to now."

I made a gesture. "I know you're not broke. I mean the interest of the situation, the unbelievable . . ."

"I'm not talking about money either. I mean I have already found out enough about her to analyze the problem without having to see her."

I was undone. Poggioli's life is a series of abstract analyses which are maddening to me. I flung at him: "I'm a story writer. I want details. And it wouldn't hurt you to dig up a few details either. It would improve your dry-as-dust lectures on criminology at the Ohio State University!"

Poggioli motioned me to hush, uncovered the transmitter, and said: "Countess, I have a friend — a most polite, tactful, intelligent, entertaining man . . ." He went on and gave me a great build-up. Here the woman said something. Poggioli answered, "No, Countess, I won't be out of the picture. You see, we live together. Anything that happens in your father's penthouse we will naturally discuss. He is a trained observer. . . ." Here he waited for several moments and finally concluded, "He will call immediately, Countess. Goodbye."

He turned to me with a droll look on his face. "What she really wanted was not an entertainer, but a criminologist. Now what earthly use would an Everhard have for . . ." He broke off and added, "You are to call at once at the villa on Ocean Drive."

I will not describe the Everhard estate on Tiamara Beach. Everybody has seen it or read about it. Guides haul winter tourists past the magnificent grounds and shout through megaphones the price of the sixty-thousand-dollar bronze gate at its entrance. So I can save myself a description.

I started walking from the gate to the villa with the peculiar penniless feeling which middle-class folk always feel in the presence of great wealth. About halfway I saw a plain smallish woman sitting uneasily in a sun-flooded kiosk. I say "uneasily" because she was peering toward the villa and the beach beyond. I wondered if this were the Countess Jalacki who had come out to watch for me and who happened to be watching in the wrong direction. I called out and asked. The woman glanced about and answered in a quick northern voice, "No, my name's Davis. Have you seen a little boy anywhere around?" I looked about, glad to be of service in such a famous place.

"Where is he likely to be?"

"Over on the beach."

This gave me pause. I wondered if it were hopelessly middle-class to look.for things where they were. Probably so. However I ventured to suggest: "If you know where he is why don't you look there?"

"Because this is little Jon's free hour," said Davis, with an ironic twist on the "free."

"I see," I said in a tone that told her I was at sea.

"It's the Count's idea," she explained. "He said little Jon ought to have a free hour to develop independence of character. At first I went with him to keep an eye on him during the free hour. When the Count found out he instructed me to stay in the villa, or here in the kiosk, while little Jon developed independence of character." Her tone told what she thought of this idea.

"Little Jon, I suppose, is the Count's son?"

"No, he's the son of Rosalie's second husband, Lord Rathmore."

Miss Davis (I had decided she was a single woman) had the Northern facility of expressing more by the way she clipped off her words than a Southern person could have said in a week.

"I take it you are little Jon's nurse?"

She said she was.

"Countess Jalacki is expecting me. Am I to go on up to . . .?"

"I don't know whether the Countess is up yet or not."

"She telephoned me."

"She has a telephone by her bed. When she wakes up, thinks of something, she telephones and has it done, then maybe she goes to sleep again."

"Uh . . . does this go on night and day?" I asked.

Miss Davis glanced at her wrist watch, then at the sun above the palms. "She's probably up now. You might go ahead."

It turned out that the chatelaine, or possibly the villaine (I really don't know what you would call the mistress of a villa), was up. A maid showed me into a sitting room with a great window overlooking the blue ocean. The Countess sat watching a youngish athletic man, a Newfoundland dog, and a small child on the beach. She turned as I entered.

"You are the man who writes Professor Poggioli's memoirs. I hope you are as clever as he is in analyzing why people do things."

I said I could hardly hope that, but that I had picked up some little tricks of analysis. . . . I saw she was not listening to me but was watching, with a troubled expression, the youngish man on the beach. He was hitting the dog with a roll of newspaper.

"Ercole is trying to break Napoleon from going into the surf after things," she said, explaining her inattention.

"I thought that was what Newfoundland dogs were for," I said.

"M-mm, ye-es, but Ercole says if Napoleon retrieves things out of the water it might encourage little Jon to play in the surf and something might happen to him."

I nodded, "I see that."

"Ercole is a real scientist," a touch of pride was in her voice, "everything he does is . . . scientific."

I paused a moment, then began again: "I believe you wanted to see me about a position with your father as his private secretary?"

"Yes, that was Ercole's idea, too."

"Now do you hire me or do you recommend me to your father?"
The Countess hesitated a moment. "I'll have to explain that to you.
The relations between my family on one side and my father and my
brother John Everhard II on the other are somewhat strained. We are
not *au courant* with what they are doing. So Ercole thought if we knew
my father's private secretary and he knew us, there would be some
connection between our two families. . . ."

I began to sense the drift of things. "But Countess, as your father's
private secretary, I couldn't give out . . . ah . . . unauthorized information."

She was annoyed. "Oh, not that sort of information. Just little
things — how he is getting on; how he slept. I don't hear anything at all.
It would be worth your while . . ."

"Well, that phase of it . . ." I lifted a hand to show that money
would not affect my loyalty, but I did wonder how much she would have
paid.

At this juncture the youngish athletic man whom I had seen
through the window entered the room.

"Ercole," she exclaimed, "I have tried to explain to this man why we
want to be on friendly terms with my father's private secretary, but I am
afraid he has misunderstood me completely." She introduced me to her
husband, Count Ercole Jalacki.

The Count was as concise and articulate as his wife was diffuse.

"It's very simple," he said, "the Countess' father is very ill and
requires a nurse. But there is almost no communication between his
family and ours, so the Countess is in continual suspense and uneasiness
about her father. It was my idea, when we learned that he needed a
secretary, for us to put in someone who would be friendly toward us and
who would keep us informed as to his condition. We would expect to
recompense you for any trouble you take on our account."

This was a very reasonable request. I said I would be glad to do that
for them, but that I would not expect or desire any pay.

"All we want to know," repeated the Count, "is when father
Everhard is feeling well and when he has his attacks."

I asked the nature of Mr. Everhard's trouble. The Count said
asthma.

"Oh, asthma," I said, expecting something more serious.

"But he is really very ill," stressed the Count, "and we want to know
the exact time father Everhard has his attacks, how long they last, what
the physician says causes them, and all such details."

I said that a daughter would naturally want to know such facts
about her father and agreed to supply them as best I could. The Count
was very pleased at this outcome, but it seemed to me that the Countess
appeared uncertain, even disturbed. I decided she must be a woman who
constitutionally never knew her own mind. The Count made immediate
arrangements for me. He said his man-of-all-work, Mr. Quinn, was

waiting for me and would chauffeur me over to the Ritz-Carlton whenever I was ready; "chauffeur" was the Count's own word.

I did not particularly relish this form of dismissal, yet there was something about the Count, a flavor to him, that made me quite willing to part with him with or without courtesy. To my surprise the Countess went along with me to the driveway. She was quite amiable now and as we talked of this and that she asked me a very odd question in a very simple manner. She wanted to know what a person could find out by learning *when* her father had his attacks.

"Why," I said, "how long they last, how severe . . ."

She stopped me. "I know that, of course, I mean . . . what else would he find out?"

I looked at her and wondered if she were quite bright. "What else could there be to find out?"

"I don't know. That's why I am so . . ." She broke off and said very earnestly, "Listen, Professor Poggioli is your friend, isn't he?" I said he was. "You'll see him today?" I reminded her that I lived with him. "Well, listen . . . when you go back home tonight, no matter whether you get the position as father's secretary or not, you ask him what else a person could find out by knowing when and how long my father had his spells."

"What else he could find out . . . I'm afraid I don't understand."

"I know you don't. Neither do I. But Professor Poggioli will, and please telephone me his answer."

I promised her I would and then wondered what in the world could be the basis of her anxiety and her question. A few minutes later I was in the car with Quinn, on my way to the Ritz Carlton Hotel.

Quinn proved talkative and as we motored along he mentioned that the Countess was about to become a mother. I exclaimed:

"Oh, that explains it." He asked me what it explained. I told him the queer question his mistress had asked me and added significantly, "Women in her condition are often very nervous and not themselves."

"I wouldn't put it that way," advised Quinn guardedly. "It's the first one that throws 'em off balance a bit, after that they get used to 'em and carry on all right. I know, Mrs. Quinn has had four."

"So you think the Countess has good reason for being uneasy . . ."

"Oh, no, but what I am saying is, it isn't her baby, because she's had one."

"Then what do you suppose she could have meant?" I asked.

"M-mm, she just wants to know what her husband could find out. You see, the Count is a very bright man, a *very* bright man."

Here Quinn drove along for several minutes in silence. Presently he began giving me the marital history of the Countess, perhaps as a background for the little riddle that confronted us.

"The Count isn't her first husband," he said. "He's her third."

"Why, she doesn't look . . ."

"No, she doesn't. A woman in her position never looks her age, but she is really older than the Count — too many years older for comfort, if you ask me. Little Jon Rathmore is the son of Lord Rathmore, her second husband. Count Jalacki was working in the Everhard laboratories and she met him there right after she had cut loose little Jon's father. So Count Jalacki caught her on the rebound. You see, Lord Rathmore was a playboy. So, of course, the Countess imagined she could be happy with the opposite. All married people imagine that. So she fell for Jalacki because he was not only a worker but a terrific worker . . . still is."

"You don't say!" I exclaimed. For I had the middle-class idea that the sons-in-law of great wealth were always idlers and wastrels.

"Oh, yes, still is. That round stone house you saw a little way up the beach from the villa is his laboratory. He's in it all day long, sometimes all night long. I know — I'm his laboratory assistant and man-of-all-work. Well, what the Countess imagined she wanted when she left Lord Rathmore was a worker. She got one all right — a very brilliant scientist. That's what caused the trouble between the two families."

"Jalacki's brilliance?" I asked in surprise.

"That's right. You see, he invented something in the Everhard laboratories before he married the Countess. He wanted credit for it. But these big companies don't give their research men credit for anything.

"Jalacki raised a fuss about it after the Countess became his wife, and she backed him. But her daddy and brother — that is, old man John Everhard I and young John Everhard II — put their feet down; said it was against precedent. They're great for precedent. The upshot was the Countess didn't get any concessions for her husband but she did get the villa, and her daddy and brother are now roughing it in the Ritz-Carlton until they can find suitable quarters elsewhere."

"Must be quite a privation," I said.

"Oh, it is," Quinn assured me, "and the two families don't have anything to do with each other any more."

After Quinn's description of the hardships of living in the Ritz-Carlton, I almost hesitated to work in such primitive surroundings. But I crushed my repugnance, went into the hotel, and had the room clerk telephone the penthouse that an applicant wanted an interview with John Everhard I in regard to a secretarial position. Presently I went up twenty-six stories in a small private elevator.

When I stepped out in the penthouse I met Miss Lemmle. She was the nurse in charge of the invalid and she was the person who really decided whether I would or would not do. After a brief interview she took me into the front "ocean" room, introduced me to her patient, then with a caution that he should not talk left us to convey information to each other in any other way we could. When she had shut the door the thin old man uttered in a wheezy whisper: "Damned bossy nurse!"

"If they weren't like that," I said, "they wouldn't be of any service to us."

"First good word . . . ever heard about her . . . she pay you anything . . . to say that?" He started to laugh but a stoppage interrupted him.

I laughed for him, then asked for some idea of my duties.

"Pretend to . . . read my correspondence . . . when she's in . . . read me the financial news . . . when she's out . . ."

"I see. Miss Lemmle forbids you to read the stock reports?"

He nodded. "Have to . . . hire a bootlegger."

"Not good for you?" I inquired, shortening my sentences after his fashion.

"Certainly it is . . . just her fool idea . . . when market goes up . . . my life goes up with it . . . it falls . . . I fall . . ." He began coughing and strangling hopelessly. Miss Lemmle entered the room, shook her finger at him, said he had talked too much. For a few moments she watched his spasm, then said sharply to me that she believed this was one of his attacks. She turned into a small adjoining room, came back with a hypodermic needle, turned up the sleeve of his dressing robe and treated his thin arm. She daubed the place with alcohol, then began to examine a number of scarifications by removing small bandages stuck here and there on his arms and chest. She looked at the scratched areas beneath them.

"This is a puzzling case," she said to me. "Dr. Mitzoff is trying to find out what he is allergic to. These attacks come on at the most irregular intervals. . . ." She shook her head over the scarified places, none of which were inflamed.

A wind was blowing in through the window from the ocean. I looked out over the blue expanse. It was dotted here and there by a sail or a wisp of smoke.

"His trouble might come from some ship in passing." I hazarded, "smoke from coal; dust from some sort of freight."

"That's what Dr. Mitzoff is trying to find out," said the nurse.

When I left the hotel I took a bus up Ocean Drive to report to the Jalackis. The Countess received me and immediately asked me what Professor Poggioli had said. I told her I hadn't seen Poggioli, that I had dropped by to report that her father had had an attack of his trouble.

"Oh, yes," she answered vaguely. "Was it bad?"

"I don't know how it compared with the rest of them, but it wasn't good."

Just then Count Jalacki entered the room. When he saw me he burst out: "Father Everhard has had an attack!" I said he had and the Countess asked him how he knew. "Because the man has come back so soon," explained the Count a little impatiently; then he turned to me. "When did it happen?"

"Why," I said, "it has just happened. I came on here at once."

The Count gave me the look of an expert who has the misfortune to deal with a numbskull. "You didn't notice precisely when his attack began?"

"Well . . . about an hour . . . or an hour and a half ago."

The Count's lean face was really impassive but somehow he conveyed to me his satiric contempt for a man who was engaged to make a report on a case and who would say that it happened about an hour or an hour and a half ago. The Countess felt it too for she asked in a suspicious tone, "What difference does it make?"

"A report is accurate or it isn't accurate, Rosalie."

He made me feel so uncomfortable that I told him I would try to be more exact in the future. As I took my leave the Countess said in a significant voice: "Now don't forget *my* question and telephone me."

Count Jalacki glanced at her. "What was your question, Rosalie?"

The Countess hesitated, then said, "I wanted to know if my father was gaining or losing weight."

"Yes, you'd be interested in that; specific physical details always catch your attention, Rosalie." The Count's voice was level and unstressed; whether he believed her or whether he was privately accusing her of fabrication, I was not sure, but I did know that she was on tenterhooks when he was around.

An hour later I recounted to Poggioli, as best I could, our odd and rather puzzling colloquy. I asked Poggioli why the Countess had tried to deceive the Count, and back of that why had she been suspicious of his inquiry into her father's illness. And, since she was suspicious, did Jalacki's inquiry as to the precise minute of old John Everhard's attacks confirm in any way Rosalie's suspicions.

Poggioli pondered these vague questions and said he could see no possible connection between the wife's suspicious attitude and her husband's questions. Jalacki, evidently, was a technical man who normally dealt in measurements of extreme delicacy, both of time and space, and the wife, soured on her husband, construed every word he uttered, every movement he made, into something inimical to her and her family.

"She's about to become a mother," I told him.

"Oh, well now, that's it."

"But it isn't her first child," I added, remembering Quinn's observations on that point.

"If she suspected her husband before her present condition, she would be a great deal more doubtful of him now. His simplest inquiry she would translate into a threat. You know yourself that Jalacki can't make any improper use of the precise time of old Mr. Everhard's asthmatic attacks. That's impossible."

I immediately telephoned Poggioli's judgment on the point to the Countess. I wanted to ease her mind if possible. But instead of soothing her she became even more incoherent. She told me with a kind of pride in her voice that her husband was a very brilliant and practical man, that he never asked useless questions, that he used his knowledge, always. After an excited pause she added that if she found out anything more she would report it to me and that I should report it to Poggioli; that he, Professor Poggioli, was the only hope she had.

For the next few days I went regularly to the Ritz-Carlton penthouse and bootlegged market information to old John Everhard I. I hit on a plan of memorizing the financial reports and repeating them to the old man as a part of our conversation instead of reading them from the papers. This ruse apparently circumvented Miss Lemmle. I must say I became quite fond of my employer. The influence which the rise and fall of the market had upon our patient amused me and at the same time touched my sympathy. It was not his reason that caused his spirits to go up with the market and fall with it; it was the habit of a lifetime. One morning he told me that he expected some day to pass out on a bear market. I warned him seriously if he didn't change his mental attitude he probably would. He seemed disappointed in my reply and told me I was talking like Miss Lemmle.

This was our status when one morning Miss Lemmle met me at the elevator door as I entered the penthouse. Very solemnly she asked me to step into her kitchen for a moment. I thought: "She's found out I repeat the stock reports to the old man."

Her kitchen was where she cooked her patient's special food, prepared his medicine, and kept her records and charts. She looked at me with the severity of a schoolmistress eyeing a small boy, and requested me to glance around the room. I glanced around the room, then back at her, a little amused and curious. Then suddenly she began asking me questions; where had I been last night, whom had I seen, when had I got home, how did I go home, from where had I started home? She was evidently giving me the third degree to the best of her ability and every moment I expected her to fling in, "Do you read the market reports to Mr. Everhard?" If she had asked that I would have denied it. Because I knew the old man couldn't last long. I knew I was giving him the last bit of pleasure he would get in this world. But to my surprise the nurse never mentioned financial reports at all. Presently she opened her kitchen door and admitted me to the patient in the "ocean" room.

As soon as I was alone with the old man, I asked him why Miss Lemmle had given me the third degree. The old fellow was amused into a wheezing and coughing fit, but finally explained that on the preceding night somebody had entered the penthouse kitchen. Today, he said, Miss Lemmle was grilling everybody indiscriminately — bell hops, night clerks, everybody — trying to find out who it was.

"What did the thief take?" I asked. "That ought to give some clue."

"That's the point," gasped the old financier, "that's why she . . . suspects anybody and everybody . . . he didn't take anything."

I was astonished. "How does she know there was anybody . . .?"

"She saw him . . . standing in the kitchen . . . standing and writing . . . that's why she has to get at him with questions . . . nothing on him she can identify."

"Why, that's the most extraordinary . . . what object could he have in *writing?*"

"That's what she's going to ask him . . . if she catches him."

"How did he get away?"

"He jumped out the window . . . by time she got out on the roof . . . he was gone . . . don't know where . . . elevator house . . . over the roof wall . . . into a top story window . . . don't know where."

"Has she checked on what guests were in the top story last night?"

"My son . . . his family . . . occupy the whole . . . top story."

Well, that was the set-up. When I went home that noon I asked Poggioli what he could possibly deduce from a burglar entering a nurse's kitchen and making notes in it, but taking nothing.

Poggioli waggled a finger at me. "One single criminal clue is like a geometrical line; it establishes a direction but doesn't locate a point. Two clues, if they are related to the same crime, should define the crime, or the intended crime, fairly accurately."

"*Intended* crime?" I repeated.

"An intruder doesn't enter a house and make notes without an object. The object must be illegal, or at least objectionable to the owner of the house, and most probably criminal, for a man to risk his liberty merely to get some notes."

I became seriously concerned for my employer. I said, "Look here Poggioli, if somebody is plotting against old man Everhard you've got to figure it out in advance and stop him in time."

"My dear fellow," said Poggioli gravely, "you have put your finger on a sore spot in modern criminology. As now practised, it isn't a *preventive* science; it is a *retributive* science. It is organized to pursue and punish the criminal *after* the fact, but it has no comprehensive machinery either to halt or to punish the criminal *before* the fact. In short, the fact in modern criminology is always a material thing — the accomplished crime; whereas the fact should be a *psychological* thing — the intended crime. Until we develop such a technique, with appropriate treatment for proved criminals, we are no more than barbarians."

"That's all very well," I said, quite out of patience, "that will be fine talk for some future time, but what are you going to do now with burglars breaking into old man Everhard's kitchen and taking notes?"

Poggioli made a soothing gesture, "I just explained to you that one line cannot locate a point, nor one clue a crime. If we are fortunate we will get another line, another clue; where those two lines cross will establish the location, personnel and magnitude of the intended crime. We must be on the alert and recognize this second clue when it . . ." He was interrupted by a buzz from my telephone.

I picked it up and the voice of Countess Jalacki asked if Professor Poggioli were in my apartment. I said he was and asked what new thing had happened to her. She asked in a rush would Poggioli please come over at once. Her husband, his man Quinn, and her little son Jon Everhard Rathmore had gone fishing.

"But listen, Countess," I reasoned with her, "is that why you want Poggioli to come to your villa — *because your husband has gone fishing?*"

"Yes, yes, it is," implored the woman. "I want him to reason out for me what Ercole means, what he intends to do, before it's too late!"

"You mean you think he is up to something because he went fishing?"

"I know it! Never before in all his life has he gone fishing! Always he works, no matter who comes or who goes, he works in his laboratory! Now he has gone fishing!"

As little sense as this made, her excitement was so contagious it infected me. I stopped the transmitter with my palm and rather nervously explained this absurd thing to Poggioli. I finished by saying, "Of course, it's her condition. What she says makes no sense at all."

"What she says is as rational as for a burglar to break into a kitchen and make notes," observed Poggioli.

"But what connection can a notemaking burglar possibly have with Count Jalacki going fishing?"

"If I knew I wouldn't have to call on the Countess Jalacki to find out. But don't you think it is very probable that they are connected? Look at the situation. Two branches of the same family, which are at loggerheads with each other, have two seemingly irrational incidents happen to them at about the same time. Doesn't that suggest a connection?"

Poggioli and I locked the apartment, went out into the street, hailed a taxi, and set out for the Everhard villa on Ocean Drive.

When we reached the villa the Countess Jalacki proved of little help in reading the riddle she had posed. Poggioli talked with her, as diplomatically as he could, trying to obtain some reason why her husband's fishing trip should disturb her, but he got none. At last he was about to return to our apartment when the mistress of the villa bestirred herself to keep him with her. She insisted that we look at her paintings, then at her antiques — in fact, we did the same sort of tourist's tour inside her villa that the Tiamara guides conducted outside. And every time we passed a clock in any of the rooms the Countess glanced at it nervously. Finally the villa ran out. There wasn't anything more to show. And our hostess suddenly thought of the Count's laboratory and insisted that we see it. By this time both Poggioli and I had become curious to know what the Countess was waiting for, so we went with her.

The laboratory was a round stone building a short distance up the beach from the villa. It was simply a chemical research laboratory and held much paraphernalia whose use I did not know. What did interest me were some charts on the wall. One was a graph of the Wall Street stock and bond market. From the graph I could see the market was in the midst of a relative depression. Then there was a detailed government meteorological report giving wind direction and velocity hour by hour, and finally a government survey of the district of Tiamara showing the bay, the city, and the keys or islands strung along the coast. Jalacki had marked in red the distances of these keys from a point on Tiamara Beach. And there was one list on the wall of irregular dates. I will not say it was a puzzling list, because I had no reason to puzzle over it. It was simply an unknown quantity. The whole set-up seemed to be that of a chemical research man who had become interested in meteorology as a hobby. And I was just thinking how unfortunate it was for humanity as a whole when a skillful research man like Count Jalacki obtained enough money through marriage to stop real creative work and take up play, even if it were highly scientific play with meteorology, when I was jerked out of my reflections by a scream from the Countess. I whirled and saw Count Jalacki, his man Quinn, and the little boy in the doorway. The next moment I realized the Countess' scream had not been from fear but from joy. She ran to her little boy, Jon, knelt beside him and caught him to her bosom. She was telling the child that he must never leave his mother again and in the midst of this was asking if he had caught any fish. The little boy answered that he had brought back some shells and corals for his grandfather and pulled around a small collector's bag to show his mother.

"Why, that's lovely, darling, that's sweet of you," praised the mother, exaggerating the importance of the shells as one does a child's gift. Here the Count interposed to say that he and Quinn had brought along some sea fans and sea anemone which he would add to little Jon's collection to form a little aquarium to interest and amuse Mr. Everhard during his confinement, "And", he added in a significant tone, "I thought it might also serve as a little peace offering."

The Countess was touched. She said, "Ercole, that is sweet of you." And then pressing the little boy to her side she started joyfully to the villa.

The only interpretation I could place on this scene and the Countess' previous nervousness was that she had been desperately uneasy about her little boy. Why she wanted to have Poggioli on hand when the fishing party returned, I did not quite know. Possibly if the child had not returned she wanted Poggioli to be present to question the men . . . but this explanation was so unnatural, not to say fantastic, that I discarded it.

Count Jalacki watched his wife and her child disappear with a faint quirk of cynical amusement on his otherwise impassive face. He said to Poggioli: "The father of that little boy, so I've been told, was simply a spendthrift of time and money, yet the Countess is utterly wrapped up in his child."

"It's her child," I interposed, "as well as his."

"Rosalie's part in the child would hardly validate its sire," observed the Count drily; then he dropped me from the conversation and turned to Poggioli with the eagerness of a brilliant lonely man who has not met an intellectual equal for a long time.

He explained his maps. They were of the waters around Tiamara. He was interested in tropical sea life and had gone out that morning for specimens. He meant to experiment in his laboratory to see if he could turn them to some commercial use. He explained with a touch of self-mockery that in his youth he had hoped to devote his life to pure science but now that he had come to America he was looking for financial returns.

His talk then returned to the Countess and her little son. He said of course the Countess was emotional and irrational about her child.

He went on to decry American democracy as being imbued with feminism and sentimentality. If we were to hold our land, he said, against the competition of other countries and peoples, our psychology would have to become hard, efficient, rational and masculine.

Naturally I had heard that talk before, many times before, but it struck me that if he spouted off such doctrines before the Countess she wouldn't take them as indifferently as I, and that she might easily be disturbed about her little son. So at this point the whole trivial mystery posed by the Countess became clear to me, and I dismissed the matter from my mind.

Poggioli and I were now ready to go home. Count Jalacki went with us to the villa where we said good-bye to the Countess. Amidst our leave-taking the Countess asked us if we were driving home by way of the Ritz-Carlton, would we deliver little Jon's present to his grandfather. All we would have to do, she explained, was to hand the little collection to the footman at the hotel door. Naturally we were glad to do this and eventually delivered the peace-making gift at the entrance of the Ritz-Carlton, then taxied on home.

As we drove along I observed Poggioli was writing something in his notebook.

"What are you writing?" I asked.

He said he was copying down the list of dates on the laboratory wall which he had read over and memorized.

"A list of dates!" I ejaculated. "Did you actually memorize a list of——"

Poggioli ticked off something on his fingers and put down another date. "I have a mnemonic system that makes this sort of thing fairly easy."

"But what object can you have in copying a list of dates?"

"He didn't explain this list." Poggioli counted on his fingers and wrote in another date. "But I know from Jalacki's mental make-up that these dates must perform some function."

I watched him with continued curiosity, touched with amusement.

"All right," I agreed, "suppose they do hang together somehow with wind velocities and wind directions and the local geographical distances of the different keys in Tiamara Bay, I still don't see why you are interested in a column of bald dates."

"My basic reason," said Poggioli, "is because Jalacki lied to his wife. I know it is quite usual for men to lie to their wives, but they seldom or never lie on points unimportant to . . ."

I was amazed. "Count Jalacki lied?"

"That child's collection of shells and coral and whatnot . . . Do you imagine a child of that age would ever have dreamed of giving a collection of anything to his grandfather? It's absurd. I know the suggestion didn't come from the child. It must have come from the Count. So . . . *why?*"

"Possibly it is the Count's peace offering to his father-in-law," I suggested.

"He would hardly have deceived his wife on that point," said the psychologist. "The Countess would have been far more pleased to know her husband was trying to make friends with her father than for her little son to have sent him a present. No, there is a logical hiatus in there. The Count has some motive which fits in and explains this situation perfectly. He makes a gift, a marine collection, and on the walls of his laboratory are charts of the bay, weather reports, a graph of the Wall Street stock market . . . and these dates."

I almost smiled: "That's why you memorized them?"

He made no answer to this but continued remembering and jotting down more figures until our taxi reached home.

In my library Poggioli took my nautical almanac and began studying it. I must say I was more interested in his method than I was in his particular problem. As a matter of fact, I didn't believe he had a real problem. He had simply exaggerated a friendly peace offering of Jalacki to his father-in-law into a chimera of suspicion which had no foundation in fact. I became more sure of this when the criminologist turned and said to me in an odd voice: "These dates are the exact hour and minute of the low tides in Tiamara Bay."

"Exactly," I agreed. "Count Jalacki is interested in sea life."

"Certainly. But these dates are very irregular. They skip days, then a month, then a week or two, then a half dozen days . . . You see, there is some *controlling factor* in here that we know nothing about."

I really was amused. "Poggioli, it's irregular because it is Jalacki's hobby. He took time off only when he could — the way a business man plays golf."

My friend made an impatient gesture. "That man never made hit-and-miss observations in all his life. He's naturally thorough in everything he does. Let me see, do you happen to have the government weather reports for these dates?"

I had them and produced them, and Poggioli began studying the weather reports for the dates on his list. Finally he straightened up, wriggled his shoulders to get a kink out of his back, then said to me in an odd voice:

"This is not a hit-and-miss list! It is a complete list of the low tides in Tiamara Bay *when the wind lay East Southeast!*"

"Every one?" I asked.

"Certainly, certainly, every one. . . . Now, Jalacki couldn't possibly have chosen an arbitrary wind. The East Southeast wind must have done something . . . maybe Jalacki didn't make this list, maybe he determined something from the list. . . . You see, don't you, how we may have been trying to work this problem backwards — trying to find out how Jalacki made his list when in reality Jalacki received the list from some source and simply used it as data, just as I am doing now, to solve some problem of his own."

Well, when Poggioli said this, a queer — I might say, a fantastic — notion flickered through my mind. "Look here, Poggioli. Do you suppose it could have any connection with that burglar writing in Miss Lemmle's kitchen? Could the burglar have been copying the nurse's report on old man Everhard's attacks of asthma . . . you know . . . their dates?"

I hardly knew what this would signify. It was just a shadowy suspicion with still more shadowy connections in my mind, but to Poggioli it must have cleared up the whole riddle. He gave an exclamation, whirled to the telephone, asked me for old John Everhard's number. I gave it. He dialled, waited, then dialled again. No response. Then he turned to the directory, got the number of the Ritz-Carlton Hotel, and twirled that. Somebody answered and Poggioli said hurriedly: "I've dialled the private telephone in the Everhard penthouse and get no response. Will you see if it's in order?"

I heard the voice of a clerk say in a pinched metallic tone: "The penthouse wire is purposely cut out. The penthouse wishes to avoid curiosity and sympathy calls. Mr. John Everhard I died of a sudden attack of asthma an hour ago."

Poggioli leaped up from his chair. He made a nervous gesture for me to follow him. As we went outside I asked him what it meant.

"The most calculated, cold-blooded murder! Here's a cab!"

We had some trouble at the Ritz getting to see the younger Mr. Everhard, but at last we entered a lift and shot upwards. A tall dark man with a banker's gravity met us at the door. Poggioli came at once to his point.

"Mr. Everhard," he said, "I have reason to believe your father came to an unnatural death. I am a criminologist by profession, I have come to place myself at your service."

The financier remained apparently calm. He indicated chairs and asked Poggioli to go on.

"Before I proceed, will you get me Miss Lemmle's report on your father's illness. If it is identical with the list I brought with me, my case is proved."

Mr. Everhard sent a man up for Miss Lemmle's chart. When he came down with it I looked over Poggioli's shoulder and managed to see that the first two entries on each list were the same. Poggioli showed the two complete records to the financier.

"The explanation is clear," he said. "Count Jalacki obtained this chart from your father's penthouse — he was the intruder. He studied it and found out that your father's attacks occurred at irregular intervals — *but always at low tide when the wind direction was East Southeast.* This gave him the direction of the island that contained the specific material to which your father was allergic. Since it was always at low tide he knew that material lay exposed at the water's edge, probably on reefs. By calculating the wind velocities he knew the approximate distance of the key. When Jalacki obtained this data, he took a boat, went out to the key at low tide, collected shells, corals, sea growth and whatnot. Then he arranged them in an aquarium and sent them as a pretended gift from little Jon Everhard Rathmore. The aquarium contained exactly the material to which your father was allergic. It brought on the last violent attack which ended in your father's death. That is what I have to tell you, and I stand ready to repeat it before a court of law — although I cannot guarantee that the nature of my evidence will secure a conviction."

The financier remained impassive. Then he asked: "Why did Jalacki do all this when my father would have probably died inside a few months at best?"

"I cannot be sure. It may have been simple revenge but I noticed a graph of the stock and bond market in Jalacki's laboratory. It forecast an inflation of values. Possibly Jalacki murdered your father now so his estate would be assessed for tax purposes at a low value, and later the administrator would be able to pay off the death dues by the sale of stocks at advanced prices. Such a maneuver would be in accord with his psychology."

Mr. John Everhard II listened to all this, then explained impassively that it was the policy of the Everhard Company never to permit legal action between its members. "Such an action would reflect on the standing of our company," explained the capitalist, "and the standing of our company is more important than retribution, Mr. Poggioli. In fact, it is more important than the lives of any of our personnel. But you must know I am deeply grateful for your offer."

Poggioli made a brief bow and said if Mr. Everhard desired his testimony inside the Everhard corporation, he, Poggioli, would still be at his service.

He was interrupted in this speech by the telephone. Mr. Everhard went to it, listened a moment, then said:

"Yes . . . yes . . . Will you please express my sympathy to my sister, Rosalie? . . . Thank you." He replaced the instrument and pressed a button on his desk. A young man appeared at an inner door. The financier said: "Henry, will you tell my wife, as tactfully as you can, that our little nephew, Jon Everhard Rathmore, has just been found dead in the surf at our old home on Ocean Drive, through accidental drowning."

I stared at Poggioli. For the first time in our long association, I saw a look of real fear — almost terror — in his eyes. . . .

A Note to Count Jalacki

In his apartment at the Ritz-Carlton Hotel the financier, Mr. John Everhard II, dialled his sister, the Countess Rosalie Everhard-Jalacki. Mr. Everhard, now senior member of the great Everhard Company, appeared deeply disturbed. He looked at the heavily built man at his side.

"I'll telephone her that you are coming right over, Professor Poggioli." As Poggioli made an inclination of assent the financier continued in his disquiet manner: "Do you suppose you can make certain about little Jon's death . . . in your usual quiet, analytical way. I don't want to disturb Rosalie."

"I see you have settled in your mind that your little nephew did not die of drowning as reported," observed the criminologist.

The financier was surprised. "Why do you say that?"

"Because when a person is drowned, people usually refer to it as a 'drowning'; but any other mode of death is referred to simply as a 'death.' That's how I know you suspect your little nephew was murdered."

For a moment Mr. Everhard made no reply to this odd observation; then he said: "I would like to get a trustworthy report on how little Jon died as quickly as I can. I know you can get it from Rosalie. I understand she has the greatest confidence in you, Professor Pog——" Here he broke off to say into the telephone, "That you, Rosalie? I wanted to know how you are feeling. You must be brave and collect yourself, Rosalie. I have a friend here beside me; I want him to go over and talk with you, Rosalie. I know he can help you. . . . It's Professor Poggioli, Rosalie; I know you tried to get him not long ago. . . . What? . . . But Rosalie, I thought you would *want* to see Professor Poggioli. . . . You say it is too late now. . . ." The financier turned to Poggioli, "She says little Jon is dead and you can do no good . . ." This was such an unexpected outcome that the brother returned to his persuasions, "But Rosalie, Professor Poggioli is such a brilliant man. . . . What? . . . *Him?* . . . Naturally, Rosalie, *he* is available, but why should you want to see him? . . . But, Rosalie, *he* is a man of no talent whatever, quite — uh — simple in fact. . . . You say you will not see Professor Poggioli? . . ." Everhard waited for several seconds until his sister finished, then covered the telephone, and turned to me with a blank expression: "Rosalie says she would like to see you, if you will come over."

I was the most astounded of the three of us. "Me! Why should . . ."

"She says you are sympathetic and kind," repeated her brother still looking completely at a loss.

We all stood pondering this queer turn; finally Poggioli asked: "Did your sister consult with someone while she was telephoning?"

"I . . . don't know."

"Between sentences, did you hear her put her palm over the receiver?"

"I wasn't listening for . . ."

"Well, she did. She was consulting with her husband. Count Jalacki thinks that if I come over I will find something about him, but if my friend comes over the Count will find out something about us. That's what is behind her selection."

"Well, I'll go," I said, "if it will do any good."

"That's the point," said Mr. Everhard, "whether it will do good — or harm."

"I'll talk to him before he starts," suggested Poggioli, "he won't do any harm." The criminologist turned to me: "You must be cautious about how you answer the Count's questions. Don't let him pump you."

"I really don't know anything for the Count to pump," I said, a little nettled at this unanimous implication that I was a numbskull.

Mr. Everhard disregarded me; he asked in deep disturbance: "Professor Poggioli, do you consider my sister's life in danger?"

"She can't be in any danger so long as she has not given birth to Count Jalacki's child," pointed out Poggioli. "The child will be the heir to your sister's part of the family estate. Through this child Count Jalacki will come into control of a part of the immense Everhard holdings."

"Yes, yes, of course," agreed the financier nervously. "Well . . . well . . . you can't go over and see Rosalie yourself. . . ." He removed his hand from the receiver which had been blocked all this time. "All right, Rosalie," he said into it, "I'll send him right over. Goodbye and good luck."

Mr. Everhard put the instrument in its fork and stood pressing it down for a moment; then he said slowly that he believed he would write Count Jalacki a note for me to take to him. "Just a line to express my sympathy for his grief," he explained. Slowly and thoughtfully he walked to the door of his secretary's office and went inside.

Poggioli and I looked at each other. To me Mr. Everhard's action seemed just a little odd but I knew that Poggioli's analytical mind dissolved this queerness into particular clues to the millionaire's present thoughts and, no doubt, to his future conduct.

Presently Mr. Everhard returned and handed me an envelope which he asked me to hand to the Count.

With my message of sympathy, Poggioli and I went to the elevator and dropped to the street floor. In front of the hotel, as we waited for a taxi, I expected Poggioli to speak and interpret the hidden meaning of the note; I mean, the motives that had caused Mr. Everhard to write a letter of sympathy to his unspeakable brother-in-law. But he said nothing. He simply stood on the sidewalk, pondering the situation. Finally a bit out of patience, I said: "You were going to give me some instructions, I believe."

"Oh, yes, yes, certainly. . . . Of course you know whom to look for at the villa to get a complete account of little Jon's death?"

I was taken aback. "Whom to look for?" I ejaculated.

"Yes, the person for whom your note is *really* intended."

"Why, I haven't the slightest idea. Isn't it for the Count?"

I think Poggioli was amused inwardly at my bewilderment.

"It is hardly a supposition, it is almost a certainty that Mr. Everhard has some informer in the Jalacki establishment and the note is really for this person."

"Why, that's the weirdest . . .why in the world do you imagine . . ."

"Do you recall this sentence that Mr. Everhard addressed to me? He said, speaking of his sister Rosalie, 'I understand she has the greatest confidence in you, Professor Poggioli.' Now a person uses the phrase 'I understand' only when some third person has given him information about another person or thing. Since the Everhard and Jalacki families have been *incommunicado* for some time, there must be a third person in the Jalacki household who furnishes Mr. Everhard with information. Now that third person is the one you should make contact with to obtain definite information about little Jon's death."

There was, of course, the usual Poggiolian hint of satire in thus reminding me of my errand, as though I were a little child. I passed over this in my astonishment that he had deduced, in such an exceedingly simple manner, the presence of an informer in the Jalacki household. I could not resist commenting on it, but Poggioli waggled a deprecating finger: "That isn't the puzzle at all."

I asked him what was. He said the real riddle was why Mr. Everhard wanted any proof or any details whatsoever of his little nephew's drowning or murder.

I was amazed. I asked what could be more natural than for an uncle . . .

Poggioli interrupted me to say, "Because I have already given him complete proof that Jalacki murdered his father. He told us outright that he would make no legal move about that on account of the reputation of the Everhard Company. Now what will he do with more proof . . . this time, of his nephew's murder?"

"He simply wants to be sure!" I cried.

The psychologist quirked his lips. "John Everhard never wanted to be sure of anything that didn't have a direct bearing on his plans and schemes for the future."

"If he doesn't really want the details of little Jon's death, what's he sending me to the villa for?"

The criminologist lifted a finger. "There you have asked a question. Why has he? It seems clear to me that the note of condolence is just a ruse to get a message through — to some stool pigeon in the Jalacki villa."

At this moment a taxicab swerved into the sidewalk. I got into it and set out for the Count's establishment. There is no use in my trying to describe the fog of suspicion and puzzlement which Poggioli had created in my head. But I finally decided he was wrong. For him to whip up all these speculations from a casual phrase, a mere word — no, it was fantastic; it was worse than fantastic, it was ridiculous. That was my decision when I dismissed my cab at the great bronze gate of the Jalacki villa.

As I entered the grounds the heavy tropical growth seemed somehow menacing in its gloom. A little way inside I saw a gardener truing the line of grass along the side of the driveway. As I passed him he straightened up and said: "These are private grounds, Mister."

I told him I was on my way to the villa, that I had an appointment with the Countess.

He looked at me suspiciously. "You have?"

"Why, yes," I said, "I've been here before, you must have seen me?"

This eased his suspicion that I was a presumptuous tourist. "No-o, I haven't seen you before, Mister. I just started work here this morning."

I pricked up my ears. It struck me that if Poggioli were here he would make something of this, twist it into some sort of clue. I asked: "Taking the place of the old gardener?"

"Of the assistant gardener."

"When did he leave?"

"Why, I understand he pulled out of here last night. The employment agency sent me over this morning."

My feeling of having hit on something of importance increased. Right in the midst of this tragedy why should an assistant gardener have flown? Then I asked in a voice as nearly inconsequential as I could make it: "This gardener who went away last night . . . know his name?"

"No."

"Know where he went?"

"Mm-mm, no-o. . . . Took a plane some'ers . . . North, I imagine . . . Did he owe you anything?"

I became quite excited that an assistant gardener had fled by plane. I said, "No, he didn't. Where's the closest phone — I mean, public telephone?"

"Don't have to go to a public phone. There's a telephone right over there in that clump of frangipanni."

"That's just a service line to the house?"

"No, the head gardener dials downtown for whatever he wants. It's a through line."

I thanked him and said I would use it. I was sharply excited that I had stumbled on a new trail the moment I had stepped into the villa grounds. I wanted to get in touch with Poggioli, tell him to go to the flying fields and find out where that assistant gardener had fled. I went over to the clump of trees and with unsteady forefinger dialled my own apartment. Poggioli was home. I kept my voice down so the new gardener would not hear me and then spoke in a roundabout fashion, so if he did hear he would understand nothing.

"Poggioli, I've got it."

"Got it? Got what? The person you were sent out to . . . ?"

Then I remembered I had been sent out to make contact with Mr. Everhard's informer at the villa. So I said, "No, no, not the s.p. I've contacted the . . . the original Mephistopheles, if you know what I mean."

Came a pause and I knew Poggioli's marvellous brain was interpreting my allusion; finally he asked in a flat voice:

"Are you telephoning in the presence of a third person?"

"Well," I said in a low tone, "maybe I am, that's why I have to . . ."

He interrupted me briefly. "Proceed as directed."

"You mean . . . after the s.p.?"

"This third person, does he appear to be a man who doesn't know how to spell simple English words?" asked Poggioli in a disagreeable tone. "Proceed as directed. Goodbye." And he cut me off.

Well, I was almost beside myself. There was what might be the vital clue and — I could have broken Poggioli's neck for his ill-timed irony. I came out of the clump of trees, nodded at the new assistant gardener, and started on for the villa. On my way through the jungly grounds I came upon the kiosk and once more the nurse, Miss Mary Davis, was in it. She had her head down on the rail of the circular seat and was having what women call a good cry. I tried to get past in silence, but I suppose I made some noise for she looked up with reddened eyes.

"It's you," she said accusatively.

"Yes," I said, pausing.

"What have you come for now?" she asked in a tone that charged me with having brought great harm on the family.

"Miss Davis," I asked, "what are you insinuating? I haven't done anything at all. I was sent here before just as I am sent here now." I stood looking at her for a space, then I asked baldly, "Look here, Miss Davis, what do you know about this business anyway?" I sat down on the other side of the circular seat, facing her.

"Don't talk so loudly," she cautioned, blinking her wet eyes and glancing around.

I lowered my voice. "Very well, now go ahead and tell me . . . was he drowned?"

She straightened. "What do you mean?"

I moved a bit closer to her. "I mean, did he drown himself, or was he drowned, or was he thrown in the sea after he was dead? Hadn't you thought of these questions yourself?"

She gave me a frightened look. "Yes, I had," she whispered.

"Well, you've seen the body . . . since they found it?" I persisted.

She sighed and wiped her eyes. "Yes, of course."

"Well . . . which was it . . . how did he die?"

She bit her lips to keep her face straight. "How would I know?"

"Why, by his face," I said, annoyed at her ignorance. "If it was white it meant he died one way, if it was purple and congested it meant he died another way. It's very easy to tell."

"Well, which is which?" she asked with a gasp.

"That I don't know," I said, "but any criminologist would know at once." Here she put her head down and began weeping outright once more. "Look here, Miss Davis, don't feel so bad. We'll get a coroner's jury on this case."

Here she looked up at me, her face changed. I glanced around in the direction she faced and there stood Count Jalacki quite close to us. How he had got there, why we hadn't seen him before, I hadn't the slightest notion.

In acute embarrassment, mingled I must say with a touch of apprehension, I wondered if he had overheard what we had just said. I supposed he had. I arose and made a feeble attempt at composure by producing my letter and telling him that I had brought a note from Mr. Everhard, his brother-in-law.

He took it and said coldly: "You lingered so long with Miss Davis I thought you weren't coming." That was an odd thing for him to say. How did he know I had lingered with Miss Davis? Then I realized that Mr. Everhard had telephoned the Count I was coming. If he came out to meet me like this, the note I brought evidently was very important. I tried to make some bold deduction, such as Poggioli would have done, but nothing came to me.

Count Jalacki dropped my note in his pocket and said we would walk to his laboratory through the grounds. Now that was exactly what I didn't want to do. The Count and I had no more in common than a hawk and a haddock. Besides, I wanted to stay and talk with Miss Davis. She had the very information I was after. I tried to excuse myself by saying that the Countess had telephoned for me to come to see her, and that I would go directly to the villa and after I had talked with the Countess, I would come to his laboratory.

To this the Count replied with his faintly ironic courtesy that he would appreciate it if I would delay my visit to the Countess for a while. He said he had just come from the villa and had found her so nervous and disturbed that he had given her a sleeping tablet. He said we would go to the laboratory first, then later go to the villa, by which time he hoped the Countess would be awake.

That, of course, kept me from further talk with Miss Davis. I was regretting this when abruptly a new and profoundly disturbing suspicion seized me. The moment I thought of it I was certain it was true. What could be more in keeping with the Count's serpentine and inhuman psychology, than for him, when Mr. Everhard had telephoned I was coming, to give his wife an overdose of some sedative! What could have been more Jalacki-like? What an appearance of innocence it would give him to tell me about the sleeping potion, have me wait with him until the unhappy woman died, then go to the villa and together find her corpse. His very frankness with me would certainly make any jury believe the overdose was accidental.

A light sweat broke out on my brow and upper lip as I penetrated his design. Also, I will admit, I felt pleased with myself that I had made a deduction quite as clever as any I had ever heard from Poggioli. But unfortunately I could think of no polite way of escaping from this Bluebeard and saving the Countess' life. Futilely I walked on with him to the laboratory.

The Count continued to talk in his usual harsh voice and with his usual smooth irony. Miss Davis, he suggested, was a very interesting woman. I agreed. He wondered if I had ever talked to Mr. Quinn, a very interesting man. I said I had once when Mr. Quinn took me in a car from the villa to town.

Count Jalacki dilated on the point. "Common people," he said, "are always more interesting than the upper classes, or even the intellectuals, because they are not specialized. Take the run of such folk — gardeners, nurses, laboratory assistants. What they know, everybody knows; what they feel, everybody feels. So they are the sympathetic bosom companions of the world at large."

I nodded. I couldn't answer him. It made me nauseated to hear him talk. I knew that in a subtle way he was really bragging to me that at this very moment he was murdering his wife.

In the laboratory we found Mr. Quinn, doing something with chemicals. The Count absently reached in his pocket, drew out the note I had brought him, and placed it in a little basket of unopened correspondence. He did this, I am sure, to show me in what esteem he held his brother-in-law, John Everhard II. Then he began telling me about Quinn. Quinn had worked with him ever since Jalacki first entered the Everhard Company's New Jersey laboratory. That was before the Count had married Rosalie. After their marriage he had brought Quinn down here as his laboratory assistant and he had laid out this new laboratory. It was an exact replica of the New Jersey laboratory. In fact, the Everhard laboratories all over the country were precise duplicates, so that a research man could be sent from one to another and always be completely at home.

"That's the American system," I said, half listening to my host.

"Correct," said the Count, "and I admire the American system. It has elevated the virtue of mediocrity to a science. Its glory are multiple parts, identical tools, and mass production. No aristocratic country ever produced inventors who would have thought of equipping other men's laboratories precisely like their own. To an aristocratic thinker his tools are as individual as his ideas, but in the dead level of a democracy identical instrumentation is an obvious and very fruitful step. I yield to none in my admiration for things American."

I listened to this not knowing exactly how much was irony and how much sincere belief when suddenly I heard a loud metallic voice in the back of the laboratory inquire: "Have you any rooted oncidiums?" And another voice answered: "We have a few just grafted to their host but can't guarantee them." One or two more questions and answers about the oncidiums, then, of all odd things, a sale was consummated there in the back of the laboratory. I looked at Count Jalacki who explained casually. "That's the assistant gardener ordering orchids from the florist over his telephone. I check on his purchases with a loudspeaker here in my workshop."

Well, it took fifteen or twenty seconds for the full import of this information to register on me. Then I realized that *Jalacki had overheard my telephone conversation with Poggioli!* I tried to remember what we had said, but I was too confused. What *had* we said? What did the Count know? Now I understood why the Count had come straight to me in the kiosk.

Without warning the Count said it was now time for us to go to the villa and see his wife.

This added to my uncertainty. My theory that he had poisoned his wife with a sleeping potion hinged on the hypothesis that Everhard had telephoned Jalacki that I was coming to the villa. That would have given the Count time to have poisoned his wife and to bring me in as a casual witness and as a proof of his innocence. Now it was apparent that he had come straight from the laboratory to the kiosk and had had no time to poison his wife. So, I deduced she must still be alive.

I am happy to say that at last one of my deductions proved correct. When we entered the villa I saw the Countess sitting in a great chair, her distended body ill at ease, as she stared, heartbroken at the sea that had drowned her little boy.

I tried to put my sympathy into words. As I did so I found it impossible to believe that Count Jalacki really had murdered his little stepson. No, Poggioli must be wrong, Mr. Everhard must be wrong, Miss Davis must be wrong; little Jon must somehow have got out of his bed and accidentally drowned himself in the surf. I talked a few minutes and then took my leave with what aplomb I could muster.

On my walk back through the jungle I tried again to recall my exact words to Poggioli over the telephone. All I could remember were the letters "s.p." which I had used as an abbreviation for "stool pigeon." I realized that such concealment would not puzzle Count Jalacki even for a moment.

When I reached the kiosk where I had talked to Miss Davis it was empty. The roadway where I had used the telephone was deserted. I walked on and presently came within sight of the fifty-thousand-dollar bronze gateway to the estate. I looked out of the gloom of the jungle onto the sunlit glare of Ocean Drive. As I walked on toward the gate I saw a taxicab waiting outside and I realized that Count Jalacki had called it for me in sarcastic courtesy. When the driver opened his door and I stepped inside, I saw on the back seat a worn leather traveling case and sitting beside it, Miss Mary Davis. I exclaimed: "Miss Davis, did he fire you!"

Her pale blue eyes were angry. "What did you tell him about me?"

I suddenly knew that I had told him she was the Everhard stool pigeon in his home. I had done this in my telephone conversation with Poggioli. I stammered, "I — didn't intend to tell him anything — about anyone."

"You don't have to intend to tell Count Jalacki anything," she said, bitingly.

"Did he tell you to wait for me here?" I asked.

"He told the driver to wait for you. He said you wouldn't be long. He paid both our fares."

I shook my head at this last delicate insult. As we drove away Miss Davis looked back at the fifty-thousand-dollar bronze gate. Suddenly she dabbed her face with her handkerchief.

"I — I've been with Rosalie ever — ever since little Jon was b-born!"

"Well, Miss Davis," I comforted her, "your job was gone anyway. Little Jon is dead."

"But — she's going to have — another baby — to — to take his place with her."

I waited till her spasm of grief had subsided.

"Where are you going now?" I asked her.

"Oh . . . to the air field."

"Going to fly . . . north, I suppose."

"Yes, of course. Where else is there to go?"

Then I realized Jalacki was getting rid of all the servants who knew anything about his little stepson's death. I said:

"Look here, Miss Davis, you know who actually did that, don't you?"

She drew a long breath and closed her eyes. "Of course I do."

"It wasn't . . . the Count himself?"

"Certainly not. His factotum, his man of all work . . . a-l-l w-o-r-k

. . . do you understand?"

"Mr. Quinn?"

She lifted her brow in disgust at my southern way of having to say everything in plain words and remained silent.

"Well, look here," I said seriously, "oughtn't you to give me your address, so if this ever comes up in court I can call you for a witness?"

"What good would that do — a trial, court, even a hanging . . . my poor little darling is . . . dead."

I didn't argue, I quit talking. I got out on Acacia Street and hurried to my apartment to tell Poggioli that he must collect these murder witnesses Count Jalacki was scattering all over the United States, get them together and electrocute the inhuman monster. . . . I unlocked the outer door and rushed into my apartment. It was empty. I called Poggioli's name but he was in none of the rooms. I was unable simply to sit and await his return. I looked out the window onto the street with some foolish hope of seeing him. Then in sharp relief I saw a note pinned to the shade of the floor lamp. I unpinned it and read: *Telephoned you at the villa, but you had started home. As soon as you read this, come to the Ritz-Carlton. Mr. Everhard has been shot. H. P.*

With a flood of regret at my own bungling, I perceived instantly the chain of cause and effect that had led to an attack on Mr. Everhard. I had betrayed the fact that Everhard had a spy at the villa and Jalacki had acted at once. He no doubt had dispatched Mr. Quinn to assassinate the capitalist. If only I had not telephoned in the garden. This thought, of my own culpability, drummed in my head all the way to the Ritz.

When I reached the hotel I was detained in the lobby until I could be identified. Finally a young man came down from the Everhard apartment. He was very solemn and turned out to be Mr. Everhard's confidential secretary. I asked him was Mr. Everhard dead or hurt very badly. He said he was not allowed to give out any information. I asked him was Poggioli upstairs. He said Professor Poggioli was closeted with Mr. Everhard and Mr. Leggett.

"Who is Mr. Leggett?" I asked.

"I'm not supposed to give out information but he is the legal representative of the Everhard Company here in Tiamara. He is employed mainly for his influence in the State legislature."

I nodded. "I now see why everything is such a secret," I said, "Can I get into this conference they're having? My information is very important, tremendously important."

"What shall I say you know?"

"Tell them I know who shot Mr. Everhard."

"So does Mr. Everhard, naturally," said the solemn young man.

That took me back somewhat. Of course, after I thought it over, I knew that Mr. Everhard would know who shot him.

"It was Mr. Quinn, wasn't it?" I asked.

"It was not Mr. Quinn."

By this time we had reached the Everhard apartment. The solemn young man went into the conference room to see if I could be admitted. Presently he came back and said that Poggioli had vouched for me.

When I entered the conference room I found the three gentlemen — Poggioli, Everhard and Leggett — seated around a table, talking and smoking with an air of distinct cheerfulness. Mr. Everhard had his left arm in a black silk sling, but he was the most cheerful of the three, his mood of gloom having vanished completely. I must admit that this fact, from which Poggioli later drew such an amazing conclusion, suggested absolutely nothing to me.

Mr. Everhard was saying in a comfortable, almost a gratified, voice that he agreed with Mr. Leggett, no good would come out of a criminal prosecution. Then he went on to suggest: "We can announce for publication that my assailant's pistol went off accidentally and inflicted a flesh wound in my left arm."

To this Mr. Leggett shook a negative finger. "I don't think we had better use your name, Mr. Everhard. We don't want to attract any attention whatever to this matter. I think we had better make an impersonal statement to the newspapers, something like this: 'An accidental shot fired in the lobby of the Ritz-Carlton Hotel slightly wounded an employee of the Everhard Company.'"

Poggioli came out of a profound study to ask: "Won't the reporters find out the details?"

Mr. Leggett smiled complacently at the criminologist. "Our organization is prepared for such incidents as this, Professor Poggioli. Our company owns two of the papers here in Tiamara outright and fifty-one per cent of the stock in the third."

This decision seemed to break up the conference. Mr. Leggett and Poggioli arose to go. Mr. Everhard turned his chair gently about and sat with bandaged arm, smiling at his confrères. No one took any notice of me or the solemn young man who had brought me up. I followed Poggioli out and went down the elevator with him. I was puzzled.

"Mr. Quinn didn't do the shooting?" I asked in the descending cage.

Poggioli came out of deep concentration. "Oh, no, no, Jalacki would never have been that obvious. The assailant was a foreigner named Schwartzen; he could hardly talk English."

"But you do think he was Jalacki's tool?"

Poggioli nodded his head.

"Well," I said, "that clears up the mystery."

"Clears it up?" ejaculated the criminologist.

"Certainly, it explains everything."

Poggioli gave a short laugh. "What I have pointed out is merely the obvious. There is still the *real* riddle."

Our elevator reached the street floor, the door opened, and I could say nothing further in the lobby of the Ritz. When we walked out into the sunlit street and were sufficiently isolated in the crowd, I asked my companion what was this new riddle — the *real* riddle he had referred to.

"I'm sure you noticed it yourself," said Poggioli. "It is Mr. Everhard's feeling of relief, of satisfaction — even of cheerfulness — which he shows plainly enough *now that he has been shot*."

I thought this over. "I believe I've got the answer," I said.

"What is it?"

"He believes Jalacki has shot his bolt and now he, Everhard, is out of danger."

"Shot his bolt?"

"Yes, made a last attempt on Everhard's life."

Poggioli looked at me in some surprise. "That's an idea . . . a last attempt. Now if this is a last attempt, Everhard must have done something to put Jalacki out of the fighting. What could he have done?"

"Mm — mm, I don't see how he could have done anything to him. The Count doesn't admit strangers into the villa grounds. Mr. Everhard certainly didn't go himself. The only thing he did was to send a note over by me."

Poggioli pondered. "That is a fact. That is all he has actually done. Did you deliver the note?"

"Yes, to the Count himself."

"Uh . . . do you know what was in the note?"

"Naturally not. Mr. Everhard placed it in my care."

Poggioli lifted a brow. "In criminology we treat any communication between the parties involved in a crime simply as evidence, not as matters of personal privilege. But go on: what else happened at the villa?"

Of course the first thing that leaped to my mind was my telephone conversation with Poggioli in which I said I was hunting for Mr. Everhard's stool pigeon, and which the Count had overheard in his loudspeaker; then how Jalacki came out and found me talking to Miss Davis, who was in fact the s.p., and how he had immediately discharged her. But I was still so chagrined over my *faux pas* on the telephone that I couldn't bring myself to mention it. I got around it by saying: "When Jalacki read my note he discharged the nurse, Miss Davis."

"He did! Why did he do that?"

"Well . . . he must have thought she was Mr. Everhard's stool pigeon."

"What earthly reason would he have to pick on a nurse?"

I grew very uncomfortable. I thought to myself: shall I tell him or shall I not tell him what an imbecile . . . I knew how sarcastic he could become.

Fortunately we were interrupted at this moment — rather I should say, shocked by the scream of a police siren. As the police car came howling past, I cried out on a sudden inspiration: "I'll bet they are headed for the villa!"

Poggioli evidently agreed, for the next moment he sighted a taxi and hailed it. As we drove off a sudden dismaying explanation came to me. I said to Poggioli, "This will be the Countess."

My companion was telling the driver to follow the police car in front of us. "No, no," he objected, "the Count would certainly do nothing to her until *after* her baby is born."

"Then it *has* been born," I cried, "and he's murdered her!"

"Maybe that police car is not going to the villa," said my friend tensely, watching the police car ahead of us; but even as he said this, it swerved into the great bronze gate of the Jalacki estate.

We whisked through the gate and were within forty yards of the police when they tumbled out at the villa.

A shocking sight met our eyes. The Countess Everhard-Jalacki came stumbling toward us from the laboratory. She was screaming, weeping, and laughing — all mixed in one hysteria. A little distance from the police she flung her arms toward them and fell writhing on the ground.

Fortunately for her the police of Tiamara are equal to any situation, even to midwifery on a hysterical woman. I stared horrified.

"Why should she call the police at such a . . ."

"It's premature," snapped Poggioli.

"Why do you think it's . . ."

"Because her obstetrician is not here. He knows the date. No, she saw something in the laboratory that caused this. We must get there before the police," and we started running for the laboratory.

I followed. Whether he knew what to expect or not, I don't know. I did not. We entered the laboratory together.

The first thing we saw was one of the maids kneeling beside a workbench with a glass of water in her hand. Then we realized she was beside a man's body and the next moment I recognized the prostrate figure of Count Jalacki. In response to a sharp question from Poggioli the girl gasped out, "I'm trying to bring him to!"

Poggioli knelt beside her, took the Count's wrist, put a hand under his shirt. "There's nothing you can do. Don't pour any more water on his face. How long have you been here?"

"I . . . don't know . . . I came . . ."

"An hour?"

"No, sir, not an hour. We couldn't get him on the telephone, so the Countess sent me here to bring him to her bedroom. I found him like this and telephoned her. She got up, came here and saw him. It upset her terribly. I telephoned for the police."

Poggioli got to his feet and looked about, "The Count was alone, here in the laboratory?"

"I suppose so, sir. When I came after him he was just like he is now."

"He was dead when you got here?"

"Is he *dead?*"

"Yes. Where was Mr. Quinn?"

"He went to town, sir, at about ten o'clock this morning." Poggioli asked her how she knew the hour. She said Mr. Quinn had stopped by the main house to report to the Countess that he was going to the city.

"Was it Mr. Quinn's custom to report to the Countess?"

"No-o . . . at least, I never knew him to do it before."

"Does Mr. Quinn ever run any errands for the Countess so that she would need to know where he went?"

"Oh no, sir. He is the Count's man," she looked intently at Poggioli for a moment. "Do you think . . . *he* did this?"

"Certainly not. How could he have done this when he went to town at ten o'clock this morning? That will do — you may go."

The girl set the glass on the bench, dropped a little pale-faced curtsey, and went out. Poggioli turned to me.

"Isn't that like a beginner in crime . . . bungle it so even the maid suspects him?"

I was shocked. "You think Quinn . . . ?"

"Quinn was merely the tool, that's all. The source of the assassination was Everhard."

"*Everhard!*" I repeated in amazement. "What makes you think . . ."

"His change of mood. His gloom and oppression when he dispatched you with the note to Jalacki — his cheerfulness only a few minutes ago. That note, of course, was Jalacki's death warrant. It was meant to be read and acted on by Quinn."

I was so bewildered that I could simply stare. Poggioli went on: "The point that oppressed Everhard was this: he was not absolutely sure that Jalacki was the murderer of his nephew. He sent you to investigate and make certain, but at the same time he was, as I say, sending Jalacki's death warrant. It was an odd situation. Mr. Everhard felt that he must act at once. However, when Jalacki's tool, Schwartzen, shot at Everhard and wounded him, then the financier was positive. That is why his mood changed from depression, uncertainty and gloom to satisfaction and confidence. It was an odd situation, Jalacki giving Everhard sure grounds for a death warrant which Everhard had *already* written."

"But how did Mr. Quinn actually kill the Count when he was in the city all morning?"

"He followed directions in the note you delivered to the Count."

"But why should Everhard take for granted that Jalacki would give the note to Quinn?"

"Because he knew the Count was extremely systematic. He knew Quinn was his laboratory assistant and secretary, that Quinn read and answered all the Count's letters and that he would read . . . and answer . . . this one."

"But Quinn had been an intimate friend of the Count's for years. He was appointed the Count's assistant even before the Count married the Countess. Why did he desert his almost lifelong boss and murder him?"

Poggioli shook his head. "That goes deep into human psychology. Men somehow cling to abstractions, not to individuals. The Everhard Company is an abstraction. It is neither the men nor the materiel in it that hold loyalty, for both of these commodities are constantly renewed. It is an idea. For this abstraction Mr. Everhard did not punish the murderer of his father or of his nephew. But when Jalacki attacked the Company itself, he had to die. Quinn was just as loyal to the Company as Everhard. Quinn had been placed as a kind of watch-dog over Jalacki when the Count first entered the Everhard laboratories as a research chemist. No doubt the Company impressed it on Quinn that Jalacki was a foreigner and gave him detailed instructions how to act in almost any emergency, how to block Jalacki, and yet not draw the Everhard Company into the evil publicity of a criminal action. Well, the time finally came for Quinn to act . . . and he did."

I stood looking at the dead man who had worked for years beside his final executioner. "Of course he would have the utmost faith in Quinn, after he had worked beside him for so long," I said slowly.

Poggioli shook his head. "No, that to me is the most elusive riddle in the whole case. Why did Jalacki ever completely trust Quinn? Jalacki was bred in the doctrine that nobody is really trustworthy. Not only that but Jalacki was a brilliant scientist. He must have known that Everhard's letter was an attack . . . a letter of condolence, that was absurd on its face. . . . It seems to me . . . in fact, I am sure . . . that something happened here in the villa that abruptly transferred Jalacki's normal suspicions of Mr. Quinn to *someone else*, and somehow those suspicions fell on, of all persons, the nurse, Miss Mary Davis. One of the queerest mistakes I have ever known a brilliant mind to make . . . and it cost him his life."

I became very uncomfortable again. I considered telling Poggioli what I knew but decided against it. Instead I said: "Well, how did Mr. Quinn actually kill the Count?"

"If you'll find me the note, I'll read it and tell you."

The note was not hard to find. It was lying in plain view on the bench among some bottles and pliers and retorts. I started to hand it to Poggioli but he stopped me.

"I don't suppose it is poisoned. That would have been too obvious — it wouldn't have caught Jalacki. But to play safe, hand it to me with those pliers." I did so, rather gingerly, because after all Jalacki was dead. Poggioli proceeded, pointing to some spots on the paper where liquids had dried. "You see Jalacki himself tested the note with reagents to see if it was poisoned. He decided it was not."

The note was typewritten on the face of a folded sheet. My companion held it flat with his pliers and I read aloud:

"Dear Ercole,

May I express my whole family's sorrow over the drowning of little Jon. I want you to know our heartfelt sympathy for you and Rosalie in this mutual grief."

This was single spaced. Then came a double-spaced interval and a second paragraph.

"We loved little Jon as warmly as one of our own children. I hope his going will unite our two families in our common grief.
Your sorrowing friend and kinsman,
John Everhard II."

I don't know exactly what I had expected, but I said, "That's just a simple note of consolation . . . exactly what Everhard said it was."

Poggioli stood glooming at the missive. "That's true . . . but Jalacki's dead."

"Maybe it's a code," I suggested.

"It's too brief to have a running letter code. Let us approach it this way: do you notice anything odd about this note?"

"Mm — mm, no-o . . . except it is a note of consolation and typewritten."

"That's a point," agreed Poggioli, "and do you observe it has a double space between these two paragraphs?"

"Yes, I see that."

"Both those details are unconventional: a note of sympathy, written on a typewriter, and a brief note like that broken into two paragraphs with a double space between them. Not only unconventional, but entirely unnecessary — unless Everhard was trying to convey secret instructions under Jalacki's guard. . . ." The criminologist shook his head. "That's what I can't understand . . . why a man like Jalacki didn't think of it instantly, and look *between the paragraphs!* Something happened here in the villa to mislead the Count, to lull him into . . ."

I became nervous about my own dumb part in the matter.

"Let's get on with the note," I suggested. "What do you find *between* the paragraphs?"

Poggioli visibly put aside his riddle, drew a magnifying glass from his pocket, and examined the empty space in question. Apparently he found nothing. He reflected a moment, then opened the folded sheet and examined the place *on the second page* that fell underneath the interparagraph space on the first sheet. Presently he looked up.

"Here it is," he said. "Everhard wrote it *with blank keys and no ribbon on the under sheet.*"

I was amazed with the certainty and ease with which Poggioli had arrived at this detail. I said as much.

"What else was there to think or suspect," answered the criminologist simply. "A child would have guessed . . . really, this is the most puzzling thing . . . a brilliant man like Jalacki . . ."

A light sweat broke out on my face. "Listen," I begged, "What does the note say?"

"Oh, I don't know . . . bring me some powdered emery dust and let's read it."

I found some of this abrasive, Poggioli sprinkled some on the faint impressions, breathed on them, and the lines marking the edge of the indentations became faintly visible. It read: "34x2365."

I don't know what I expected, but certainly not two numbers to be multiplied together.

"There's your code," I said.

"Not likely," objected Poggioli, "Quinn wouldn't have such a code at his fingertips."

"Well, what does it mean?" I asked.

Poggioli glanced over the bench, then he pointed. "That bottle marked Tincture Merthiolate hasn't it got a number under the name?"

I looked. It had and with an indrawn breath I said, "And it's number thirty-four."

I started to hand it to him but he stopped me quickly. "No, my friend, don't touch that. That's a business double. It has killed one man already. Now see if you can find bottle number twenty-three sixty-five?"

I started searching through the laboratory with a kind of flustered concentration.

The number was not difficult to find. Every item in the place was arranged according to a numerical system. I found the bottle and called to Poggioli:

"This one is Potassium Cyanide."

"I see. Well, it *isn't* Potassium Cyanide," analyzed Poggioli at once. "That is your simple antiseptic, Merthiolate. This container marked Merthiolate is the Cyanide. When you and Jalacki left the laboratory this morning, Quinn read this note and *switched the contents of the two bottles* — then replaced them according to their numbers. The poison, masked as an antiseptic, simply waited till Jalacki should scratch a hand or a finger and need to dab the scratch with Merthiolate. He must have done that fairly soon after he came back from the villa, directly after he had discharged Miss Davis for being a spy. Miss Davis. . . . Miss Davis. . . . Do you know, I believe that somehow or other Count Jalacki overheard our conversation on the telephone this morning . . . it's the only possible solution. Let's look around this laboratory and see if we can find a loudspeaker somewhere. . . ."

The Mystery of
the 81st Kilometer Stone

Poggioli and I arrived in Tacuba last night. This Sunday morning we were aroused by multitudinous church bells ringing in all directions. Mexican church bells ring very fast, like village fire alarms. To the old-fashioned orthodox churchmen they were, in a way, just that. I called to Poggioli from my bed, "Hear that? You realize now they have three hundred and sixty-five churches in this town, one for every day in the year."

Poggioli lifted his head and said around a yawn, "No, they don't . . . days of the year have nothing to do with it."

"There's three hun—"

"I understand that. But those churches were built to mask Aztec temples. That was their real purpose — not a church for every day in the year. Now, the Aztecs undoubtedly erected three hundred and sixty-five temples, one for each day in the year —"

Such hair-splitting annoyed me. "Isn't that the same thing?"

"Is it the same thing for one man to build an airplane to go somewhere and another to wreck it so he can't get there?"

I made no answer to this. It was just some more of Poggioli's habitual, college-professor's sarcasm. I asked him presently why he supposed the Aztecs had a temple for every day in the year. He said that was what he had come to Tacuba to investigate.

From the piazza of the Reina de Espagna, the hotel where we lodge, Poggioli and I watch the crowds stream by to mass and to the cockfights. On the wall of an ancient church across the *calle* I can see the advertisement of a bull fight. Poggioli philosophizes on the connection between religious rites and fights. He wonders if it is possible that the cockpit and bull ring are halfway houses between old Aztec ritual and present-day worship? The old Spanish conquistadors were extraordinarily practical men. They took what they found in the Indians, physical and spiritual, and moulded it into something viable. We English in the North eradicated our autochthons, saving nothing, either physical or spiritual.

In the crowd an old peon in a red blanket hurries past holding under his arm a grey gamecock. Poggioli comments on the accidental stylistic perfection of this composition. Had the colors been reversed — blanket grey, cock red — stress would have fallen on the fowl, not on the peon. As it is, there is something arresting, even startling, in the old man's tortured face. However, it may be that the old cockfighter is not tortured at all. That is simply the way old Mexican Indians look, as is proved by the canvasses of Orozco and Rivera.

Presently Poggioli asked me why I supposed the crowd was in such a hurry. I said I didn't know. Poggioli continued with his coffee and presently Belita came out to the hotel's sidewalk tables with more rolls. The criminologist asked her the same question. She began impulsively, "*Ca, Señor,* the moon is full to —" then seemed to catch herself and finished casually, "They are always in a hurry . . . the peons."

This last was so funny that when she went inside I began laughing. For some reason Poggioli was not at all amused. He looked after the old Indian with the grey cock who was just disappearing around a church corner.

"I wonder what Belita is concealing," he said slowly. "What could she possibly want to hide from us, a pair of perfectly haphazard tourists. . . ."

"Why, a crime," I said, "certainly a crime!" I began laughing at Poggioli because that man can twist the slightest, the most trivial, *lapsus lingua* that anybody makes into a remote but unerring clue to some sort of crime. It's a mania with him.

Poggioli paid little attention to my satire. He finished his coffee, got up. "Let's walk to the cockfights."

"I thought you came here to study religion," I replied.

"I did," he said, "but who knows — their religion may begin with cockfights."

"Now, why make a rationalization like that?" I demanded.

"The moon," said Poggioli. "Belita's accidental, but truthful and immediately corrected reference to the moon, and the further fact that the old Aztecs did have a lunar religion."

Since I make my living out of Poggioli, writing down his dull and pompous efforts at satire along with his criminological deductions, I finished my coffee and followed.

There is no use describing a Mexican cockfight; the circle of tense aficionados, binding on the gyves, pitting the birds, the tragic momentary flutter of two utterly fearless little creatures and the death of one or both. I wouldn't describe it if I could. But this time Poggioli called my attention to the tenseness, the air of expectancy — I might almost say, apprehension — that seemed to hang over the crowd; not only in the midst of a fight but between duels. It was a constant. Poggioli asked me what I made of it. I said, "Heaven knows I don't know. What do *you* make of it?"

He gave a little shrug and said, "As a rule tension is relieved by some expected dénouement."

The Indians had loads of cocks, all of them wanting to fight. They reminded me of military organizations. We again saw our old Indian with the red blanket and the grey fighter. His face was still in tortured wrinkles but so were most of the other faces. His must have meant nothing at all. I presently quit noticing our particular peon because there was a tall, dark, aquiline man by the cockpit who gradually became for me the center of the crowd. Everybody knows what I mean. There is always one person who becomes the personification of the crowd. Different spectators pick different persons for their "centers." I often choose a fat round man or a beautiful woman as my barometer, and I keep glancing at him or her to see how the show goes. This time, however, it was this tall, Romanesque sort of man, not exactly gloomy but certainly not cheerful.

Eventually, our peon pitted his cock against another. The two birds flickered through their usual passes. I glanced up at my Romanesque Indian to judge by his expression how the fight was progressing, because I really knew nothing about the sport. When I looked back again, the other rooster was down and our grey one was crowing. I felt a certain relief that our old peon had won, for I assumed that the possible loss of the fight was what had given him such an anxious, tortured face. I saw him stoop to pick up his excited cock when the bird leaped upward and fluttered a moment over his wrist.

I hardly noticed this maneuver of the fighting fowl; it didn't occur to me that it could mean anything; but a kind of sigh, a sort of tense exhalation, arose from the spectators. Poggioli beside me said in an undertone, "So that's what the crowd was waiting for."

"Waiting for what?" I asked.

"That cock cut the old man's arm as he picked it up."

I looked and sure enough, I saw blood dripping from our peon's wrist. The old man stood looking at the wound the bird had inflicted with one of its gyves. The sight somehow gave me a queer feeling. I said, "How could the crowd be waiting for that when they couldn't have known it was going to happen?" Poggioli lifted a hand to express his own ignorance.

I kept looking and finally I said, "Isn't the old fellow going to do anything about it? He's hurt badly enough to make a splotch there on the ground." But he didn't do anything, just stood looking at his arm; everybody else was watching it, too. Finally I pushed my way through the crowd to the old man. I had in mind that I at least would do something for him because, in a way, he was mine and Poggioli's peon. We had, you might say, artistically adopted him.

What I got to him I was shocked at his yellow, clayey face and bloodless lips, and his wrist was still bleeding. The old fellow sat down. I pulled out my handkerchief and picked up a little stick off the ground — to improvise a tourniquet. As I knotted my cloth and bent over, a hand on my shoulder drew me back and a calm but severe and positive baritone voice said in blurry Spanish, "*La ley, Señor,*" . . . the law, *Señor.* The man who had stopped me was our Roman senator in copper.

Then I realized there must be some sort of law in Mexico analogous to our own law about wounded motorists. Our law says that nobody can assist one of them without becoming responsible for his death, if he dies. The strict legal procedure is to wait for an ambulance. If there is no ambulance coming, one just waits. That was what this crowd was doing. I started back to our hotel. If I couldn't do anything, I didn't want to be there.

Poggioli joined me on the outskirts of the crowd. "Why in the world did you think you could stop something the whole crowd had been waiting for?" he asked.

Poggioli lifted a shoulder with a kind of logical reproach in his tone. "You saw the crowd waiting for something to happen . . . this happened . . . suddenly the suspense was over. Since the crowd was obviously waiting for him to be wounded, then letting him alone after his mishap must be customary."

"Poggioli," I said, "there is nothing wrong with your reasoning if I admit the cock spurring the old man was a part of the program — but that's impossible."

"Which do you consider the more convincing? — your logic or the reaction of the whole crowd?"

As I had no answer, I asked him what was his explanation of a large group of sportsmen actually feeling relief when one of their number got hurt. He said he didn't know, that somehow it might link with Belita's hesitancy in answering our question that morning as to why the crowd was hurrying. I broke into incredulous laughter at the thought that Belita's boggling over a very simple question could possibly have any connection with this rooster cutting the old peon's artery. There was no link conceivable between the two incidents.

(I jot these things down in my notes just as they happened; I don't believe they can ever take on a story form.)

We didn't see Belita again until next morning, when she brought coffee to our room. She seemed gay and uplifted, as if she had been delivered from evil. Poggioli asked in a casual tone, "Belita, the old peon died yesterday, didn't he?"

"*Si, Señor.*"

"Belita, is that why you seem so relieved this morning?"

The girl stared at him antagonistically: "Why should I seem relieved, *Señor,* at poor old Juan's death?"

This evening we went to Swilly Bill's night club for dinner. It caters particularly to American tourists but everybody goes. There are similar spots in all the larger Mexican towns, called variously, Sloppy Joe's, Swilly Bill's, Messy Mat's, and so on. Whether these clubs are named to attract Americans or to express their owner's opinion of Americans, I don't know. All have jazz bands manned by Mexicans and these bands play under artificial palms made of cork, even when real palms grow all around the place. I suppose it is to make the Americans feel at home. And the Americans all gather there to see native life and the Mexicans come to see American life. This gives both a pleasant sense of superiority.

I often take my chessmen to the night clubs and after I have eaten, I set them up on my table and nearly always get a game. Tonight I was not disappointed. A Mexican gentleman in modish English clothes stopped at our table and with a gesture indicated my men. I am sure he knew by my appearance that I couldn't speak Spanish. I nodded an invitation for him to have a seat and concealed a black and a white pawn in my hands for him to choose a color. As I looked fully into his face, I received a queer shock. The fellow was the Roman-senator peon who had been the "center" of my crowd at the cockfight.

Naturally it surprised me that a man who wore a blanket at one place should appear in very stylish attire at the night club, but surprise wasn't the core of my emotion. It was uneasiness; it was some vague kind of apprehension; what of, I did not know.

Now I like riddles and problems; that is why I play chess and write mysteries; but I don't like them to backfire on me. And this man impressed me, both at the cockfight and here at the chess table, as an excellent person to let alone. Behind this feeling was not only the Mexican's grim appearance but the fact that he really had stopped me from saving the life of the old Indian with the grey cock. He was heartless — I could see that much in his face.

As we played, I was eager for Poggioli to notice my opponent. I kept glancing at the criminologist, trying to catch his eye, but my friend seemed to be immersed in some problem of his own.

Naturally, under all these stresses, I lost the game. Our Roman-senator arose and bowed his thanks with the dignity that all Mexicans possess, and then walked away from our table toward the street, in the direction of the Mexican orchestra under the artificial palms.

The moment he was out of hearing I whispered to Poggioli, "Did you see who that man was?" He asked who, and I said, "Why, the peon — the old Roman peon at the cockfight! Here he is coming to the night club dressed like a politician in a silk-stocking ward!"

Poggioli nodded. "They do look alike."

"Look alike! They're the same man!"

"Mm-mm . . . no-o . . . different aura."

"What do you mean . . . aura?" I said.

"Oh, personality . . . atmosphere . . . impression. That something about every man which you can feel but can't see."

"It was his English clothes," I said, "which threw you off."

Poggioli dismissed our argument with a wave of his finger. "The point about him that we've got to decide is something else entirely. Why does he want to see me?"

I stopped placing my chessmen back in their box. "See *you*?"

"Yes. You saw him, didn't you, signal me to follow him out in the street?"

"Why, no-o! Did he? I watched him walk away. That's all he did."

"Yes, true enough, but in what direction did he walk?"

"Toward the jazz band," I said.

"There you are — toward the jazz band," repeated Poggioli, with the satisfaction of a wrangler who has made his opponent concede a point. "You certainly admit that is a signal to me to follow him outside?"

I just sat and looked at Poggioli. I hadn't the remotest idea what he was driving at. So he went on. "He walked toward the jazz band. Now do people ordinarily, when they leave a club like this, depart in the direction of the music?"

"No, I don't suppose they do. So what?"

"And especially if it were disagreeable music — harsh, dissonant music — in fact, not music at all, just braying, for that is what American jazz is to these Mexicans. For a Mexican to have got up and . . . walked . . . toward . . . such . . . music. . . . What must that have meant?"

I tried to think of something deep but finally I had to say, "He wanted to get out and go home."

Poggioli gave the brief, hopeless laugh that he uses in his class at Ohio State University. "Now, listen," he said, "I'll analyze his action. He knew that if I were the psychologist that I am reputed to be I would notice his leaving in precisely the opposite direction he would normally take. If he wanted my attention that badly, he could easily have spoken to me here at the table, but he didn't do it. By saying nothing and walking in the direction of the jazz music he accomplished two things: he tested me to see if I really were an acute, sensitive psychologist, and secondly, it told me of his dire — I might almost say, desperate — need for the assistance of such a trained psychologist."

"Poggioli," I said, "would you mind telling me, as a friend, what you are talking about?"

"I am saying that man, for some reason, did not want to ask me in so many words to come outside with him; so he gave me a very subtle signal which no one but a psychologist would catch. I therefore analyze him as a highly educated man of great sensitivity. Furthermore, he must have some enemy here in the club tonight from whom he wants to conceal his meeting with me; otherwise, he would simply have asked me to go home with him. He is standing outside the club building now waiting to see if I will follow him."

I can hardly express my feeling for such a fantastic notion. The idea of deducing all this rigmarole because a man walked out of a night club in the direction of the jazz band! I told Poggioli flatfooted what I thought of the matter. He said he wouldn't have dreamed of placing such an interpretation on the fellow's action if it had not been for the other things that have been happening. I asked him what other things. He said the peon getting killed at the cockfight and Belita's shifting her reasons when questioned that morning. I said to him, "Poggioli, you are trying to string together things that have no earthly connection."

"Possibly, possibly," agreed the psychologist, "but sometimes I find that a number of inexplicable details link together and make a quite explicable whole. That's my only reason for . . ."

"All right," I interrupted, "to prove you are completely wrong in this instance, I'm going outside and see if the man is waiting for you."

Poggioli pursed his lips in doubt. "I had thought of that myself, but I came down here for rest, not work, and besides I am sure neither of us wants to incur any personal danger."

I couldn't help smiling at that.

"The old peon with the cock got killed," recalled Poggioli gravely.

"Then what are we supposed to do?" I asked. "Go to a cockfight and get ourselves killed?"

"No, no, certainly not," he said soberly, "it wouldn't be *that* method."

"You sound as if somebody had hundreds of different methods of inflicting . . ."

"You'll simply have to wait," advised my friend, "until enough of these incidents occur for us to construct a theory around them, and . . . we don't want to be one of the incidents ourselves."

Now, I remembered that Poggioli's theories, grotesque as some of them are, always seem to work out. So I sat looking at him and pondering. Heaven knows I don't court personal danger, but if there is a story in the thing . . .

"Poggioli," I said, "as a favor to me will you permit me to follow that man and see if he is really waiting out in the street?"

"Mm-mm . . . I hate to become involved even as a counselor in an affair like this . . . completely outside the psychology of our Anglo-Saxon civilization. Oh, go ahead . . . it may fit in with my own researches . . ."

If I hadn't been almost positive that Poggioli had imagined a mare's-nest, I don't believe I would have gone. For him to attribute such subtlety to a man who couldn't even speak English amused me. I know it's provincial to think like that, but we Americans do feel that if a man doesn't speak our language, he can't be so very brilliant, and it would take a genius to signal Poggioli in any such fashion as he had imagined. So I got up and walked to the door behind the orchestra, rather amused at the futility of my own gesture. Still it would show Poggioli how far astray his deductions could wander, which would be an indirect feather in my cap. I was still smiling when I opened the door and stepped out into the street.

There stood the man on the narrow sidewalk looking at the moon.

I came within a squeak of closing the door and walking back inside again. The thought flashed across my mind: "Poggioli's string of deductions is correct . . . this fellow is connected with the cock murder, Belita's guilty conscience, and our own danger." Then came the thought: "What a story this will make if I ever get an explanation for it!" So I walked on.

Yes, there he stood on the two-foot sidewalk looking up at the moon between the spires of the cathedral. The moment I appeared he started away; but in his going he walked so close to me that he touched me — in fact, he slipped a bit of paper in my hand. Then he disappeared around the corner. Neither of us said a word.

It was all so impossible that I just stood there for two or three minutes, looking at the moon above the church, with all sorts of vague fantasies floating through my head. I turned and went back inside to Poggioli. As I approached him at the table, he lifted a brow at me. I nodded. He took the note without a word and opened it. To our surprise it was in English:

DR. HENRY POGGIOLI, ESTEEMED SIR,
   I have a request to make of you which is vital to me. I stand in great need of the assistance of a psychologist. It means life or death to me. Will you have the great kindness to meet me tonight at two fifty-eight o'clock at the eighty-first kilometer stone? P.S. Read this note once, then destroy it.

We sat and looked at each other. Then Poggioli drew out a cigarette lighter, flipped it open, and burned the note.

"Why that?" I asked.

"Why a kilometer stone at two fifty-eight o'clock at night?" said Poggioli. He pulled at his bluish chin for a moment in thought, then said, "Well, let's get going."

We turned out of Swilly Bill's, walked to our taxicab, and woke Pancho in the driver's seat. Poggioli glanced at his watch and told our driver that we were due at the eighty-first kilometer stone in exactly sixteen minutes.

"*Si, Si, Señores.*" Pancho jumped out and began to crank his jalopy. In the midst of his preparations, he suddenly straightened and asked as if he had not heard right. "Where did you say you were going, *Señor?*"

Poggioli repeated: "To the eighty-first kilometer stone."

Pancho did not resume his tinkering. He put his hands on his radiator. "*Señores* . . . it is nothing to me, *certainamente*, but . . . but *porque*? Why would you want to go to . . ."

"To tell you the truth, Pancho," said Poggioli, "we don't know."

"You don't know?"

"We haven't the slightest idea."

"Hadn't I better take you back to the hotel, *Señores?*"

"No, the eighty-first. . . ."

Pancho thumped his radiator in regret. "*Señor*, I remember now. . . . I am so sorry . . . but I took out my spark plugs to clean them when we first came to this night club . . . then I sat down and went to sleep. . . ."

"Pancho, where are your spark plugs?" asked my friend.

Our little man looked about aimlessly in the semi-darkness. "I took them out. . . . I laid them. . . . I wonder if somebody stole them while I was asleep!" His loss seemed not to disturb him; he pointed down a glimmering *calle*. "Why don't the *Señores* walk? It isn't very far and you will have a light to walk by — the moon goes down at two fifty-eight tonight."

He eyed us obliquely as he made this last observation. If he were looking for some sign from us, he was disappointed because neither of us knew anything.

Now, when a Mexican chauffeur turns down an American fare, something is seriously wrong. Poggioli and I walked on down toward kilometer stone eighty-one, speculating on what it could be. I could hear my friend repeating to himself in an undertone the links in our problem . . . expectant crowd . . . game cock murder . . . servant girl knew something . . . chess player . . . chauffeur quits . . . moon goes down. . . . Of course, the trouble was that he had no assurance that these incidents really were connected. They might not be incidents at all, just accidents. I spoke aloud as we walked past one after another of the dark mysterious churches. "You think Pancho was afraid to come with us?"

"Mm — mm, it could be fear, or it could be fidelity to some religious faith or superstition. Most likely, fear."

I picked a flaw here. I said, "You bring in religious faith and superstition only because you are studying the old Aztec religion."

"Certainly. I realize any habitual train of thought tends to corrupt logical judgment. An ideal detective, I am sure, would be a man who never had an idea in his head about anything." This last was probably academic sarcasm. I was framing a suitable retort when we reached the end of the city. Mexican cities do not straggle off into suburbs as do our American towns. They end as definitely as a loaf of bread. We had come to the end of town, the *calle* turned into a *camino*, and just a little way beyond where the houses stopped and the street changed into a road, I saw the glimmer of the eighty-first kilometer stone.

Beside it stood our chess player. Before we actually joined him the moon sank and left us in the velvety star-shot darkness of a tropical night. Poggioli whispered to me, "Remember this: it was arranged, it will fit in somehow." That was all he had time to say. He referred, I think, to the moon-set.

The man in the gloom greeted us in excellent English and still more surprisingly, spoke with an Oxford accent. Why hadn't he talked to me over the chess game in Swilly Bill's? This was just one of the many riddles our conversation with him developed. I am sorry I cannot reproduce our entire talk, but it was a black night and I couldn't even see the pad on which I attempted to make notes. The best I could manage were brief sentences summarizing the different subjects the two men discussed. Later in our hotel I expanded some of these from memory. Here is the list:

1. Power of the suggestion of death.

The fellow introduced this theme into what seemed to be a purely impersonal conversation between two scientific men. Poggioli's observation was this, and it struck me as a good one. "To suggest death to a man might lead to serious illness. It would be impossible, however, really to produce death because as the mind weakened its own power of lethal suggestion would decrease; so, on the very brink of death, the mind would become inert and the body would continue to live."

The unseen man said, "That's assuming that what men call the soul is simply a function of the body, not a separate entity." I agreed to this. "Then if suggestion can slay a man," went on the unseen speaker, "would not that tend to prove the independence and possible continuity of the soul?"

I answered that the mere suggestion of a soul was so far removed from American materialistic thinking that I would not attempt to follow him in that realm of speculation.

2. The next theme I have on my list was a discussion between Poggioli and the man on "soul energy," whatever that may mean. The man in the dark drew a macabre analogy between the development of energy through the destruction of the atom, and the possible use of energy through the destruction of the human soul. He suggested ascending gradations of power — simple matter as we know it, molecules, atoms, electrons and protons, soul. And he pointed out that the human will or the human soul could perform labor at a distance without actual physical contact. This was as dramatic an advance over atomic power as atomic was over molecular power. In proof of this "soul power" he cited experiments recently performed with dice at Duke University, Durham, North Carolina. There it was proved that the unaided human will could influence the fall of dice. Here I interposed to say that the fall of a die was such a trivial exhibition of power. He agreed to that but pointed out that for decades scientists had known of atomic power only through enormously magnified photographs of liberated ions. Comparing that to controlling the roll of a die would be like comparing a feather with the weight of the earth. Which, of course, as queer as it may sound, is perfectly true. Then he went on to press the point that this "mind force" operated at a distance, without contact, lifting it completely above our ordinary conception of energy into a realm new and unexplored by Western science.

Of course, that too was true, but I didn't see what all this was leading to.

Then he spoke of the fertility of the Mexican land, how it had borne crop after crop for unnumbered centuries, whereas the soil in America required fertilizers and some of it was already abandoned as nonproductive. All this had nothing to do with the mystery in hand; it is every citizen's right to praise his own country and decry other lands.

The man in the darkness drifted next into local history. He mentioned again Tacuba's three hundred and sixty-five churches, and the fact that they were built to cover up old Aztec temples. On the heels of this statement he related a very queer story. He said all monastic institutions had been banned in Mexico by law ever since the days of Juarez. However, a nunnery had managed to exist in Pueblo, Mexico, through all those years. It was camouflaged by shops and houses and was discovered accidentally by a police officer who put his hand on an oil painting which in reality was a bell cord at the entrance of the nunnery. A door opened in a blank wall and the abbess appeared and asked him what he wanted.

Finally our host — I suppose I might call him our host, since he invited us to meet him at the kilometer stone — asked Poggioli in a very serious voice if Western psychology had developed any defense against the power of suggestion.

"No mental defense," said Poggioli; "some physical defense, possibly, like a stimulant or a sedative. You see, Western psychology, in contradistinction to Eastern psychology, does not credit the existence of the soul. Its experiments are purely physical, conducted in laboratories with mechanical equipment. It contrives no defense against black magic and no aid of white magic because it does not believe in such things. Actually Western psychology stands in the grotesque position of a science built around a vacuum; a psychology without a psyche; or, in plain English, 'words about nothing.'"

Our host stood for a moment, silent in the darkness, and finally he asked, "And that is your scientific creed, too, Dr. Poggioli?"

"Certainly. I am a trained Western scientist."

On this completely irrelevant note our visit ended. The man bade us goodbye and Poggioli and I started back to our hotel. I must admit I was disappointed. I had nothing writable, no mystery story — just a faint suggestion of the eerie which is the Western reaction to the idea of soul; nothing by any stretch of the imagination solid enough to mould into a mystery story saleable to the American public.

As I say, I was disappointed, and then, as a sort of sop to my typewriter, chance tossed me one little touch of the mysterious that is writable.

We were passing a Mexican cemetery. There was a hooded lantern in the brick wall above the iron gate, and just as we passed, the gate opened and who should walk out but the chess player we had just left behind us — the same dark, saturnine face. Now, however, he wore an ordinary peon's *serape* thrown around him, for the night was cool. It gave me a sort of start. I tried to recall whether he had worn the *serape* when he talked with us at the kilometer stone. I didn't remember it. Poggioli, of course, saw him too, and when the man passed, Poggioli said, "The cockfighter."

"Sure," I agreed, "and also the chess player."

"No," objected my friend. "Why would an educated man like that run ahead of us, appear in a cemetery's gate in a *serape* . . ."

"Didn't he have on a *serape* at the kilometer stone?" I asked.

Poggioli shrugged.

"Will you please tell me why he asked us to meet him at the kilometer stone at all?" I asked.

Poggioli turned and tried to see my face. "You don't know . . . when he told us just as plainly as he possibly could without using so many words?"

"What did he tell us?" I snapped in annoyance, "without using so many words?"

"He told us . . . Let me see . . . a lot of things: that there is still an old Aztec temple going full blast in Tacuba."

"For Heaven's sake, Poggioli, how did you ever . . ."

"Why should he have mentioned the nunnery hidden for decades in Pueblo if he hadn't meant . . ."

"That was just gossip," I said.

"That man would not gossip — not when he was trying to get some sort of magical formula to save somebody's life, possibly his own."

"Save his . . . why do you imagine that?"

"That's why he mentioned the richness of the Mexican land after centuries of cultivation. The priests at this Aztec temple still offer human sacrifices to the gods of fertility."

"But, Poggioli, that wouldn't have anything to do with the actual richness of the land!"

"Sure of that?"

"Certainly I am — that's the crudest superstition!"

"Of course, I think you are right. I'm an American the same as you . . . but think of the energy in an atomic bomb."

"All right, I'm thinking of it. What about it?"

"Try to imagine a subtler energy than that, a more refined energy, a something or other that doesn't require any physical contact whatever to operate on matter. Energy that will work at a distance just as efficiently as if brought in direct contact."

"You are now talking the same twaddle he was giving us about experiments with dice at Duke University."

"That's precisely what I am talking about. Imagine such a force, controlled, stepped up to the nth degree and then utilized for the enrichment of the soil of this country in what we would call savage fertility rites. . . ."

I made a gesture in the darkness. "Why, that's the most unbelievable —"

"Then why do you suppose the Aztec priests used to sacrifice thousands and thousands of human lives? It was brutal, repulsive work, but they stuck to it. Why? Only because they must have had proof that they were directing the concentrated soul power of hecatombs of victims into the fertilization of their soil . . . fertility rites. And they are still doing it! That old peon whom the cock killed . . . The whole crowd expected a victim; nobody knew who it would be; that was the reason for such enormous relief when the victim was finally revealed. The rest knew it would not be them."

I walked along in a daze. I felt sure that Poggioli was wrong this time. "That copper-colored Roman — he didn't kill the peon himself," I objected.

"I think he did — not with an obsidian knife, but with psychic power. You see the Western world entered Mexico with Cortez and stopped simple physical sacrifice. The priests made the most of their necessity and evolved psychic murder — *the control of matter at a distance through the human will.* We Westerns are just beginning to touch the fringe of that science by, say, controlling the fall of dice at Duke University." I could feel Poggioli was laughing inwardly at me, at himself, at Americans in general, at our grotesque and lopsided materialistic development. He turned to me again, suddenly. "It follows so perfectly the contrary patterns of life in the Orient and the Occident," he said.

"What does?" I asked.

"The use to which they put their extremest achievement in science. We developed the atomic bomb amid peaceful labor and used it to destroy cities. They developed the transformation of the energy in the human soul amid scenes of bloodshed and agony and used it to build up the peaceful soil. One is as horrible as the other, but there is more intelligence in theirs."

"Poggioli," I cried, "you don't really believe that, do you?"

"Certainly not. I'm an American the same as you. I don't believe there is any power guiding anything; all is accident. It was an accident that the crowd expected the peon's death. It was an accident that he died. It was an accident that our new friend waited outside Swilly Bill's night club with a note. It was an accident that we found him . . ."

"Then what did the eighty-first kilometer stone have to do with all this?" I demanded.

"The kilometer stone," Poggioli replied, "was one of two things. It was either the finial of a still-operating Aztec temple . . ." here I interrupted in amazement to ask why he suggested such an idea. He said, "To conceal an Aztec temple under a public highway would be a highly Indian ruse." The only reason he toyed with this idea, he explained, was because he knew there was an Aztec temple in Tacuba and he did not know where else to look for it. Also it would explain why our taxi driver absolutely refused to drive us to that particular road marker.

His alternate hypothesis was that the kilometer stone marked the limit of clairaudience for priests in the Aztec temple, wherever it was. That explained why the chess player would say nothing to us in Swilly Bill's Club, but invited us outside the limit of audibility before conversing with us.

We walked the rest of the way to our hotel in silence.

Well, I realized then that I had thrown away my time investigating such an alien situation. I knew I would never be able to work it into a good standard mystery. Still I couldn't get it off my mind. I lay awake nearly all night long thinking about it. Finally, just before I went to sleep, I decided there was one thing more I could do: make Belita tell me whether the cockfighter and the chess player were one and the same man or different men. I was sure she knew.

So next morning at the breakfast table I questioned her. No, no, she knew nothing whatever about the matter. She seemed rather frightened at the idea of knowing something. Deliberately I laid a hundred-peso note on the table.

"Belita," I said, "are you sure you know nothing about the chess player and the cockfighter?"

The girl wet her lips; her face turned a sickly yellow. *"Señor,"* she whispered, "I . . . I can't tell you . . . anything . . . here."

"Then where?" I asked with rising interest.

"Señor . . ." she looked at the money but seemed about to faint, "if . . . if you will drive me beyond the . . . the eighty-first kilometer stone . . ."

"Sure, sure," I agreed, "have Pancho bring around his car. I'll drive it myself, just you and me and my friend here . . ."

"Si, Si, Señores . . ." Her hand shook so the coffee spilled.

We stopped eating breakfast, went out, and all three of us got into Pancho's car and started for the kilometer stone. We didn't tell Pancho where we were going; we probably wouldn't have got his jalopy. Belita began talking as soon as we left the hotel. Her story was very simple. The cockfighter and the chess player were brothers. Their father had been the *alcalde* of Tacuba and he wanted one of his sons to continue as the leading man of the city. He sent one son to Oxford, England, for an education. The other son he kept in Tacuba in order to give him a native education. If the people of Tacuba desired a man of Western education, one of his sons could fill the position; if they desired a man of native education, the other son would be chosen. So these two sons became political rivals and, in the end, deadly enemies.

I interrupted: "Belita, just where and from whom did this other son get his native education?"

"Señor," whispered Belita, "here in Tacuba is an . . . an old . . ." She was staring ahead at the kilometer stone which we now approached.

Suddenly she broke into a violent scream. A buzzard, one of those Mexican buzzards which form the street-cleaning department of every Mexican city, was sailing through the air quite low. Revoltingly enough we struck it. Its noisome bulk crashed through our windshield. I, too, was shocked, but mainly for the girl. She was so tense and apprehensive already, in such a taut condition, that I knew this accident would wreck her nerves.

I cried to Poggioli to do something. He was already bending over her. He snapped back, "Get to the hospital quick! A piece of glass has cut her throat!"

As I slewed the car around, I remembered some of Poggioli's words: "*Psychic murder* — the control of matter at a distance through the human will . . ."

AUTHOR'S NOTE: *I accumulated the notes on "The Mystery of the 81st Kilometer Stone" in the ancient city of Tacuba, Mexico, and spent considerable time trying to string them into a proper mystery story. I'll mention here my method of writing mysteries. I take any batch of unexplained facts and try to invent some sort of clue which might run through and connect them into one complete mystery. Sometimes no such explanation is possible — then I have wasted my time and labor. That happened in Tacuba. I was so disgusted that I took the results of several weeks of effort and tossed it into our wastebasket.*

I left our hotel, the Reina de Espagna, and took a long walk out in the city to get over my frustration. Tacuba possesses three hundred and sixty-five churches, and I had intended to make that fact one of the points of my mystery — if I could have managed it. It would have been such an unexpected detail in a detective story.

I took my walk, looked at some of the churches, and when I returned to our sitting-room, Poggioli was at his desk. I was amazed when he looked up and said, "I want to congratulate you. This is by far the best story you've ever done." Then I saw that he had my notes. I asked him if he had fished them out of the wastebasket. He said no — he had found them on his desk; he supposed I had put them there for him to read. Then I said it must have been Belita, our maid, who had rescued the notes. She probably had thought they were his, Poggioli's, work, and had fallen off his desk accidentally. My friend asked why the notes were in the wastebasket at all.

"Well," I replied, "I can't think of any explanation to hold the incidents together."

"Explanation!" ejaculated Poggioli. "You don't need an explanation! That's the trouble with you mystery writers — you think you need long-winded explanations at the end of your stories. Fortunately, this story needs none: it flows in perfect sequence, with complete clarity, and the end, while not a surprise to me, should startle many readers."

I stood looking at my notes, considering what he said.

"Then you'd send them on to 'Ellery Queen's Mystery Magazine' — as they are?"

"I certainly would," said Poggioli.

So I did . . .

Poggioli and the Fugitive

When Gebhardt of the *Tiamara Times* telephoned in for help, my friend, Dr. Henry Poggioli, asked if the reporter were at the fish docks. I repeated his question over the wire and answered, "No, he's at the morgue."

"Then tell him I'm busy for the day," Poggioli said.

Such abruptness, and I must say such irrationality, puzzled and disturbed me. I popped my instrument in its fork.

"All right, say it." said Poggioli.

"Would you have gone if he had been at the docks?"

"Yes, I would."

"Will you please explain why the docks are so much better as a setting for a criminological problem than the morgue?"

"I have a general and a specific reason," Poggioli said. "The fish docks are a center of local and Latin-American activity and a good deal of it is questionable. The morgue is a dead end where action has stopped. When action ceases mystery dies."

I argued that mysteries were just as mysterious after the death of their actors as before. But Poggioli said no, they ceased to be mysteries, and became simply the records of mysteries, a field in which he had no interest.

I didn't agree with this but I didn't debate his point. I said, "That's your general reason. Now give me your specific one." I wondered what he'd say.

"The case I'm interested in lies at the docks. That's why I'm willing to go down there this morning." To amplify his answer he picked up his copy of the morning paper. "This is from Alex Alexson's column, SEAWEED, SHIPS AND SKIPPERS," he informed me. "It is written in Alexson's usual silly style, but the hint he gives is a genuine one. It always is." And he read again, "*'A little minnow whispered into this reporter's ear that a certain trawler's slip was showing.'*"

"What does that mean?" I asked.

"If I knew I would turn to something else," said Poggioli.

"Yes, I'm sure you would. Now let me tell you the situation Gebhardt has just described over the phone. A Cuban schooner, the *La*

Laguna Serena, has just brought a decapitated American soldier from down among the keys, and has left a guard over his body in the morgue until the army identifies it. Isn't that more of a mystery than Alexson's minnow whispering about a certain trawler's slip?"

"That's no mystery at all," said Poggioli. "It's simply an accident."

"Accident?"

"Certainly. The schooner was an auxiliary schooner. The soldier fell off the stern into the screw and suffered a fatal and gruesome accident. The Captain has brought the body into port. That's all there is to it."

"Why did the Captain station a guard over the corpse?" I asked argumentatively.

Poggioli made an impatient gesture. "The guard is there. Gebhardt is certainly able to ask him without my help."

His stubbornness angered me. I said I thought I would go over and help the reporter in any way I could.

Poggioli warned me that I would be throwing away my time, that Gebhardt's request for help merely meant that he had a simple one-paragraph story of a death which he hoped to expand into a whole column of mystery.

Knowing Gebhardt, I had to admit that could easily be. However I called him up again, and asked him why he didn't question the guard as Poggioli had suggested.

The reporter's unhappy voice came back, "The fellow speaks Spanish."

"Oh," I said, "so *that's* the reason. I'll be right over."

Poggioli sat watching me. "The guard speaks Spanish," he affirmed.

"You heard Gebhardt's voice over the wire," I said.

"No I didn't. It simply occurred to me that your Spanish was all you've got that Gebhardt could use."

I paid no attention to this. I went out, caught a taxi and drove to the morgue. Twenty minutes later the reporter met me at the entrance of the melancholy building.

"I'm sure glad you can talk Spanish," he began gratefully. "This stacks up to a front page story for me, if I can just get it. You go in there and find out from the sailor why they ever brought the body here in the first place. That at least would be a lead."

We went in together. The sailor was a brown man and he was standing formally at attention beside the sheeted figure on the table. He turned out to be Pedro, of the schooner, *La Laguna Serena*, out of Santiago, Cuba.

I didn't quite like to ask a Cuban sailor why his ship had brought home the body of an American soldier. It wasn't a delicate suggestion, so I switched to the accident itself which I knew Gebhardt would want.

"How did the fatal accident occur, Pedro?"

"I don't know, Senor."

"Then you didn't see him fall overboard into the propeller of your boat?"

"Senor, he didn't fall off our boat," the brown man assured me earnestly.

"Did he fall off some other boat in your fleet?"

"We have no fleet, Senor. *La Laguna Serena* trawls alone."

I was a little puzzled. "If he didn't fall off your trawler where and how did you find him? Just floating in the sea?"

"No, Senor, we found him lying in the middle of the little dock on Doce Key."

"Didn't you ask some resident of Doce Key how the body got there?"

"No one lives on Doce Key, Senor. It is just a rock where fishermen dry their nets. It has a little quay where they can get ashore. That is where we found the body."

I was somehow taken aback at this departure from Poggioli's prognosis. "So you don't even know who he is?"

"No, Senor. The Captain saw the military identification tag around his neck, so we brought him here and telephoned the military to come and claim his body.

This really surprised me. When I translated it to Gebhardt he said, "There is enough mystery in that for you to get a fiction story out of it, too."

I shook my head. "To find a headless dead man on a bare rock in the ocean is sensational and a good filler for the newspapers, Gebhardt. But I couldn't put it into a story. My art requires general truths, not accidents."

Gebhardt brushed this aside, plainly annoyed by my implication that his trade was not an art. He said, "Find out why the Captain brought his body to Tiamara. That's the only reason I telephoned you in the first place."

When I passed the question on to Pedro the brown man was astonished.

"Would Captain Jiminez, Senor, sail away and leave unhonored a soldier of the army that is fighting the battles of all free nations at this very moment? Do you think that, Senor?"

When I translated Pedro's reply to Gebhardt I'll frankly admit I was thrilled. No newspaper man, however, can believe an heroic or unselfish thing about anyone.

"Ask him if there is no other reason why he is standing guard over this body?"

When I did this, Pedro explained simply enough that Captain Jiminez had hoped for a reward from the military for bringing in the body. The Latin fisherman saw nothing ironic in the situation. He had told me first his moving fundamental reason, and then, his incidental one. But as might have been expected, my journalistic companion reversed this order instantly.

He said, "I'm half a mind to write this up as humor. If I can't get a better lead I'll do that."

I was disgusted. I am reasonably cynical and hard-headed but when Gebhardt seized on a completely incidental motive and raised that up to obscure one that was fine and unselfish, I really was disgusted.

I said, "Gebhardt, that would be an outrage."

The reporter began arguing in an attempt to justify himself. If I had run into as many welchers and pretenders as he had and so on, all the trite excuses of the ungenerous.

In the midst of this Pedro said he was thirsty. I was sympathetic. "Haven't you had anything to drink since you went on guard? I'll get you a glass of water!"

The sailor lifted a hand. "Senor, no, not water. Not here among dead men."

I understood his Latin distaste for water at any time or place, and especially in a morgue."

"Gebhardt," I directed, "Get Pedro a coke. Get a whole carton. I'll go on with the questions, and tell you what I find out."

The reporter departed and I continued with my catechism. I wanted a little atmosphere for Gebhardt's story.

I said, "This barren island, Pedro—who built the quay on it? The fishermen?"

"Oh no, Senor. No one knows for sure but they say the pirates built it back in the old days. Gasparilla, Teach, Captain Kidd."

There was color in that, romantic mystery. If Gebhardt got nothing more out of it than an historical sketch for the Sunday edition, it would be something. In the middle of my questioning Pedro interrupted me to say, "Senor, I am so sorry."

I asked what about, and it turned out that what he wanted to drink were not cokes at all, but, of course, wine. He had Latin fears about imbibing any sort of drink in a foreign country unless it had first been rendered germ-proof by at least a minimum of alcohol. He could not imagine why he had not mentioned the unfortunate fact before.

Naturally I went out at once to get the wine, and had the good fortune to meet Gebhardt coming out of a grocery store with a carton of cokes. I explained Pedro's mistake to him, and he immediately became suspicious.

"It's the power of advertising," I said. "It's the result of seeing hundreds and thousands of 'When Thirsty' signs."

"Yes, but Pedro can't read English," argued Gebhardt holding fast to his doubt.

"Maybe not. But you're forgetting he has read the very same signs in Spanish all over Cuba."

"Yes, of course, that's right. Did he say anything further about why his Captain had brought the body here to Tiamara?"

"No, he didn't. But I found out for you that Key Doce was a resort of pirates in the old days. Pirates built the quay on the island."

"That's something," admitted the reporter. "If nothing better turns up, I might rig a column of pirate stuff, and run that."

We went on back to the morgue, planning Gebhardt's article in the event that nothing more exciting and timely came our way. When we reached the place and went inside we saw an army sergeant standing by the table inspecting the headless body of the soldier. Pedro had vanished.

The sergeant was examining the metal tag around the dead man's neck and also looking at a tattoo on the left forearm. When he saw us he recognized our kind for he said, "You fellows from the paper?"

Gebhardt said, "Yes. Can you identify this man?"

The sergeant glanced at the tag again. "Sure. He was Robert Mears, Waycross, Georgia. Height—five eleven. Weight—one hundred and eighty pounds. Blonde. Thin light hair; tattoo mark on left forearm. Funny thing about the tattoo. It's sort of smeared. Sea and the sun, I imagine."

"Did Pedro turn the body over to you when you arrived?" I asked. "Did you bring him any reward from the Army?"

"No, there was no reward offered, and when I came in there was nobody here. I had no trouble finding the body however. The sheet was turned back just like it is now."

Gebhardt tried to make something out of this, but I assured him that Pedro had simply grown tired of waiting for us, and had gone out to get himself a drink. We talked for some little bit, with Gebhardt getting more and more nervous all the time until finally he said:

"Look here, I'm going to telephone Poggioli again."

"What about?" I asked.

"About that tattoo," he said. "Did you ever hear of a tattoo blurring?"

We went to a telephone in a little railed-off corner, and Gebhardt called up my apartment. He evidently got Poggioli, for he talked for a few moments in an undertone, possibly to keep the sergeant from hearing. Presently he put up the receiver and turned to me with a queer expression.

"The dead man isn't Robert Mears," he said.

The moment I heard this and realized that it had been relayed from Poggioli, I knew it had to be true. But how and why, I had not the faintest idea. I made a guess.

"Is it the smeared tattoo—"

"Poggioli said the tattoo was merely a corroborative detail," repeated Gebhardt with his strange look. "No, what proves that the body is not that of Robert Mears is his identification tag."

"His what?"

"That's right, his identification tag. Poggioli said if he really were Robert Mears, he wouldn't have his tag on in perfect shape. He said if the head had been cut off by a ship's propeller the tag certainly would have been damaged or lost in the sea."

"Well, it would have been," I said. "Is Poggioli coming over here? Is the problem mysterious enough for him now?"

"Yes, he's coming right over. He said to ask the sergeant to wait for him."

When we made this request of the sergeant he dismissed it with military brevity. But when I explained it was Dr. Henry Poggioli, the well-known criminologist whom we were expecting, and that he was looking at the man who had written the accounts of Poggioli's investigations which he had read in the magazines, it made all the difference in the world. He shook my hand, and introduced himself. He was Sergeant Roy P. Floyd, from Reading, Pennsylvania.

In a short while we heard a motor outside, and Poggioli entered the morgue. He had brought with him a little vial of kerosene, and he used it immediately and effectively to remove the tattoo mark from the dead man's forearm, thus proving his contention that the dead man was not Mears of Waycross, Georgia. I must mention that this was the only time I ever saw Poggioli use anything in pursuit of criminals except strict psychologic deduction.

Poggioli set his bottle aside. "Your record of Robert Mears shows him to be absent without leave?" he asked. At the Sergeant's quick "Yes Sir," Poggioli went on: "What you want to know, Sergeant, is where Mears is now. What *we* want to know is how he got this body substituted for his own, and shipped here in an obvious attempt to be declared dead, and have his case dropped by the Army."

Gebhardt interrupted, hopefully, with his pencil out. "Did Mears himself murder this man, decapitate him, and try to make the switch?" he asked.

"That's a detail," dismissed Poggioli. "The question is how did he get a fishing boat to bring the body here, deliver it to the military, and why should the guard vanish? Such manipulation would require the financial power of a racketeer. Do you know him, Floyd?"

"He was in my company, sir." Here the Sergeant smiled. "He didn't have a dime in the Army. He shot craps and bummed his cigarettes."

"Did he ever talk to you about his plans? Were they practical or romantic?"

"I would say romantic, sir. He tried to borrow a dollar from me once. He said he had a system that would beat any crap game, and all he needed was a dollar."

"Then he didn't murder this man," said Poggioli, looking at the body with its severed neck.

"How do you make that out, Dr. Poggioli?" asked Gebhardt almost with reverence.

"He wasn't practical enough," said Poggioli. "But that makes the mystery deeper than ever."

"What mystery, Poggioli?" I asked, somehow on edge about the matter.

"How he ever got the body delivered here. Could it possibly have been Mears in disguise who was standing guard over the cadaver, when you arrived?"

"No. Pedro was a Cuban who spoke only Spanish." I turned to Sergeant Floyd. "Mears couldn't talk Spanish, could he?"

"He couldn't talk English a month ago when he was in my company."

Poggioli shook his head. "I can't quite make this out. I will have to talk to Mears and get the feel of the fellow before I can say how he ever got this body brought here to impersonate him."

"Where will we go to talk to him?" asked the Sergeant in a brittle tone. "I was sent here to bring him into camp."

"He's probably down around Key Doce in a boat of some description."

"What description?" demanded Sergeant Floyd.

"Probably in a very poor craft, possibly owned by a fisherman who sympathizes with Mears in his flight from the army."

"That seems improbable," said the Sergeant who knew Mears.

"Such was my implication when I said 'possibly,'" said Poggioli, in the tone of a lecturer who dislikes interruptions.

Gebhardt began planning how to get to Key Doce. As a *Times* reporter he knew the art of reaching unscheduled destinations in tropical seas. He said we might wangle something to get us to the Key in Oceanfront Park where there were fishing boats, cruisers and private yachts for hire. Sergeant Floyd decided his assignment could be stretched to permit him to go with us.

The patrons of the big beautiful boats we found in the municipal yacht basin gave me a sad insight into the distribution of luxuries in America. We, a group of intellectuals, could find absolutely nothing within our economic orbit, whereas we saw fat, well-feathered men waddling blithely about seeking still finer yachts for their cruises. And these were men devoid of any genius whatsoever except, of course, the sort they had.

At last Gebhardt went to a telephone, and called up his managing editor. The rest of us stood just outside the glass door, listening to him stressing the mysterious features of the story: discovery of body on empty key, brought to Tiamara for unknown reason, military tag of A.W.O.L. soldier switched to dead man, guard, Pedro, mysteriously vanishing.

It really was quite a bill of particulars. Gebhardt sat in the booth, nodding and arguing and gesticulating with his free hand.

Finally he came out and said to Captain Marks, "You can send your bill to the *Times*. Do you want to confirm it over the phone?"

The Captain was delighted. No, no, he trusted us implicitly. But in the midst of this confession of faith he somehow managed to step inside, and check Gebhardt's authority. He came out expressing his delight at such passengers. He usually carried dull business men, for intellectuals of science and literature, as a class, never seemed to care much for yachting.

At first I thought Poggioli and I were going along free. But it turned out that Gebhardt had arranged with his paper that we should do some work to repay him for our passage. Poggioli was to keep a lookout for the craft in which he hoped to find Mears. I was to help Gebhardt with his reporting.

It sounded simple enough. I thought I was merely to help the reporter interview Mears if we succeeded in finding him. But it was not that at all. Gebhardt's editor had concocted quite an assignment.

My duties were to keep a sharp lookout for all pleasure yachts of impressive dimensions, get in touch with them by radio, take down the names and addresses of their owners, and his list of guests. If any young woman on board were about to get married or was already on her honeymoon, I was to get the girl's name, the name of her fiance or new husband, and every conceivable tidbit of gossip or scandal ever associated with their private lives, and deliver the information to Gebhardt's private cabin to be whipped into shape for transmission to the *Times*.

In short we had turned into a sea-going society column. We did all of this by radio naturally, and when I spotted one yacht and began my questioning other boats for miles around picked us up, and began radioing in their guest lists voluntarily. My trouble was not in finding yachts, but in keeping them separated, with the right women engaged or married to the right men.

On our first night Gebhardt got a radio message from the managing editor saying he had received over two thousand subscriptions by wireless to be mailed all over America and would Gebhardt consider a handsome offer to cruise through the Canal, and straight up the West Coast?

On the third day Gebhardt was instructed to tell my yacht owners that if they were equipped to send wireless photographs the *Tiamara Times* would gladly receive them. Apparently the *Times* had tapped a salt water gold mine.

In the midst of this buzz of social publicity Dr. Henry Poggioli kept a lonely, almost unnoticed, watch for a small craft with a runaway soldier in it.

Well, on the fourth day, while I was busy relaying the guest list of the yacht *Ingobar* out of New York for Cairo, Captain Marks' voice bawled through his megaphone for us to stand to port and prepare to drop anchor.

I looked to port and saw a great flattish stone thrust up into the intense blue of the sea. In its lee lay a nondescript little craft with something bulky in its stern, and a stub of a mast in its middle.

Poggioli and Captain Marks were studying the boat through binoculars. The skipper said, "There's a winch and an air pump in its stern. I can't make out whether the man is white or colored."

Poggioli said, "He's white."

"Your glasses must be better than mine."

"No, he's the man we're after. He's Mears of Waycross, Georgia."

"Why do you say that?"

"It takes two men to use a diver's outfit like that. It isn't likely there would be two such expeditions among the keys at the same time. So the man that isn't there must be the body we left in the morgue at Tiamara."

The deduction was so obvious it brought no comment from Captain Marks. But he did ask sharply, "Did Mears murder his partner to use him as an escape from the army?"

"I don't think so. But I'll know a good deal more about it when I've talked to him. I'll get something of his temperament, and I ought to be able to make a guess."

When our mahogany hull had whispered to within earshot of the little hulk, Poggioli called through a speaking trumpet, "Boat ahoy! How's your grub and water?"

The skipper now had begun to follow the criminologist's program with curiosity.

"Why the grub and water, Dr. Poggioli?" asked Marks.

"Men are more communicative when they are desperate," said Poggioli. As he spoke, his answer came back.

"Purty skimpy!"

Whether the man in the boat were a murderer or not, all of us began smiling at his dialect. It so completely underwrote Poggioli's deduction that he was Robert Mears of Waycross, Georgia.

Captain Marks became active. He called to the steersman to telephone the cook for a platter of food and coffee. He suggested to me that I tell Sergeant Floyd to stay off deck until Poggioli talked to the man.

I rushed to the cabin and found petty officer Floyd helping Gebhardt with his radio society news. Both men were sarcastic about brides to be and debutantes. I broke in on them and said, "Sergeant, Poggioli's got your man!"

Sergeant Floyd wheeled toward the cabin door, but I stopped him. "You're to stay out of sight until Poggioli gets all the details. Then you can come out and take him over."

Gebhardt jumped up. "I don't have to stay here working on this tripe." He changed his tone. "Sergeant, you can't come on deck anyway. Will you finish interviewing the Baroness de Traut over the wireless?"

"I won't know what to ask her."

"You don't have to ask anything when you interview the Baroness. Just listen and write."

He turned over his head phone, paper and pencil to the soldier, caught up some extra sheets for himself, and hurried out on deck to question the man who either had or had not murdered his diving partner, and tried to palm off the dead body as his own.

When we reached the deck again the cook had lowered some grub to the derelict and the lone survivor was eating ravenously. Poggioli was saying, "You eat like a man who has been out of grub a long time."

The soldier maneuvered his food so he could mutter, "I did not start with no grub, suh."

I smiled at the double negative.

"But why should you and your partner start on such a junket without grub?" Poggioli asked.

Mears stopped swallowing. "How come you know I had a pardnah?"

"You've got a winch and an air pump. You had to start with another man to run them."

The fellow began eating again. "That's right. You're a smart man. The reason we started out without grub was—we decided to try that Frenchman's experiment."

Gebhardt began writing. "What Frenchman?" he called down.

"That there Frenchman that started across the Atlantic on a raft with nothin' to eat or drink, not even watter."

I myself remembered reading of that fantastic French experiment when it broke in the press. In the queer world of the newspapers it had not seemed so suicidal. But it *was* suicidal, and for this Georgia boy to be alive at all was surely a miracle.

"Did you actually live on fish and mollusks all during your cruise?" I called down

"If I'm still alive an' this ain't a dream, I done it."

Gebhardt, still scribbling, called down, "Do you mean you came on a junket like this to see if you could survive with just a fishing line and a net?"

Poggioli answered for the fellow. "No, he and his partner were searching among the keys for buried treasure."

The sun-blackened youth stopped eating abruptly. "How'd you know that?"

"Very simply. Men don't risk their lives without an object. The Frenchman wanted to write a book. You have an air pump and a winch, so you must have been looking for buried treasure."

"I be hanged," ejaculated Mears blankly.

"Did you find any?" rapped out Gebhardt.

"They found some," answered Poggioli for the man, "that's how his partner got killed."

At this the youth in the boat stared up at Poggioli with his mouth hanging open.

"How . . . how did you know?"

"I didn't know it," said Poggioli calmly, "but it seemed likely. If your partner sent you up a bar of precious metal, you certainly would be greatly excited, and stop working the air pump. Naturally he would drown."

Mears shook his head earnestly. "It wa'n't the way you think, sir. He come up with it hisself. Then he went down ag'in an' got hung. He signaled. I hauled as hard as I could, but he was hung. I could feel somethin' give, and he came up. His neck was tore, an' broke. He was dead. I held to the winch an' looked at him. There we was, rich—but him dead. Then I knowed people would think I done it. They would say I kilt him after he helped me find the treasure."

"How much treasure was there?" asked Gebhardt.

The youth reached under his seat, and produced a single small barnacle-grown brick. He got to his feet and handed it up. He had already scratched off a spot that showed the pale gleam of silver.

"You didn't kill him intentionally, Mears," said Poggioli. "It was the fact that there wasn't any more silver down there that really killed your partner.

The lonely man looked enormously relieved, but he stared hard at Poggioli as the latter went on:

"You both thought there was a trove here at the foot of the quay. Your partner was as excited as you. He began groping and pushing among the coral formations and got hung. You hauled up on the winch as hard as you could. It was all you could do. When his neck tore he came up. But he had been dead before that, for you couldn't lift and work the air pump, too."

"Sir, I—I didn't know what had happened. He come up dead with his throat tore."

"That's right, Mears. Came up dead. And you took your identification tag from around your neck and you put it around his neck. You laid his body out on the dock."

"How do you know I done all that?" cried the soldier.

"Because the tag would have been lost in such an undersea struggle—or bent, or damaged. But it lay on your partner's neck like an ornament put there by an undertaker. You couldn't have told the world more plainly in words that you were away without leave, and that you hoped your partner's body would be mistaken for your own. Isn't that so?"

The soldier simply sat holding a bone of meat staring at Poggioli. He looked down at his own boat, then at the cook who had hauled up his brick of silver.

"Who gets that?" asked Mears.

"It isn't worth more than a hundred or a hundred and fifty dollars," Poggioli said. "The Government will get part of it and you the rest. What I want to know, Mears, is this. How did you get the body to Tiamara?"

"Tiamara?"

"Yes, Tiamara."

"Is that where it went?"

"You didn't know it had gone there?"

"No, I jest laid it out on the dock," said Mears. "I hoped somebody would come along and take the tag back an' git me wrote off as dead, and shut of the army. I didn't figger nobody would take the body back, too."

He blinked bewilderedly.

That ended the case. When Floyd came out he recognized Mears and immediately took charge of the prisoner. Gebhardt was happy. He turned his marine social column over to the radio man who had learned how to handle the matter, and went to his cabin to write up the fabulous story.

I followed him to the cabin and watched him warm to his task.

"There's material here for a great short story," he mentioned cheerfully to me.

I shook my head. "No, it runs too smoothly and predictably. It's newspaper stuff—not life . . . or literature."

"What do you mean, too predictably?" he demanded.

"The characteristic feature of life, Gebhardt, is that you can't forecast how anything will turn out. That's why good mystery stories have such an appeal. They mirror the unpredictable. This business is like a demonstration out of Euclid."

I left Gebhardt joyous, triumphant, amused and a bit scornful, and went out on deck which was deserted now except for Poggioli walking up and down.

I joined him as one seaman falls in with another, step for step, although I don't think he liked it.

"Well," I said finally. "I wish it had had a quirk to it."

"Quirk to what?" he snapped.

"To the incident you have just unraveled!" I said in surprise.

Poggioli gave a brief snort, then after a moment relented a little. "Our unraveled incident leaves us in a more complete mystery than ever."

"How is that, Poggioli?" I said. "It seems to me that we have . . ."

"How do you explain Pedro walking off and never coming back?"

"He probably got drunk," I said. "He drank too much."

Poggioli gave another disagreeable snort, and went into the cabin. I never care to be alone. Presently I went into the cabin, too, and met Gebhardt just coming out with his copy.

"Taking it to the wireless, eh?" I called after him. "Well, it should win acceptance from newspaper readers."

"There are eight hundred thousand of them," called back the reporter, "and in the morning my byline will greet each and every one of them on the front page!" He was quite elated over it, the fool.

I went into the cabin and sat down. Poggioli moved back and forth swaying to the swing of the sea. His disturbance was the antithesis of the reporter's.

I said to him, "Poggioli, don't worry over imaginary problems."

He hushed me up with an effacing movement of his hand, crossed to a lounge and sat down. A newspaper lay on the lounge. He picked it up, and I saw it was an old copy of the *Times* which we ourselves had brought aboard the *Tarpon Queen*. But when I mentioned that fact to him he informed me coldly that he was able to read the date for himself. So I hushed, and simply sat there watching Poggioli read a three-day-old *Times*:

Presently to my surprise he paused, scratched his bluish chin, drew out a pencil and marked something in the paper. Then he tossed it aside and went out on deck.

I followed him, and saw him enter the radio room just as Gebhardt came out. The reporter was in high good spirits. He took a turn on deck, expanding his lungs and ignoring me completely. Once he gave himself a thump on the chest.

For some reason Gebhardt's euphoria depressed me. I went back into the cabin, sat down on the couch and presently picked up the *Times* which Poggioli had discarded. As I looked it over absently, I noticed the sentence he had underscored. It was the same one he had read aloud to me in our apartment, the quotation from Alex Alexson's shipping column, "A little minnow whispered in this reporter's ear that a certain trawler's slip was showing."

I wondered what Poggioli could possibly have seen in that on his second reading. I decided he had simply thought of some unrelated topic as I quite often do when I'm reading some passage of trivial nonsense.

I wondered gloomily if I would have been happier as a journalist like Gebhardt, writing about uncombed combinations of chance instead of stamping the flow of life under my eyes with the pain, passion and intricate designs of fiction. The first was the easier, and certainly the more profitable insanity. I went to my private cabin, and turned in.

I believe I have as little envy in my make-up as the next man. But I must say that when we eased into Tiamara quay the next morning and I heard the newsboys screaming, "Great Decapitation Mystery Solved"

I felt what an unjust world this is.

Gebhardt came out on deck in high fettle. I am sure it was the first time one of his stories had ever made the first page. He didn't wait for the gang plank, but jumped from the taff rail to the wharf, and got out nickels for the newsboy.

He took three copies, tossed one to me, and another to Captain Marks and nosed into the remaining copy himself. I felt an impulse to throw my copy into the water. I opened it up instead, and read the secondary headlines under the decapitation streamer.

*International Smuggling Gang Busted by Times Crime Expert,
Dr. Henry Poggioli. Takes Tip from Times' Shipping Column. His
Wireless Warning Enables Police to Catch Gang Agent, Pedro
Alfiero, a Sailor, Bringing Dope Into Tiamara Morgue in Clothing of
Decapitated Corpse, Found Accidentally on Key Doce by Gang.*

I turned nervously through the pages looking for the story
Gebhardt had wirelessed in. On the society page I read a great splash,
"The Baron and Baroness De Traut are cruising off Tiamara as guests of
Amri B. Pendiver, the Roasted Peanut Magnate on his Yacht, *Shalimar
III.*"

I felt a tap on my shoulder and turned.

Dr. Henry Poggioli stood at the quayside, smiling at me.

"There's your twist, your quirk, whatever you want to call it, my
fine feathered friend," he said. "I wirelessed the police last night, just as
Gebhardt was sending in what he thought was the complete story. I
knew that Pedro must of necessity have disappeared for a very good
reason, for a man does not go out into the hot sun for one little drink
when he has a great responsibility to fulfill. From what you told me, he
would have wanted you to think well of him — if he had been the Pedro
you described.

"He had to be another, different kind of Pedro, and Alex Alexson's
column supplied me with the key. Tipping off the police by wireless was
then just an automatic gesture. You could have done it yourself."

I returned his stare, unflinchingly. "Perhaps," I said. "But only Dr.
Poggioli could have done it with such a fine flourish and kept mum
about it. You might at least have warned me."

"Then you would not have enjoyed so delightful a surprise when
you opened that paper just now." Poggioli said.

To that — what answer could I give?

The Mystery of
the Personal Ad

The ex-university professor, Dr. Henry Poggioli, was questioning me in his faintly disagreeable and didactic manner about the personal advertisements in the late edition of last night's *Tiamara Times*.

"Take this one," he said. "Just what would your interpretation of this be: 'Henry, forgive my carelessness and come back. Bessie.'"

I said I thought Bessie wanted Henry to come back. This irritated Poggioli — as I intended it should.

"I mean, what is the relationship between Henry and Bessie?"

"Married, I imagine."

Poggioli lifted a shoulder. "I don't know whether Henry is married or not, but Bessie is and Henry is her lover."

"What earthly proof have you for that conclusion?"

"No proof — only probability. Notice the position of the words 'carelessness' and 'come back.' If she had been his wife she would have advertised, 'Henry come back and forgive my carelessness' — because carelessness would have been the basic point at issue. But when she says, 'Forgive my carelessness and come back,' that places the stress on getting Henry back again. That isn't wifely — it is, if I may coin a word, 'mistressly.' Wives know very well that their husbands will come back, and they are in no stew about it."

"Well, there's no way," I pointed out, "to check up whether you are right or wrong."

"No, not conveniently. Let's try another. What can you do with this: 'J.L.J. deliver package to Fourth and Orange, twenty-three twenty-three, last notice.'"

"No signature?" I inquired.

"J.L.J. undoubtedly knows who wrote it."

"M — mm. Well, my interpretation is that somebody known only to J.L.J. wants J.L.J. to deliver a package to twenty-three twenty-three Fourth and Orange."

"What do you mean, twenty-three twenty-three Fourth and Orange?"

"That's the street address."

Poggioli made a hopeless gesture. "Did you ever hear of one address on two streets?"

"No-o, I don't believe I ever did. But why does it say twenty-three twenty-three?"

"That is the time it is to be delivered."

"Time? It couldn't be the time — there are only twelve months in the year. . . ."

"It's the hour and minutes on a twenty-four hour clock. It would mean twenty-three minutes after eleven P.M."

"But why should any man pick out eleven o'clock at night to deliver a . . ."

"I don't know. That's what makes it interesting — and a bit sinister. We can be sure there is some illegality in it somewhere."

There is no telling how much farther my companion's deductions would have led him, but at this point our doorbell rang and Poggioli broke off to wonder, "Maybe the man at the door will throw some light on this advertisement?"

This also annoyed me — his presumption in thinking that every little mystery he was interested in would eventually float around to him. I was glad when it turned out not 'to be. Our caller was a Captain Scambow, Chief of the Tiamara Homicide Squad. I knew little of Chief Scambow's ability as a detective — I never heard of him catching anybody, but I did have an impression that he found his calling highly profitable, if not to the city and society at large, at least to himself.

I knew he had come to see Poggioli about some case or other, and as I invited him in I asked what he wanted. He said it was a matter of robbery and disappearance; a kind of bank had been rifled and a kind of banker had disappeared.

"Not one of the big city banks!" I exclaimed hopefully, for that certainly would have meant a story big enough for me to write and sell.

"No, a little concern — in fact, a loan company."

"Oh, I see." My enthusiasm vanished as we moved through the hallway. To make conversation I said, "Well, a little man like that will probably get caught."

I did not especially mean this for cynicism; it was just a fact that if men took only small amounts of money in Tiamara, they were very likely to be caught.

When we joined Poggioli he asked no questions — he always prefers to form his first impressions on the actual scene of the crime. So the three of us — Poggioli, Scambow, and I — went out, got into the Chief's car, and rattled off downtown to the Teachers' Ever Ready Loan Company, located on the second floor of 321 Orange Circle.

It was a single, bleak room with a table, two or three chairs, a wastebasket with a newspaper stuffed in it, an old-fashioned breast-high bookkeepers' desk, and an old iron safe in the corner, its heavy door ajar.

A little man was on guard — a smoked, expressionless little man who looked like a janitor and turned out to be one. We learned later that when he entered the Loan Company's office that morning he found the safe in its present open condition, and so gave the alarm. The first thing Scambow asked him was if he had heard anything from Jones yet.

Poggioli inquired who was Jones.

"The man who was manager of this company," explained Scambow.

"You say 'was manager,'" picked up Poggioli, with his usual finical attention to language. "You don't think he's manager now?"

"M — mm, now, that I don't know," hedged the Chief, "with the safe standing open and the money gone and Jones himself vanished. I suppose that is what caused me to say 'was manager.'"

"I see. And just what did you expect to hear about Mr. Jones from Mr. Peevik?"

"I didn't know. I sent a man to Jones' home to find out whether he was sick or not. I thought maybe my man had telephoned back and talked to Peevik here."

"No, Mr. Jones isn't sick," stated Poggioli.

His assurance amused me. I knew my friend had some reason for saying this so positively, but he always tried to play up his omniscience before strangers. Scambow asked how he was sure. Poggioli answered that the probability of the manager falling ill on the very night his company was robbed was too remote to be considered. He said he was sure Jones was in excellent health — or had been murdered.

Scambow gave a little shrug at this. "Well, my department doesn't reach conclusions in such a high-handed way. We check along, one thing after another, and see what has happened."

"You sent your man out to see if Jones were at home, but before you heard, you came and got me?"

That did seem queer. I hardly know why it seemed queer, but it did. Scambow waved the point away and indicated the rifled safe.

"I didn't expect Jones to be at home either. This shapes up like the same old story."

The psychologist stood there, looking carefully at the Chief and at the janitor. "Same old story, eh? Then why, Mr. Scambow, did you call me in on such an elementary situation?"

"Dr. Poggioli, it's like this. It's easy enough to see that Jones has run off with the firm's money. I got you to come here and tell us where he went. I wanted to know Jones' psychology of flight, where he'd go. Just tell me that, and I'll save the city of Tiamara thousands of dollars searching for him."

"Do what?" asked the scientist.

"Save the city considerable expense looking for him," repeated Scambow.

It was only in thinking it over afterwards that I realized the cynicism in Poggioli's surprise that Scambow should do anything to save the city money.

"You want me to deduce, from this lay-out, where Jones went?" summed up the psychologist.

"That's my idea, Professor," nodded the Chief. "I don't see how it could possibly be done — however, I have seen you do many things that couldn't possibly be done . . ."

Poggioli began his job by a long series of questions to Peevik, the janitor. So far as I could see, he got nowhere. Peevik had been working for Jones for nineteen years. Yet he knew nothing about his employer. The manager of the loan company was about fifty; Peevik didn't know whether he was married or not, but he didn't think he was.

Scambow, puttering through the drawer of the old desk, remarked casually that fifty was the age a man often broke loose, whether he was married or unmarried.

"Tell me something else about Jones," continued Poggioli to Peevik. "Did he have any intimate friends that you know of?"

"I don't think he did."

At this point the office telephone rang. Scambow took it. It was the report from his man at Jones' home. Jones was unmarried; he rented a single room, and his landlady said that he had not been in his room that night.

This, of course, was expected; nevertheless, when it emerged as a certain fact, all four of us stood looking at the gutted office, a little shocked, as if we had not known it before. Finally, Scambow said, "In this miserable place, for nineteen years, without a wife or a friend. . . . I don't much blame him."

"How much money did he take?" asked Poggioli, off on a fresh start.

"We don't know," said the Chief.

"Maybe we can find out," suggested the psychologist. "The amount he took would determine more or less how far away he could go."

This sounded reasonable, so Poggioli took an old ledger from the ancient safe, carried it to the bookkeeper's desk, and began going through it. Scambow was doing research of his own at the table and at a receiving teller's cage that faced the door; but he kept a curious eye on Poggioli. Presently, the psychologist looked up from the ledger and said that Jones had got away with fifty thousand dollars.

Both the Chief and the janitor were obviously surprised.

"How did you find that out, Professor?" asked Scambow.

"This is the beginning of the month," explained my friend. "I took the income received last month, subtracted the accounts payable, added about ten percent as a reserve fund for a shoestring business like this, and arrived at about fifty thousand dollars. But what is surprising about that?"

"Well, that you got it at all."

"Maybe I didn't; maybe I'm all wrong."

The homicide detective gave a little laugh. "Maybe you didn't, but you sound like you did." Then he pointed to the table he had been examining. "Here's our lead, Professor Poggioli, as to what's behind all this.

"Jones has been following the ponies. Look at that . . ." He indicated a pile of old horse-racing tickets in the back of the table drawer.

Somehow this didn't seem exactly right to me, but Poggioli nodded in agreement. "That could be a reason for embezzling, Chief."

"Certainly it is, and it tells us where Jones has likely gone . . . Saratoga . . . Santa Anita . . ."

The betting slips were of various dates, reaching back for several years. In the drawer, along with the betting receipts, lay a small, ordinary, wooden screw. When Poggioli picked it up, it left its print in the dust. My friend turned to me and said, "Make a note of this screw."

"Why?" I asked.

"It will probably have a bearing on the outcome of this case."

I didn't quite believe this. Poggioli likes to make a monkey out of me occasionally, for his own pleasure; but I wrote down in my notebook that there was a wooden screw in the table drawer.

My friend picked up the racing tickets and the screw and stood looking at them in the abstracted manner he has when plunged in abstruse criminal analyses. Finally he said:

"Gentlemen, Mr. Jones could not possibly have taken that money."

I wondered if the wooden screw had anything to do with it. It seemed to have. All of us asked the psychologist why Jones couldn't be the thief.

"Because no sane manager of a Loan Company would leave the evidence of his horse-racing activities here in an open desk, subject to the inspection of any stockholder who happened to enter this office."

Peevik, the janitor, licked his lips. "I never knew a stockholder to come into the office."

"Well, it's a business company, isn't it? Didn't they ever have directors' meetings?"

Peevik became more confused. "Not that I ever heard of."

"In nineteen years?"

"That's right."

"If it's a legally organized company, it has a stockholders' book. Let's look for that book."

He turned back to the safe, found the stock book, and started going through it. As he did so, he began talking of other things. He mentioned that he himself always had been interested in horse racing and had given some thought to betting theories.

This caught the attention of both the other men, as naturally it would; because if Poggioli should turn his marvelous powers on horse racing, he would almost certainly be able to pick the winner, or at least the horse that would place. Chief Scambow asked the savant to tell him his theory.

"And I imagine Mr. Peevik is also interested, aren't you?" inquired the psychologist genially.

"Y-yes, I really am," hesitated the janitor. "But why did you think I would be interested, Mr. Poggioli?"

"On account of your ring."

"My ring!"

"I never noticed that he was wearing a ring," said Chief Scambow.

"You wouldn't. Ordinary persons never notice rings unless they are expensive. Peevik's is a brass ring in the shape of a serpent holding its tail in its mouth."

"But what has that to do with horse racing?" asked Scambow.

"Not much, except that men who wear serpent rings lean toward the mysterious, the subtle, the bizarre, and the hazardous. That is why I knew he would be interested in my theory of horse racing."

"Well, yes, I am," agreed Peevik, pleased at being singled out as an exceptional man. "I worked out a horse-racing system of my own, but it wasn't much good."

"I imagine you and your employer, Mr. Jones, were very congenial when it came to racing gossip," suggested Poggioli.

"No-o. . . . no-o. . . . We really never mentioned the matter to each other," said the janitor.

Chief Scambow broke in with another wise smile. "Anybody connected with a financial company, Professor, can't very well afford to mention horse racing to anybody anywhere."

"Nevertheless, you would have thought . . . two racetrack fans . . . during nineteen years of association . . ."

"Oh, no, never at all, Professor. A finance man bets absolutely on the q.t. He has to."

My friend apparently agreed with this, and presently came to a pause in his search through the stock book. "Here it is — a list of the stockholders and the amount of . . . Oh, this is one of those dummy companies. There are only five stockholders — four owning one share each, and J.L. Jones, the manager, owning all the rest."

"Well no wonder he didn't mind leaving his old racing tickets in his desk drawer," observed Scambow.

"I don't know about that," objected Poggioli. "Mr. Peevik here might have seen them."

"What do you mean — Peevik might have seen them?"

"I mean that Mr. Peevik is one of the other four stockholders. William Peevik . . . isn't that your name, Mr. Peevik?"

"Why . . . yes . . . that's me. I remember now . . . about sixteen or seventeen years ago, Mr. Jones asked me if I would take a share in his company. He said it was free, wouldn't be any liability and . . . and it might be a asset when . . . when he was dead . . ." Peevik broke off, staring, not so much at the stock book as at space . . . and time.

In the midst of this, Chief Scambow's mouth dropped open and suddenly he began laughing, incredulously at first, then uproariously.

Peevik now remembered the other three stockholders: one was a Jim Fredericks who had been Mr. Jones' barber; the others were a junk man and a tinsmith. All three were dead. At this Chief Scambow again broke into irrepressible laughter, and then abruptly said, "Well, I think I'll keep on looking around the office and see what else I can find."

Personally, I wanted to go home. I had about decided there was no salable story in the situation when Scambow drew the newspaper out of the wastebasket, spread it out on the desk, and looked at it. From an inner page a very small rectangle had been clipped. Scambow looked at this, was about to turn on through the paper, but then paused to look at it again. "Wonder what that was?" he said aloud.

"What?" asked Poggioli.

"This clipping. Somebody's cut a clipping out of this paper."

"Where is it?" asked the psychologist.

"Here among the personal ads. We can get another paper and find out what it was."

"Let me see . . . I read the personal ads every morning. They are the most human things a paper prints — tell more in less space. . . . Oh, this one! I remember it. Let me see . . . it said, 'J.L.J. deliver package to Fourth and Orange, twenty-three twenty-three, last notice.'"

A little breath went through me. Poggioli, you will recall, had suggested that our caller might have something to do with this advertisement. Scambow's face became illuminated. "What a memory you've got, Professor! That's our clue, with shipping directions attached. That ad undoubtedly was meant for John L. Jones . . . J.L.J. . . . see?"

"It probably was," agreed the psychologist.

"The package it refers to, of course, means the money. Jones owed somebody money — bookies, I imagine, from these slips. Peevik, did your boss attend racetracks in person or did he place his bets over the 'phone?"

"He never . . . uh . . . went to the races, Mr. Scambow, but . . . but I never heard him telephone a bookie either."

"Cautious man. He was cut out for a banker, but he evidently must have telephoned — these slips prove it — and he got a long way behind in his account with the bookies. But, of course, they would trust a banker . . . for a while."

"Why didn't the bookie call for his money?" inquired Poggioli. "Why didn't he telephone, why did he run a personal ad?"

"To keep everything on the q.t., Professor."

"But why should Jones have taken all his money?"

"Evidently he owed it all, and then some."

"Why do you say 'and then some'?" queried the psychologist.

"Well, Jones hasn't come back, has he? If he could have paid off in full, it's reasonable to assume that he would have come back, isn't it?"

"What do you suppose happened?"

"It seems to me there are two possibilities, Professor: when Jones read that notice in the paper, he could just have taken his money and beat it; or he could have gone out and tried to settle with 'em and got into trouble. Of course, I'm not looking at it from your viewpoint — that's why I got you to come here. I wanted an expert's opinion."

All this struck me as being very clear reasoning on the Chief's part. There was nothing foggy about it. I had no trouble in following it, as I always do in following Poggioli's deductions. In fact, I could have thought up Scambow's ideas myself, and it seemed to me that the chief was a very well balanced man indeed.

That I was wrong, however, became clear when the four of us started out in the Chief's car for Fourth and Orange Streets, which was the address given in the personal ad. Scambow and Peevik sat in the front seat; I rode with Poggioli in the rear. The motor was not new and it made enough fuss so that Poggioli and I could talk privately. I said to my friend, "He's a pretty clever reasoner, isn't he?" and nodded at the front seat.

"A clumsy bungling thief," answered the psychologist.

I was amazed. "*Thief!*" I whispered; then I thought I understood. "Oh, I see — you mean his previous record with the Police Department" — because Scambow had been up before the courts, for conduct unbecoming to an officer.

"No, I mean thief in this particular case. He's got that fifty thousand dollars."

"Then why did he consult you?" I asked in a whisper.

"He wants me to second his theory — that Jones paid all the money to some bookie or other. My say-so would quash any further investigation."

That threw a very strange light over what I had thought was a simple case. I rode on in silence for several minutes, trying to get my new bearings. Finally I said, "Why do you think Scambow has the money?"

"Because when I guessed fifty thousand dollars both he and Peevik were greatly surprised. There was nothing to surprise them — *unless I had guessed the correct amount!* Both knew I was going to make some sort of estimate. If they hadn't known the correct amount, nothing I could have said would have stirred them up. But when I actually hit on the right figure, both of them were amazed. In fact, that is why I took so much trouble to figure out the exact loss. I knew Chief Scambow's reputation, and that was a simple way of finding out immediately whether or not he had the money."

I was utterly flabbergasted — Poggioli, so seemingly innocent and straightforward, laying such a mine under the feet of his apparent co-worker. At last I collected myself enough to whisper, "But what happened to Jones?"

Poggioli lifted a finger and shrugged imperceptibly. "I thought Peevik had murdered him until I found out positively that he did not."

"How do you know he didn't?"

"By Chief Scambow's laughter. There is something funny about Peevik being a stockholder. It couldn't be Peevik's murder of Jones — that isn't funny, even to Scambow. I am now trying to decide just what Scambow considers so funny."

"Then what could have become of J. L. Jones?"

"I don't know unless Peevik, for some reason, ran that idiotic ad in the paper and scattered his old racetrack tickets in the table drawer — perhaps to make it appear that bookies murdered him. That's why I called your attention to the print of the wooden screw in the dust. The old tickets left no print — they have just been put in the drawer. Peevik has to be the one who put them there — his system furnished him with plenty of losing tickets. Jones himself was no race-horse fan. Two racing men couldn't possibly have worked together for nineteen years and not become confidants. . . . No, that ticket business and the ad in the paper was just the sort of false trail some fool would think up who invented betting systems for horse races and who wore brass serpents on his forefinger."

"But that suggests that Peevik did kill his boss."

"Yes, it does."

"But the Chief's laughter suggests that Peevik did *not* kill him."

"That is also correct."

"Then which is right?"

"We are on our way to inspect the body now — to find out."

I myself was not so sure there would be a corpse at Fourth and Orange Streets. Yet, I must confess, I looked forward to one. You see, my interest and that of Jones were directly opposed. Nobody can sell a detective tale to an American magazine unless there is a murder in it. If Jones were alive, he won; if he were dead, I . . . but there's no use going into that.

I must say that what we found on the corner of Fourth and Orange Streets was a sorry sight. Jones' scalp was beaten and bloody, and his neat banker's clothes awry. A policeman guarding the body called out:

"Chief, I thought you would never get here! I've had you paged in every police station and radio car. . . ."

"Don't worry, Sergeant, the murder is solved."

"You mean it?"

"Yes, this is the body of a banker, J. L. Jones, of the Teachers' Ever Ready Loan Company. He got behind in his gambling debts to the bookies. They lured him out here last night by an ad in the paper, took his money, and then killed him."

"Which bookies, Chief?"

"Who knows? With five thousand bookies all doing a brisk business in Tiamara, it is like trying to decide which mosquito bit a man."

"Why did they kill him?" asked Poggioli.

"Professor, that's a difficult question, and one I hoped you could answer. You see, we guardians of the law really don't grasp the psychology of law breakers . . ."

"I see that," nodded the criminologist.

"If I had to theorize, I might go astray. I depend more on my legs than on my theories. I don't know anything except what I look up. . . . I wish I had a brain like yours . . ."

"But you do have a theory after all?"

"Yes, it's this. I don't know whether Jones paid up his full debt to the bookies or not — probably not; but they killed him as an example — to scare other customers into paying off promptly, with no dillydallying. They can't lose anything by it, Professor. This murder will get results — wide publicity in the papers — hundreds of telephone bettors will read about it and come in and pay off their gambling debts. That's really why they ran that personal ad in the paper — the start of an advertising campaign."

Well, to my mind, there was a simplicity, an easiness to understand, about Chief Scambow's theory that drew me over to his side of the argument.

As for the criminologist himself, he stood studying the inert figure on the street corner in the deepest abstraction; he stood, one hand in his pocket, the other pulling at his bluish chin. I knew he was trying to form some hypothesis which would pull together all these very contradictory elements.

But that, of course, was impossible, and I cannot deny a certain secret satisfaction in my heart to see my friend's intellectual arrogance brought low. I watched him finally take out his handkerchief, stoop, and daub it on the stained head of the dead man. Of course, that meant nothing to me. He might just as well have taken the banker's coat or tie or one of his ears, so far as I was concerned. He walked over and gave the stained cloth to the policeman.

"Young man," he said, "get on your motorcycle and take this to Dr. Anson, 1516 Bougainvillea Avenue. Tell him I'll telephone him within a half-hour. I want to know the blood of these stains."

"Professor, I don't understand," began the Chief.

"I simply want to know if the blood on the outside of this man is the same as the blood on the inside. Very simple request . . . get along, my son."

The policeman looked at Scambow, who nodded grudgingly. Poggioli then turned to the three of us. "All right, Mr. Peevik, we will now go to your room."

Peevik and Scambow glanced at each other, but the four of us reentered the Chief's car and set out for Peevik's room, wherever it was.

"Uh . . . Mr. Poggioli, did . . . did you want any particular thing from my room?" asked the janitor, twisting around in the front seat.

"Just wanted to use your telephone. I'm going to telephone Dr. Anson pretty soon . . . I thought you and I and the Chief could analyze this case more quietly in your room than, say, at the Police Station."

"Oh, yes, we can," agreed Peevik eagerly.

I felt sorry for the murderer, for now I realized that Poggioli had settled on Peevik as the criminal. The way the little man grasped at not being taken to the Police Station moved me with that feeling of pitying contempt which we Americans feel for all criminals who have taken less than a quarter of a million dollars.

Peevik lived on the third floor, in the slum district which has made Tiamara famous. And as Poggioli predicted, he had a telephone, although it looked incongruous in that bare cubicle.

"Now, Mr. Peevik," said Poggioli, "in these dirty walls somewhere you have a spring which, if you touch it, opens a hidden closet. . . ."

Peevik wet his lips. "Mr. Poggioli, why in the world do you say that?"

"Because of your ring, Peevik, your brass snake ring. Men who wear such trinkets are of the intellectual age of boys — the type of boys who dig caves and form secret societies with mysterious rites and terrible oaths. Where is your secret closet?"

Peevik pointed an unsteady finger. "Right there, sir."

"The money's there, too?"

"Y-yes, sir."

The Chief of the homicide squad spoke up. "Peevik didn't kill Jones, Professor."

"I know that, Scambow."

"How did you know it?"

"By your laughing . . . Tracing murders is your work, Scambow. Men never laugh at their own work — only at something apart from their work."

Poggioli went to the telephone and dialed a number. "Hello . . . hello, is this Doctor Anson? . . . Anson, you got the handkerchief I sent you? . . . Well, I want to know the type of blood on it. I think it is probably of a different type from the real blood of the dead man I found it on. . . . If that's true, I'm going to take that fact and save the life of a janitor named Peevik. I'm going to prove that Peevik did not kill his employer . . . What? . . . What? . . . *Cat's blood!* Well, I'll be . . ."

Poggioli broke out laughing, and presently hung up. Answering my look, he said, "Certainly, I'll explain. Jones dropped dead in his office — overwork, heart attack, whatever it may have been. The janitor found his body, took the money in the safe, and then cooked up a wonderful scheme to make it appear that Jones was killed by bookmakers. He ran a personal ad in the *Times* and planted old betting tickets in the table drawer. The janitor then beat the dead man over the head to simulate foul play. But of course the corpse didn't bleed. He took the body out to dump it at Fourth and Orange Streets but was met by a police officer of the Tiamara Police Department. The two agreed on a split of the money, but they still needed some blood. So the officer shot a stray cat and . . . What? . . . What was the Chief's laughter about? . . . Chief Scambow was the officer. He couldn't help laughing at the thought that the janitor — *as the only surviving stockholder of the Loan Company* — could have had the whole business for himself, simply by *not* stealing the ready cash and *not* carting the body away."

The Telephone Fisherman

My friend, Professor Henry Poggioli the criminologist, is an incorrigible show-off. When Dawson Bobbs stopped his jalopy in front of my yard, Poggioli looked at him for several moments, then said to Mrs. Alma Lane, his croquet partner, "Your town marshal is looking for me. He has just received a telephone message from a woman reporting a crime on her husband."

Mrs. Lane naturally replied, "Now, Mr. Poggioli, you and Dawson Bobbs have made this up."

I promptly gave Poggioli a character recommendation, for I had seen him do that sort of thing many times. I said, "No, they haven't, Mrs. Alma. Poggioli's analyses are always genuine."

"But how could he possibly know?"

"Well, for instance, he knew that Mr. Bobbs is the Lanesburg marshal by his badge."

"Yes, but that's just a start. How did he . . .?"

The rest of it, I assured her, was just as simple.

"Mr. Poggioli, won't you please . . .?"

"I am sure he will," I said. "Instead of hurrying him, you'd better find yourself a soft seat on a bench in the shade."

"You're jealous of him," she said to me in an aside.

"What man wouldn't be," I said, "when he monopolizes the ladies?"

My friend, whose extraordinary genius I am the first to admit, did explain his deductions very simply, just as I was sure he would. He said he knew by the way Bobbs looked over our group that he was hunting for someone he did not know. The fact that he came to my home indicated that Bobbs had heard there was a criminologist visiting Lanesburg. The marshal did not appear to be an intellectual — therefore his interest in a criminologist must be practical. If that were true, he had just heard of a crime over the telephone . . .

At this point Helen Stevens, the auctioneer's wife, caught him up; she didn't see how the telephone came in.

"That followed very logically, Mrs. Stevens," explained Poggioli. "Mr. Bobbs was clearly in a hurry. He had just heard his news. There is no telegraph line running into Lanesburg, and it has only one mail a day which has not yet arrived. So his information had to come in over the telephone."

At this explanation the astonishment of our Croquet Club decreased, I would say, about 20 per cent. Then Taylor Lane, the banker — Mrs. Alma Lane's husband — asked how Poggioli knew the marshal's message was from a woman.

"Not only did I suspect a woman," replied Poggioli, "but I was almost positive it was some woman telling on her husband. Mr. Bobb's informant evidently gave him a mere hint and then rang off, or he would never have needed me. If it had been a woman in no way related to the criminal she wouldn't have hinted, she would have given full details. If it had been a man his message would have been terse but complete. Therefore, the message must have come from the criminal's wife."

The astonishment of our club decreased proportionally as Poggioli explained his deductions.

"The wife must have been jealous of some other woman!" exclaimed Mrs. Stevens.

"Good, extremely good, Mrs. Stevens," praised Poggioli, with the pleasure of a college professor who has discovered signs of life in his class.

Poggioli had passed what might be called the Q.E.D. of his original proposition. The interest of the crowd now turned to Marshal Bobbs, who stood in my gate amazed, no doubt, at hearing a stranger tell so much about himself. Mrs. Stevens now turned to the marshal.

"Exactly what did the woman say to you over the phone, Mr. Bobbs?"

"She said Sam Wagham had committed a hanging offense," repeated the marshal, and this corroboration followed so naturally that nobody was surprised at it.

"And what did you want to find out from Mr. Poggioli, Mr. Bobbs?" asked Mrs. Alma.

"Nothin' from him. I wanted to ast Jim Stevens did he know any Sam Wagham around here?"

At this everyone was amazed. "And you weren't looking for Mr. Poggioli at all!" cried Taylor Lane.

"No, I was looking for Sam Wagham!"

"Then what made you study Mr. Poggioli the way you did, Mr. Bobbs?" asked Mrs. Stevens.

"Because I thought maybe he was him," said the marshal, in the complaining tone of a person who is explaining something too simple to require an explanation.

At this, everyone began laughing with the unrestraint of small-town folk. I think Poggioli was a bit disconcerted, but he observed with surprising aplomb that pulling out a single brick didn't necessarily tear down a wall.

Mrs. Stevens, who was good-natured, relieved the situation by saying, "Jim, do you know any Sam Wagham, and where he lives?" And Mr. Stevens, who had the waggishness of an auctioneer, replied, "No, I don't, but undoubtedly Mr. Poggioli does." Mrs. Stevens gave her husband a reproving look.

Poggioli, however, was like a derailed engine that had been put back on the track; he steamed ahead as briskly as ever.

"Mr. Bobbs, are you acquainted with the people of this village?"

"Absolutely ever'body, Mr. Poggioli."

"But Wagham evidently lives in Lanesburg or his wife never would have telephoned you?"

"Mm — mm, y-e-es, I guess that must be so."

"Now there you are," said Poggioli brightly, turning to the group. "That is what I call an indicative contradiction. It is an X marking the spot where you must search."

"What spot?" asked the officer literally.

"One that is clear enough," said Poggioli. "You know every man in town, yet you don't know Sam Wagham who is *in* town. Therefore, Wagham must be a transient, one of your floating population."

Marshal Bobbs was suddenly enlightened. "Oh, you mean the fishermen in their shackboats on the river!"

"You don't know them?"

"No, I don't know them — they come an' go. But it ain't likely they committed any hangin' crime. A little telephone fishin' maybe, but they don't do nothin' of importance."

"But a jealous wife sometimes exaggerates things, Mr. Bobbs," put in Mrs. Stevens, who had started the jealousy idea.

"I'll say they do," nodded Mr. Stevens, mainly at his wife.

"You ought to find him on a houseboat, Mr. Bobbs," suggested Poggioli briskly. "Since his wife has run off and left him, you will find him living alone. All the other boats will have couples on them."

Mrs. Helen Stevens was so pleased with having dipped her thumb into Poggioli's criminological pie that she exclaimed, "Let's all go down and see how Mr. Poggioli's explanation turns out!"

"Come on, come on," invited the marshal heartily. "I debbytize all of you to come down and he'p me arrest Sam Wagham. If he resists, I'll let you all take a shot apiece at him with my Police Special." And he indicated the gun in his inside coat pocket, where it didn't show.

Under this compulsion of the law, The Croquet Club piled into the marshal's jalopy and set out for the fishermen's boats moored below the village.

There proved to be three of them that week: a down-river boat, a middle boat, and an up-river boat. We took them in that order.

The down-river boat had on it a woman, twin babies, three other assorted children, and a sign, *Fish, 25 cts a poun.*

Mr. Bobbs called out, "Is this Sam Wagham's boat?" No reply came, and when he repeated his question a woman's nasal voice yelled back, "What do you-all want to know fer?"

"Want to buy some fish!"

"We-all sell fish!"

"But is this Sam Wagham's boat?"

"We-all sell fish same as Sam Wagham."

"This isn't the boat," diagnosed Mrs. Stevens. "Let's go to the next one."

"How do you know it isn't, Helen?" said Mrs. Lane.

"Because if it had been she would have said, 'Yes, you-all come aboard.'"

The rest of them laughed at Mrs. Steven's imitation of the poor white dialect, but it didn't amuse me. It has always seemed to me if the rest of the country could express itself with the delicate pronominal precision of the Southern poor whites, it would represent a considerable advance for the less vocal masses of Americans.

The next shackboat was empty. A crude pigsty stood on the bank in front of it. The bottom of the sty was still muddy, but it had no pigs in it. Bobbs was about to drive on when Poggioli suggested we go aboard.

"What's the use lookin' in a empty boat for a missin' man?" asked the marshal.

"Trained men like Mr. Poggioli," I answered for the criminologist, "will observe details, Mr. Bobbs, which an ordinary man would miss."

"I could see the sense to it," said Bobbs, "if we was lookin' fer whiskey, but not if we're lookin' fer a man."

Nevertheless, we teetered across a narrow, cleated plank, got aboard, and looked in the cabin. Mrs. Lane said it was cleaner than she could get her maid to keep her home.

"This has been kept by a Northern woman," diagnosed Poggioli. When Mrs. Stevens inquired into the why and wherefore of this, he added, "To be exact, it has been occupied by a Vermont woman. Those are the sort of curtains Vermont women put over their windows."

"She is not very particular about her bedstead," criticized Mrs. Alma Lane, who was an actively defensive pro-Southerner.

Poggioli went in and examined the bedpost, which had a missing finial. "This knob was broken off recently," he stated, "at about the same time the occupants took their pig out of the sty."

"What pig and what sty?" asked Jim Stevens.

"I don't know whose . . . yet. The sty is there on the bank."

"Mr. Poggioli," asked Mrs. Alma, "what connection has the broken bedpost with the sty?"

"None that I know of, Mrs. Lane, except in point of time. Everything that occurs at about the same time may possibly have some causal connection; then, of course, they may not have any such connection."

Poggioli always answered such questions in the most uninteresting way, but of course he had been a professor in a university for a great many years of his life.

At this point we were interrupted by a woman calling out with an incisive Northern pronunciation, "What are you persons doing on that boat?"

The moment we heard her, Mrs. Lane said to Poggioli, "There's your Northern woman, but she's on the wrong boat."

We turned briskly out on deck, for the shouter was in no pleasant temper. Marshal Bobbs called back to say that we were looking for fish. We could now see the woman standing on the aft deck of the up-river boat.

"Where did you persons expect to find the fish," she inquired with Yankee pointedness, "in the bedroom?"

"We wasn't expectin' to fin' the fish in here, Ma'am," explained Mr. Bobbs with hill courtesy. "We was hopin' to find Mr. Wagham in here an' get the fish from him."

"Well, you can come on up an' 'git' your fish from him up here," mimicked the up-river woman.

"She is not only a Vermont woman," said Poggioli, "but at some time in her life she has taught in a girls' private school in the East."

Our two women glanced at each other and lifted their brows to indicate how clever the marshal was to get at the identity of his man without asking his name. The Northern woman naturally suspected no trap; she asked us to come on up and Mr. Wagham would attend to us.

As we got into the car and rode up to the third boat, Mrs. Alma said a little uncertainly, "I thought we were going to find Mr. Wagham on a boat by himself." But we had no time to develop this thought before we were getting out again.

We found a hulking, whiskery, leathery man aboard the up-river boat who answered to the name of Wagham. As he came out on deck the woman, who wore a snood, went into the cabin where we could glimpse her through the door, returning to work. Mr. Wagham said, with a touch of apology in his Southern hill voice, "She's a workin' womern. Well, how much fish do you-all want?"

We skirted around another pigsty with a sow in it. "What sort of fish you got?" asked the marshal.

Mr. Wagham picked up a dip net and began stirring in a fish box in front of his home. "I reckon you-all'll want cat. I got any kind an' size of cat you want — yaller cat, channel cat, spotted cat . . ."

"Ever'body here wants a two or three poun' cat, don't they?" asked Mr. Bobbs of us.

We guessed that for some reason it was expedient for us to want "a two or three pound cat" — so we all did.

"Gertie," called Mr. Wagham to the woman in the cabin, "can you step out here a minute an' string these cat when I dip 'em out?"

The woman said, "Certainly, Sam," her clipped enunciation sounding almost droll after the way her husband talked. She came out on deck again.

"All them cat?" queried Mr. Bobbs peering into the fishbox.

"Mm — mm. Yeh, they're all cat. Say, you-all want jest one apiece?"

"B'lieve I'll take two," said Mr. Bobbs. "I've got a frien' who'll want a good cat, if you'll let me telephone him." He indicated an old-fashioned wall telephone fastened to a plank leaning against the front of the cabin.

"Why, I'm afeard that phone ain't connected," said Mr. Wagham.

"Oh, it ain't," said Mr. Bobbs, and he stopped.

Poggioli stood surveying the peaceful scene. "You'll excuse me, Mr. Wagham, but you two certainly are a congenial couple."

"Mm — mm, I guess we air at that, don't you, Gert?"

The woman said, "I feel that way, Sam. I don't know how you feel."

"Naw, I'm shore you don't," and the grizzled fisherman laughed.

"How long have you been married, Mr. Wagham?" continued Poggioli, with the admiration everyone feels for a happy couple.

"Mm — mm, six year," said the shackboat man.

"And where did you meet your wife?"

"In Decatur, Alabama."

"Right up the river a hundred or so miles and floated down?"

"That's right," said Sam.

"Jim," said Mrs. Helen Stevens to her husband idyllically, "why can't we live on a fish boat, too?"

With that we paid for our fish and went back to the car, each of us carrying a cat on a string. On the way Mrs. Alma Lane said, "I never would have dreamed detective work was like this. What's this we've got — evidence?"

"A kind of evidence," said the marshal dryly.

"Evidence what of — murder?"

"Naw, the little ol' misdemeanor of telephoning fishes. It was like that fool woman on the boat to telephone me her husband committed a hangin' crime, then rush back to him and he'p him out when I come to git him."

"Mr. Bobbs, what do you mean by 'telephoning fishes'?" asked Mrs. Lane.

"That's what he uses that telephone fer on deck. I knowed it wasn't connected. It's a new way of ketchin' fish an' it's agin' the law. All you do is to throw yore telephone wire in the water an' ring yore bell, an' up floats all the fish in yore neighborhood. I mean up floats all the slick fishes like cats an' eel. Scaly fishes like carp an' buffalo, it don't do nothin' to. That's why his box was full of cat."

Such was the mystery we had come to fathom. It was disappointing — like hunting a lion and jumping a rabbit.

"Are you going to arrest them?" asked Mrs. Stevens.

"Mm — mm . . . naw. I'm not the game warden. Besides, I've telephoned up fish myself. Of course, I don't want you-all to mention that."

"Why did his wife phone you word that Wagham had committed a hanging offense, then come back and help him with the very crime she was complaining about?"

"Oh, that's jest like a woman," said Bobbs, "mad one minute, over it the next."

Poggioli interposed, "I can't quite agree with you, Mr. Bobbs, in the light of the other evidence."

"What other evidence? All the evidence they is point to Wagham's guilt. Telephone box settin' out in plain view, his fishbox full o' nothin' but cat . . ."

"It struck me, in the light of the other evidence," persisted Poggioli, politely but didactically, "that those things may have been put out as a blind to make you *think* he had been telephoning catfish, as you call it, and to hide a crime of violence. Possibly murder."

This came as a shock to everyone. "What in the worl' makes you think that?" asked the marshal.

"Primarily, his *stressing* the idea of telephoning fish."

Mr. Bobbs blinked his eyes. "What do you think he is trying to hide?"

"His wife practically accused him of murder over the phone."

"Yeh, but she's come back to him, as honey-dovey as pie."

"I'm certain she is not his wife," said Poggioli.

"What do you mean?" asked Mrs. Lane, with a woman's quick interest in such things.

Poggioli turned to her. "Did you ever know a wife of six years' standing to stop in the middle of housework and help her husband string fish without a complaint?"

Everyone saw this at once. "She really isn't his wife!" agreed both women.

"I don't think so. And the rest of the evidence corroborates my suspicion."

"What is the rest of the evidence?" asked Taylor Lane.

"The pigsties, the clean and unclean boats, and the fact that the woman owns the lower houseboat while the man owns the upper."

When pressed by everyone to explain his explanation, Poggioli began with the last item.

"I knew the woman owned the middle boat, because when we were on it, it was she who shouted down for us to get off. If the man had owned it he would have walked down and inquired into the matter. So, you see, although the two are living together they are not married; and they have a very clear understanding of what property belongs to each of them."

"Now, what's the next point?" asked Mrs. Stevens, evidently determining to make a better showing on that.

"The next," said Poggioli, smiling, "are the pigsties."

We fell into a deep study over this problem, but none of us could make anything out of it.

"The two sties," elucidated Poggioli, "show that Wagham and the woman intend to make their relation permanent. The pen in front of the middle boat was old and empty, the one beside the Wagham boat was recently constructed and had a hog in it. Evidently when Wagham's wife left him, this woman's husband deserted her and she came up to Wagham's boat."

"How do you know she had a husband, Mr. Poggioli?" interrupted the banker.

"Because women never live alone in houseboats; men do occasionally, but women never do."

"Mm — mm, I follow you there. Now, go ahead about the sties."

"There's nothing more to it. The woman brought the pig up from her sty because she was sure this new arrangement with Wagham will be permanent and that her own husband would never return."

A faint grue came over us at the end of Poggioli's statement. Mrs. Lane asked, "What do you suppose happened to her husband?"

"Since the present Mrs. Wagham, in fleeing her first husband, telephoned Marshal Bobbs that Sam Wagham had committed a hanging offense, the most natural conclusion to come to is that Wagham killed him. It could be something else, but it isn't likely."

The simplicity of Poggioli's reasoning amazed us. Indeed, whenever I heard his conclusions I wondered why I hadn't thought of them myself.

"Are those all the implications of the affair?" inquired the banker.

"We could never possibly analyze *all* the implications," said Poggioli professionally, "because every new arrangement readjusts all the units in it. Of course, the greater part are unobservable by the human senses. In this instance, the very clean down-river boat and the woman beginning to clean up Wagham's boat show conclusively that she had just moved in with Wagham, and that fact may have some bearing on the crime itself. But I can't follow that indication to any positive conclusion; it simply leads off into the unknown."

Marshall Bobbs wanted to know if Wagham murdered the woman's husband with a gun or a knife? Poggioli thought neither; Wagham was not the type of man, Poggioli said, to use either a knife or a gun; the broken bedpost suggested a rough and tumble affair.

The Marshal was distraught. "How're we ever goin' to git a case aginst him with nothin' but pigpens an' bedpost knobs and a house-cleanin' Yankee woman for proof?"

Poggioli made a gesture. "Legal proof is an entirely different matter, I know. All I can suggest is to subpoena the real Mrs. Wagham and have her testify as to what she knows."

"Yeh, subpoeny the real — Where *is* the real Mrs. Wagham?"

"I would say she is in Decatur, Alabama, Mr. Bobbs."

Our whole Croquet Club wanted to know Poggioli's source of information on this point.

"That was why I asked Mr. Wagham when and where he had been

married," explained the psychologist. "I was sure that on the spur of the question he would tell me where he married his real wife. The first Mrs. Wagham is obviously a poor housekeeper, suggesting that she may have come from some indolent Southern family. The condition of her houseboat confirms Wagham's statement that he was married in Decatur, Alabama. Since such a woman could not and would not make a living for herself, she undoubtedly has returned to her people in Decatur."

After a while Poggioli's prescience palls. He was like an adding machine: punch the numbers and receive the correct answer.

Marshall Bobbs said, "I'm going to Decatur and git that woman, then I'm comin' back here with her an' hang Sam Wagham!" After driving on a little further he cautioned us, "Looky here, don't none of you-uns talk none of this; it would jest make it harder for me to ketch ever'body and git 'em together in Square Smith's courtroom."

We all promised we wouldn't discuss the Wagham case. But I am afraid Mrs. Lane and Mrs. Stevens did mention our junket confidentially to some of their women friends, and they in turn confidentially to other women friends, and so on. I am putting this on the women purely through custom. Our expedition had not been particularly exciting, but it was a very talkable affair; of course, the men could have discussed it just as easily as the women. But the upshot was the same: Wagham received news of his danger from some source. He did not run away, as I think Marshal Bobbs anticipated. He did a much more devastating thing from a social and sociological standpoint: he retained the Honorable H. Hall Hickerson of Savannah to defend him.

The Honorable H. Hall Hickerson was a criminal lawyer famous for never having lost a case. An admiring people praised and honored him for having set free in their midst sundry thieves, firebugs, burglars, murderers, and whatnot. Whether he really never lost a case or not, I don't know; but as dramatic counterbalance to the invincible H. Hall Hickerson there arose on every tongue an equal fame for Poggioli. He, it was said, was a detective who had never failed to hang his man. I knew for a fact this was not true. Poggioli had never convicted anybody for anything. He pursued his investigations purely for his own entertainment and, I suspect, to amaze and bewilder his various audiences. Now his deadliness arose purely as an echo of the Honorable H. Hall Hickerson's invincibility. The result was that on the day of Wagham's trial one of the largest crowds Lanesburg had ever known funneled into our town.

Nor was it an altogether peaceable gathering. Friction immediately broke out between the partisans of the Honorable H. Hall Hickerson and those of Poggioli. The Poggioli men were the scattering of Yankees in and around Lanesburg, while Hickerson's adherents were, of course, the native-born. Several quarrels arose, including a few street fights over the relative merits of the two heroes, but usually the antagonism took the form of betting. Gambling may be looked upon with disfavor by press and pulpit, but there is no telling how many public affrays it has prevented. No partisan is going to club the opponent from whom he hopes to collect a wager, although he may feel like doing both. It was fortunate that Wagham's preliminary trial was not going to be held before a jury, for there were not twelve unprejudiced men in all Lanesburg.

Squire Smith heard the case in the lock-up down the alley from the Universal Feed, Furniture & Undertaking Company. Marshal Bobbs summoned The Croquet Club as witnesses — not that he ever used us, but merely to get us front seats in the lock-up; other auditors stood behind us, while the main crowd swarmed about the doors and barred windows and filled up the alley.

The only witness used was the real Mrs. Wagham, whom Marshal Bobbs had brought back from Decatur. She was a pretty woman in a kind of wild-deer way, the sort a man picks out in a crowd, vaguely regretting that her good looks are wasted on a woman of her class.

The warrant Marshal Bobbs had written out for Sam Wagham was complicated; it charged Wagham with murder in the first degree, in the second degree, with voluntary manslaughter, with involuntary manslaughter — for he had no idea what sort of testimony Mrs. Wagham would offer.

There was no State's Attorney in the case; there seldom is in a preliminary hearing. So the great criminologist, Professor Henry Poggioli, conducted the State's side.

I am embarrassed to relate that the odds on the Honorable H. Hall Hickerson gradually went up as the trial progressed. The great criminal lawyer objected to nearly every question the great criminologist put and to nearly every answer Mrs. Wagham gave. When Poggioli asked her if she were the wife of Sam Wagham, the defendant, she faltered out that she "reckoned she was" and the Honorable H. Hall promptly objected to this "on the ground that it sounds like hearsay evidence!"

Poggioli, however, pressed the point. "What do you mean, Mrs. Wagham, by 'you reckon you are'?"

"I mean I don't know sence Gertie Longmire moved in."

"Did you move out when Mrs. Longmire moved in?"

The Honorable H. Hall Hickerson lifted a bored voice. "Your Honor, I object to the prosecution leading the witness. Let her tell her own straightforward story with no suggestions from anyone."

This disconcerted Poggioli. "All right, Mrs. Wagham, tell your story."

"What story?"

"Why you left Mr. Wagham."

"Mm — mm. . . . Hit was because he traded me off."

"He did what!"

"Traded me off to Bill Longmire for Gertie there."

A sensation buzzed through the courtroom as the Honorable H. Hall got to his feet.

"Your Honor, I object. My client is indicted for murder in all its various degrees. I don't know what this woman means by 'trading her off' — my client is not arraigned for illegal merchandising, merely for murder. So I object to both the question and answer."

But the court had become interested along with the crowd. "Go on, Mrs. Wagham, what do you mean by Sam 'tradin' you off'?"

The woman spread her shapely hands. "Jedge, it's like this; me'n Sam got on fine tull we landed alongside of Bill and Gertie Longmire . . ."

"Mrs. Wagham, will you confine your answer to the question His Honor asked you?"

Mrs. Wagham became silent; like many simple persons she could not pick a particular answer out of her experience, she had to tell everything.

The Judge started her again. "You said until Bill and Gertie Longmire landed alongside of you-all."

"Oh, yeh, yeh. Then Sam begun to complain about me: Why couldn't I cook like Gertie, why couldn't I keep house like Gertie, why couldn't I do this an' that like Gertie? I got sick an' tired of hit an fin'ly one day I says to him, 'If you think Gertie Longmire is so much smarter 'n I am, whyn't you trade me off fer her?' He said Bill wouldn't trade. I says, 'I bet he would,' for I seen Bill noticin' me though Sam hadn't . . ."

"Your Honor, I object! All this is utterly irrelevant, superfluous —"

"Go on with your testimony, Mrs. Wagham. Did Sam an' Bill ever ackshelly trade?"

"They shore did, Jedge. Bill brung Gertie up halfway betwixt our boats an' Sam brung me and they swopped us an' me an' Gertie went to each other's boats."

It required minutes for Squire Smith to obtain order and hush the laughter, the gasps of horror, and the ejaculations of amazement in his court.

Poggioli, as chief interrogator, interposed again. "How did this trading of wives lead to Bill Longmire's murder, Mrs. Wagham?"

The Honorable H. H. H. jumped to his feet.

"Your Honor, the counsel for the State is putting words in the mouth of the witness. She has said nothing about murder!"

"How did the men start quarreling after you women done all you could to please 'em?" asked the judge of his own volition.

The woman hesitated; the court rapped for order so that she could be heard. Then Gertie Longmire, who was sitting beside Sam in the dock, spoke up in her clipped voice, "Go on, admit it, Sarah. Admit my Bill wanted to trade back quick enough and your Sam wouldn't do it!"

The pretty woman nodded reluctantly and her answer was lost in another outbreak of laughter from the room, windows, and doors.

Poggioli lifted his voice. "Is that how the murder happened, Mrs. Wagham — Bill Longmire trying to trade you back for Gertie Longmire?"

Mrs. Wagham flushed as the courtroom quieted for her answer. "Yeh, Bill brought me up to Sam's boat; he said he had come to swap back. Sam said he wouldn't do it. They argued, then they got to cussin', an' fin'ly Bill grabbed Gertie an' begun draggin' her back to his boat, yellin' out it was against the laws of God an' man the way we was doin'. All three of 'em went into Bill's boat together. Pretty soon I heard a big rumpus in there an' Gertie yellin', 'Sam, you killed him!' Then I cleared out. I half run and half walked to town, caught a truck goin' out to the highway, bought a ticket for Decatur, an' then while I was waitin' for the bus to come, I telephoned Marshal Bobbs what had happened."

When Squire Smith rapped down the uproar he asked, "Is that all?"

"That's all, Jedge."

"Mr. Hickerson," directed the court, "you may take the witness."

The great criminal lawyer lifted a declining hand. "No questions, Your Honor. The defense rests."

"Rests?"

"Yes, Your Honor, and the defense moves that all the testimony the court has just heard be stricken from the record."

"On what grounds, Mr. Hickerson?"

"On the grounds that Sarah Wagham is the wife of Sam Wagham and a wife cannot testify against her husband."

A queer kind of shock went through the courtroom. The oddness of it arose from the fact that everyone knew the point of law but somehow had overlooked it in the strain of the trial. Now the ease with which the great criminal lawyer quashed the indictment lifted him to new heights in the public esteem and caused especial rejoicing among the men who had played him for a favorite. When the alleyway learned the news the lucky sportsmen whooped and hollered and beat their hats against boxes, telephone poles, and, in extreme cases, the ground.

For once, I believe Poggioli was really disconcerted. Usually he had not the slightest interest in convicting a wrongdoer; indeed, he had never actually brought a criminal to justice and had never attempted to. I had always supposed that his interest in crime was purely intellectual, following the tradition of our finest amateur sleuths. Now a painful suspicion filled me that he really got his pleasure out of astonishing his audiences with his feats of ratiocination, and when his audience were not intellectuals and did not appreciate his amazing mental performances, he was driven to the vulgar objective of hanging his man. I had never before realized that my idol had feet of clay. My disillusionment was especially painful, for it came suddenly and without warning when Poggioli arose in court and asked Squire Smith to recess the court and give the State opportunity to produce the dead man's body. What a sordid alternative for my usually transcendental criminologist!

The Honorable H. Hall Hickerson moved the case be dismissed, and I for one heartily agreed with him. But the bettors who had put their money on Poggioli were tremendously excited; out in the alleyway they argued they should be given a sporting chance for their money. A general sentiment that this was only fair gradually crept through the crowd. Of course, this had no influence whatever on Squire Smith beyond the fact that our J.P.'s hold elective offices; at any rate, the Honorable H. Hall Hickerson's motion was dismissed.

At this a new rash of betting broke out. The whole trial now hung on finding the body. There was no question but that Wagham had murdered Longmire and flung his body into the river. The crux of the case now emerged: Would Poggioli find the body, and if so, how? The odds teetered now up, now down. The Lane County spectators figured that a great modern criminologist would have some new hydro-electric device for placing a finger instantly on the drowned man. Hill Davis, who ran a garage and had four mechanics working for him, picked on the exact term, "hydro-electric device," because it sounded to him like something that would work under water. At this, the odds on Poggioli went up. But as soon as the crowd flowed down to the river bank and learned that Marshal Bobbs was going to resort to the old-fashioned method of dynamiting the river to raise the body of the missing man, the betting evened off again. The officials always dynamited the river to bring up drowned persons but nobody had ever seen one actually brought up. However, there was one good feature about dynamiting the river for the drowned: it had high entertainment value.

Marshal Bobbs deputized three mussel-shell scows and their crews to handle the court and three well-drillers to handle the dynamite; then we all set out to raise up the dead. We began above the town and floated down. When the muffled thumps of the dynamite began piling up mounds of roiled water in the blue-green river, the crowd on the banks saw dead men everywhere. They shouted, "Yander it is, Mr. Bobbs!"

"I see it! Looky yonder, Square Smith!"

"There she floats right at you!"

But it all turned out to be dead fish or debris from the bottom.

In the midst of all this, the boat containing Mr. Bobbs and his two prisoners, Wagham and Mrs. Longmire, and their attorney drew by our scow. The Honorable H. Hall had a request to make of the court. He asked the court's permission for his client to pick up the dead fish. He explained that since Wagham had been unjustly accused and his good name libeled, the least the State could do to repair these injuries was to allow his client to recover and sell the dynamited fish. Squire Smith was a good-hearted man, lenient toward criminals, or he never would have been elected squire; so he told the men in the opposite scow to go ahead, he didn't want to waste any fish.

They proceeded when a very shocking situation came to light. Wagham brought the fish to an ice truck which in the confusion had parked unnoticed at the regular boat landing. When this obviously premeditated arrangement fell under the eyes of the crowd, an astonishing variety of opinions were bawled out from the bank.

"What kind of a skin game is this?"

"That crook, Hall Hickerson, worked this whole racket so Wagham could pay his fee!"

"Watch 'em, Mr. Bobbs, they'll stow the dead man on ice an' sell *him*, too!"

"Call the game warden an' have him arrest the whole shootin' match!"

The people were genuinely angry that somebody other than themselves was cleaning the river of fish. Squire Smith was also incensed. He did not object to Wagham having the fish so long as it was purely incidental; but the moment he saw the ice truck and realized it had been planned, he was outraged. He called out to the mussel digger who ran our scow, "Ketch up with them fish thieves. I'm goin' to put a stop to this business!"

I asked Squire Smith what he was going to do with the fish — let them spoil?

"Naw, I ain't goin' to let 'em spoil. I'm goin' to distribute them free among these people. They're the people's fish an' I'm goin' to give 'em back to the people!"

I began to see why the Squire had been elected Justice of the Peace these past eighteen years. His heart went out to the people, at the right time and in the right place. We sped our boat toward Marshal Bobbs' scow on our patriotic errand.

Now I don't really know if this too was prearranged on the part of the Honorable H. Hall Hickerson or was improvised, but the moment we came within call he began waving his hand and shouting to us to help them drag Mr. Wagham's net out of the way of the dynamiters, so it wouldn't be damaged.

The court was outraged again. "Us drag it out! Why should we drag it out?"

"This whole operation, Your Honor, is under your direction!"

"Then I direct Sam Wagham to git his own net out of the way. These fish he's pickin' up, I can't give 'em to him. They belong to the people!"

"Very well, Your Honor, all we wanted was your authority to drag Sam's net out of the way." And Bobbs' boat turned and set off down the river.

My friend, Professor Poggioli, the great criminologist, had sat in the stern of our scow all through this, wrapped in what I can only call analytical divination or some such paradoxical state. Suddenly he came out of his trance, and said sharply to Squire Smith, "Help him move his net!"

"Help that —? Let him move it hisse'f!"

Poggioli turned to the mussel digger who was running our scow.

"Lend Marshal Bobbs' boat a hand!" he ordered. "Cut between it and the net!"

There is an authority about Poggioli in moments like this that is not to be denied. Our boat cut in, and Squire Smith did not object.

When we hitched onto their line, Bobbs' and Hickerson's boat had already dragged the net forty or fifty yards. I had not the faintest notion what all this stir was about until Poggioli turned to the justice himself and snapped, "Here, Squire, lend a hand. Let's raise this net and see what Sam Wagham has caught!"

I must say that single sentence clarified the whole macabre situation for all of us. Poggioli explained to me afterwards how he had come to see the truth. Wagham's cold-bloodedness in asking for the dead fish and his having arranged in advance for an ice truck revealed the fisherman's crime. Then, as corroborative proof, there was the box of catfish which Wagham tried to pretend he had caught by telephone fishing; Poggioli knew cats were a scavenger fish and would be attracted by exactly such bait — a dead body.

Strangely enough, neither Wagham nor the Honorable H. Hall Hickerson seemed at all perturbed at our boatman cutting inside and running the net. They came up in their own boat to watch us, and as the telltale contents of the net appeared above the surface of the water, the Honorable H. Hall Hickerson actually stepped over into our scow to inspect it.

He shook his head. "Your Honor," he said, "isn't it too bad that the court has no means whatever of identifying these pathetic human bones! Whom did they belong to? No one knows, and there is no way to find out. You see, the net tore as it dragged along the bottom, and somehow it picked up these old disarticulated bones. I wish I knew their origin. If it be an accidental drowning, I would hasten as a patriotic Southerner to telegraph the next of kin; if it be a crime, I would be the first, as an American citizen, to demand that the culprit be brought to justice. But as I say, all that is in the realm of idle speculation. All this honorable court can do is to convey these remains to the city cemetery, bury them, and carve on a headstone: *Name Unknown, Sex Unknown, Age Unknown, Date of Death Unknown. Found in the Tennessee River and Buried in the Lanesburg Cemetery by order of Malcolm R. Smith, Justice of the Peace for the Second Civil District of Lane County, Tennessee. R.I.P.*"

It was a moving funeral oration. I almost forgot that Longmire had been murdered, in my sympathy for his anonymous and lonely death.

Poggioli, however, was not victimized by Southern eloquence. He fished the skull out of the net, turned it over in his hands, and said factually, "Your Honor, I want you to notice the fracture in this temporal bone; it has been crushed in by some rounded object. Let us take it to the Longmire houseboat and fit it onto one of the three remaining knobs on Longmire's bedposts. I want to show you where

Sam Wagham lifted Bill Longmire bodily, smashed him down on his own bedstead, and killed him!"

Naturally, the Honorable H. Hall Hickerson hooted at such sleazy proof, such diaphanous accusations. But when it turned out that the knobs, any one of them, actually did fit the fracture in the skull, Squire Smith bound Wagham and Mrs. Longmire over to the Circuit Court under a five-hundred dollar cash bond. The fisherman, I feel certain, could have made the bond if the Squire hadn't changed his mind about the fish and given them away to the crowd. But by the time Wagham had paid the rental for his ice truck and the fee to his lawyer, he didn't have enough cash left; so he and Mrs. Longmire had to spend the entire summer in the hot Lane County jail, which isn't a pleasant place to be, anyway.

The whole affair was a run of bad luck for Wagham. I am sure he never meant to kill Longmire; he was not that sort of a man. Then, if only his lawyer had told Squire Smith in an eloquent sort of way that Wagham had gone to the trouble to save the State's fish, or something like that, everything would have come out all right for him: the Squire never would have got mad and given away the fish; Wagham could then have made his bond; and by the time Quarterly Court came around, the two defendants would have been gone and forgotten, the money would have been in the court's pocket, and the whole case would have blown over.

The Mystery of
Andorus Enterprises

The tallish youth in the living room of our Acacia Street apartment asked Professor Henry Poggioli if he could tell by just looking at him who he was and what he wanted? Now a question like that, somewhat flattering and completely silly, irks me; but my friend took it as an opportunity for an exhibition.

"You want me to analyze *someone else* and you offer yourself as a test of my ability to deduce accurately?"

Our caller seemed slightly disappointed. "Naturally you would know that much."

"And you must be in a hurry or you would go about your mission more deliberately," continued Poggioli.

"Yes, that's true, I am in a hurry, I've got to get over to the . . ."

"And you have a sheaf of yellow second-sheets in your coat pocket, three lead pencils in your vest pocket, and your two forefingers are spatulate with their nails worn away. . . . The only persons who hurry out for copy, then hurry back and typewrite it with two forefingers, are newspaper reporters. You are out after some sort of story that has you puzzled. . . ."

"No, you're wrong there." The tall young man seemed pleased to have caught Poggioli in the wrong. "It's not a puzzling case at all — it's really a tear-jerker, but I'm not good at that sort of thing. I thought if you'd go with me and make some sort of mystery out of it. . . ."

The naïveté of the request surprised me. Poggioli, however, seemed interested.

"Just who are the principals of your story, Mr. ——"

"Gebhardt," supplied the young man. "The principals are a Mrs. Dawson and the Andorus Enterprises, Incorporated. It isn't a criminal action at all. The city court is investigating the qualifications of Andorus Enterprises to receive Mrs. Dawson's last baby and find a home for it. So you see, there is really nothing to the story, but I thought if I could get you to work up some sort of psychological angle . . ." He broke off vaguely.

"I don't know Andorus Enterprises."

Mr. Gebhardt was astonished. I interrupted to tell him that

Poggioli read nothing in newspapers except the criminal news; then he analyzed the various crimes, figured out who did them, the criminals' motives, where they had fled, and so forth.

"How does he find out these facts?" asked the young journalist curiously.

"Oh, from the stories themselves, or by putting two or more stories together, or by reading the personal advertisements. But often, when there is a real mystery afoot, and because he is so widely known, somebody — an officer of the law or occasionally the criminal himself — will come here, give him all the facts, and ask him what to do."

Young Gebhardt was amazed. "Doesn't he ever double-cross the criminals and have them arrested?"

"Certainly not. They are merely pieces in a chess game to him."

"Then I'm sorry there is no mystery about Mrs. Dawson," he said regretfully.

Poggioli took up the conversation again.

"You say she is giving away her last baby? How many others did she have?"

"Nine, I believe. She's giving away her tenth because she and her husband can't support that many children."

The psychologist considered the point for a moment. "Doesn't that strike you as queer? — a couple giving away their tenth child because they can't support it?"

The youth thought for a moment, but finally said, "Why no-o. . . . I'm afraid it doesn't, sir."

"Don't you know that the first child any couple has is the most expensive to rear, the second less so, the third still less, and so on. Finally, when a woman has nine children, she can rear the tenth without any perceptible extra cost, beyond the hospital fees for her confinement. So to give away a tenth baby to save expense doesn't make sense."

The reporter was surprised at this commonplace reasoning. "Then I wonder why she is giving it away."

"That I don't know. What I find interesting is why you should come to me with a story that you obviously considered dull and hardly worth writing."

"Well, I . . . because it is dull, and I knew if anybody could make it interesting . . ."

"Oh, no, that won't do! Nobody seeks expert advice over trifles. If you don't consider the story of any importance, then, somehow, the actors in it are important to you."

"The actors!"

"Exactly. Something is important. . . ."

"Why, I never heard of Mrs. Dawson before! She's nothing but a scrubwoman in the Andorus Building. . . ."

"A scrubwoman in the Andorus Building is disposing of her child to Andorus Enterprises!"

"Yes, what of that?"

"Nothing at this moment. Let us continue with your own personal aversion to the story. Just what grudge have you got against Andorus Enterprises, Mr. Gebhardt?"

Mr. Gebhardt was astonished. "Why, nothing, what could I have?"

"That is what we are trying to fathom. In what business is this company, Andorus Enterprises, engaged?"

The reporter gave a brief smile of distaste. "It would be a lot easier to tell you what they don't do. They engage in semi-philanthropic works. They bought up a big slum area here in Tiamara and are building model housing for the colored. They have started to work on a stadium and are going to give the city professional football. They are back of a plan to build a glass subway under the bay to allow tourists to walk out to a submarine tea room, where they can drink cocktails and look at the fishes. Now, of course, their last project is to find homes for unwanted babies, so they start with their own scrubwoman, Mrs. Dawson."

From Gebhardt's manner and tone he might have been charging Andorus Enterprises with highway robbery.

"Well, what's the matter with all these things?" asked Poggioli curiously.

"Why, the company came from Central America!" exclaimed the reporter. "Imagine a Central American syndicate, backed by millions of dollars, coming here to . . ."

Poggioli dropped his hands. "I see what you mean."

I looked at my friend and said, "I don't."

The psychologist nodded slightly. "I am sure you don't," he answered me, "and I am also sure that neither does Mr. Gebhardt." Here he broke off into one of his professorial lapses. "As a matter of fact, gentlemen, this is one of the most extraordinary instances of subconscious logic — which we ordinarily call 'hunches' — that I have ever encountered."

I realized we were about to wander off into a long theory which I couldn't possibly use in my notes about the case — that is, if there *were* any case — so I said, "Don't tell us how Mr. Gebhardt's mind worked — just state the objection he had to Andorus Enterprises, and let it go at that."

Poggioli was dampened, but he continued. "Well, it's very simple. Central America is an undeveloped country. There is never a flow of capital from a province to an industrialized state such as ours; money always moves from centers of industry outward. Gebhardt felt that, and subconsciously he realized that Andorus Enterprises did not and could not originate in Central America. He felt they were sailing under false colors, which undoubtedly they are. So there lies the basis of his psychological aversion to the corporation, and why he came to me hoping I would be able to discover something — say, criminal — about the company."

Gebhardt was astonished at this analysis. I was amused and began to laugh. The reporter turned to me and inquired why I was laughing.

"Look at the situation, Mr. Gebhardt," I said. "What could be more absurd than to investigate this vague bugaboo, this international fraud, in the city court of Tiamara, on the tiny question of whether or not the company is competent to convey a child from the child's mother to adoptive parents. That is like pulling a tack out of a skyscraper and expecting the building to fall down — that is, if Poggioli's wild deductions are really true."

"My dear man," retorted Poggioli angrily. "I didn't say Mr. Gebhardt's subconscious plan was practical. Subconscious plans seldom are. I simply told you why he felt an antagonism to Andorus Enterprises, and my diagnosis is correct."

Young Mr. Gebhardt arose with a reporter's nervousness. "Gentlemen, this phase of the discussion is academic. I would like Professor Poggioli to honor me by accompanying me to the city court and analyzing Mrs. Dawson herself. If there really is a fox in the canebrake, nobody could scare it out as quickly as he."

The psychologist arose. "You are coming along?" he asked me.

"Oh, yes, I'll come along — but this is a waste of my time. I can't possibly work anything as simple as a baby-adoption case into a good salable mystery story."

Gebhardt laughed and Poggioli shrugged. The three of us went outside to a car the reporter had waiting.

On the way to the city court there developed what I am sure was the real reason for young Gebhardt's visit to Poggioli. He was fishing for a sensational twist to the Dawson adoption to compete with another reporter's story about the waterfront hotels. The other reporter was named Jenkins, and Jenkins had discovered that a yacht owner and his wife had come ashore and engaged the penthouse suite of the Del Mar Hotel for twelve hundred and fifty dollars a night.

That exorbitant price was all that Jenkins had at first, which on Tiamara Strand was not as startling as it sounds. But Jenkins had dug up the accessory fact that the yachting couple were suffering from a nervous breakdown, and that a Dr. Majoffsky had come to visit them at ten o'clock on the following morning.

As Gebhardt was telling us these facts, Poggioli interrupted. "I read that story in the morning's paper," he said, "that feature of it — the ten o'clock visit by Dr. Majoffsky. It aroused my curiosity."

Both of us looked blankly at Poggioli, as the reporter's jalopy trundled downtown toward the city court.

"What's odd about a doctor's call at ten o'clock in the morning?" I asked.

"Why didn't the sick couple go to a hospital? Why did Dr. Majoffsky call at the hour when most city practitioners receive patients in their offices? Family visits usually come before ten o'clock in the morning and after two in the afternoon."

"That's a rather farfetched question, don't you think, Poggioli?" I asked, somewhat ironically. "There's no ironbound rule about it. It just happened to be at ten o'clock in the morning. Maybe the yachting couple were late sleepers."

"Not with nervous prostration."

"What could the hour have to do with it?" inquired Gebhardt curiously.

"Mm — mm. . . . I hardly know . . . ten o'clock. . . . All I know about ten o'clock is that banks usually open at that time."

Both Gebhardt and I were astonished. "What could that possibly have to do with it?"

The psychologist stressed his points with his fingers. "Gentlemen, I haven't the faintest notion, and I will not surmise. A premature guess may throw us completely off the track, and we may never get on it again. No, the thing for us to do is to wait for the next bit of evidence and see how it . . ."

"But, Professor Poggioli," interrupted Gebhardt, "aren't we working on the Dawson adoption case?"

"Certainly, but both those questions are on my agenda for today. I try to solve all the little equivocal points that arise in my morning newspaper. I do it to keep my hand in."

When the three of us reached the city court, we found that the matter in hand was not a criminal suit or a civil suit, or indeed a suit of any kind. It was simply an investigation brought on by the uproar raised in the newspapers over what they called the "black market in babies."

Mrs. Dawson and her infant were before the bar and Andorus Enterprises were represented by their attorney, a Mr. Nock. Nobody had committed the slightest offense. There is no law against a mother giving away her child. But Mrs. Dawson's neighbors had read about the black market in babies, and three different ones had telephoned to police headquarters that Mrs. Dawson was about to give away her last baby; this investigation was the result.

As the three of us listened to the testimony, young Gebhardt got out his paper and pencil, but he had nothing to write. He grew more and more fidgety. Poggioli touched his arm.

"Very suggestive point. Why don't you put that down?"

Gebhardt concentrated. "What point?"

"Mrs. Dawson telling the whole neighborhood that she was going to give away her tenth baby."

"That's just woman-talk."

"Yes, but they don't usually talk about matters which reflect on themselves. Normally, Mrs. Dawson would have said nothing whatever about giving away her baby until it was all over, and then she would have explained it the best she could."

The reporter was a little surprised. "Why did she talk then?" he asked.

"I am sure I don't know. It's a point you should remember — something may arise later to explain it."

"I see. So it might." Mr. Gebhardt wrote the fact down on his yellow paper, and I could see him wondering what that particular little point could mean.

Since I have a mystery-story writer's slant on life, I usually pick out somebody to be the hero, somebody to be the villain, and so on. My villain in this instance was Mr. Nock, attorney for Andorus Enterprises. He looked the part. His manner and voice were oleaginous — exactly the way a questionable lawyer's would be. He reminded the court of all the good things Andorus Enterprises had done for the city. He pointed to Mrs. Dawson and said there was no mission more sacred to mankind than the care and nurture of the young. Of course, as a writer, I felt that any man who would use clichés like that must have a bad heart.

Mr. Nock continued that Andorus Enterprises had business connections not only throughout the United States but all over the world. It was no trouble for such a vast concern to make contact with wealthy but lonely couples, who would be glad to adopt a baby and rear it in comfort, even in luxury, as their own. Andorus Enterprises had done this for Mrs. Dawson. Andorus Enterprises had reached a helping hand down to their own scrubwoman and would lift her excess baby out of poverty into wealth and love and happiness. . . .

There was some sniffling in the crowded courtroom at this — from the women, of course.

Owing to Poggioli's previous comments on the cost of babies, this speech irked young Gebhardt very much, and finally the tall young man arose in the middle of Mr. Nock's oration and requested permission to ask a question.

There ensued a little byplay: Mr. Nock objected to any question; Gebhardt said that since the state was conducting the investigation and since he was a citizen of the state, he had the right to ask a question.

This was a new idea to the audience, who never thought of themselves as citizens of the state but as neutral third parties watching what the state was doing. The judge, a big impassive man, held that as a citizen of the state Gebhardt could ask his question. The reporter then expounded Poggioli's idea and asked if it were not true that a woman's tenth baby was almost no financial burden at all to its parents.

Mr. Nock answered this, saying, "It is clear to me, your Honor, that this young and inquisitive citizen of our great commonwealth has never had either a child or a wife, but I predict that by the time he has ten of one and one or two of the other, he won't have to come into the city court to find out whether or not a baby, no matter what its number may be, is v-e-r-y e-x-p-e-n-s-i-v-e."

An uproar of laughter broke out at this and young Mr. Gebhardt sat down with a hot face. In his embarrassment he looked in different directions over the courtroom and caught sight of another young man, somewhat older than himself, pushing his way around the wall and eventually kneeing his way between the benches to where we sat. When the newcomer got within whispershot, Gebhardt said, somewhat defensively, "What are you doing here, Jenkins?"

"I bumped into some stuff I thought it wouldn't hurt you to know," whispered the other reporter.

"Well, what is it?"

"It's this," said Jenkins impressively. "Dr. Majoffsky, who called on the yachting couple in the Del Mar penthouse, dropped by the First National Bank on his way back to his office."

Gebhardt started to say, "Well, what of . . ." Then he suddenly remembered Poggioli's remark about banks and banking hours, and he broke off suddenly. "How do you know he did?"

"I followed him in a taxi. I couldn't get into the penthouse, I couldn't get a phone call through, and I couldn't get a word out of the hotel management. So I followed the doctor. When I finally got into his office, he refused to talk. But I noticed something. He didn't carry a little vest-pocket case — the sort some city doctors carry; he had a bag, like an old-fashioned country doctor's. Then I decided to go back to the bank. There's a clerk I know very well. I went to him and said, 'Jim, did you see Dr. Majoffsky come in here a while ago?' He said he had. I said, 'Did he deposit money or take some out, or what did he do?' Jim said, 'You know, Jenkins, I can't tell you that.' I worked on him, and finally Jim said, 'Jenkins, why don't you guess how much Dr. Majoffsky deposited in our bank this morning?'

"I saw what he meant, so I said, 'This is for Majoffsky's medical services?'

"'I imagine so.'

"'Mm — mm . . . say, fifty bucks. These yacht owners are usually millionaires.'

"My friend shook his head, and jerked his thumb upward.

"'One hundred?' I said.

"My bank-clerk friend jerked his thumb 'way up.

"Well, I went up and up until finally I got too high. So I came down five hundred, and that was what it was. I had guessed it."

"Well, how much was it?" I asked.

Jenkins didn't look at me — he kept looking at Gebhardt as he answered the question.

"Forty-two thousand five hundred dollars!"

"For a morning's visit! I don't believe it!"

Jenkins made a slight gesture in my direction, and began listening to Mr. Nock's speech, which was still going on.

"As a matter of fact," said Poggioli, "I am sure Mr. Jenkins has discovered something more closely connected with this case than Dr. Majoffsky's fee — or he never would have come to this trial."

Jenkins seemed surprised at the psychologist's deduction, and Gebhardt immediately asked Poggioli what it was Jenkins had found out.

"I am sure Mr. Jenkins will tell us himself," said Poggioli.

"You don't know Jenkins. In the office they call him the clam."

"But under the present circumstances, with our information so disconnected and patchy, I certainly think it would be wise to pool what we know and see if we can't make something intelligible out of it."

With the two men whispering about him, as if he were a robot, Jenkins abandoned his secrecy. He said he wasn't sure that what he had found out had any connection with the case, but it popped into his head to look into the title of Hotel Del Mar, and to his surprise he found it belonged to Andorus Enterprises. What that meant he didn't know, but since Andorus figured in the baby-adoption case, he thought he would come down and see if he could pick up anything more.

This, of course, started all of us speculating on the possibilities. The ownership of the hotel proved nothing at all; still the exorbitant penthouse rate, the huge medical fee, and the complete seclusion of the occupants of the penthouse might possibly have some connection with the Andorus baby investigation.

I think I have a right to a certain pride when I say that I got the first glimmering of the situation. I broke out in a somewhat excited whisper. "Andorus is getting this baby for the couple in the hotel and that's the fee they are charging!"

Both reporters were against this theory.

"Why should the couple pay that much for a baby?" demanded Gebhardt.

"I don't know," I said, "but the papers are full of stories about baby black markets. Somebody seems to be paying for babies, and very stiff rates, too."

Poggioli nodded. "That is the interesting feature of this whole situation, gentlemen. Wealthy persons seem to be paying large amounts of money to be allowed to perform a charitable and humanitarian act. Right on the face of it, that's a contradiction. That's why it is so interesting."

"Look here," said Gebhardt, "we'll never have a better chance to find out than right now. Suppose I ask Mr. Nock a few more questions, and he'll have to answer."

I tried to stop him. "Gebhardt, that's no good. You might just as well try to put your finger on a drop of quicksilver as to ask questions of that lawyer."

But Gebhardt got to his feet and in a loud voice asked the court's permission to interrogate the witness. When Mr. Nock saw who it was he remarked, "By all means, Judge, allow the single, sole, and solitary citizen of our state to do his civic duty."

Again laughter arose in the courtroom. Gebhardt, however, stood his ground. "The question I want to ask is this," he proceeded. "There is a couple renting the penthouse of the Hotel Del Mar at a fabulous rate per day. They have also just paid an astronomical doctor's bill. What I want to know is — is that the couple to whom Mrs. Dawson's baby will be delivered by the Andorus company?"

A sensation went through the courtroom, but Mr. Nock seemed only blankly surprised. "What possible connection, your Honor, could there be between a hotel bill and a doctor's fee —"

Gebhardt interrupted. "I'm not asking what connection. All I want to know is whether or not the Hotel Del Mar couple is scheduled to get the Dawson baby."

For once in his life Mr. Nock seemed disconcerted. He said, "I am sorry I can't answer the young man's question."

"Does that mean you don't know the answer or that you will not give the answer?" pressed Gebhardt.

"May I explain a point in the philanthropy of Andorus Enterprises?" requested the attorney.

The judge tapped his desk. "The attorney has a right to state his corporation's position in this matter."

"Now listen to Nock crawl out of it," whispered Jenkins bitterly.

And sure enough, Mr. Nock did. He said that for reasons of humanitarianism he could not possibly divulge any information whatever concerning the adopters of the Dawson baby. Then he went on to point out that the great drawback to the adoption and successful rearing of adopted babies was publicity. When the child finally learned that it was an adopted child, that fact shook its feeling of security. Andorus Enterprises handled any children who came under its care in a completely different manner. Nobody would ever know the identity of the adopting parents — not even the mother of the child. Nor would the adopting parents know the identity of the mother. Andorus Enterprises arranged matters as humanly as possible so that the life of the child would be the normal, loved, and loving life that every child has a right to expect.

Now he, Nock, attorney for Andorus Enterprises, was neither admitting nor denying that the couple in the Del Mar penthouse were or were not the adopting parents, but he certainly trusted to the judgment and good will of the court that he would not be forced to destroy all the bulwarks of psychological safety for the child which his company had so painstakingly erected.

A great outburst of applause followed this explanation which the judge rapped down. He ruled that Mr. Nock would not be required to answer the interrogation.

The two reporters were disgusted. Poggioli touched Gebhardt's arm and whispered. "Make a note of that — it may be part of your story."

"You mean when he refused to answer?"

"I mean, his demurrer to answering was too smooth, too adroit not to be premeditated. He evidently was expecting somebody to ask him a question like that."

"Yes, I suppose he was. What of it?"

"It means the couple in the Del Mar penthouse really are paying thousands of dollars for the Dawson baby. Mr. Nock's ready-made defense proves it."

"That's it!" exclaimed Jenkins. "Plain as the nose on an elephant. I'll get back to the office and write a follow-up on the penthouse story."

In the courtroom the investigation was finished, and Mrs. Dawson was delivering her baby to Mr. Nock for the good of the child and the goodness of Andorus Enterprises, Inc.

When Jenkins had left, Gebhardt looked at Poggioli ruefully. "Now isn't that the devil? Here Jenkins drops in and gets a follow-up for his story, and I have absolutely nothing to write about —"

"You didn't observe anything else worth writing up?" asked Poggioli, with a certain expression on his face.

"Mm — mm . . . no-o . . ."

"You didn't notice how Mrs. Dawson handed the baby to Attorney Nock?"

"Why-y, she just handed it over, didn't she?"

"Exactly, just handed it over. Can you imagine a mother parting from her baby forever just handing the child over to a stranger, without kissing it and embracing it and weeping?"

Gebhardt looked blankly at the psychologist as we got out into the street. "Just what are you driving at, Professor Poggioli?"

"I mean that wasn't Mrs. Dawson's baby."

The reporter was bewildered. "Why, that seems impossible! She seemed such an honest woman. . . ."

"I'm not questioning Mrs. Dawson. She is honest — she is transparently honest. . . ."

"Of all the crazy . . . I've got to look into this. I can't take it on . . . you know . . . *just* reasoning. I've got to know. Good-bye and a thousand thanks for the tip!" And with that young Gebhardt got into his ancient car and set off for the Dawson home.

When we had hailed a taxicab and started for Acacia Street, I told Poggioli that the case interested me personally but not professionally. I explained that the situation was not sufficiently dramatic to make a good mystery story, and the solution was too simple. Then I added, a little regretfully, that if I had the knack I might doctor it up with a little imagination, but I simply didn't have the imagination.

Poggioli asked me what I thought the solution was. I said, obviously Andorus Enterprises was carrying out their policy of secrecy to the furthest possible extent. When they received a baby to place in a home, they hired a wet nurse for it in order to conceal completely the identity of its mother.

"Assuming that's true," agreed Poggioli, "how do you explain the couple in the Del Mar penthouse willing to pay thousands of dollars to receive an unknown and mysterious baby?"

"They are evidently wealthy people," I said, "and would expect to pay well if Andorus Enterprises took so many precautions to present them with a baby completely free from any undesirable family background."

"Why should Andorus Enterprises make its charges through doctors' bills, unreasonable rentals, and things like that?"

"That is merely an assumption," I pointed out. "But even if it's true, the adopting couple are perhaps millionaires who wish to aid in such good work and are glad to contribute considerable amounts to Andorus Enterprises."

"How can Andorus Enterprises be in a position to receive private charity with one hand when with the other it turns around and makes large and aggressive investments in stadiums and housing projects and submarine promenades?"

"I can't answer that," I said. "In fact, your questions are getting a little remote from the subject, aren't they, Poggioli?"

This pinked Poggioli. He answered acidly, "The trouble with ordinary minds is, they have trouble reaching obvious conclusions."

"You don't seem to know any more about this matter than I do," I said, in perfectly good humor.

"At least I know what *not* to believe," snapped the ex-college professor.

I let the matter pass. Poggioli once taught criminology in the Ohio State University, so naturally he loses his temper when he gets the worst of an argument.

We had just got out of our cab and I was putting my key to our front door when I heard a great racket coming down the street. The cats and dogs in Acacia Street have learned to scuttle out of the path of a speeding auto, and these occasional animals were now making their disappearances. I wondered what maniac could be driving at such a dangerous speed, when the uproar calmed down to a rattle, and out scrambled young Gebhardt. I looked at him with that natural dismay which an older man feels when a younger man pays him a second visit right on the heels of his first.

"I'm glad I got here in time!" cried the young reporter, tumbling out of his steaming vehicle and hurrying up to us.

"In time for what, Mr. Gebhardt?" I asked.

"To join you before you start for the Del Mar."

"Why do you think we are going to the Hotel Del Mar?"

"To investigate the baby Mr. Nock is taking there. It wasn't Mrs. Dawson's child after all."

"So what, Mr. Gebhardt?" I asked. "We already knew that."

He was quite taken aback. "Aren't you going over there to find out whom the stray baby belongs to?"

"Professor Poggioli is not a miracle man," I said, "or a mind reader. There is not one chance in a thousand that he could look at the adopting couple and tell whose baby it was."

Gebhardt said he would still like Poggioli to go with him to the Hotel Del Mar.

"But you can't see them," I objected. "Nobody can. That also is part of the Andorus benevolent secrecy."

"I've figured out a way for us to get into the penthouse," said Gebhardt, "so that we can interview both the millionaire and his wife to our hearts' content."

I asked him what he had in mind. He said we could put on overalls, get a box of tools, and enter the Hotel Del Mar as three plumbers.

I shook my head. "We can't do that, Gebhardt. Poggioli would never stoop to disguise himself as a plumber. In fact, as I told you before, he rarely goes out of his study to investigate a crime. He is a consultant, and he wouldn't dream of stooping to disguise himself —"

"I'll go with you, Gebhardt," interrupted my apartment mate.

I turned on him. "Look here, Poggioli, whose notes am I writing up anyway, a criminologist's or a gumshoe detective's?"

Poggioli is not a man without pride. He said to me, "If it wasn't for the extreme mystery of this case, and its duplication in many other parts of the United States, I wouldn't consider going with Mr. Gebhardt. . . ."

"I don't see much of a mystery in it," I retorted. "Some woman wants to get rid of her child. . . ."

"Not much of a mystery!" ejaculated Poggioli. "Never in history was there such an irrational demand for babies — a black market in babies. Imagine such a thing!"

Young Gebhardt was tremendously impressed. "Why do so many couples pay such fancy prices for babies?"

"That's the point I'm trying to solve. If I knew that I wouldn't need to go to the penthouse. So let's go."

On the way into town my two companions obtained three pairs of overalls and a kit of plumber's tools. At the entrance of the Hotel Del Mar we found a sizable crowd drawn both by the newspaper publicity and the city court investigation. They were evidently awaiting the arrival of Nock and the baby. Young Gebhardt did not stop here, but drove on around to the service entrance in the rear. Here we found a milk truck backed up to the curb, with two men delivering bottles and picking up empties. A guard stood at the back door. When we started in, the guard stopped us and said he was sorry but he couldn't admit us. Gebhardt got out a little book, thumbed through it, and said, "This is the Hotel Del Mar, isn't it?"

The guard said it was. "Then what does your manager mean,

ordering us to come here and then not letting us in?" demanded the reporter.

The watchman became nervous. "Look here," he said, glancing into the hotel, "I think if you'll stick around for just a few minutes, I'll be able to let you in."

Naturally, we knew what that meant: the adopting couple were going to leave the hotel and every entrance would be blocked until they were gone. Gebhardt put down his kit and consulted his little book again. "Look here, if we can't get in, we're going to our next job." He began thumbing through the pages for our next appointment.

The guard became even more nervous. "Say, don't run off . . . couldn't you wait half an hour?"

"No, we won't wait half a minute."

We turned to go, when the guard stopped us. "Okay, you men go on in quietly — hurry, now!"

The basement of a big hotel is a maze. It is full of narrow concrete corridors leading past drab doors saying *No Admission*.

Gebhardt said, "We've got to find the freight elevator and get to the penthouse right away."

We were now hurrying along these endless basement corridors, and the probability of stumbling on a freight elevator was zero. I was as nervous as a cat, and the barb in my feeling was that I had no reason to be nervous. There was no real mystery —

Gebhardt cried out, "There's a bellhop. Hey, boy, where's the freight elevator?"

The blue uniform turned and pointed. "Go back the way you came — second turn to the left, third to the right, first to the right, then four doors further on . . ."

The three of us hurried away. We had followed directions as far as third turn to the right, when we heard the bellboy come running behind us. When he saw us down the long corridor, he hallooed, "I forgot to tell you, the freight elevator isn't running!"

All of us stopped. I was trembling and sweating without any reason whatever to tremble or sweat. Gebhardt called back, "Where's the passenger elevator? We hate to take these tools in the passenger elevator, but we've got to get upstairs."

"You can't take the passenger elevator — that's not running either."

"Is the electricity off?"

"Oh, no — just everything's stopped . . . for a short while."

That drove Gebhardt almost frantic. "Well, where's the office? Where's the telephone system? There must be something somewhere that's working!"

The bellboy gave us detailed instructions how to reach the office, and we set off again, double-quick, and finally we reached some wide steps going up into the lobby. We ran up them and into the lobby. Through the front entrance we could see the crowd still besieging the hotel. Gebhardt breathed, "Thank heaven we're in time!" We made for the office, keeping our attention on the bank of passenger elevators across the lobby. Gebhardt got the attention of a clerk in his cage. "When can I go up to the penthouse to fix some plumbing?"

The clerk glanced at a clock. "Mm — mm, I imagine pretty soon. . . ."

"Elevators not running?"

"Not at this moment, but in a few . . ."

"How about me telephoning up there and finding out what I'm supposed to repair?"

"There's the house phone," said the clerk.

Gebhardt reached for it. Then he said to Poggioli, "You take it, you'll be able to tell a lot from their voices."

Poggioli got a connection with the penthouse. He jiggled his cradle two or three times. Finally he said, "Nobody answers."

Gebhardt grabbed Poggioli's arm. "Too late — they're gone!"

Poggioli started toward the basement again. "We're dumbbells," he snapped. "That milk truck wouldn't be delivering milk at this time of day! They were waiting for the couple and the baby, of course! They came down by the freight elevator!"

The three of us went helter-skelter down the basement steps and into the lower maze again. Fortunately, Gebhardt had a fine sense of direction. We raced to the service entrance and just as we saw the distant rectangle of light, a man and a woman carrying a baby, surrounded by bellboys, appeared and moved out to the milk truck. As we came running out, the woman screamed and hugged her baby closer in her arms.

The man said, "Darling, they're just some workmen!"

The woman said shakenly, "Yes . . . yes, I see they are."

Poggioli, who was fairly close now, called out in his quiet, authoritative professional voice, "Madam, you and your husband are from Long Island, aren't you?"

"Y-yes," trembled the woman, "we are."

"On what day, Madam, was your baby stolen from you?" asked the psychologist.

"On Easter Sunday. . . ." Then she caught herself. "But who are you?"

Poggioli began asking more questions when the man hurried, "Come on, Mary, let's get out of here while we can!" And man, woman, and baby got into the truck and rumbled off.

Gebhardt started running for his jalopy. "How in the world did you know they were from Long Island. . . ."

"Dialect, almost a patois, my boy. The people around New York, especially the wealthy, speak in a particular —"

"What a scoop this will be . . . kidnapers . . . how did you ever come to think of . . ."

"Why, it was so simple," said Poggioli, "this whole black market in babies is kidnaping. How can wealthy parents pay ransoms without the law knowing? Andorus Enterprises worked out a clever scheme. They have a child to be adopted. If the parents will pay a certain amount they can adopt a child. The fact that the child is already their own isn't mentioned by anyone. . . ."

Gebhardt was beside himself. "What a story! What a scoop!"

We were dashing away now toward the office of the *Tiamara Times*. Poggioli laid a hand on the car's rickety wheel. "Gebhardt," he called, "you mustn't go the *Times* office right now!"

Gebhardt glanced around. "Where should I go?"

"To the Federal Building."

The young reporter gave a snort. "Why should I. . . ."

"Because you are a citizen of this state . . . and of the United States."

"I don't get you."

"Listen, the baby black market is all over the country. This is one section of a vast criminal organization. You publish this and it warns all the others. They'll close up, go underground, maybe get clear away. Take this to the F.B.I. office in the Federal Building — the man in charge will guarantee you your scoop — but go there first!"

We parked at the curb and the reporter went inside the Federal Building. A policeman presently came along and gave me and Poggioli a ticket for improper parking. We continued sitting in the car, waiting. After a while Gebhardt came out. He appeared in a sort of daze. Poggioli said, "What's the matter?"

"N-nothing."

"You saw the F.B.I. head?"

"Yes, I saw him."

"Did he say he would take care of you when the story broke?"

"Oh, yes, yes, very appreciative. He said if I had published that story today it would have ruined everything. He'd been working on it for months. He said his men would move in on the Andorus bunch within twenty-four hours, and after that I should have the exclusive story."

"Why, that's fine for you," I cried. "Of course, there's no story in it for me, but it's O.K. for a newspaper. . . . By the way, do you know the name of the officer who is in charge of the F.B.I.?"

"Yes."

"What is it?"

Gebhardt was still in a daze.

"Who is the F.B.I. head?" I repeated.

"Mr. Nock."

The Mystery of
the Seven Suicides

When Scargrave, reporter for the *Tiamara Times*, and a smallish
gentleman entered our apartment, I knew at once they had come to
consult Poggioli about the Jalatti tragedy. My reasoning was this:
nobody visits my criminologist friend except about mysteries; as the
Jalatti affair was the only local mystery in the morning paper, this visit
had to be about that. I thought this was a rather snappy bit of deduction
and mentioned it to Poggioli.

He seemed not impressed. He stood appraising our visitors a
moment and then said, quite loudly enough for them to hear him, that he
was surprised that these two men should call upon him together. I knew
no reason why they should not come together and I am sure neither of
them did either. Scargrave the reporter, who was always on the *qui vive*
for a lead into a Poggioli interview, asked the criminologist's reason for
making such a remark.

"Because you two want diametrically opposite solutions to Joe
Jalatti's death," explained Poggioli, "and it is only ordinary prudence
for men on opposite sides of a controversy to employ separate
counselors."

None of us knew what he was talking about. Scargrave got out a
pad of paper and asked why Poggioli supposed that he and his friend
were on opposite sides of Jalatti's death, and how there *could* be
opposite sides to such a matter?

"You want to prove Jalatti was murdered and your friend wants to
prove him a suicide," said the psychologist.

The reporter opened his mouth to say something, but obviously
changed his mind, for he asked a little bewildered, "How did you know
Mr. Wilks wanted to prove Jalatti a suicide?"

"Because I can see he has come here on a business mission. He
shows no emotional disturbance whatever; his relation to the dead man
is obviously one of property. Now the simplest property relation
between a business executive and a dead man is life insurance. Could be
something else, but life insurance is most likely. Mr. Wilks is an adjuster,
an insurance claim agent. The only point he could possibly want to
know is whether Jalatti killed himself or was murdered. Jalatti's policy is

evidently of the type voided by suicide. So he wants Jalatti's death proved a suicide in order to save his company money."

Both our visitors gave the brief laugh of surprise and admiration that usually follows one of my friend's *tours de force*.

"And why do I want him murdered?" asked Scargrave.

"Because you are a newspaper man. Murder is more dramatic than suicide — it's front-page stuff."

Scargrave gave an odd little twist of a smile.

"No-o," he said slowly, "I'm on Wilks' side. I also want you to prove Jalatti's death a suicide."

I was amazed. On impulse I blurted out the very indiscreet sentence, "Surely the gangsters haven't bribed the . . ." and there I stopped.

Scargrave turned to me with more dignity than I thought he possessed. "No, the gangsters haven't bribed the *Times*. Quite the opposite: this is for the advancement of the public welfare."

Poggioli pondered, then looked at the reporter attentively. "You don't mean the murder was . . . for the public welfare?"

Scargrave laughed a little ruefully. "No, no, not at all. I know the public in general regards these intra-gang killings as good riddance of bad rubbish. I mean the shift from murder to suicide is for a great public good. And that's why I've come to you: to prove, if possible, that this murder was suicide . . . for the public good."

Poggioli nodded slowly. "I see . . . I see . . . but I've never before deliberately twisted the evidence in foul play, Mr. Scargrave."

"Listen, I don't ask you to twist it. All I ask is that you come along and give me any evidence or suggestion of suicide — and murder too, if you like — and let me publish what I please . . . for the good of our state."

Poggioli tapped the table reflectively. "Very well . . . I'll give the *Times* my complete analysis." And the four of us started for the street.

Well, I can hardly express my perturbation at such a bargain struck before my eyes with my hitherto immaculate friend. "Poggioli," I exclaimed, "how can covering up a murder be for the public good?"

My old friend turned and was about to explain when Scargrave interrupted. "You'll treat my information as a privileged communication between client and counsel?"

"Certainly, if you put it that way," said Poggioli. So the four of us walked on out into the street and I learned nothing more of the strange point.

We hailed a cab and Scargrave directed us to the Ritz Hotel. I sat in the front seat with the driver and kept looking around at the three men in the back, wondering what earthly cause could have persuaded Poggioli to falsify murder. Presently he misconstrued my looking back, for he said, "You want to tell me we are being followed. I am aware of it. I have been noticing it in the mirror."

Now, I hadn't meant that at all. I never look to see who's following me; I never suppose anybody is following me. But I had no chance to explain this. The news excited our visitors. They turned around and began staring out the back window. Scargrave asked which one it was. Poggioli said the Cadillac. Scargrave asked why Poggioli thought that fellow was following us.

"Because he stops behind us at red lights, which is the place a car like that always passes a car like this."

"Cadillac," repeated Scargrave, "that could easily be Boni's car."

"You mean the murderer?" asked Poggioli.

"I am sure it's his car," said the reporter. "Boni's the czar of illegal gambling in Tiamara, and Jalatti was muscling into his field. Yes, that looks like Boni's car and the driver looks like Boni himself."

"Look here," I suggested nervously, "our jalopy can't lose a car like that. Why don't we slow down and see if he passes, or stops, or what?"

Scargrave nodded and instructed our driver to pull up to the curb.

We had no sooner stopped than the big car was slowed up beside us. A small, impassive man called out to ask if this were Professor Poggioli's cab. The insurance man said it was. The motorist handed something across to me in the front seat, "May I ask Professor Poggioli to read this carefully." With that he placed an envelope in my hand, and drove away.

I think we were all glad to see him go. The insurance man asked what was in the letter, as I handed it to Poggioli. I said I didn't know. Scargrave guessed it would contain a five or ten thousand dollar bill. There is a certain suspense even in watching such a communication opened, but when Poggioli tore open the envelope, no money dropped out — just a note.

Scargrave said, "I hope your professional ethics won't keep you from letting us know what he wrote?"

The criminologist finished the missive, then lowered it thoughtfully. "No . . . no . . . under the circumstances I feel justified in showing this communication. It's an attempt to deceive me. It isn't the honest effort a criminal makes when he goes to a lawyer for protection."

We were amazed at the audacity of the Cadillac driver. I even laughed at the imbecility of anyone trying to deceive Poggioli. Scargrave asked the nature of the deception.

"Very simple," said Poggioli, "this is really an admission of Jalatti's murder, but on the surface it denies it. The fellow evidently didn't realize that a murderer can't write a denial of his crime and not fail to include incriminating phrases which actually admit his guilt. You see, the trouble is," went on Poggioli, falling into one of his academic moods, "a written statement more or less divulges what is really in the writer's mind. There is no way for the writer to avoid it. The writer will be too blunt, or too diffuse, or go too far around a point, or cut across it too sharply — in other words, he can never write his denial naturally. All criminals should have lawyers for secretaries and put all their correspondence in strictly legal forms."

Scargrave begged him to read the letter.

"Very well, and as I read I want you gentlemen to be on the alert for critical phrases revealing murder, just as a check on my own deductions."

Naturally, that put us on guard and we listened with minute attention as Poggioli read the following note:

DEAR DR. POGGIOLI,

May I, as an admirer of your criminological skill, request your investigation of the death of Joseph Jalatti at the Ritz Hotel on Tiamara Beach. I ask you to check the details of this tragedy carefully and I feel you will reach a verdict of suicide. What details you will find I have no idea, but I am sure they will be something the police and the detectives would never observe

Your sincere admirer,
Henry Boni

The three of us looked at each other and then at Poggioli. I broke the silence by saying, "I don't see a word in that to convict him. In fact, if he weren't innocent he never would have dared to invite you to the scene of the crime."

"I am going to quote this note in my story," said Scargrave, "and let my readers draw their own conclusions."

"That probably was Boni's idea," observed the criminologist drily.

"What is your explanation, Professor Poggioli?" asked the insurance man a little anxiously.

"I quote from the note," began Poggioli academically. "'What details you will find I have no idea, but I am sure they will be something the police and the detectives would never observe.' Why should anyone make a remark like that?"

This, of course, was a rhetorical question, but the insurance man was so on edge that he answered, "Because he has read stories about you, Professor Poggioli, and you always — at least, in the stories — find out things in the most extraordinary manner." And Mr. Wilks' voice was a plea, begging Poggioli to do that again.

"But those instances were murders," snorted the psychologist. "A suicide — why, that's written all over the place! It doesn't take a microscope to see an elephant track! But suppose we get on to the Ritz and see what delicate and subtle clues our gentleman has contrived to make a murder look like suicide."

The Jalatti apartment was in the penthouse of the Ritz. We went up in a private elevator which landed us on a tiny platform where we had to press a bell and be examined through a peep-hole before we were admitted to the penthouse proper.

A ghost of a woman did this peeping and when she let us in, she went back to a table and sat down and put her head in her hands. This was so tragic and touching that only after several moments did I observe a dead man on the floor with an automatic near his hand. Then I glanced about for other details; a huge window which gave on the ocean had a bullet hole in its upper half; a modernistic painting on the south wall resembled the woman at the table in a vague sort of way. There were many other things in the room but I mention only these three because later on they turned out to be clues, and I am putting them down for what they are worth. Naturally they told me nothing.

The insurance man seemed fascinated by the woman. He touched my arm and whispered, "If she can prove her husband was murdered, she will collect a quarter of a million from my company." I made no reply.

Scargrave acted as spokesman. He began by extending his sympathy, then said he was from the *Times* and his paper wanted to know the facts of the tragedy. The woman looked up in a dazed fashion and said that Boni had done it.

"You didn't see him do it, did you?" asked the reporter.

"No, I was in there." She pointed to a bedroom door.

"Then how do you know it was Boni and not someone else?"

"Because when we heard the bell, Joe looked through the peep-hole and nodded it was Boni and motioned me to go into the bedroom."

"Then you didn't actually see Boni when he came in, or while he was here, or when he went out?"

"No."

"And your husband didn't *say* anything to you — just motioned?"

She nodded.

"How can you be sure your husband meant Boni?"

The woman's face grew a shade paler. "Because that's the way Boni works. First he telephones . . . then he sends a man . . . then he comes himself." There was something grisly in the way she uttered this last phrase.

"Then you and your husband were *expecting* violence?" I suggested.

"I was, he wasn't."

"What had you done to arouse Boni's anger?" I asked.

"We'd muscled in on his racket."

When I inquired what racket, she seemed surprised at my ignorance.

"Why, the gambling racket! Joe put in a casino and fixed it up with the city police and the county officers. We paid off everybody we were supposed to. Then Boni cut in and telephoned Joe to bring him seventy-five per cent of our take. I thought we'd better do it, but Joe told him to come and get it, if he could."

Such a percentage shocked me. Apparently the racketeers were no more considerate of each other than business men. "What happened then?" I asked. "Is that why he came?"

"No, he sent a man over who asked for eighty-five per cent, and I told Joe he'd better pay it and then try to get it lowered, but he said no, he wouldn't, we were in the South."

"What has the South got to do with it?" I asked, puzzled.

"Why, it was our first trip down here," said the woman, with a spark of withered resentment. "We'd read in the papers that the gangsters didn't kill each other in the South, that they carried their feuds back North and killed each other up there. Joe figured we would just stay in the South and not go back North at all. That's why we fixed up this penthouse like it is . . . and he's lying there on the floor."

Seeing I understood none of this, Scargrave said in an undertone to me, "The papers here did play up one instance of Tiamara gang feuds being settled in the North. It was part of our public policy."

I remembered the headlines from the previous tourist season, but before I could dig into his reference to "public policy," Poggioli took over the questioning.

"Did you hear their conversation from your bedroom, Mrs. Jalatti?"

"No, when we leased this apartment, Joe had it sound-proofed."

As Scargrave wrote this down quickly, he exclaimed, "So you didn't even hear the shot fired!"

The wife gave a brief, shaken nod. "I could hear that."

Poggioli asked, "And you rushed in and saw your husband lying here on . . ."

Mrs. Jalatti gave a little gasp. "I — didn't rush in."

The criminologist looked at her carefully. "Were you afraid?"

She shook her head in silence.

Poggioli brightened. "Oh, I see — you thought your husband had killed Boni! You didn't go in because you wanted to give him a chance to clear the room before you entered!"

Scargrave began writing rapidly again. Presently the reporter paused to ask, "Mrs. Jalatti, how long did you wait after you heard the shot — *before* you entered this room?"

She said ten or fifteen minutes.

"And how long did you wait in your bedroom after the unknown man came up the elevator — *before* you heard the shot?"

I did not know why the reporter reversed the time element like this, and neither did the woman, for she replied in weary bewilderment, "Oh, I don't know. Maybe thirty minutes."

Scargrave pointed his pencil at her. "Then Boni, if it was Boni, had plenty of time to go back down the elevator and get out of the building — *before* you heard the shot?"

The widow looked at Scargrave antagonistically. "You are not trying to make out my Joe killed himself?"

"No, no, not at all. I am simply trying to get the facts."

"Of course, he had time — but my Joe didn't kill himself."

"That's all I wanted to know."

The wife seemed quite shaken at the possibility. The insurance man went over to her and told her that no matter what the papers printed, it would have no influence on the settlement of Jalatti's life insurance policy. He then suggested that she go into the bedroom, lie down, and try to rest. This seemed to me commendably neutral on Wilks' part, since he was trying to rob her with one hand and assist her with the other. Mrs. Jalatti swayed as she rose from the table. Wilks took her arm, assisted her into the bedroom, and softly closed the door behind them.

I will admit I had a bad taste in my mouth, realizing that all three of these men were working with all the professional skill at their disposal to prove Jalatti's murder a suicide. They wound a machination of words around the widow, like spiders webbing a fly. I could not understand at all how public policy entered the case, but of one thing I was sure: the three were out to cheat the widow of a quarter of a million dollars.

After Mrs. Jalatti and the insurance man had gone, Scargrave cleared his throat ruefully and said, "I suppose it must have been murder — couldn't very well have been anything else." To this Poggioli's silence acquiesced, then the reporter went on with business-like briskness, "Well, you are here, Professor Poggioli, to ferret out the smallest suggestions of suicide. . . ."

"Clues of suicide which Boni arranged for us to find, and about which he wrote us the note — in case we miss them altogether," agreed Poggioli ironically.

"I suppose that's the size of it," agreed the reporter. "Now let's find them and I'll play them up in my story."

I can at least say for these men that neither of them had any appetite for the job. Still, they went to work systematically to aid and abet some hypothetical "public welfare" which I did not understand.

As for clues, they were practically nonexistent. I've already given you three — the body on the floor, the hole in the window, and the modernistic portrait on the wall of the dead man's wife. It was Poggioli's task to twist these innocent details into a refutation of murder and a proof of suicide. Under the circumstances I could not even know whether my friend was sincere in his deductions or whether he was weaving a required theory out of a vacuum. It was very simple and can be told briefly:

The police had developed the fingerprints on the handle of the automatic. They were the dead man's fingerprints. Scargrave wrote this down. But Poggioli pointed out that these prints were blurred, as if someone had pressed Jalatti's fingers against the pistol butt after Jalatti was dead; so the fingerprints themselves were an indirect proof that the dead man was murdered. Scargrave did not write that down.

The other clue — the bullet hole high up in the window pane — was of the same tenor. Poggioli looked at this with the appreciation of an expert appraising the work of an amateur.

"This is not so bad as the fingerprints," he said. "Notice the bullet hole is three or four feet *above* the level of Jalatti's head. Now, it is a fact that suicides, when shooting themselves, always train their bullets upwards, whereas murderers level their guns — aim at your own head, then at something else, and you'll see what I mean." Both Scargrave and I pantomimed and we saw the psychologist's point. Poggioli went on not without a touch of admiration for the murderer, "It's amazing that Boni hit on so delicate a proof of suicide and was cool enough to carry it out. He must be an expert in his way, he must have killed dozens of men. I understand now why he wrote me a note asking me to look for and admire the artistry of his job."

Scargrave wrote rapidly at this and nodded his head with satisfaction. "Maybe Jalatti really did kill himself and I'm writing an honest story after all," he said wishfully.

Poggioli shrugged. "Unhappily, Scargrave, in this particular instance it is an absolute proof of murder."

"But how can it be, when it's a proof of suicide?"

"It isn't a proof of suicide, it is a proof of great cunning in the killer — but not quite enough cunning. You see, the trouble with concealment of murder is this: it is still murder in the killer's heart and thoughts. All traces left in matter must eventually expose the actual psychology of the person who leaves them. In other words, in this case the murderer has left not the concealed traces, but the traces of his *effort to conceal them*."

In a spot like this we naturally didn't want a lecture. So Scargrave flung out, "What's wrong with the hole in that window?"

"It's in the wrong place," said Poggioli, "it doesn't belong in the window."

"Wrong place how?" demanded the newspaperman.

"If Jalatti had been alone in the room and shot himself, the bullet from his automatic would have lodged either in the right wall or the left, according to whether he was right-handed or left-handed; but it would never have gone through the window facing the sea."

"But why do you say that?" cried Scargrave in frustration.

"Because a suicide, in destroying himself, always fixes his last look on the light, the sky, the world he is leaving. He would have been staring through the window at the ocean and his bullet would therefore have lodged in one of the walls."

Scargrave glanced about for some counter-argument. "He could have faced his wife's portrait," he offered, pointing to the picture on the wall.

Poggioli shook his head. "Quite the reverse," he said. "That is a modernistic portrait. All modernistic painting is an unconscious effort to flee a despised reality. Husbands order modernistic portraits of their wives as an escape and to revenge themselves for having to live with the original. This is all unconscious, of course, but it would effectually prevent a husband from turning *toward* his wife's portrait when he killed himself. He *would* have turned away from it."

Scargrave twiddled his pencil nervously. "That's much too deep for the readers of the *Tiamara Times*. I'll just say that Jalatti did face the portrait of his wife when he killed himself — that will give the story a sympathetic touch and appeal to the public."

At this moment the bedroom door opened and the insurance man entered the living room.

"She's asleep," he said, in the tone one uses when an invalid is at rest. "A terrific strain is off her mind. How did the examination come out — murder or suicide?"

"Suicide," said Scargrave.

"Murder," said Poggioli.

The insurance agent said sharply, "Of course, it was really murder! All of us know that."

Scargrave widened his eyes at Wilks' change of front.

"We know nothing of the sort. Every detail shows it was suicide. See that bullet hole in the window! See those fingerprints on the automatic! See this picture of the man's wife! They all spell suicide!"

The insurance man was bewildered, and Scargrave explained the suicide theory earnestly.

Wilks turned to Poggioli. "But you, Professor, said they meant murder!"

"Do you *want* them to be murder?" cried Scargrave.

"Yes, I do," declared the agent.

"What's come over you? What's changed you?" And even I was as bewildered as the reporter.

"I'll tell you," stated the insurance man with righteousness, "I got to thinking in there about us men cheating that woman out of a quarter of a million dollars, and I decided . . . I decided I wouldn't be a party to it!"

I couldn't repress myself. "Good!" I cried. "I'm glad one man in this crowd has got a conscience!"

Poggioli wiped the ghost of a smile from his lips with his tongue. "You talked to Mrs. Jalatti — before she went to sleep?"

"Certainly," said Wilks, belligerently.

"You eased her mind . . . on financial questions? That's why she went to sleep, isn't it?"

Wilks said, "I don't know what you mean, Professor Poggioli," in a tone that showed he did.

"It's a pleasure to explain it," said Poggioli, with his ghost of a smile showing again. "You sold Mrs. Jalatti a large life insurance policy contingent upon collecting her husband's insurance. So now you want him to have been murdered."

Wilks started to speak, then didn't; began again and said, "You say the proof here shows murder. Will you please explain that to me?"

The criminologist dismissed the fact that Wilks had changed horses midstream and explained very clearly his interpretation of the fingerprints, the bullet hole, and the portrait.

"Is that all?" asked the insurance man in quite an unsatisfied voice.

"That's all. We need nothing more. That's conclusive — he was murdered."

"It may be conclusive to you, but that kind of proof won't stand up for a minute in a court of law. She couldn't collect thirty cents on that!"

"Mm-m. . . . That's the proof, that's all there is."

"Well, it won't do! We've got to get some *solid* proof." Wilks shook his fist to show how solid. He began moving about the apartment, looking here and there, evidently seeking a more patent proof of murder.

As I was in sympathy with him anyway, I watched him and wished him well, but I knew it was hopeless. How could any mortal man hope to wipe Henry Poggioli's eye? To my knowledge no clue had ever escaped him; no crime had ever eluded his analysis. I felt sorry for Wilks, even if his motive was purely mercenary.

However, the insurance adjuster made his inspection with a certain professional touch. He evidently had done this sort of thing before. In his orbit he picked up the automatic and examined it minutely. As the fingerprints already had been developed, I wondered what he was after. He studied the firearm, turned it bottom side up and looked at it, then walked across the room to a telephone, with the gun in his hand. He gave the dial a single flip, got Information, and asked the number of the County Courthouse. I lifted my brows at Poggioli to inquire what all this meant. In a low tone Poggioli said to me, "He's calling the firearms register at the County Courthouse to see if the automatic has been registered."

"Oh, yes," I whispered, and then the absurdity of the idea — that a Northern gangster would come South and *register* his gun — struck me forcibly. I didn't laugh. It was too grotesque.

"If he should find the gun registered," whispered Poggioli, "he will be completely undone."

"Why?" inquired Scargrave.

"Because the only racketeer in town who hoped for a peaceful life in Tiamara was Jalatti. Since he believed feuds were not fought in the South, he might possibly have registered his gun and decided to become a law-abiding citizen, more or less."

At this point the insurance man began speaking in the telephone.

"Will you please connect me with the register of small arms? . . . Hello, is this the department where citizens register their guns? . . . World Insurance Company speaking: will you see if you have on your registry a Colt's thirty-eight automatic, No. 856743, and give me the name of the owner. . . . Yes, I'll hold the phone."

Scargrave wet his lips with his tongue, stepped over and touched Wilks on the shoulder. "Look here, if that gun's registered by Boni, it would absolutely prove murder!"

"Sure. . . . That's what I want," replied Wilks, without looking around.

"But listen, you can't take that chance! As a citizen of this state you can't afford to prove this is murder!"

"Why can't I, as a citizen of this state?" With the phone to his ear, Wilks turned and looked at Scargrave.

The newspaperman studied him a moment. "It's hard to tell in a breath, but . . . but the finances of this state depend in a large part on horse racing, dog racing, jai alai, all of which have been legitimatized, and these taper off into hotel bookmakers, gambling casinos, numbers racket, honkytonks, which have not been legitimatized, and they are all cogged in together —"

"Everybody knows that," said the insurance man.

"I know they do, but here's the point: As long as the state has its income and crime doesn't appear too bad, the people will stand for it — it's good business. But if murder happens too often, the people will start a house-cleaning. They'll tear down our whole financial structure — schools, hospitals, roads — why, we'll have to put on a sales tax, and a state income tax. It'll scare off tourists . . ."

"What am I supposed to do about that?" snapped the insurance man.

"Hang up that phone. Let this go as suicide. Don't take the risk it's Boni's gun and therefore murder!"

"But I'll get a fifty thousand dollar commission —"

"All right, what would you do if you got fifty thousand and ruined your state?"

"I'd move to another state. . . . Hello, hello. . . . Yes, this is the World Insurance Company. . . . You've found it? Well, who's the owner? . . . Jalatti. . . . *Joseph G. Jalatti!*" And he replaced shakily the instrument in its fork.

Scargrave flung out in amazement, and relief, "It really was a suicide!"

"This contradicts your theory, doesn't it, Poggioli?" I said, with a certain pleasure of my own.

"Seems to," answered the criminologist briefly.

"Seems to!" cried the insurance man hotly. "What are your fantastic proofs of murder compared with this?"

"Still valid, still irrefutable," snapped Poggioli. "It's this suicide that is fantastic. It's motiveless. Jalatti had dug in here, to live permanently. Then to kill himself? Impossible!"

Wilks said he was going to get another investigator, one not so theoretical and rarefied as Poggioli, an honest flat-footed investigator who would prove this murder was a murder if it was the last act he committed on earth.

The four of us rode down the elevator together, in no pleasant temper; then we separated and went our ways. As Poggioli and I taxied back home he said to me, "I knew those men, whose interests were

diametrically opposed, shouldn't have come to the same counselor."
The fact that he had interpreted both of them incorrectly didn't seem to
disturb him.

The drama, I must say, stuck in my head for days. It was so
inconclusive. I couldn't figure out what had really happened. Then one
morning the whole mystery was opened afresh by my morning paper. I
picked it up on our lawn and ran to Poggioli at the breakfast table.
"Look at these headlines!" I cried.

Tecumseh Sherman Wilks, Tiamara Manager World Insurance
Company, Kills Himself. . . . Legal Bar to Payment of ex-Gangster's
Quarter Million Dollar Policy Led to Deed. . . . Slew Himself in
Company's Office. . . . Used His Own Smith and Wesson."

I can hardly describe my shock. "What do you know about that?" I
ejaculated. "Killed himself over losing a commission!"

Poggioli dropped his hands on the table. "So that's the
explanation . . . Heavens, how simple . . . Why didn't I think of it at the
Ritz and save the poor devil's life!"

I said, "Poggioli, what do you mean? These headlines don't explain
a thing."

He leaped up from the table and started for the street. "Come
along," he snapped, "you'll see it in time, even you. . . . So that was what
Boni's note directed me to discover . . . all the subtle clues of suicide
must have been accidents . . ." Poggioli made a sharp gesture.

Outside we took a taxi. I asked if we were going to the insurance
company's offices. My companion was annoyed. He said certainly not,
we were going to the County Courthouse.

I cried, "Poggioli, this has upset you! You are crazy! You have to go
look at the dead man to find out what killed him!"

We went on to the County Courthouse, went up to the seventh floor
where firearms are registered. An official lounged behind a desk.
Poggioli went to him, spread the paper, rapped the headlines.

"Look at that! Mr. Wilks registered his gun in your office only a few
days before he died, didn't he?"

The man became defensive at once. "How do I know who registered
what when — my memory's not a filing-card system!"

Poggioli pointed his finger. "You remember perfectly or you
wouldn't answer like that!"

The fellow backwatered a trifle. "Maybe I do — three days ago, I
believe." Then with a return of spirit, "What of it?"

"What of it? Just this. I think you are an accomplice in the murder.
Jalatti, who was supposed to have killed himself a week or so ago — he
registered his gun in your office a few days before his death too, didn't
he?"

The man was obviously frightened now. He wet his lips with his
tongue, "T-Two days before, I believe."

"And all the other five suicides before Jalatti — they all registered their pistols a day or so in advance — and then killed themselves?"

The clerk opened his mouth, then closed it. Finally he stammered, "One — one actually did kill himself."

"Don't you realize you are an accessory to murder when you permit a gangster or racketeer to enter your office, register a firearm *in another man's name*, then go out and shoot the man with the same gun, leave it on the spot, making each murder look like suicide? Don't you realize you are an accomplice?"

The man started to get up, then sat down again. "Well, I . . . we thought . . . so long as they were killing each other . . . it was good riddance . . . but now that they've begun to shoot respectable Southern business men . . . Still, if we make a fuss it'll upset the whole system. . . . We don't know *what* to do!"

The Warning on the Lawn

The morning headlines only depressed me: *Senate Crime Investigating Committee Sits in Tiamara; Topflight Criminals Flee Subpoena Servers* — and so on and so on.

My depression, I am somewhat embarrassed to admit, was not that of a patriotic citizen, eager for the purification of his city and country. No, it was peculiarly personal to myself. The Senate Crime Investigating Committee clarifies and eliminates criminal mysteries that I otherwise could collect, write, and sell. Every mystery the Committee solved, every criminal they unmasked, was so much bread off my pantry shelf. So, with some despair, I turned to other criminal news: *Miss Mona Moon, the movie star vacationing at the Sherry-Plaza, has lost her jewels along with her sixth husband.* I called Poggioli's attention to it across the breakfast table.

"Now here is a case that will undoubtedly come to us," I said, pushing the story to him.

My friend read it. "Why us?" he inquired.

"Because female movie stars, although they appear very prodigal and all that, are really a very thrifty set. She will come to you in order to get herself written up in my notes on your cases, so that she will gain the widest possible publicity for the loss of her jewels. If they are costume jewelry, which she would never admit, she'll be getting a bargain — not to mention a change of husbands, which is also excellent advertising."

Poggioli didn't think so. He never thinks very much of my ideas. Just at this point a very large, expensive car drew up in front of our apartment, and a little later our bell rang sharply.

"There she is now," I said.

I went out and was not surprised to see on our threshold a plump, personable, synthetically young woman who looked like a six-goal player in the hard-riding game of American matrimonial polo. I thought I would pull a Poggioli trick and astonish her with my deductions.

"You want to see Professor Poggioli about your jewels, isn't that so?"

"No — about my husband."

I was surprised at what she chose to recoup; then I realized my first guess was right, so I said, "So the jewelry you lost really are costume jewels after all."

She looked at me in a perplexed way. "I'm afraid I don't know what you are talking about. I haven't lost any jewels."

"Aren't you Miss Mona Moon, the movie star?" I asked.

My visitor flushed with pleasure. "Do I really look like Miss Moon? Some of my friends have said so. No, I'm Mrs. T. T. Thompson of the T. T. Thompson Plastiglass Corporation. I came to see Professor Poggioli, the criminologist."

I suspected that she wanted to inveigle Poggioli into making a speech before some women's club or other. She now looked exactly like the women's club type. I said to her, "Professor Poggioli is not a speech-maker, Mrs. Thompson. He is a retired university lecturer, so he has no ability whatever as a public speaker. He would simply put your club to sleep."

The mature, good-looking woman made a nervous, negative gesture. "I'm not here to look for a speaker. I want him to tell us who burned that warning on our lawn."

I was shocked. "Burned a warning on the lawn of the president of the T. T. Thompson Plastiglass Company!" I had meant to solve her problem myself. In fact, I always mean to solve the problem of Poggioli's next client, in order to get my hand in and not have to rely so heavily on Poggioli's deductions and researches into crime. It certainly is high time that I begin to stand on my own feet and do my own reasoning and criminal investigating, instead of depending on such a curmudgeon as Henry Poggioli. But every time, just when I'm ready to get started, some peculiar twist develops and I am simply forced to turn it over to Poggioli — which I now did.

In our dining-room, where Poggioli still sat over his newspaper and coffee, the criminologist looked up, then rose and offered our visitor a chair and a cup. She took the chair but was too nervous for coffee. I explained for her: "This lady is the wife of T. T. Thompson, president of the T. T. Thompson Plastiglass Company, and they have had a warning burned right on their lawn."

Poggioli's eyes became instantly concerned. "They are always burned in some conspicuous place like that. Let me see the note."

Mrs. Thompson began a search through her purse. "Yes . . . I have it here somewhere." She started pulling out things and piling them on the breakfast table. "Here it is."

I wondered annoyedly why I hadn't asked her for the note. They always leave a note, such people do, stating the moral objections they have to the person they warn. If I had only thought to ask for the note, I could probably have cleared up the mystery myself.

Poggioli took the note and read it aloud. "*DROP ADA . . .* (signed), Committee of Public Safety." The great criminologist nodded his head in satisfaction. "Very, very interesting — well worth investigating, Mrs. Thompson."

I said, "I don't see how a note and a warning in fire can be very interesting when they happen so often through the years."

"Ordinarily you would be right," said Poggioli, "but in this particular case you are wrong. You see, it is almost a contradiction in terms."

"How?" I asked, a little blankly.

"Heretofore, all castigation for moral offenses has been given by a class just *above* the class being warned. That is the normal course of moral correction. Usually, the immorality of a higher class — and in America that means a wealthier class — is not condemned and punished, but imitated by the classes just below. Now for this group, whoever they are, to threaten Mr. Thompson merely because he has a mistress, is completely atypical. Ordinarily, if the lower classes could get the money, they would imitate him; if not, they would envy him; but they would never dream of correcting him or threatening him."

The moment Poggioli explained, I saw that he was right. I said, "That is peculiar, isn't it?"

"Very odd . . . very unnatural. I assume, Mrs. Thompson, that you know this Ada and her relationship with your husband — to judge by your resenting the note and your trying to conceal it from your women friends. At least, you have been trying to pretend that you didn't know anything about it, because I know how a woman feels if she admits outright that she knows her husband has a mistress — very bad for her morale, makes a kind of hanger-on out of her . . ."

"I know who it is," said Mrs. Thompson in a bleak tone.

"I imagine it's his secretary," I said, with a sudden flash of insight.

"Well, yes. I'm sure it's his secretary," said Mrs. Thompson.

"What do you mean . . . you're sure it's his secretary? When you say you're 'sure it's his secretary,' it means you are faintly doubtful that it *is* his secretary. Now who else do you think it could be?" Poggioli gazed at Mrs. Thompson.

"Nobody, nobody at all. All I meant was, they have spelled her name wrong. It isn't Ada — it's Ida."

Poggioli looked first at her, then at me, in amazement. "That certainly does throw a mystery over the whole affair."

"Why?" I said. "Simply spelling a woman's name wrong?"

"Utterly improbable that they would spell her name wrong. Men never make a mistake in the name of an easy woman. That is part of the evolution of the human male, Mrs. Thompson — to identify correctly a woman he can safely approach. So the probability that the warning burners would write *A*da when it was *I*da is infinitesimal . . . "

"But her name *is* Ida — Ida Leonard."

"Listen," proposed Poggioli, "let us run over to your home, Mrs. Thompson, and see if we can pick up any other scrap of evidence identifying 'Ada'."

"It's just simply Ida Leonard, but I'd be glad if you would come with me and see what you can find out. It's awful, Professor Poggioli, to have to pretend you know nothing about your husband's affairs. If they don't believe you, they think you are dumb for not getting a divorce and alimony, and if they do believe you, they think you are just dumb."

Mrs. Thompson drove us to her mansion in a new Cadillac. In Tiamara the new-rich drive Cadillacs, and the newer their wealth the newer the Cadillacs. On the way over another bright idea struck me.

"Look here, Poggioli, I've got the whole thing solved. We don't have to bother going to Mrs. Thompson's home."

The lady lifted the precisely curved brows she had acquired in some swanky beauty shop. Of course I shouldn't have said "*bother*" going to her home.

"What have you thought of?" asked Poggioli.

"Just this," I said. "Mr. Thompson's got *two* mistresses — one named Ida and the other named Ada. That explains everything. It even makes clear your lower-class people criticizing and threatening upper-class people. Because they don't approve of two mistresses at one time. That's the truth, Poggioli — the American people don't. One at a time, yes, but two, no. Why? Simply because we sympathize with the first mistress. We feel that a married man has no moral right to be unfaithful to his first mistress. If a woman has that much love and confidence in a man to live with him without a legal shred to hang onto, we feel he is a dirty skunk if he isn't loyal to her. That's why this group, whoever they are, threatens the rich Mr. Thompson. They don't want to imitate him — they disapprove of his morals."

Poggioli listened to me carefully, a very rare thing for him to do.

"Your reasoning," he said, "is original and excellent. In fact, it is convincing — except for one detail."

"What's that?" I asked.

"The law of probability," said Poggioli. "The probability that Thompson would fall *out* of love both with an Ida and with an Ada is too remote to be considered."

"Is that your only objection to my theory?" I cried.

"That's all."

"Well, you will find, Poggioli, that such pernickety, petty . . ." Mrs. Thompson cleared her throat. "I'm afraid you'll find you are wrong," I concluded.

I will state here frankly that the remainder of my own personal observations and speculations on this case were aimed at proving that T. T. Thompson kept two mistresses. I felt if I could wipe Poggioli's eye just once, he would never treat me so cavalierly again.

We went on to Mrs. Thompson's home and there was very little to see. She spent nearly two hours showing us the designs for some new decorating in her library. Her books consisted of a premium-gift dictionary and a single shelf of best-selling fiction. I don't know why she had the dictionary — even a free one.

Quite by accident, I think, she had come upon the warning that had been burned on her lawn. It was made of two hard, clear sticks, tied together.

"What are these sticks made of?" asked Poggioli.

"Oh, my husband manufactures that. It's plastiglass."

"Then this came from his own factory?"

"Yes, I suppose it did. I guess it's his own men who are criticizing his carryings-on with Ida."

"But every one of them would know it was Ida — not 'Ada'."

"Yes, I suppose they would. Maybe they wrote it 'Ada' not to hurt Ida's feelings, if it got back to her." That was a strictly feminine way of looking at it. I still stuck to my theory of a real flesh-and-blood "Ada."

"What are you going to do now?" asked Mrs. Thompson, who wanted to show us some more designs, this time for her living-room, I think.

Poggioli said he would run over to the Plastiglass factory and see what he could find out there.

"I don't think they'll let you in the stockade," said Mrs. Thompson, "especially if you are looking for evidence against T. T."

"But the signers of this note — the workers — are evidently antagonistic to your husband."

"Why, that is a fact," exclaimed Mrs. Thompson, as if she had never thought of it before.

"I'll take you over there and get you inside the stockade. All of them know me and it won't be any trouble. But I won't go in myself. I'll just tell the guard who you are, then I'll turn around and come back. I don't want to see anybody."

We started out again in her car and Poggioli said this was one of the most extraordinary cases he had ever known — for a millionaire's workmen to criticize the private morals of their employer . . .

"They wouldn't," I said, "unless he had two mistresses."

"What I don't understand," put in Mrs. Thompson in disgust, "is what T. T. sees in Ida Leonard — such a washed-out creature, and no personality at all!"

"That's why he found a second one," I said.

Neither of them paid any attention to me. "There's the stockade and the guard at the gate," said Mrs. Thompson. She drew up to the entrance and motioned the man to come to her car. "Let these two men into the plant," she directed, and when we stepped out, she turned and drove away.

It has never been my habit to be brusque with men who carry pistols, even if they are as relatively harmless as policemen; so I stood before the guard, not knowing quite what to do next. The guard himself was under no such constraint. He looked at me and Poggioli, and said, "You two lads are on the Thompson side of this matter, aren't you?"

Poggioli began talking diplomatically. I can always tell when he is going to be diplomatic by the way he clears his throat.

"No, no, I wouldn't say exactly that we are on the Thompson side . . ."

"Well, exactly which side would you say you were on? You came here with Mrs. Thompson."

"Yes, we did, but purely as private investigators. By profession I am a criminologist."

"Criminologist . . . Just what do you do?"

"I study crime."

"Brother, you couldn't come to a better place! But you are bound to be on one side or the other . . ."

"I was not properly introduced to you," said my companion. "My name is Poggioli — you may have heard . . ."

A complete change came over the guard. "Why, of course! You are the great detective who doesn't take pay. Glad to meet you, Mr. Poggioli. Who do you want to talk to in here?"

"Well, anyone who knows the details of the trouble in this here plant."

The guard nodded cooperatively. "Mm — mm, I see . . . I wonder now who would know the details of the trouble in this plant?"

Poggioli said, "How about one of the foremen?"

"Certainly, Mr. Poggioli. Just walk down past that toolhouse yonder and call for Jim. Jim'll know everything and tell you anything you want to know."

On the way to the toolhouse we naturally passed a number of men, some walking, some in trucks, some on motor scooters, and finally a very odd fact dawned on me. I said to Poggioli, "Do you see what I see?"

He said yes, he thought he did.

"The point is," I continued, "what have they got in their pockets? It is very odd that so many men should carry tools with curved handles. Why should everybody have a leather cutter or a curved-handle knife in his hip pocket?"

"I feel sure they are not knives or leather cutters," said Poggioli.

The foreman, Jim, also had one. He kept his back turned rather studiously from Poggioli, but I saw the outline of his tool, or whatever it was, in his back pocket.

Jim was a largish, hail-fellow-well-met man, but today he seemed preoccupied, or worried. When Poggioli introduced himself, Jim knew him and said that he always thought detectives visited a place after a crime had been committed. I noted a little stress on the word "after" and said, as lightly as I could, "And not before, eh?"

Jim laughed a little. "I hope not before."

"Is this a special day," I went on, "when everybody carries leather cutters around with them?"

"Leather cutters?"

"Yes," and I nodded at his hip pocket, which he had turned from Poggioli.

"Oh, that's not a leather cutter," he said. "It's more in the nature of a punch." Then he said more seriously, "I brought mine down today to get it fixed."

"Has it anything to do with . . . Ada?" I went on in my same light vein.

"Ada?"

I saw that he was really at sea. "Well, it could be Ida," I admitted. "Ida Leonard."

"Oh, Miss Leonard. She's the boss's secretary. Well . . . no-o . . . I brought my gun down on account of Miss Leonard's traveling bag." And the good-natured foreman looked at me with the expression of a riddle-maker propounding a conundrum.

The reference to Ida's traveling bag floored me. I gave up. Poggioli began talking seriously to Jim about the company and the company's organization. He asked if the workers held any stock in the company. Jim said, yes, they did. All workers who had been in the plant more than twelve months were eligible to buy stock, and that everybody, or almost everybody, had purchased some. "They had a right to," concluded the foreman, "for at the time it looked as if the company would make big money."

"And now," I began subtly, "it doesn't look as if . . ."

Poggioli frowned slightly at me and shook his head, "I wonder if there would be any way," he interrupted, "to bring about a peaceful settlement between the workers and the management?"

"I don't know anything about that," said the foreman. "It would be a very good thing to do, however."

"I wonder if there is somebody I could see . . ."

"Mm — mm . . . It might be Mr. Hicks, our department manager. But you wouldn't be able to see him today."

"Would you telephone him and find out for me?"

"Why, yes . . . what'll I say to him?" Jim walked into the toolhouse and we followed.

"Just tell him that Professor Poggioli, the criminologist, would like to see him in reference to averting a sudden drop in the value of the company's stock."

Jim looked around in amazement, "You mean you could do that!"

"I can try," said the criminologist.

Jim nodded, did the telephoning, and said, "He'll see you. Walk three blocks straight down to the Administration Building and go to Room 781."

Mr. Hicks was a smallish, very serious man, cut after the pattern in which all department managers seem to run. On the walls of his office were photographs of plastiglass motor cars, furniture, utensils of all

sorts. When he grew tired of selling plastiglass he would rest his brain by
looking at these photographs.

He was pleased, in a serious, sober way, to see so great a man as
Poggioli. He confessed he had always thought of Poggioli as being a
rather lightminded man. Poggioli said the reason for that was because I
had always written up the notes on Poggioli's cases in a rather trivial
style. Mr. Hicks then asked Poggioli what he thought of corporate law
and corporate practice.

That floored me again. I wanted to ask about Ada and Ida, and
settle the point, and here they were discussing corporate law and
corporate practice.

"Exactly which point are you referring to?" inquired Poggioli, "in
your distinction between law and practice?"

"Well . . . say, bonuses," said Mr. Hicks.

"Bonuses?"

"Yes, the amounts the higher executives of a corporation vote
themselves above their regular salaries. You know, the stockholders
have nothing whatever to say about that matter."

"They have a legal right to enter suit for its recovery. In fact, I
believe stockholders have recovered bonuses in several instances."

"But such a suit isn't entered once in a thousand times."

"No, it isn't. In large corporations the bonuses are a very small
percentage of the company's gains, and the amount taken from each
stockholder is small, almost nothing."

"That's true," agreed Mr. Hicks somberly, "but if the management
can vote themselves a small percentage, they can also vote themselves a
large percentage. If they can vote themselves a bonus once a year, they
can vote bonuses twice, three times a year — as often as they want to and
as much as they want to."

For the two men to go on gabbling like that, with the whole
working force of the plant wearing pistols in their back pockets, began
to get on my nerves.

"If the stockholders don't like it," I said, "they can outlaw it."

Mr. Hicks became suddenly aware that I was in his office. He
turned on me with the controlled scorn of a department manager.

"Make a law against it! How can we make a law against it? By what
legerdemain can we influence the lawmakers in Washington to
introduce a bill to outlaw corporate bonuses?"

Before I could say anything else, Poggioli thanked him for his
courtesy and inquired the way to Miss Ida Leonard's office.

"You're going to see her?" asked the manager with interest.

"I thought I would."

"Would anything she could do have a bearing on the situation at
this late hour?"

I had no idea what it was a "late hour" for, but Poggioli seemed to
understand. "Yes, it may be possible to arrange something with Miss

Leonard to give the men in the plant a little more time to reach a peaceful solution."

At this Mr. Hicks was moved. He came around from his desk, took Poggioli's hand in both of his, and pressed it. "God speed you, Professor Poggioli," he said earnestly. "I hope you rescue our company from the utter ruin it now faces. The easiest way to get to Miss Leonard's office is to go downstairs, ride on the conveyor belt to Station 13, get off, take a small escalator on the left, ride to the top, get on a moving platform, and then get off when you come to the sign saying 'Executive Offices.' Walk through the General Filing and Accounting Department, and Miss Leonard's office will be the fifth on the right."

As we started off to follow these instructions, I said, "I wish I could find out the 'Ada' end of this business."

"You mean 'Ada' as a woman?"

"Certainly she is a woman!"

Poggioli shook his head. "No. 'Ada,' I regret to say, is not a woman. She is three initials — A — D — A — which undoubtedly stand for an association of gangsters which have bought out President Thompson's stock, are going to take over the management of the company, and in the future confiscate all the profits of the corporation through the device of bonuses. At least, that's what manager Hicks and all the rest of the men believe."

I was shocked. "How in the world did you find all that out?"

"Manager Hicks told me just as plainly as he could. He thinks it is going to happen today — I mean the take-over; and I know the workmen-stockholders are going to make a desperate stand against it. Your question — the one you put to the foreman, Jim — brought out the fact that the men expect the sell-out of the plant and the elopement of Thompson and his secretary today."

I searched my head in vain for the question I had put to the foreman. "What did I say to Jim," I finally asked, "and what did he say to me?"

"You asked about Miss Leonard, and Jim said it was not Miss Leonard that had roused the workmen, it was her traveling bag. That meant they cared nothing about her morals; they were rebelling against the desertion of the plant by the President and his secretary."

"O-oh . . . traveling bag!"

"That's right."

"Now explain Ada to me again. What do the letters actually stand for?"

Poggioli has no patience with a man who digs for details. He snapped, "Oh, anything — anything at all! African Dromedary Association . . . Allbright Doodling Activities . . . anything! The point is, Thompson is selling out to A.D.A. and the corporation is going to be gutted."

"Why did he sell out?"

"A dozen possible reasons. Maybe he's tired of his business and wants to cash in. Maybe he's tired of his wife and wants to go off with Miss Leonard. Maybe he's getting a big share of stock in A.D.A. in return for the Plastiglass Company."

"I wish Ada was a woman," I said.

"Why?"

"So I could sell this story — not for myself — but for the benefit of the reading population of the United States. Half of them own stocks. This story is very important for them to read and reflect over, but they won't read or reflect over it unless it's about a woman."

Poggioli nodded. "That is the first correct judgment you have made."

By this time we had reached the office of the secretary to the President.

Miss Leonard was not the sort of person I had expected to meet. She was a slender, pleasant efficient-looking girl — the kind a man would marry, not elope with. As we entered her office she was sitting at a pink plastiglass desk, looking out through the clear plastiglass side of her office onto the long boulevard that led to the entrance of the stockade. On her desk was a small pink plastiglass clock, which she glanced at now and then. On each article of these plastiglass furnishings, I noticed the company's slogan: *Stronger than Steel — Clearer than Glass — Cheaper than Wood.* It really was a remarkable product.

Miss Leonard turned from watching the avenue. "How did you get in, Professor Poggioli? I didn't see your car."

Poggioli told her how we came, then added, "You've been watching the driveway for some time, have you not, Miss Leonard?"

"Yes, I have," she said nervously.

"A great deal depends on the arrival of someone soon?"

The President's secretary moistened her lips. "A very great deal, Professor Poggioli."

"Will you tell me how much time there is left — before you expect these callers?"

The young woman glanced at her jewel-like clock once more.

"In . . . six and a half minutes, Professor Poggioli."

The psychologist went taut. "Listen, Miss Leonard," he said rapidly, "which do you put first — the general good of your thousands of co-workers, the economic stability of American industry, or . . . your own personal plans?"

It was a brutal way to put it. It gave the girl absolutely no moral escape.

"Why . . . why do you ask me that, Professor Poggioli?"

"Because I'm a criminologist. I try to foresee and forestall violence. I am also trying to prevent a precedent being set in American corporate existence that threatens our whole financial structure . . . and incidentally you will prevent bloodshed here in the plant."

The young woman stared at him. "I . . . I can do all that?"

"You can — by putting your personal interests aside and acting for the common good. But it will mean a great sacrifice for you."

She drew a long breath. "What . . . what do you want me to do?"

"Merely delay your elopement for a half-hour, an hour — as long as it takes . . ."

"For what?"

"Call up Orange 54321, ask for Captain Blake, let me talk to him, and you'll understand."

I couldn't imagine what Poggioli wanted, and neither could the girl. She got Captain Blake on the line and handed the receiver to Poggioli.

"Captain Blake, this is Poggioli. You now have about four and three-quarter minutes to act. Call all your radio cars in this section to converge on the Thompson Plastiglass Company. In a very few minutes a car or cars with some half-dozen men in it will enter the Plastiglass stockade and drive toward the main offices. Seize them all, subpoena them to appear before the Senate Crime Investigating Committee now sitting in Tiamara. Accept no excuse, no alibi, no pleas of important business. They are among the leading criminals of America."

I was amazed. I said to Poggioli, "Look here, you've hit the nail on the head. Your plan will make the Senate Investigating Committee one of the strongest powers for justice in our nation. We cannot, of course, put all the topflight racketeers in the penitentiary, but why not summon them all before a Senate Investigating Committee and keep them waiting in the anteroom for the rest of their lives?"

Nobody paid any attention to me. Poggioli turned to Miss Leonard.

"Young lady, I want to thank you for what you will do for American finance. If the police are not here in time, don't run off with President Thompson. Delay the proceedings . . ."

"Oh, I will indeed, Professor Poggioli. You see, T.T. stood me up. He planned, after he had sold out, for us to fly to Mexico. But at the last minute he shifted from me to Ada Delehanty. He is now going to elope with her, or so he thinks. I put that warning and note on T.T.'s lawn myself."

Poggioli stared at the girl. Then he turned to me with an expression as if he were about to launch into one of his profound and amazing, yet perfectly simple, explanations.

But he closed his mouth and said nothing.

The Man in the Shade

He was merely a tourist standing under the shade of the banyans around the Tiamara Yacht basin watching the boats come in. Nothing about him even caught my attention, much less tickled my suspicion, yet Poggioli, after only a couple of appraising glances pondered, "Wonder what he's spying on and why?"

This disturbed me. Not that Dr. Henry Poggioli, ex-professor of criminal psychology, has not a right to suspect whom and when he pleases. He has. But I did not want him to head into a research so obviously empty of fraud, crime, deceit, murder and malfeasance as was this healthy, well kept, genial gentleman, standing in the shade. Time spent on such a man would be a direct financial loss to me for I make my living by writing and selling my notes on Dr. Poggioli's criminal researches. I tried to ease my friend away from this pointless extravagance.

"He's standing in the shade because the sun's hot," I said casually.

"Do you believe a tourist would do that?"

"Certainly, why not?"

"These tourists," he nodded at the spatter wandering around the basin, "pay forty dollars a day to come here, get blistered in the sun so they can go back North and prove they have had a vacation in Tiamara. No thrifty Yankee would waste time and money standing in the shade."

I should have let it go at that. Poggioli might have come along and stirred up some real mystery and illegality for my daily literary provender but I didn't stop talking in time. I said:

"He's watching the yachts come in," for there really were an uncommon number of yachts heading into the basin.

"Not that precisely, he's watching for some particular yacht to come in."

"How do you make that out?"

"If he were looking at the yachts in general he would continue walking as the others are doing, but when a man wants to pick out some particular boat, he stops and looks carefully."

Here I made my second mistake. "Why would he get back among the banyans to do his looking, why wouldn't he stand on the seawall?"

The criminologist nodded approval. "Good question, excellent question! That shows some surreptitious intention, an instinct to hide while he watches. It's why I knew he was a spy of some sort."

I laughed. This was the limit of the absurd. I asked Poggioli: "Don't you know the man is more conspicuous among the banyans than if he were walking around with the crowd?"

"Possibly he has something which he doesn't want anybody to see, not even fellow sightseers. Is he carrying a package of any sort?"

"I don't see any."

"Of course you don't see any. If you saw one I'd see it too. I'm asking you doesn't his posture suggest he is carrying a package in his left arm away from traffic?"

"I don't know what his posture would be like," I said.

"It would be like he's standing now," uttered Poggioli a little impatiently, "with his left shoulder a trifle higher than his right."

I, too, was out of patience. "You think he's a spy of some sort because his left shoulder is fractionally higher than his right!"

"It's one, just one, indication of all I've mentioned. It would mean little or nothing taken by itself, but the sum total . . ."

Once well started there is utterly no end to Poggioli's deductions. Among the sightseers I was glad to see coming Bill Gebhardt, the *Tiamara Times* crime reporter. I hoped I would turn Poggioli away from this unfruitful will-o'-the-wisp onto some good solid crime which I trusted Gebhardt was investigating. When I hailed him and asked what he was up to, Bill gave me the high sign of a man in a hurry and called that he was on his way to a stockholders' meeting.

I hurried after him and joined him. So did Poggioli.

I said, "Gebhardt, you're not holding back something from me, are you? Wouldn't do that, would you? You are no financial writer, you're a police reporter and you know that I have always taken your stories and worked them up into something readable . . ."

"Sloane, the city editor, sent me over here, to a stockholders' meeting at the City Yacht Club." He seemed evasive to me.

"He couldn't have sent you to a stockholders' meeting at the Municipal Yacht Club because the club hasn't any stockholders." I felt quite a logician catching Gebhardt up like that.

"He means all the stockholders of this company are yacht owners," explained Poggioli absently, "and they sail in here and use the yacht clubhouse for their convenience. It explains why so many boats are coming in this morning."

Gebhardt seemed relieved that Poggioli had found out something which he had not been at liberty to tell.

"That's it exactly," he agreed, "this is strictly a blue chip company."

"I imagine the chairman of the board must have asked the city editor to send you specially," hazarded Poggioli, "or he never would have sent you."

The crime reporter seemed a bit surprised at the psychologist's deduction. "I believe I was sent for," he admitted.

It seemed this might be something of interest from a mystery writer's viewpoint even if it weren't out and out murder, which of course, I would have preferred. So I said:

"Look here, Gebhardt, take me and Poggioli along with you. No telling what's going to pop up and three experts are better than one."

"Have only one ticket of admission," regretted Gebhardt, "and only one photograph to prove that I am myself. Awfully sorry. Wish I could wangle you both in but I can't," and he started around the basin toward the clubhouse.

"Listen," called Poggioli after him, "if you need me send a boy."

"Thanks, I'll do that, Dr. Poggioli, I certainly will," and he was gone.

I was never more reluctant to see a man go. I had utterly nothing to write about. I said to Poggioli, "Do you suppose we could follow him and somehow get into the room next to the stockholders' meeting? I want to see why a big corporation asked the city editor to send a crime reporter to cover their meeting."

"I think we'll find out anyway, and if we don't it won't make any difference."

"How do you mean, 'we'll either find out or it won't make any difference'?"

"If the problem is too deep for Gebhardt, he'll send for us. If it isn't too deep for him, it would hold no intellectual interest for me."

"Yes, that's all right for you," I said drily, "your bread is already baked but I've got to eat. I'd like to know more about this story Gebhardt's after. It might sell, if it could end up in a murder or something."

"That's not likely," said Poggioli.

"Well, what are we going to do now?" I asked. "Let the morning slip away without any copy at all?"

"I believe we'd better go back to the man under the banyans," said Poggioli.

I was never so outdone. "That fellow!" I ejaculated. "Leave a vague but rather hopeful hint to go stare at a tourist under a banyan!"

"We have nothing to do now, unless Gebhardt sends for us," said Poggioli. "We might drop back and talk to this fellow. If he is communicative, we'll go off and leave him. If he is reserved I'll probably be able to find out why and that might be something for you to write about."

As he started back the way we came there was nothing I could do but follow him. If I went to the clubhouse and bribed my way into the room adjoining the board meeting I knew I wouldn't be able to make any of those acute deductions which Poggioli seems to turn out effortlessly, and which I sell. My dependence upon this obstinate old criminologist, poling off in the wrong direction, galled me. If I could have deserted him and lived, I would have done so. Back we went around the curving promenade among the usual pedestrians until again we reached the particular banyan under which the fellow had stood. The place was empty. An ironic gratification filled me.

"So here we are," I said, "with our walk for nothing."

"Nothing!" snapped Poggioli, looking at me, "him not being here is the very thing I expected, because it is now past twelve o'clock. However, I wanted to check on him and make sure."

Now I was quite at a loss. "What do you think went with him at twelve?"

"That's the hour the board of directors meet. Evidently his boat came in. He either joined it at the wharf or went on to the clubhouse for the meeting."

I was completely up in the air. "Listen, you said he had a package he was concealing . . ."

"Yes, I noticed he held his left shoulder higher than his right."

"Then what do you think it was?"

"Since he was looking for a special yacht to come in, I don't know. Now if he had been a tourist with a package as you thought he was, he'd have carried a kodak, a pair of binoculars, a bottle of sun lotion, dark glasses, swimming fins for his feet and a watch guaranteed to run under water."

Poggioli's flippancy annoyed me. Somehow I myself had begun to feel the man was not an ordinary tourist. "What are we going to do now?" I asked. "Just stand here like this?"

"It's all we can do at the moment."

"Don't you want to find the banyan man again and see what he's doing now?"

"Certainly, that's the problem, what's the fellow doing now?"

"Let's go look for him," I suggested under a certain nervous pressure.

Poggioli took hold of my arm. "No, wait. Gebhardt left us here and said he'll send a club attendant here to find us."

"But will he certainly send a boy?" I questioned uneasily.

"If the man under the tree has anything to do with the stockholders' meeting, Gebhardt will certainly send for me."

"Why do you think so?"

"Because the situation will be complicated; he will need my help."

"Suppose he can work it out by himself?"

"In that event the problem would be too simple to interest us in the first place."

"I don't believe the man under the trees had anything to do with the stockholders' meeting."

"Maybe not, in that instance, Gebhardt, of course, won't send for us."

"Then what will we do?"

"Let's wait a few minutes. If nothing happens, we'll take a taxi home."

I was exasperated but mainly at the correctness of Poggioli. If there were no complications between the man and the meeting then neither one really furnished dramatic stuff. But I wanted to see what each one was. The idea of just walking off and leaving an unresolved situation gaffed me even if it all turned out to be a very simple matter. Poggioli on the other hand was philosophic, the moment he saw a situation lacked intellectual complications, he was through with it. I wished I were like him but I wasn't. Presently he got to his feet, glanced at his watch and obviously began looking for a taxi. He hailed one which drew up near our bench. He motioned me inside and followed me. As he did so a boy with a blue cap came running up the promenade with a letter.

"Is this Dr. Poggioli?" he gasped out of breath.

My companion said yes and reached for the letter.

My relief squeezed my chest. I said, "Boy, how did you guess this was Dr. Poggioli?"

"Mr. Gebhardt described you, sir. He said you would be with Dr. Poggioli, and there was no way to miss you, sir, among these wealthy tourists, sir."

I was somewhat taken aback. I said, "Yes, I see; there probably wasn't."

Poggioli said, "Driver, take us to pier twenty-three."

It is my misfortune when I'm following a clue like this one to get so excited that I can hardly put heads and tails together.

I asked in a low tone, "Will Gebhardt be at twenty-three?"

"Gebhardt sent the note from the club," said Poggioli.

"I see, so Gebhardt is at the clubhouse!"

"Presumably."

"What did he say in the note?"

"Go to twenty-three and use your discretion."

"Is that all?"

"That's all."

"What does he mean?"

"I don't know. If I knew I wouldn't go."

This in a way was allegorical. It meant if he understood the whole mystery on which we had embarked, he naturally, would finish the business by going home to lunch. His interest in criminals and crime was always admiring and purely intellectual, never retributive. In fact it was the typical American standpoint. In the midst of these reflections, I suddenly ejaculated:

"Look! Look, Poggioli, yonder's the man we saw under the banyan!"

And sure enough it was. He was one of a kind of receiving group on the deck of a large Latin-American vessel; rather too large for a yacht, but it evidently was a yacht nevertheless. Everybody was shaking hands in the manner of very wealthy men who have not been financially scuttled up to now.

There was a crowd on the quay, of course, watching the scene on the yacht. Poggioli paid off our taxi driver and we moved together through the sightseers to the boat's gangplank. I don't know whether anyone would have stopped us or not, I mean if nobody had recognized our criminological importance, which no one seemed to do. But just at this moment that collective resistance which keeps social and financial groups separated from intruders was broken up by a very peculiar happening.

A man, an outsider whom I know, a customs inspector named Sloane, had also come aboard, whether professionally or as sightseer, I don't know. At any rate he was walking around over the polished deck and paused at the well containing the anchor chain. He reached down into the well, finally lifted himself over into it and came out with a bundle.

The whole matter was simply nothing. No one paid him the least attention. But Sloane looked at his bundle, examined it, then with a queer expression walked straight into the felicitating group to the yacht's owner. He showed the bundle to the owner. I am sure nobody would ever have paid any attention to Sloane at all but he wore the cap of a customs inspector. Amid the genial chatter he said something to the skipper. The skipper said *"Qué?"* and looked at him. Sloane repeated whatever he had said. A circle of surprise, then of amazed embarrassment spread over the group on deck and reproduced itself in excitement and curiosity among the sightseers on the dock.

"¿Ça, Señor, that ees emposseblay," ejaculated the skipper in amazement, "the presidential yacht with a theeng like that on board!"

Sloane made a gesture. "It's always a surprise to the crew of a boat. It is even to me, in a case like this."

Everybody heard them. Nobody was talking but the two. The officer said:

"Señor Inspector, I am truly shocked. I suppose you will confiscate that. Eef you do eet ees all right with our crew. We did not even know eet was there . . ."

"As a matter of fact," said Sloane, "it is my duty to confiscate your boat and everything on it. Nothing can be removed from the boat . . ."

"*Pero, Señor* . . . but, Señor, we did not know eet was there!"

"I know that, Captain, a complete surprise . . . !"

"But, Señor, *Dios mío!* Do you eemagine we would have risked the ship and her cargo for a . . . a . . . leetle package like that. What ees it worth?"

"It's about fifteen thousand dollars' worth of marijuana, Captain."

"Feefteen, thousan' . . ."

"That's right."

"Leesten, ees eet sensible, ees eet reasonable that we would risk two hundred and twenty meelion in stock securities, not to mention our boat, to smuggle in feefteen thousand dollars worth of marijuana?"

"No."

"Then, Señor, let us go. We come to a stockholders' meeting with stock and proxies . . ."

"Captain, if we let people go who do idiotic things, the government might as well abolish customs and discharge its inspectors."

Suddenly all the guests aboard began talking. "It was absurd!" "Stake a vast fortune for a penny!" "Something was wrong!"

"Leesten," suggested the captain suddenly. "Eet was not taken ashore. Eet would never have been taken ashore. I myself am a . . . an addict . . . a slave to the drug . . . my liquors, eef I keep them een my bar, closed up, they are legal till I sail out again, no? Would that be true also weeth my marijuana?"

"Not dropped down in the well of your anchor, Captain, and it is more than you could use for the rest of your life."

"Listen, my frien's," called the captain to the group, "weel not some of you vouch for me and my ship, and let us go to the stockholders' meeting in the clubhouse?"

Came a rush to do this. The man whom we had seen under the banyans came forward to protest for the captain. "If the captain was subject to a weakness, it was not the duty of American customs officers to seize on his ship which was visiting our port to cast a majority of votes in a great financial decision. He arrived as a guest, he should transact his business and depart as a guest!"

It's a great pity that rhetoric no longer rules the South. Sixty years ago it did and at that time the captain would certainly have got off free. Now it was different.

"Nothing goes off this boat, Captain," repeated Sloane, "the boat itself stays here where it's moored until the government disposes of this case."

The sightseers on the quay began a kind of mumbling, shuffling protest at this ruling. In the midst of this Poggioli approached the official. "Inspector Sloane," he suggested reasonably, "the question is not whether el capitán Guiterrez uses a narcotic, it is whether or not he brought this package of narcotics in with him on his boat."

"He practically admitted he brought it in when he said he smoked the weed himself."

"That's true but he thought by that he might get some important business property ashore. Those two things contradict each other. A smoker of reefers would never be put in charge of a million dollars worth of securities at a stockholders' meeting. So you can forget the captain's vague plea of personal privilege."

Now a great many persons recognized Poggioli and the inspector was grateful for his assistance.

"That's my opinion. I hate to tie up a yacht but I'll have to do it."

"Wouldn't a good deal depend on whether the package really came in on the yacht?"

"Certainly, that's the gist of the charge."

"Wouldn't it be proper for you to look at the matter in action and see for yourself?"

The inspector looked at his parcel undecidedly. "I don't see anything on it that says where it comes from."

"The knot," suggested the criminologist. "A new knot is fairly easy to untie but an old knot, long in salt air, is quite difficult."

Somebody on the quay broke into relieved laughter and called:

"Go to it, Poggioli! That's a fact, Inspector!"

Inspector Sloane did manipulate the tie of the string and I could see that it slipped easily.

"I couldn't let him off on a point like that, Dr. Poggioli," said the official between a question and a statement.

"No, certainly not, just a beginning. The string, what about the string? It's the flat, waxed variety which you don't find in this boat's port of origin."

Delight from the quay, a mixed reaction on the yacht's deck. The man from the banyan shade seemed quite at a loss at Poggioli's simple analysis. The tourists on the shore began calling, "Turn the captain aloose, he's all right!"

"He could have got some American twine," said the inspector half to Poggioli and half to the onlookers.

The criminologist waved the matter away, "A mere detail, Inspector, which proves nothing just as you say. How about testing the salinity of the paper?"

"The . . . what?"

"Salinity."

Inspector Sloane rubbed a tentative finger over the parcel. "If it did have salt on it, Dr. Poggioli . . . then what?"

A laugh went up from the quay at the inspector's ignorance although all of the sightseers were probably in the same boat.

"It would mean this," explained the scientist, "if that package came here on the yacht it has been in the salt air for several days and must be highly saline. If it has just been put aboard it may or may not be salty. The person who tied up the parcel might have known enough to rub salt on the paper, or sprinkle it with salt water. A microscopic test would show either method. On the other hand he may have been innocent enough to forget all about the salt air. In that instance proof that this package came aboard here in Tiamara is complete. In short a test for salinity could clear Captain Guiterrez but it can't convict him with certainty."

Some of the crew members cried, *"Bien! Bravo!"* From the dock, "Go to it, Inspector, give the captain a break!"

I do not believe the inspector knew how to test for salinity. I myself thought of chewing a bit of the paper around the bundle and then noticing the middle of my tongue where I believe salt is tasted.

"All you need," explained Poggioli casually, "is an alcohol lamp. Burn a piece of paper which you know has been on the yacht all the time, then burn a bit of this wrapper. The first flame will certainly show the yellow of sodium, that wrapper may or may not show yellow when it burns. That's what we want to find out."

The moment he said this everybody knew all about the experiment and there was much relief on deck and dock. One of the crew went to get an alcohol lamp. In the interim I made a note of how to test for salinity because if the time ever comes when I will be forced to unravel criminal mysteries for literary purposes on my own, I certainly want a scientific technique to fall back on.

As I wrote the man from under the banyan came across deck to me and Poggioli.

"I had no idea there were so many ways to tell where a parcel came from," he said, looking at the inspector manipulate the alcohol lamp.

"Those were just a few gross methods," said the criminologist. "If you go into microscopy, chemical analysis, a Latin-American package would bear no more resemblance to a North American package than a rabbit to an elephant."

This, of course, was putting it on a bit thick, as Poggioli sometimes does. But it impressed the man from under the banyan.

"Would you like a position, Dr. Poggioli, where you would have very little to do and draw say about forty or fifty thousand a year?"

A cold chill ran over me at this proposition and I was deeply relieved to hear Poggioli say he had an honorarium quite sufficient for his needs.

I felt sure, in fact everybody felt sure, that the test would come out clear of salt and it did. A great cheer went up from dock and something that passed for a cheer from deck. A guard instantly assembled on deck bringing envelopes containing stock certificates and a big leather bag full of proxies.

They marched off the gangplank to the applauding quay and then on around the tiled surface of the promenade to the rococo entrance of the Tiamara Municipal Yacht Club.

Frankly I was heartsick. We had spent that entire morning utterly for nothing. Not a murder, not even a smuggling case. The only thing that was smuggled was going the wrong way; trying to get out, apparently, not in.

I said to Poggioli, "Call a taxi and let's get home."

"Look here," he said. "Doesn't it strike you as odd that somebody should spend fifteen thousand dollars trying to get a visiting yachtsman into trouble?"

He was trying to defend himself and I had no interest in his defense.

I saw a taxi and waved it in. As the man drove up, I stepped inside. "Twenty-three Acacia Street," I said.

Poggioli hesitated and then exclaimed, "Wait, wait just a minute!"

"What for?" I said, "I need a lunch and a drink."

"It's Gebhardt," said Poggioli. "He's coming this way. He's running!"

I was half-minded not to wait for him. Gebhardt always runs or seems to and he never writes anything but journalese.

Gebhardt called to us while he was still some distance away.

"Did you let 'em go? Did you turn 'em loose?" He came up breathing from his hurry and his excitement.

I wondered whom he meant. I looked at Poggioli and was not sure he knew. However, he said, "Yes, yes, I thought it was best to get it over with."

"I'm sure it was," nodded the reporter in a disturbed manner. "It was such a corny trick we could hardly have done it a second time. I told the board when they planned it, it would be entirely up to you whether you would let it go through or not."

At this point a suspicion dawned in my head. "Gebhardt," I said, "do you happen to be talking about that marijuana somebody dumped on that foreign yacht?"

"That's right. Elderson did it. He was trying to sequester the boat and its cargo to keep a great load of sugar stock and a bunch of proxies being voted at the stockholders' meeting."

"What earthly interest," I cried, "did Captain Guiterrez have in the South Eastern Sugar Growers Association?"

"Dr. Poggioli knows all about that," said Gebhardt, brushing me off.

"He may know it," I said, "but I don't."

"It's simple enough," said the reporter. "Guiterrez himself is a poor man, a naval officer in charge of the presidential yacht. The shares and proxies were placed in his name so he could vote to change the South Eastern Sugar Growers Association into the South Eastern Tung Growers Association."

I was utterly bewildered. "Who wanted it changed?"

"The president of the republic . . . and the republic itself."

"How did anybody know such a question would come up?"

"It's been on the agenda for this meeting for the last six months. Some of the stockholders were just about to go crazy over it. Nobody knew whether tung oil would make money or not. But they did know it would not cash in for at least six years to come."

My head seemed to spin. Nothing seemed to make sense.

"Why did the president of a foreign country buy up stock and proxies in an American sugar growing company, and why shift it to tung oil."

Gebhardt made a hopeless gesture.

"Because his country raises sugar and it doesn't raise tung oil. If Guiterrez pulls this, it will raise the international price of sugar some fractional part of a cent. This isn't a big company, but some of the stockholders have their entire fortunes in it."

Did Poggioli know all this from the time he first glimpsed the man under the banyans? I don't know.

"Who thought up the package smuggling aboard the yacht?" I asked, wondering if it were possible to work such a quiet undramatic move into a salable mystery story.

"Bill Elderson, the President of the company himself. Bill always lands on his feet somehow, but he hadn't counted in Dr. Poggioli here. I knew the doctor would see right through President Elderson's grammar school scheme and break it up if he thought best."

"Well," I said, "since he's got the Sugar Association in such a mess as this, how's he going to get 'em out?"

"I imagine he has decided to sacrifice this company so Congress will make proper laws about the voting of stock in American corporations. Our Labour is protected from foreign competition. Our manufacturers are guarded by tariffs. But the poor devils of millionaire stockholders can see their businesses snatched up and shunted into some new and untried path in the twinkling of a stockholders' meeting by foreign financial competition. That is what Dr. Poggioli had in mind to correct by allowing Guiterrez and his gang to walk off their boat with the stock and proxy certificates."

The Mystery of
the Sock and the Clock

The delicate, some might even say, the presumptuous errand on which I had come to the American Hospital in Cuernavaca was chased completely from my head when I saw my old friend, Professor Henry Poggioli, standing in the patio — Henry Poggioli, Professor of Criminal Psychology of the Ohio State University, no doubt on another sabbatical leave. After our flurry of greetings he continued his conversation with Dr. Beveridge, physician in charge. The two were talking, of course, about Poggioli's professional field, crime. In the morning paper Dr. Beveridge had read that a woman's body had been found in an old Spanish well near Taxco. Here Dr. Beveridge turned to me and suggested casually that I might use the incident in a detective story.

I said it would make a very trite beginning, that every detective-story reader expects to find mangled bodies in old wells, or else why drag in an old well. And I added, there was no mystery attached to such a find since the body evidently had to be thrown in from the top.

Here Professor Poggioli smiled and said, "You came to the hospital this morning on some rather annoying matter, didn't you?"

I had to think back to see why I had come.

"Since you mention it, I believe I did. But how did you know that? I'm not disturbed now."

"Because your humor about Dr. Beveridge's suggestion was a little abrupt, not to say tart. I gathered it was a carry-over from some annoyance already in your mind."

I was too well acquainted with my old friend's subtleties to lift an eyebrow at this one. Dr. Beveridge, however, was startled. He discussed my friend's deduction at some length, then eventually turned to me and wanted to know my trouble.

Played up to like this I hardly knew how to start my complaint. It really was nothing. I told them so and tried to beg out of it, but both Poggioli and Beveridge would not have it, so finally I said baldly:

"Well, it's about one of the nurses here, a Miss Birdsong."

The physician was surprised, "Emma . . . Emma Birdsong! What has Miss Birdsong done that could possibly affect you or anybody else adversely?"

"Well, not me, personally," I admitted, "but all of us American residents in Cuernavaca." Then I went on and explained that Miss Birdsong had been attending a sick child, a little José Mendez, at the Quinta Catalina. When the little boy recovered and Miss Birdsong was leaving the Quinta, Doña Catalina, the child's grandmother, had invited the nurse to remain and make the Quinta her home. Such an invitation, of course, was pure Spanish formality, but Miss Birdsong turned around, went right back into the old manor and did make it her home.

"Now I learned all that from my Mexican *criada*, Concepción," I explained, "and I hope it isn't true. But if it is true I want to protest for the benefit of other Americans. The natives here charge every boorish act of one American to all the other Americans collectively, and it isn't doing right by the rest of us for her to act like that."

Poggioli as a newcomer was amused, but the physician who had twenty-odd years in Mexico was serious. He said my *criada* had misinterpreted the whole incident. He explained when little José recovered, Miss Birdsong had not wanted to remain at the Quinta, but Doña Catalina had begged and implored the nurse to stay there nights. She, the Doña, said it was the greatest benefit that little José could possibly have. So much against his will and convenience, Dr. Beveridge permitted the nurse to sleep at the Quinta and report for work at the hospital every morning. That was the real status of the case. I was about to return the conversation to the woman in the well because, after all, murders are pleasant and interesting events and I don't know what the human race would do if they should all suddenly stop. But Poggioli sidetracked me by saying:

"If the little boy was well, as you say, Doctor, why did Doña Catalina want the nurse to stay on?"

"I meant that little José was physically well."

"Is he mentally unwell?" I asked with some concern because I knew the child and his grandmother.

"Don't leap at conclusions," soothed the house physician, "there are other disturbances besides a mental breakdown. This little boy developed a great fondness for Miss Birdsong and Doña Catalina asked that she might live at the Quinta for the child's sake."

Here Professor Poggioli stroked his chin. "Now just what are you holding back, Doctor?" he inquired good humoredly.

"I'm not aware that I'm . . ."

"Possibly not aware, but of course you really are. You say the little boy had a mental disturbance, but this disturbance turns out to be a great love for his nurse — which is no disturbance at all but a perfectly healthy reaction. So there must be something you are consciously or subconsciously trying to conceal because your explanation explains nothing at all."

Dr. Beveridge was a little taken aback. "I believe there *is* a gap there." He tapped his cigarette and looked at its coal. "I may have been covering up one little detail unconsciously. Little José's unfortunate psychological twist is not his affection for his nurse; it's his aversion to Doña Catalina, his grandmother. She told me her little grandson was very unhappy with her and he seemed to love Miss Birdsong. She thought every child ought to have someone to love, and so did I. That is why I allowed Emma to spend her nights at the Quinta."

Here the psychologist asked if Doña Catalina drank, if she were sadistic, if she were cold-natured and strict?

"Nothing of the sort. There's no better woman alive. She tries in every way to please the child but he won't have anything to do with her."

"Why doesn't she give him back to his parents?"

"His parents are dead."

In the little pause that followed a taxicab drew up in front of the hospital and a moment later Miss Birdsong entered the doorway.

Now I barely knew Miss Birdsong but all Americans in Mexico are on a hail-fellow-well-met footing, so I called to her as she came down the patio.

"How does it happen that American nurses rate taxicabs in Cuernavaca?"

Dr. Beveridge replied for her that every day the Señora Mendez sent her up in the family car.

"But," I said, "the auto I see through the door is not the Mendez. . . ."

Here to my surprise Miss Birdsong gave me a slight shake of the head. I hushed, wondering why a taxicab should be a delicate subject. The nurse sensed my puzzlement for she immediately asked me in a significant voice if I had seen the hospital's new X-ray machine.

Dr. Beveridge answered for me: "Emma, he's a story writer; he has no interest in mechanics."

Now it irritates me to hear people classify story writers as if we were a separate species of animals; so I told Miss Birdsong I would be glad to see the machine, although I really hadn't a breath of interest in mechanics. So I followed her into the electrical appliances room just off the patio.

Inside, Miss Birdsong pointed to a bulk under a dust cover. "That's it," she said, evidently to fulfill her promise to show the instrument, then added in an embarrassed voice, "I've been wanting to see you for some time. You don't mind me . . . running off with you like this, do you?"

With some curiosity I said I didn't; then she drew breath to reinforce her own courage, and asked: "You write detective stories, don't you?"

Then I knew why I had been closeted. I began smiling. "Are you another one of those persons who has a wonderful plot . . . if you could only write it. . . ."

She flushed abruptly. "Why, I'm nothing of the sort. I wouldn't waste my time thinking up story plots. I want to do some good in the world while I'm alive. . . . Now you've seen the machine, we can go back." And she turned toward the entrance.

"Wait a minute," I begged, "I'm sorry I got off on the wrong foot."

"Oh, it's all right if you don't want to help me."

"But I didn't realize you needed help."

"Why did you think I signaled you to follow me in here?"

"I — I don't know."

She relented a little at this. I have noticed that as a rule women always relent in time to put you to work for them.

"It's that taxicab I drove up in. You saw me shake my head so you wouldn't mention it before Dr. Beveridge, didn't you?"

"M-mm . . . yes . . . but why shouldn't I mention a taxicab?"

"Well, there's something about it that's very . . . disagreeable . . . and mysterious."

"About a taxicab!"

"Yes . . . exactly . . . about a taxicab, at least about that taxicab."

"Then why do you ride in it?"

"I . . . I can't help it." I stared at her in astonishment and she went on, "It's the most mysterious thing, and . . . and since you write detective stories, I thought maybe you could solve it for me."

I shook my head. "No, I can't solve it."

"But you do solve mysteries in your stories."

"No, I don't. I *make up* mysteries, but I already know the solution. My only job is to keep the reader from finding the answer too soon."

The nurse was painfully let down at this. She turned toward the door again. "Well, we might as well go back. . . ."

I was not only interested, I was moved. "Listen," I said, "why don't you consult Professor Poggioli? He's probably the greatest criminal analyst in America."

"This isn't a regular crime, it's just . . . disagreeable . . . and . . . mysterious . . . and a little scary."

"That's all right, he'll answer any kind of question. Stick your head out the door and ask him to come and see the new X-ray machine."

Miss Birdsong went to the door and called, and Poggioli came in.

"So you weren't able to answer her questions about the taxicab, eh?" he inquired lightly of me.

The nurse was bewildered by his penetration but I told her to think nothing of it, that when he explained how he knew, it would sound very simple. Here Poggioli took up the matter for himself. He said that when I had mentioned taxicabs as Miss Birdsong entered the hospital, she had shaken her head at me — so he had supposed there was some kind of trouble about the cab.

The criminologist now began questioning the nurse and the account she gave really was quite odd. It seemed that a very handsome, aristocratic, but annoying and even threatening Mexican paid her taxicab fare every morning from the Quinta to the hospital. That was why she did not want the taxicab mentioned before Dr. Beveridge.

"But it seems to me you would have wanted it mentioned!" I stressed in amazement.

"No-o . . . on account of little José . . ." began the nurse.

"Wait a minute," interrupted Professor Poggioli, "let's not jump into the middle of this. Begin at the beginning, Miss Birdsong, and tell us how any man could maliciously and with ill will furnish you with a taxicab every morning and why you *have* to ride in it?"

"Does sound funny, doesn't it? I first saw him standing outside José's nursery window, in the alley outside the Quinta. He wasn't doing anything, just standing there, gazing at the roses . . . and I didn't like his looks."

I stopped her. "Hold on, Miss Birdsong. Why didn't you like the looks of a rich, handsome, aristocratic young man. . . ."

"Because I could see he was one of the idle rich, and just wasting his time, without a single thought except to indulge himself," she replied warmly.

"Miss Birdsong," interposed Poggioli gently, "how could you decide this young man was self-indulgent on your first glimpse of him through the nursery window?"

"I . . . I didn't say 'glimpse,' Dr. Poggioli, I said 'sight.'"

"They don't mean the same thing?"

"No, 'glimpse' means just a short look at anybody; 'sight' means seeing everything he did while you watched him."

"I see. . . . So he did something besides just look at the roses?"

"Yes, he did," she nodded, with an adverse compression of her lips. "He was waiting for someone."

"And for whom?"

The nurse hesitated. "I don't think you ought to mention people unless you can say some good about them."

The criminologist nodded understandingly. "So it was a woman?"

"How did you know that?"

"Because you say evil things about this man and think nothing of it at all; yet you boggle over somebody else. So it must be a woman . . . in fact, a young woman, of your own age."

The girl gasped in admiration.

"Now why," continued the psychologist, "did you decide he was self-indulgent?"

"Well . . . that's very plain. A rich handsome man like him waiting at the Quinta fence for Socorro, the maid, to come out and talk to him; and for them to talk very intimately and uneasily, too. Socorro looked around several times to see if anyone saw her."

Dr. Poggioli nodded. "I see. It would be a natural construction."

"Well, don't you believe it, too?"

"I don't know yet. What else happened?"

"Nothing right at that moment. But a little later when I started to walk over to the hospital, who should drive up in a taxi but this man whom I had seen flirting with Socorro and ask to take me to the hospital!"

"You refused?"

"Certainly I did!"

"And what did he do?"

"He went away that morning."

"But came back the next morning?"

Miss Birdsong gave Dr. Poggioli a questioning look, but finally she answered a simple, "Yes."

"And then how did he *make* you ride in the taxicab, Miss Birdsong?"

The girl's face warmed in anger. "Why, he simply slowed down the cab and drove along the street beside me. When I walked faster, he had the chauffeur go faster; when I walked slower, he went slower. Once when I stopped, he stopped. I said to him 'Why don't you go on?' He said, 'This is what I came out for, to place a taxi at your convenience.' And I said, 'Well, I don't want it!' and he said, 'Well, you don't have to have it but if you change your mind it's ready for you.' I said, 'This is more conspicuous than riding with you!' And he said 'I hadn't thought of that but it is, isn't it?' I appealed to him, 'Listen, this could cost me my job. I'm working in an American missionary hospital. If people see you following me like this they would misunderstand it.' 'Then why don't you ride?' asked the man, 'nobody would notice it then.' So-o . . . I rode . . . it was all I could think of doing."

I shook my head. I had lived in Mexico over a year and I knew of a great many crazy things the Mexicans did, but this was the craziest I had heard of. I glanced at Poggioli to see what he was thinking. The criminologist stood tapping the dust cloth on the X-ray machine. "Is it possible he's trying to drive you away from the Quinta?"

"You think so?" asked the nurse, quite impressed and frightened.

"Ye-es, I think so."

At this point a doctor entered the laboratory to take an X-ray photograph, so our conversation ended. Poggioli said he would think over the matter and try to decide what the nurse had better do. Miss Birdsong was very grateful and thanked him as if he were some superhuman being who had promised her aid.

It was tacitly understood that Professor Poggioli would be my guest while in Cuernavaca, so after saying good-bye to Dr. Beveridge and the nurse, we set out for my apartment on Ignacio Abad *calle*. When we reached my place we were still debating the cause of the Mexican's strange persecution of Miss Birdsong. Poggioli gradually developed an hypothesis of *jealousy*.

It was perfectly absurd, of course, but his reasoning held together in an odd way. He said the only connection Miss Birdsong had with the Quinta was the little boy. If this Mexican wanted the nurse *out of* the

Quinta, it was because the little boy loved her. The Mexican wanted the little boy to love only him. . . .

"But Poggioli," I cried, "that makes no sense at all! How can you be sure the Mexican even knows the little boy?"

"He must know the household of the Quinta very well," declared the criminologist.

During this discussion, my Mexican *criada*, Concepción, slid back and forth from refrigerator to living-room, from dining-room to kitchen, with an odd mixture of timidity and ironic amusement, as if she were some sort of supercilious mouse. Whether she understood our English or not, I don't know. She never spoke it. But I did observe that when I gave her an order in Spanish I usually had to repeat it in English before she knew what I meant.

Well, Poggioli developed his theory of the little boy's kinship with the unknown Mexican man all afternoon, and after dinner, in the evening, he decided we would walk over to the Quinta Catalina to interview the little boy and find out why the child didn't love its grandmother. He seemed to feel that somehow or other this would shed light on the case.

I knew, of course, that it wouldn't. I was sure there could be no possible connection between a little child's aversion to his grandmother and a strange Mexican annoying an American nurse. They were logical incompatibles. However, as host I was showing the town to my guest anyway, and as the Quinta was the third tourist attraction in town, the first and second being the cathedral and the native market, I was very glad to walk over with him.

It was a typical Mexican evening; one of those marvellous evenings that made an American wonder how the town could be so dirty and yet seem so poetic and lovely. The Quinta looked mysterious half seen behind a high iron fence, with four or five dim lights pointing up the gloom of the eucalyptii and the rose trees. Everything was fragrant, with a hint of surface sewage in it.

I went to the tall iron gate and reached to ring the bell when I heard a woman's voice give a brief suppressed cry. It startled me for an instant but I was immediately reassured by a child's voice imitating a grown-up's reprimand.

"What you squealing about, Emma? Nothing to be afraid of. . . ."

A moment later woman and child came toward us out of the shadows and the woman said in a nervous undertone, "I thought he had come back."

"What if he had; he couldn't eat you, could he?"

By this time the woman recognized us and came forward eagerly. "Oh, it's you! Has . . . has the Professor decided anything?" She evidently was using the slight obscurity of speech with which grown-ups puzzle childish ears.

I answered in the same vein by saying Poggioli thought that by talking to some one in the Quinta he might get a clue to the information she desired.

"You mean by talking to . . .?" asked the nurse, coming up to the inside of the gate.

"Yes," I nodded.

"Why, what would that have to do with it?"

"Just a possibility," said Poggioli behind me, "nothing certain at all. He and I could just have a little talk together. . . ."

"I see. . . . Well, come in." She attempted to unlatch the tall gate but found it locked. "Darling," she said, "will you run and get the key from Socorro?"

The child standing three or four yards behind her said no.

"Why, José, darling, won't you go for me?"

The boy repeated his no, and after a moment added, "And I won't talk to him."

We three grown-ups stood with the frustrated feeling of having been understood all the time. Miss Birdsong called Socorro's name and presently Socorro appeared out of the darkness.

"Socorro," explained the nurse in a reproachful voice, "I asked José to tell you to bring me the gate key and he refused."

"Ça, José," chided Socorro, and then added, "I'll go get it, Señorita."

The combined disapproval of all the grown-ups turned little José around and sent him walking slowly into the Quinta. We watched him until his little figure moved under the illumination of the dome light over the entrance. Then Socorro went for the key.

Poggioli turned to the nurse. "We seemed to startle you when we appeared at the gate. Are you nervous all the time?"

"No, I thought . . . he had come back."

The psychologist moved to see her more plainly through the bars. "I understood he annoyed you only in the mornings, in the taxicab?"

"Yes," she said in a worried voice, "but this afternoon as José and I started for a walk he came up with a little gun to give to José. . . ."

"Oh, a toy gun," interrupted Poggioli.

"Yes. He was very polite and self-effacing about it, in a sarcastic sort of way." She shivered. "He's the most disagreeable man I ever met. When he came up on José and me this afternoon, so unexpectedly . . ."

"How do you mean, unexpectedly? Didn't he just come walking along the street?"

"No, he came from the alley," she pointed, "around the corner, where I saw him that first morning, and he was right on us all at once. . . ."

Here she was interrupted by Socorro appearing in the shadows again.

"Señorita," said the servant, "I can't find the regular gate key. Somebody has misplaced it. Shall I get the Doña's master key?"

Poggioli stood a moment in silence. The whole situation seemed somehow to rest completely with him.

"No, no, that's all right, Socorro," he said at length, "we were just going anyway."

Naturally both Poggioli and I were disturbed over the missing gate key. For some time we walked silently through the darkness toward my rooms on Ignacio Abad *calle*, then finally I said, "Do you think that man got the gate key from Socorro?"

"Whether he has or hasn't got it, I don't believe he will do any physical harm to Miss Birdsong," said Poggioli thoughtfully.

"Why do you say that?" I asked.

"From Socorro's manner. It was quite casual. Either the key has been mislaid as she said it was or she has given him the key so many times that it no longer disturbs her poise."

"But I don't see what that has to do with physical harm. . . ."

"It's very simple. He couldn't have entered the Quinta a great many times and worked physical harm to anyone without discovery and action from the law, even Mexican law."

"That sounds to me as if you were hanging Miss Birdsong's safety on a rather thin limb. I think we ought to tell the police and have them watch the . . ."

"And stop him?"

"Certainly stop him — if he attempts anything!"

"And have him put off his attempt, whatever it is, until we are off guard, and miss this opportunity to trap him?"

I was taken aback. "I hadn't thought of it that way," I admitted, "I was thinking of Miss Birdsong."

"You were thinking of her present," said Poggioli, "I was thinking of her future."

"Yes, I see. But if he kills her tonight, she won't have any future."

"He won't kill her, Socorro was too calm for that . . . and besides she really may have mislaid the key."

I personally didn't like to gamble on such a narrow margin. I was so disturbed that when I got home and to bed I couldn't sleep at all. I heard the cathedral clock strike every hour. When it tolled one, I thought that at that very minute he could easily be doing Miss Birdsong to death. And for me and Poggioli to lie here like this, when we knew an attack and 'perhaps a tragedy was imminent . . . that is, if the key were not really lost . . . it was horrible. Finally I must have gone to sleep because the next time I woke up it was high Mexican daylight.

Poggioli was up, apparently had been up for some time. He had the morning paper and when he saw I was awake, called out cheerfully, "Listen to this. 'This morning at an early hour, a train carrying forty American tourists was held up at La Victoria, robbed by armed bandits, and then sent on to Mexico City. The robbers relieved the travelers of cash and jewelry.' That's an out of the ordinary crime. I was wondering if you could get a mystery story out of it?"

I had a headache. I said, "Poggioli, if the friends of a writer would only forget about plots, it would make the writer's path through life a lot smoother and pleasanter." And then I added, as a dig at the way he had treated Miss Birdsong, "It seems to me a criminologist's duty ought to be as much to prevent crime as to detect it after it has been committed."

"Now, wait," argued Poggioli, "how could I possibly have prevented forty American tourists from being . . ."

"Forty your foot! You know I'm not talking about forty American tourists!"

"Oh, that. Well, I don't think anything's happened; nearly ten o'clock and we haven't heard anything."

At that moment Concepción put her head in our doorway and said big-eyed and in frightened Spanish, "Señor, a man has come for the police!"

"For the what?" I said.

"For the police, Señor."

"You mean *from* the police!"

"No, Señor, *for* the police," and she looked at Poggioli. "Is he not a policeman?"

I got into a dressing gown and Poggioli and I went outside.

A private automobile, one of those large, expensive, resplendent cars such as rich Mexicans always own, stood at the foot-wide curb outside my doorway. In the rear seat sat a suave, agreeable gentleman with his chauffeur in front. The gentleman began begging our pardon, but he had noticed in the paper that Professor Poggioli, the American criminologist, was visiting at this street and number, and he had also noticed in the same paper that an American woman had been robbed. He said he was afraid that we didn't read Spanish, or that we didn't take the local Cuernavaca paper, therefore he was taking the extreme liberty of calling to the attention of a great American criminologist the fact that a fellow countryman of his, a woman, was in distress. He hoped we would consider this a friendly gesture. . . .

I am sure he would have gone on talking and apologizing in excellent English all day if I had not interrupted with a guilty pang.

"Was it Emma Birdsong . . . at the Quinta Catalina?"

The Mexican gentleman referred to a paper in his hand. "I believe that is correct, a Miss Emma . . ."

"We are very, very interested," I interrupted him, giving Poggioli a condemning glance. "We will go over immediately."

"Might I run you gentlemen over in my car?" offered the samaritan.

"No, we won't put you to the trouble. We'll do that much for ourselves," I said significantly.

The gentleman was agreeable and signaled his chauffeur to drive ahead.

"Why didn't we go with him?" asked my guest.

"You wouldn't understand if I told you, Poggioli!" I said bitterly.

My friend looked at me. "Why are you so disturbed?"

"For heaven's sake, man," I cried, "How can you stand there calmly and talk like that? She's been robbed! Maybe she's also been attacked, hurt, killed . . . and it's our fault!"

Poggioli clicked his tongue at my simplicity. "Why, she can't have been hurt. That would have been the headline in the paper, not the robbery."

"Poggioli," I said, "you are too scientific to make a good friend, and you may be wrong, too. These Mexican papers report things according to their whim, not according to psychology."

Here a taxi came in sight. I first whistled at it American fashion, then remembered and hissed Mexican fashion, and it came to us. I rode to the Quinta in the greatest self-reproach.

When we reached the place everything was in confusion. The police were there; the grounds were being searched; the servants questioned. Little José watched everything with dour unchildlike eyes. Doña Catalina herself seemed suddenly aged. I asked her where the nurse was and the poor old dowager pointed to a room. I hadn't the hardihood to ask if Miss Birdsong had been injured. When I entered the boudoir and saw the girl, I still wasn't sure; she seemed so pale and shaken. She was so glad to see us. I asked her if she had been harmed. She shook her head. "Oh no, nothing like that." Then I asked her had he taken much of value.

She shook her head as if she were ill. "No, no particular value."

"What did he take?"

"A sock."

"A what?" ___

"A sock." She lowered her voice to a whisper. "He woke me up, talked to me, took my sock . . . and went away."

I looked at her, trying to understand. "Did it have money in it?"

"No, no, that's what makes it so frightening! What can he want with a sock?"

Poggioli was behind me, pulling at his chin in deep thought. He spoke out of his cogitations. "I believe this man is the cleverest criminal I have ever met."

I turned impatiently. "Say what you mean, say it plainly! My Lord, this is no time for . . ."

"I mean, stealing a sock, and the psychologic effect he aimed to produce. If he had stolen money, jewels, it would have been a commonplace. But a sock! It throws an air of mystery, almost of menace, over the crime. It suggests a strand in some unknown plot . . . and it's terrifying. Miss Birdsong is much more frightened than if he had taken her rings. Isn't that true, Miss Birdsong?"

"A rich man, he wouldn't have taken money," said the nurse.

"Perhaps not. So the object of the sock is simply to be mysterious, to frighten you, to drive you away from the Quinta. That's the explanation and you needn't really be frightened any more. This fellow is bluffing."

The nurse was enormously relieved. "I suppose that is right. I hope it's right. But why does he want me to go away? What on earth have I . . ."

"As I explained to you, I can't go into that, Miss Birdsong. I haven't enough facts, and probably I haven't the Mexican psychology either. You haven't told the police what you know?"

"No, indeed. I'm afraid to. . . . Think what he would do if I told the police on him. He might murder me."

"But he would be put in jail," I pointed out.

"Maybe. . . ."

Poggioli interrupted. "Miss Birdsong, you'll have to make a decision: whether you'll give up little José and go back to the hospital, or whether you'll use the law, fight this man with it, and stay here with your patient."

"But would they put him in jail . . . just for stealing a sock?"

"Now there you are," I said, "I hadn't thought of that. I don't know whether you'd better tell the police or not."

Still undecided we went out on the Quinta grounds where the little Mexican police were busy with their investigation. The police captain was explaining to the Señora that it was an inside job because the vines on the iron fence were unbroken. This proved that no one had climbed over the wall. Moreover, it proved that an amateur burglar was at work because a professional always broke vines when a servant let him in — to clear the servant of complicity. So the marauder had had an accomplice in the Quinta. ". . . at what hour did this burglary take place?"

The robbery was committed at four o'clock. The Doña was sure of that. She had heard Emma scream, had got out of her bed and noticed the clock in her room; it was exactly four o'clock.

"How did you come to look at the clock in the excitement, Señora?"

"It struck just as I got up."

"*Exactamente.* May we look at the clock?"

The whole crowd of us, servants, policemen and all, marched into the Señora's bedroom to look at a grandfather's clock in the corner. The hour was then three minutes past ten.

"The time is correct now," stated the little officer, glancing at his own watch. "It must have been correct then." He turned to Miss Birdsong. "Señorita, did you mark the hour?"

"Yes — it was two o'clock."

"*Two* o'clock!" exclaimed the officer, "but Señora says *four* o'clock and her clock is right!"

Miss Birdsong shook her head, half in stubbornness, half in bewilderment. "When I woke up it was two o'clock — I looked carefully."

"Señorita, if you woke up frightened by a thief, why should you note the hour?" inquired the chief officer.

"Because I'm a nurse and trained to observe the exact time when anything happens — and it was two o'clock, not four."

"*Si*, may we now enter your bedroom and *con su permisión* examine your clock, Señorita?"

"Certainly. This way."

The crowd moved into the nurse's bedroom. Miss Birdsong's clock was an ormolu, standing on her dresser.

The chief officer smiled broadly and spread his hands. "There is no mystery," he said, shrugging. "Look. The Señorita's clock is two hours *slow*."

Miss Birdsong's ormolu stood at four minutes after eight.

"Did this clock ever lose time before?" asked the officer.

"Never," replied Miss Birdsong.

Here Poggioli spoke to Miss Birdsong in English and in a casual voice: "It's all right now — no more danger." And we made our adieus to the Señora and the nurse, and went away, leaving the nurse plainly a little frightened. I myself was uneasy for her. Outside the Quinta I asked Poggioli why in the world he said there was no danger now when this new clock mixup seemed to complicate the situation?

"Why, don't you see through that?"

"No."

"Do you really suppose that Miss Birdsong's ormolu actually lost two hours, precisely two hours, not a second more, not a second less, since early this morning?"

"Why, I hadn't thought of it that way," I said. "It would be odd."

"Odd? It would be impossible!"

"Then what happened?" I asked.

"Think, man!" Poggioli lectured me as if I were a stupid pupil. "The robbery actually took place at four o'clock — we know that from the Doña's clock, which is on time now, and from Miss Birdsong's ormolu, which is now two hours slow. Don't you see? The intruder was in Miss Birdsong's room at four in the morning. Before waking her, he turned back her clock two hours — from four to two."

"But why?" I asked.

"To make Miss Birdsong think that her room was entered at two o'clock — therefore, to make her testify that the robbery was committed at two o'clock. All he stole was a sock — yet even for so petty, so trivial a theft, he has obviously arranged an unbreakable alibi for two o'clock. We are dealing with a timid man really. He's no more to be feared than a toy terrier. But we shall fool him, for all his tricks."

I couldn't help saying admiringly: "Poggioli, old man, frankly you're a wonder."

Later, when we were back in my rooms on Ignacio Abad *calle*, the telephone rang. I strode to it with a premonition of a new alarm. Sure enough, no sooner had I spoken my name into the transmitter than Miss Birdsong's voice cried unhappily in my ear.

"This is Emma! They've got him! They've summoned me down to the court to identify him!"

"Well, look here," I soothed, "don't be so down-hearted. We wanted to get him — now we have!"

"Ye-es," she wavered, "but I have to identify him — I'm so afraid."

"Listen, Miss Birdsong, Poggioli has reasoned him out to be a complete coward. He says you need have no further fear of him whatsoever."

"Oh, does he!" she exclaimed gratefully. "I'm so glad. But you two men must go with me to the courthouse. I'd never have the nerve to sit and testify against that man alone."

"We'll go with you, Miss Birdsong. Just drop by on your way over and pick us up."

I was quite excited, naturally, and even Poggioli seemed keyed up. When Miss Birdsong arrived in a taxi, we joined her eagerly; but as we drove away, I saw Concepción standing in my doorway and there was a queer expression on her sallow face.

"Now, listen," said Poggioli to both of us in the cab. "He expects Miss Birdsong to swear that he was in her room at two o'clock. Then he will prove that at that time he was somewhere else, not in the Quinta. His alibi will be perfect — so he will go scotfree. But we'll fool him. Miss Birdsong, you explain how your clock was tampered with, put two hours behind; you insist — insist, mind you! — that it was really four o'clock when he stole the sock. His carefully prepared alibi for two o'clock will then be meaningless, will fall to pieces. You understand?"

Miss Birdsong nodded her head in agreement. Poggioli's clear instructions braced both me and the nurse. We even began to laugh a little over the coming trial, not very heartily, but a little.

When we entered the courthouse, I instantly saw the prisoner at the bar, and the strangest feeling of my life came over me. I turned to my friend and whispered: "For God's sake, Poggioli, do you see what I see?"

Miss Birdsong heard me and ejaculated in an undertone: "What — what is it?"

"That man in the prisoner's dock," I whispered, "he's the *same man* who drove up to my apartment this morning and told us you had been robbed!"

This new discovery completely unnerved me. Miss Birdsong was white as a sheet. Poggioli gripped her arm and whispered confidently: "Remember, do exactly as I told you. If you follow my instructions, there will be no danger, I assure you."

Miss Birdsong went to the witness stand and was sworn in. The trial came off without a hitch. The nurse identified the man, identified the stolen sock, and fixed the time of the theft at four o'clock. The Mexican did not even offer a defense. He was found guilty and sentenced to prison. As he was led away, he bowed gallantly to Miss Birdsong.

Strangely enough, he seemed to bear no resentment — he was smiling as he walked off between two officers.

We left the courthouse, got into a taxi, and started back. At Ignacio Abad *calle*, Miss Birdsong dropped us and our last words to her were not to be afraid; the fellow would be in jail for a while and could not continue his persecutions.

Concepción was once more in the doorway, waiting our return. As we came up she called out: "The Señorita witnessed for him. I knew she would — everybody does."

"No, Concepción," Poggioli corrected with satisfaction. "Miss Birdsong witnessed *against* him. She sent him up for a jail term."

"But Señor, Socorro told me over the telephone that the Señorita swore he was in her room at four o'clock this morning."

"That's right," said Poggioli.

"Si, Senor." Concepción burst out, "but he was not in her room at four o'clock!"

"What do you mean?" demanded Poggioli. "Of course he was!"

"No, Señor — not at four o'clock. He was at the Quinta *at six o'clock* in the morning. All the clocks were fixed — the Doña Catalina's, too. Socorro told me how she set all the clocks back, the Doña's to four o'clock, and the American lady's to two o'clock — just as he instructed Socorro to. Later Socorro changed the Doña's back to the right time, but she left the Señorita's two hours slow."

"But why?" I demanded.

"So that the Señorita would be twice as sure that he came at four. He *wanted* the Señorita to testify that he entered her room at four o'clock!"

"But *why?*" I demanded again. Poggioli was strangely silent, although his lips were moving angrily.

"*Caramba*, Señor, everybody in Cuernavaca knows why! At four o'clock Señor Carlos Mendez was at La Victoria — robbing the forty Americans in the train! It takes him two hours to drive from La Victoria — so he is in the Quinta at six. But if the American lady insists he was in her room at four, he would be convicted of *small stealing*. Then he cannot be accused of *big stealing* at exactly the same hour!"

My house seemed to reel.

"He always escapes some way, Señor," said Concepción, her eyes shining. "You see, he is Doña Catalina's son and the father of little José."

"But I thought Doña Catalina said little José's father was dead!"

"He is to her, Señor. Such a life as her son leads, robbing and shooting — he is dead to her."

Poggioli never discusses this case. To one who was accustomed to really serious crimes and important trials, this little affair, however piquant, had seemed only a trifling matter to the great Poggioli. But that brilliant criminal, Señor Mendez, hoodwinked the Professor completely. He permitted Poggioli to win a minor skirmish, but the major battle — Poggioli lost. It was Poggioli's greatest failure.

The Case of the Button

At the prolonged ringing of our doorbell, Poggioli stirred his coffee a little more violently than usual, glanced across the breakfast table, and said, "That is surely Gebhardt."

I didn't doubt him for a moment. Gebhardt would have had no scruples at all about getting us up even at two in the morning.

"What's his problem?" I asked.

"Murder," said Poggioli.

The bell continued ringing, but Poggioli did not stir. Finally I said impatiently: "Aren't you going to let him in?"

Poggioli grimaced. "No, why should I? If I let him ring himself out he may go away."

I was profoundly shocked. "Poggioli, such an unethical attempt at evasion should not even occur to a reputable criminologist. It is simply incredible on the face of it. In five minutes you'll be going through the paper looking for an interesting crime to investigate. You always do, except on Sundays."

"That's the very point," said Poggioli. "The particular crime that Gebhardt's so agitated about isn't interesting."

I considered this surprisingly new and unexpected facet of my old friend while the bell kept ringing impatiently.

"Exactly what kind of a murder would you classify as dull?" I asked with thinly-veiled irony.

"Political."

The cocksureness of his answer startled me. Worse, its far-reaching implications frightened me. If Poggioli was becoming too indolent or temperamental to investigate his murders I'd be out of a job. I wouldn't have anything to write about. With perhaps unjustified alarm I thought to myself: "I ought to make a start in this business on my own."

I very nearly did so, by getting up and going to the door to admit our agitated caller. Then I remembered that in all our years of living together in Acacia Street, no visitor had ever elected to discuss his problems with me. But that did not prevent me from becoming irritated at Poggioli's assumption of omniscience.

"Poggioli," I protested, "why do you sit there like an unwrapped mummy insisting that Gebhardt has nothing interesting to discuss. You admit yourself that he has latched on to a murder. Why should it be political and why dull?"

"Simple enough," answered my friend casually. "The tourist season is over. All the yeggs, gangsters, confidence men, all the impressively individualistic artists in crime have gone north for the summer. All we have left in Tiamara now are the local politicians."

That was perfectly true. Poggioli can be beguilingly persuasive when he dons an armor of verbal logic. But now I was convinced that his logic was wholly gratuitous and completely off beat as to facts. I decided I would test him.

"Listen, Poggioli, I'm going to the door and if our visitor doesn't happen to be Gebhardt, I intend to admit him anyway."

"That's agreeable to me," he said.

"Furthermore, if it *is* Gebhardt, and he's not on a political murder, I'm still going to let him in."

Poggioli made a patronizing gesture. "It takes a primitive mind a long time to develop faith in logic."

I paid no attention to his ridiculous thrust. I went to the door and opened it, rather fearing it would be Gebhardt. It was.

"Gebhardt," I said in a flat voice, "have you come here about a murder?"

He stared at me and nodded, obviously taken by surprise.

"A political murder."

"Well, yes . . . a politician has been murdered. I presume it's a political murder."

I stepped outside and closed the door after me. "You can't get in," I said. "I'm sorry, but that's the way it is."

The young *Times* reporter was shocked and angered as he had every right to be. "What do you mean, 'Can't get in'?" he demanded. "Have you and Dr. Poggioli been discussing me as if I were a panhandler or a bill collector or something?"

I was in a jam. I liked Gebhardt in a way — although he wrote on an ephemeral journalistic level and in a slapdash fashion which I intensely abhorred.

"It's like this, Gebhardt," I tried to explain. "Poggioli knew you had come on a political murder and he just told me he wouldn't see you. He claims that political murders are too trite and dull and machine-made to entertain him."

"What does he mean—machine-made?"

"I'm sure I don't know. Political machine, maybe. It's unfair to ask me."

"Well of all the conceited, complacent, asinine—"

"Not so loud Gebhardt. He's right in there."

"Let him be in there! Let him stay in there on his fat— Look, I came here with the most mysterious, baffling, stupendous, brain-mangling mystery—" I shuddered at Gebhardt's choice of adjectives.

"Gebhardt," I said, to placate him. "I'll go with you."

"What for?" he demanded.

"I'll help you investigate."

He did not seem impressed— or even pleased. "Whose notes will you take?" he asked. "I write up my own."

"I'll do some theorizing," I said with some dignity. "I have been following Poggioli's methods for a quarter of a century. No one is better qualified to apply his criminological principles in a case of this sort. I have often wished for a chance to go on my own, and not have him throwing me off the scent with his over-elaborate theories."

He looked at me and said nothing.

"Where is this murder?" I asked.

"Nineteen Bayfront Drive."

"Are you going there now?"

"Certainly," Gebhardt replied. "I should have been there an hour ago. But I naturally assumed that Poggioli would join me, and that having him along would more than compensate for the delay. How was I to know he'd go prima donna-ish on me?"

"Who was murdered?" I asked.

"Mark Fanoway. He's a city councilman and boss of Ward Ten. You probably know him. He's the most reactionary old coot that ever slowed up the progress of a metropolitan city. The man who did it was a public-spirited citizen, if you ask me."

"I never heard of him," I said. "Fanoway, I mean."

"Why, his pictures came out as big as the side of a house every election year."

"I might know his face," I said. "But I don't remember his name."

"How do you vote for the candidates if you don't remember their names?"

"Like everybody else," I told him. "I give my ballot to the first name on the list. I figure if a candidate has pull enough to get first billing he must be a good politician."

"Then you've voted for Mark Fanoway without knowing it ever since you came to Tiamara," said Gebhardt, who seemed, for some reason, to be disgusted with me.

I got into Gebhardt's rattling old Press Chevy and we dashed to 19 Bayfront Drive at a speed which was certainly illegal and probably ill-advised. The building proved to be a relic of Tiamara's lush but artistically misguided past, its shrubbery and flowering plants mercifully concealing the twice-lifesize statues on the front lawn.

At its rococo entrance a policeman stopped us and demanded that Gebhardt show his press pass. Even then he remained surly and insisted that we wait while he went inside to confer with his superiors on the telephone.

"That's odd," I said. "Deliberately keeping a reporter from a crime."

"A political crime," Gebhardt emphasized.

"I suppose that would make a difference," I said.

"Your friend Dr. Poggioli would certainly think so."

"Look here, Gebhardt," I said. "You'd better make a note of that. It's unusual for an officer to hold up a reporter. Poggioli in his practice always has me make notes of every variation from normalcy, no matter how trivial. Then he puts them all together, and—feels he's making progress."

"Is there anything else around here that you'd advise me to note?" asked Gebhardt.

I looked around the big marmoreal entrance. "Well, let me see. Did you notice those mailboxes over there? They are extremely individual; I mean for the tenants. They might give us some clue as to the personality of their occupants. It's little details like that, Gebhardt, which ordinary men would completely overlook which gives Poggioli his wonderful—"

"You understand Poggioli's methods and I don't," Gebhardt interrupted. "Why don't you go over and look at the mailboxes yourself and report back anything you discover."

"Mmm, all right, I'll do what I can to help you, Gebhardt," I said—and went across to look at the mailboxes.

After studying them carefully and memorizing every detail so that I would be able to recall it instantly to mind, as Poggioli always did, I returned to Gebhardt.

"What did you find out?" asked Gebhardt.

"They have the names of the tenants on them," I said. "One of them is marked 'Fanoway,' and that, of course, belonged to the murdered man. The Fanoway box has a button sticking in its grille."

"Button, button, who's got the button," intoned Gebhardt.

"Look here, Gebhardt," I said, "don't be frivolous. You've got to take the smallest detail with the utmost seriousness and try to connect it with any other relevant detail you may find. That's what Poggioli always does."

Gebhardt was sufficiently impressed to walk across to the mailboxes with me. He looked at the button.

"Somebody probably snapped it off as he was leaving the hotel and stuck it in the Fanoway box for safe keeping," he said.

"An odd place to stick it—in the grille," I pointed out.

"It wouldn't quite go through. Don't you see? The fellow was obviously in a hurry and didn't want to unlock the box, so he just stuck it in the grille."

"Yes, but it's wedged in from the inside," I said. "The box was apparently open. In fact I think it is still open. Why push a button into the grille from the inside?"

"Perhaps he was afraid he wouldn't see it when he came home, or would forget about it if he just laid it in the box."

"Yes, I know. But it's Mr. Fanoway's box, and he's been murdered."

"That wouldn't prevent him from trying to save a button he had lost off his coat," said Gebhardt. "I suppose if he had known about his murder he wouldn't have bothered about the button. But, happily or otherwise, he didn't know. In fact, the button itself shows that Fanoway's murder was a complete surprise to him. Wouldn't Poggioli agree to that?"

Gebhardt's satiric mockery infuriated me. But before I could think of a suitable reply the policeman who had gone into the lobby emerged and approached us.

"Who is the gentleman with you, Mr. Gebhardt," he asked. "Does his name happen to be Doctor Henry Poggioli?"

Gebhardt stared at him in astonishment. "Wouldn't Dr. Poggioli be admitted to the murdered man's apartment?" he said sharply.

"Mr. Gebhardt, my orders are to keep a record of visitors to Mr. Fanoway's apartment. If this gentleman is Dr. Poggioli—"

"This is not Poggioli," Gebhardt assured him.

"Very well, you may go inside. Ninth door to the right."

Gebhardt looked at me triumphantly. "We caught him in his own trap," he said.

"What do you mean?"

"He said he was keeping a list of the people who passed inside but he didn't demand your name. All he actually wanted to do was to follow orders and *keep Poggioli out.*"

My respect for him went up a peg. His assumption was undoubtedly true, but it would never have occurred to me. Whatever his shortcomings, he had more analytical power than I had thought.

"Then it is just as well Poggioli didn't try to come with us," I said.

"Just the opposite!" exclaimed Gebhardt. "An attempt by the police to keep Dr. Poggioli away from a murder would make a bigger scandal than the murder itself! Good Lord, what a story I've missed by his not coming with us!"

"At least it proves pretty conclusively that the murder was political," I pointed out. "Just as Poggioli said."

"Who ever doubted that?" retorted Gebhardt, seemingly quite depressed because Poggioli had not come along to be insulted.

The hallway beyond the lobby narrowed in economical fashion and presented a darkened passage through which we more or less had to grope our way. We had advanced perhaps forty feet when we almost stepped on a body lying on the runner with one arm rigidly outstretched in the shadows. I halted abruptly, a coldness encircling my scalp.

"They haven't moved him," I gasped.

"No," Gebhardt said, apparently unperturbed, "they're waiting for the homicide squad to come and make photographs." We stepped over the dead man, opened the apartment door gently and went inside.

The room had one occupant—an old woman who sat huddled in a chair looking out of a great picture window. From the misery in her eyes I knew she did not see the blue sweep of the bay, with its crowded shipping, and the towers of Tiamara beyond.

When we had advanced almost to the window and were hesitating as to how best to question her, she spoke without looking at us.

"Well . . . they killed him at last."

"Who killed him?" asked Gebhardt, instantly alert.

"Whichever one shot him," said the old woman. "I was his housekeeper."

"Who was likely to shoot him?" pressed Gebhardt.

"Any of 'em. He didn't have no friends. He was the soul of honor."

I did not find the statement difficult to believe. A man who was the soul of honor would not be likely to have too many friends in Tiamara. I saw that she was weeping and tried to comfort her.

"You have a beautiful view here," I said.

"Yes, sir. Mr. Fanoway tried to—to keep it like that."

Gebhardt leaned toward her, his eyes searching her face. "You say Mr. Fanoway kept the bay beautiful? How could a man keep our bay beautiful?"

"He—he stood up for it, sir."

"Stood up for it?"

"Yes, sir, he loved all sorts of beauty, sir. That painting there, on the wall, 'General Custer's Last Stand at the Battle of the Little Bighorn' – he rescued that out of a junk shop."

We tried to draw more important facts out of her but apparently she knew none. According to her story, she had come there that morning, and found the politician dead at his own door. She had instantly raised the alarm and had been detained pending the arrival of the homicide squad. It struck me that probably her presence in the apartment was the chief reason why the guard had been instructed to check visitors at the door. The prosecution would not want the main witness tampered with.

Solely to forestall the possible ire of his city editor Gebhardt measured the distance of the dead man from his door, from the picture window, and from the opposite side of the hallway. In short, all that battery of figures which newspaper writers fill in so voluminously when they have nothing else to print about a murder.

When he had finished this wholly unnecessary undertaking, I said, "Let's examine that mailbox again as we go out. It's the only thing here with a touch of mystery about it."

"Listen," said Gebhardt impatiently, "you fiction writers are always over-sold on mystery. What I want are the *facts*."

"Well, the button is a fact!"

"Certainly the button's a fact, but what does it prove? What possible connection can it have with this case?"

"I don't know," I said. "Poggioli always gets all the little facts, and later weaves them together in a quite wonderful manner so that the explanation seems to work out by itself."

"That may happen in this case," said Gebhardt drily. "I'm becoming convinced that otherwise it may not be worked out at all."

As we went back through the entrance I insisted on stopping for a last look at the mailboxes and the button.

"I wonder if it could have been ripped off of Mr. Fanoway's sleeve," I said.

"You didn't think to look, when you were there?"

"No, I really didn't," I admitted unhappily. "I can run back now, and—"

"Don't trouble yourself," he said. "I looked. Mr. Fanoway had all his buttons."

I glanced at the guard who was sitting slumped in a wicker chair by the small telephone stand in the vestibule. He had fallen asleep, which did not surprise me too much, for he had all the earmarks of an irresponsible, self-indulgent individual.

"Was there anything else in the Fanoway box, besides the button?" I asked in an undertone. "I should have looked. It was stupid of me not to."

Gebhardt unconsciously lowered his own voice. "Two or three letters," he said. "You can see them through the grille."

"How do you know they don't contain something that would give us a lead?" I asked.

"Do you really think they might?" he asked with a derisive inflection.

"I don't know," I said. "But anything Poggioli doesn't know, he investigates thoroughly. Remember, I told you when you asked me to come with you that I'd help you all I could."

Gebhardt scowled, and then glanced cautiously at the guard again. Then he put his finger under the little steel door and lifted it open. He took the button from where it was caught inside the door and handed it to me.

"That's *your* clue," he whispered.

"Go on, run through the letters," I urged, impatiently. "Maybe we'll find something to go with the button that's a great deal more conclusive."

Gebhardt's expression became slightly amused and slightly ironic. "The next clue we find is mine," he said, and reached in for the letters.

There were almost a dozen in the box. He riffled through them and turned to me in startled incomprehension.

"A lot of these envelopes are empty," he said.

"Which ones?" I asked.

Gebhardt re-examined the entire batch. "Business envelopes from—" Here he began going through them more carefully. "From banks, industrial corporations, brokerage companies, investment houses . . . Look here," he whispered quite seriously, "this is the month when quarterly dividends are mailed out, isn't it?"

I nodded. "Do you suppose that fact had something to do with Fanoway's death?" I asked with an odd feeling that we were groping blindly in the dark.

"I don't know," he replied. "I don't see why he should have taken out the checks and put back the envelopes. I don't see why anyone would do that."

"Maybe he took the checks to the bank and meant to pick up the envelopes when he returned to his apartment."

"But he didn't pick them up," said Gebhardt, "they're still here."

"Naturally they're still here," I said. "He got shot in the meantime, remember? He probably had already drawn the money on them."

"He couldn't get into the banks so early in the morning. It's just bank time now."

"Well, don't neglect the details," I said, "that's the way Poggioli proceeds and our problem always works itself out."

Gebhardt reached into the box again. I glanced uneasily at the guard, as I was not entirely certain that we were within the law. Just then I heard Gebhardt cry out. I looked around, and saw him standing almost at my elbow with a small .25 automatic in his hand. If he had been clasping a snake I could not have been more shocked.

"You found that pistol in the box?" I whispered.

"That's right. Did you think it was mine? Shooting you would hardly make sense—just to keep this exclusive."

"Why . . . that's the weapon that killed him!"

"Of course it is."

"Maybe it isn't," I said, reconsidering. "We'd better go back and see if he was shot with a twenty-five."

"I've already looked. The wound was quite small—not ragged and gaping. A forty-five automatic, even a thirty-eight, seldom makes that kind of wound."

"But how did it get into his mailbox?"

"I don't know," Gebhardt said.

"Listen," I whispered, "he must have committed suicide, put the pistol in his mailbox and staggered to his apartment door."

"Why would he put it in his mailbox?"

"To make a last mystery, perhaps," I said. "To get talked about one last time. A good many politicians are hams at heart."

Gebhardt stared at the little weapon. "That's not the reason," he said. "Listen. I've got to make the afternoon edition. I don't really need to know *why* the pistol's here—not for a while anyway. Just our finding a pistol will make front page copy for two or three days!"

With that he put the gun back in the box, closed the lid, and walked out to his jalopy. I was utterly at loose ends. Unless the lethal weapon's presence in the mailbox could be logically explained I could not share his elation.

When we arrived at the *Times* Building, Gebhardt jumped out with merely a nod to me and disappeared under the big electric clock over the entrance. I was simply left as so much waste material. I had every reason to feel embittered, because if it hadn't been for me he would never have looked in the mailbox in the first place. I even had to pay my own taxi fare home.

The puzzle of the gun and the empty envelopes in the mailbox continued to torment me all the way to my apartment. But then, just as I paid off the driver, the whole matter straightened itself in my mind with Poggioli-like simplicity. An insane man must have shot Fanoway. That was quite obviously the reason why I had been unable to make heads or tails of the affair.

In its essence it was irrational, perhaps, but it satisfied me intellectually, if not financially. No writer can sell an irrational murder mystery. A bewildering but strictly logical dialectic is at the very core of the mystery writer's craft. I thought enviously of Gebhardt. A newspaper reporter spontaneously welcomes any phase of life without let or hindrance. The cross-section of reality he deals with doesn't have to be logical, lyrical or laughable.

He simply waits for something to happen. He makes use of it and gets paid for his pains. I could not repress the dry, wry smile of the penurious intellectual for the pampered proletariat.

As I walked into our living-room on 23 Acacia Street, Poggioli glanced up at me, with almost genial solicitude, and asked me how I had made out with *my* political crime story.

"It was a murder, just as Gebhardt reported," I told him. "But it was not a political crime. In a strict sense, it wasn't a crime at all."

Poggioli honored my paradox by lifting his brows and reflecting for a moment. "Oh, you mean the murderer was insane."

I was struck dumb for a moment. Then my astonishment abated a little, and I shrugged off what I should have taken for granted— Poggioli's amazing perspicacity.

I was still resentful because Gebhardt had not even had the courtesy to bring me home in his car after I had presented him with an exceptionally fine newspaper story.

"Wait a moment," said Poggioli, "I hope you're not forgetting you voluntarily started out to investigate a political crime?"

"Why should I want to forget it?" I countered.

"And you found instead it was the work of a maniac?"

"That's what I found."

"Well, how can you draw any hard and fast lines between insanity and politics?"

He was being funny in his elephantine fashion and I was in no mood for it.

"Poggioli," I said, "I've had an exhausting, disappointing day and I've no intention of standing here splitting hairs with you."

He chuckled wryly.

"You are bitterly disappointed because you can't convincingly write up a murder mystery involving a crazy man?"

"That's right," I said.

"Couldn't you make it a simple blood-and-dark-drapery horror tale?"

"I am not a simple writer, Poggioli," I said with dignity. "I always adhere to a bewildering, paradoxical but intrinsically exact logic, and that is what my readers have come to expect of me."

"Mmm—mmm . . . I see. What's that you've got in your hands?"

I lowered my eyes. I hadn't known I had anything in my hands. "A button," I said.

"Really? Is it connected with your maniac somehow?"

A vague sort of apprehension went through me. I didn't want Poggioli's help with this problem. I was determined to solve it entirely on my own.

"Why do you say that?" I asked.

"Because you are nervously playing with it, passing it from one hand to the other. You are very uncertain about something. Since you are thinking about this 'maniac' of yours, he must be the reason for your agitation. You don't really believe he *is* a maniac. You're taking refuge in rationalization because you are up a stump and don't want to admit it to yourself."

I really felt miserable. I couldn't deny the truth of his statement. My first effort to go out and solve a murder case all by myself, after countless years of apprenticeship to Poggioli, had ended in complete failure. I would never in the world be an autonomous mystery story writer. I would always have to depend on somebody else.

"Precisely where did you get the button?" asked Poggioli.

"Out of a mailbox," I said flatly.

"Out of the mailbox of the murdered man!" demanded the criminologist.

He seemed just about to unravel the mystery and I felt a completely irrational objection to his doing so.

"Let me see the button," said Poggioli.

I handed it to him, still in the grip of a senseless reluctance. He took it and examined it painstakingly, turning it over and over on his palm. I wondered if he would suddenly start questioning me about the empty envelopes and the gun.

I was afraid, from just one button, that Poggioli would deduce more about the crime than I had been able to discover by examining the mailbox, the corpse, the old woman and the whole apartment building. He did not, however, build a structure of deductive logic linking the button with the envelopes and the gun.

"This is a sleeve button," he said.

"Is it?"

"Yes. It was torn off a very expensive suit of Scottish wool tailored in London."

Somehow I was glad his line of thought appeared to be veering away from the murder.

"The man who wore this," he continued, "was a very expensive, but conservative dresser. A bit more ostentatious than a banker, but more subdued than a salesman. It could easily come from the coat of a very dignified politician."

"Where did you say the button came from?" I asked.

"Off his sleeve."

I thought I saw a gap in Poggioli's logic.

"It's odd," I said, "that such a well-dressed man should allow a sleeve button to work loose and fall off."

"It didn't work loose and fall off," said Poggioli. "It was snapped off with great force. The threads in it are torn—not worn."

That threw my entire theory out of focus. I had assumed that Fanoway had dropped one of his buttons, picked it up, and put it in his mailbox, meaning to retrieve it when he returned home.

Poggioli seemed to read my thoughts. "The murdered man, Fanoway— Was he a careful dresser, or did you forget to observe that point?"

"No, he wore very ordinary clothes," I said.

"Then he hadn't lost a coat sleeve button?"

"Gebhardt made sure of that when he examined the corpse."

"I'm glad Gebhardt took the trouble to look, although I was virtually certain the button didn't belong to Fanoway."

"Poggioli," I ejaculated, "how can you be so sure?"

"Because the Bayview Apartments are very old-fashioned and a man who lived there wouldn't be likely to wear modish, imported English clothes. You didn't notice anything else of importance, did you?"

"Poggioli," I said, "I'm nervous and overwrought now. I'm going to my room to lie down. When I've rested and feel capable of taking up the problem, I really want you to help me."

He made a gesture of acquiescence. "Oh, all right. It may not be much of a mystery anyway. Politicians more or less run true to form." And he put the button in his pocket.

I went to my room disappointed and disgusted with myself. The simplicity with which Poggioli had demonstrated that the button could have had no connection with Fanoway irked me. Why had I failed to think of so obvious an explanation?

I tardily reconstructed my own theory. A well-dressed man had somehow snapped off a button. For safe keeping he had picked it up and put it in Fanoway's box. He had pushed it in the grille from the inside so it would be clearly visible and not fall out. He did so with the intention of returning and retrieving it again later. The only reason he used Fanoway's box was because it was unlocked, and hence highly convenient.

The painful part to me was that the plot, the dramatic involution that is absolutely essential to a good mystery story, did not exist. Poggioli had wiped it all out with a mere glance at the button.

I toyed with the idea of starting from scratch and inventing a completely new story, one in which a succession of surprises *did* hang together in an ever-mounting crescendo until it culminated in an unforgettable climax. My mental perturbation became so great that I lost consciousness.

I suppose Poggioli in his disparaging way would have said that my brain stopped functioning and I went to sleep. In any event, I did not wake up all that afternoon, and indeed not until almost nine o'clock the following morning.

I might well have continued on as one of the Seven Sleepers, if it had not been for Poggioli shaking me sharply awake.

"Do you know anything about this?" he demanded rattling a paper in front of my face.

"About what?" I asked, struggling dazedly to sit up.

He smacked the paper with the back of his fingers, and I read the streamer headlines:

Mailbox Thief Murders City Councilman Fanoway.
Killer, Jake Flippo, Hides Pistol in Fanoway's Letter Box.
Evidence indicates slain councilman surprised thief looting box when Flippo shot him.
Slayer had removed dividend checks, leaving only empty envelopes. Stolen checks later found on Flippo's person.

Bill Gebhardt, Times *reporter, summoned police and developed Flippo's fingerprints on pistol. Flippo arrested in afternoon of day he committed crime. Admits he stole checks but denies murder. Trial at City Criminal Court at twelve o'clock.*

When I read Gebhardt's masterly summary of the mystery, done in such short crisp paragraphs, my admiration for the fellow mounted.

"Poggioli," I exclaimed excitedly, "that's a marvelous solution to the mystery. Gebhardt is just about as good as you are!" I couldn't have said a more unfortunate thing.

Poggioli cried angrily: "Solution to the mystery! Haven't you enough elementary discernment to see that the 'solution' was planned?"

"You mean— Gebhardt planned it?"

"Certainly not. The man who killed Fanoway planned it. He wanted the police to make this discovery and arrest some mail thief, or other. The thief just happened to be Flippo!"

That *really* startled me.

"Then Flippo *didn't* kill Fanoway—even though his fingerprints were on the gun?"

"Certainly not," Poggioli replied. "Flippo's innocent, I'm telling you. I suppose you knew about that pistol in the mailbox all this time?"

"Yes, I did," I told him.

"Imagine that! The pistol *explains* the button. You've caused me to spend a sleepless night trying to solve the mystery of the button!"

"Oh, that," I said. "I've an explanation for that. Some well-dressed man simply picked the button up when it snapped off his sleeve and put it in the mailbox until he could return for it on his way home from work. He used Fanoway's box because it just happened to be open. I'm convinced now that the button has nothing to do with the murder."

Poggioli looked at me both pityingly, and with undisguised contempt. "The button and the pistol form the plainest possible signposts pointing out the murderer. The question now is—simply to pick him out."

"You're *sure* it wasn't Flippo?" I stammered.

Poggioli made a hopeless gesture. "A mailbox thief kill Fanoway! Did you ever hear of a sneak thief carrying a gun and shooting anybody? If a man has spirit enough to kill, he has spirit enough to go in for big hauls. He wouldn't stoop to filching checks from a mailbox and putting their envelopes back."

I hated to give up Gebhardt's idea. I made a desperate, last try. "Couldn't there possibly be a many-sided genius of a criminal who could do both?"

Poggioli came to a pause, staring hard at me. "Did you and Gebhardt think to go through every part of the dead man's apartment, while you were there?"

"Yes, we did. The guard stopped us and asked if I were you. When we replied in the negative he let us go on."

Poggioli laughed briefly. "How transparent. The whole plot is childishly simple. But the question still remains, which one of them did it."

I realized Gebhardt's fine solution was being demolished brick by brick. "That's usually the question in a murder mystery isn't it . . . who did it?" I said.

Poggioli paid no attention to this although my question was logical.

"In the dead man's apartment," Poggioli went on, "what did you find out?"

I tried hard to remember. "That Fanoway was a lover of beauty," I said, after a moment's thought.

"And how did you discover that?" Poggioli asked.

"From the original painting on his wall of 'The Death of General Custer at the Battle of the Little Bighorn,'" I told him.

Poggioli stared at me. "You mean the actual original of all those prints we used to see in saloons?"

"That's right. At least, it didn't look like a reproduction."

"How did anyone come to mention beauty in connection with that painting."

"The elderly housekeeper, who was sitting in the apartment, mentioned it," I told him.

"Then *you* must have said something about beauty. I'm sure that in the midst of the excitement and horror of a murder the old woman didn't begin lecturing about the pictures on the wall."

"Well, as I recall it, she said that Mr. Fanoway was a great lover of beauty, and then she pointed out that particular picture."

Poggioli became hopeless. "But exactly how and why did beauty come up in the first place?" he pleaded.

It is extremely difficult to recall conversations backwards. It's like trying to repeat the alphabet in reverse.

"Oh, yes," I said, after a pause. "To comfort her I mentioned that Mr. Fanoway had a very beautiful view out of his window."

"Then what? Try to remember everything that was said."

"Then the old woman remarked that Mr. Fanoway tried to keep it like that."

"She remarked what?" Poggioli asked.

"That Mr. Fanoway tried to keep the bay looking beautiful. Then Gebhardt said—"

"Didn't that strike you as being an amazing and pregnant statement?" he interrupted. "Didn't it?"

"Why-y . . . no. It didn't strike me that way particularly. I remember Gebhardt did ask her how Fanoway could keep the bay beautiful, and the old woman replied that he stood up for it. Gebhardt asked how a man could stand up for the beauty of a bay. The old woman replied that he loved and protected all sorts of beauty, and then she showed us the 'Death of General Custer' which he'd rescued from a junk shop."

"And you two dropped the subject of Fanoway's defense of the beauty of the bay?"

The harshness in Poggioli's voice made me feel a little incompetent.

"I'm afraid we did. From there on out we discussed the 'Death of General Custer.'"

Poggioli drew a long breath. "It's at least helpful to know the motive of the murder. Now I won't have to depend entirely upon this button to identify the criminal."

My head, figuratively speaking, went round and round. Here I was, at this late date, off on a completely new and unknown tangent after Gebhardt really had nailed down an excellent solution. I realized with the darkest forebodings that the new track might throw me off entirely.

Poggioli would tell me nothing further. He was too thoroughly disgusted with me and Gebhardt and when I asked him what he was going to do he said only that he would attend Flippo's trial at twelve o'clock and liberate an innocent thief.

Beyond that, he apparently meant to do nothing. In despair I watched him turn back to our morning *Times* and begin reading it to try to find some crime of the day of sufficient interest to hold his attention.

I must admit I was utterly torn up over his attitude, for I am a conscientious writer. If I do not believe my story to be solidly grounded in a bedrock of verifiable facts, I simply cannot write it at all. I resolved to go to the prisoner in the city jail, interview him and see what he had to say about the crime.

Of course, I expected him to stoutly protest his innocence but I hoped, with my mind trained in psychological analysis by long association with Poggioli, that I would be able to winnow out the truth from whatever he might choose to tell me.

When—a half hour after I'd made my decision—I was admitted to Flippo's cell in the top story of Tiamara's skyscraper jail, the prisoner naturally did deny his guilt, emphatically. He was a smallish, dried-up little man and looked pathetic sitting on the edge of his bunk.

I talked to him outside his bars. I told him that I was a professional writer and would like to know, man to man, why he had shot Mark Fanoway.

I put it to him with extreme candor, hoping he would slip into a confession unthinkingly, in an effort to boast, and justify himself.

He must have seen through me because he protested at once that he not only hadn't murdered Mr. Fanoway, but had never even met the man. How could I think him guilty?

"I know," I pointed out. "But if you were robbing his mailbox and he came out and caught you in the act, you'd probably murder him without an introduction."

His defense was precisely what Poggioli had already indicated to me that it would be. "Me shoot a patron!" he said. "I am a mailbox operator. I never carried a gun in my life, as that would automatically up my sentence to the penitentiary. I'd as soon carry a snake in my pocket.

"Besides that, I do no man any harm, even in my work. Why should I put a sin on my conscience by murder? When I'm caught, and occasionally I am caught, I talk my way out. I say, 'Oh, I'm sorry. I'm in the wrong box.'"

I got interested in the fellow. He seemed a very honest person. "Look here," I said, "you say you do no man any harm. But you go through his mail, take out his checks and cash them?"

"That annoys him, yes," admitted Mr. Flippo, "but it doesn't harm him financially. He can have his check duplicated by writing to the company that issues it. I cash them usually in some department store during the rush hour. When my signature comes back to the company as forged, they lose nothing because they are insured against bad checks. When the check finally turns up at the insurance office and gets paid off, they lose nothing because they expect that in their business.

"As insurance men, they know approximately how many bad checks they will have to pay off each year and arrange their insurance rates to make a profit on the year's transactions. I'm simply a cog in the commercial machinery of our nation. If I, and everybody like me should go on a strike, it would throw thousands of men out of employment."

I saw Mr. Flippo was to all intents and purposes a conventional businessman. But there was a mystery about him.

"Mr. Flippo," I said, "how do you account for that gun in Fanoway's mailbox with your fingerprints on it?"

The mailbox operator wet his lips. "That gun, sir, was in the box when I opened it. I was getting out the small checks, opening the envelopes and picking them out. I never take a check for over a hundred dollars, for that would be grand larceny and get me into serious trouble. That was all I was doing, going on with my regular business, harming nobody, when I reached in and touched this gun.

"It nearly scared me to death. I thought, *This is a trap!* But then I thought again, how could it be a trap? I figured some night watchman had stashed his gun in the mailbox and would pick it up again when he went to work in the evening. The only reason in the world my fingerprints are on that gun is because I had to pull it out before I saw what it was."

Well, Gebhardt's story was thoroughly punctured, just as I feared it would be. Now I had no ending at all unless I could worm the truth out of Poggioli and I knew he wouldn't tell me after I had told him that Gebhardt was as good a criminologist as he was. I felt sorry for myself and sorry for Flippo who had got arrested in his somewhat unconventional trade.

I said to him, "Well, Mr. Flippo, you'll come out all right."

"What makes you say that?" he asked in surprise.

"Did you ever hear of Dr. Henry Poggioli who used to lecture on criminology at the Ohio State University?"

"Who hasn't sir? I have studied many of his cases in the magazines—always with an eye to improving my own style."

"I'm the man who writes up the accounts of his cases," I said.

Mr. Flippo was overcome. "Imagine me talking to such a man . . . and in a place like this." He made a gesture of apology for his condition, got up, came over and shook hands with me through the bars.

"Why do you say I'll come out all right?" he asked gripping my hand.

"Because I heard Poggioli say that you had not done this murder,

that your psychology was not the homicidal type and that he was going
to see to it that you got out of the murder charge."

"Praise be," said Flippo, "this comes of leading a proper life. Help
comes to you in the most unexpected ways."

Just a few minutes later the jailer came to take Flippo to the
criminal court on the sixth floor. I went along with them.

It turned out that the case was up by the time we reached the court
room. Several councilmen were in court to see that the murderer of their
colleague got condign punishment.

Poggioli moved among them looking from one to the other. I
hadn't the faintest idea what he was looking for. Finally he nodded to
one of them to follow him into the anteroom. I went with them—hoping,
but not really expecting to hear something that would help me on my
story.

Poggioli introduced himself and said, "You are Councilman
Collyman? I hope you'll excuse me for breaking in like this, but you're in
the real estate business?" Collyman said he was. Poggioli went on, "I'm
looking for a water-front building lot. I wondered if you had any?"

Mr. Collyman considered. "How soon do you want this lot, Mr.
Poggioli?"

"No particular date. I just want one eventually."

"Mmm-mmm. Now my company is about to make a development
in the bay, Mr. Poggioli, a small real estate development, a fill-in of
about five hundred acres. It won't take us too long. We'll get the
authorization when our board meets next Thursday afternoon."

"Very good, I'll wait for you," Poggioli promised. "You and your
company are fortunate in being able to add these improvements to our
city."

"I think so, too," Collyman replied. "Of course there was some
opposition to it. Aesthetics before utility, you know. But that's not
American. Well, it's overcome now."

"Very good. By the way Mr. Collyman, you have political influence
here in Tiamara?"

"Mmm-mmm . . . some."

"I wondered if you would help me nolle pros the murder charge
against the little mailbox thief up before the court?"

"I help?"

"Yes, if you want to see justice done."

"But this man Flippo murdered my colleague, Mark Fanoway! If
ever a man deserved to hang—"

Poggioli held up a hand. "No, this man didn't. The actual murderer
is still at large, Mr. Collyman, and who he is is a complete mystery. And
he will never be discovered. He executed one of the most clever crimes I
have ever known.

"He put on gloves, shot Fanoway, and hid his pistol in Fanoway's
mailbox. That alone is clever. But he didn't stop there. This unknown

man knew it was the end of the financial quarter of the year when mailboxes were full of dividend checks.

"He reasoned correctly that some mailbox thief would come around and steal these checks. If no thief came the mystery of the gun in the box was still insoluble. But if a thief did appear and touch the gun, then his fingerprints, don't you see, would be on the gun, and the thief convicted for murder."

"Mr. Poggioli, that's the most amazing theory I ever . . ."

"Isn't it? And the most brilliant. But unfortunately, one little accident left . . . I won't say a clue, but a sign of the real murderer. When he pushed his pistol into the box, a button from his sleeve hung in the grille on the inside of the lock box door and snapped off. I have it with me."

Poggioli showed the button, then went on. "You see in the murderer's excitement, he never felt his button hang and jerk off. It couldn't be Flippo's button. It came off of an imported English suit made of Scottish wool.

"Flippo never wore such clothes as that in his life. So it wasn't Flippo. That little man merely touched the pistol, then fled—with his checks, of course." Poggioli smiled at an inner vision of the little man fleeing with the checks. "Now I am sure that you, as a public servant, will be glad to quash the murder charge against an innocent man and let him go. As to who did it, that, no doubt, will never be known."

Mr. Collyman moistened his lips. "If what you say is true, Mr. Poggioli, I will do my duty as a councilman, of course."

"Thank you, I knew you would. I don't know this Flippo. I never met him, I just wanted abstract justice done."

As I followed Poggioli out into the hallway toward the elevator bank I asked him how he had picked out Collyman. Four of the board were real estate men and it could have been anyone of them, I thought.

"Easily enough," said Poggioli. "Collyman wore an English suit, made of Scottish wool, but it had a new set of American buttons on its sleeves."

A CATALOGUE OF SELECTED DOVER BOOKS
IN ALL FIELDS OF INTEREST

AMERICA'S OLD MASTERS, James T. Flexner. Four men emerged unexpectedly from provincial 18th century America to leadership in European art: Benjamin West, J. S. Copley, C. R. Peale, Gilbert Stuart. Brilliant coverage of lives and contributions. Revised, 1967 edition. 69 plates. 365pp. of text.

21806-6 Paperbound $3.00

FIRST FLOWERS OF OUR WILDERNESS: AMERICAN PAINTING, THE COLONIAL PERIOD, James T. Flexner. Painters, and regional painting traditions from earliest Colonial times up to the emergence of Copley, West and Peale Sr., Foster, Gustavus Hesselius, Feke, John Smibert and many anonymous painters in the primitive manner. Engaging presentation, with 162 illustrations. xxii + 368pp.

22180-6 Paperbound $3.50

THE LIGHT OF DISTANT SKIES: AMERICAN PAINTING, 1760-1835, James T. Flexner. The great generation of early American painters goes to Europe to learn and to teach: West, Copley, Gilbert Stuart and others. Allston, Trumbull, Morse; also contemporary American painters—primitives, derivatives, academics—who remained in America. 102 illustrations. xiii + 306pp.

22179-2 Paperbound $3.50

A HISTORY OF THE RISE AND PROGRESS OF THE ARTS OF DESIGN IN THE UNITED STATES, William Dunlap. Much the richest mine of information on early American painters, sculptors, architects, engravers, miniaturists, etc. The only source of information for scores of artists, the major primary source for many others. Unabridged reprint of rare original 1834 edition, with new introduction by James T. Flexner, and 394 new illustrations. Edited by Rita Weiss. 6⅝ x 9⅝.

21695-0, 21696-9, 21697-7 Three volumes, Paperbound $15.00

EPOCHS OF CHINESE AND JAPANESE ART, Ernest F. Fenollosa. From primitive Chinese art to the 20th century, thorough history, explanation of every important art period and form, including Japanese woodcuts; main stress on China and Japan, but Tibet, Korea also included. Still unexcelled for its detailed, rich coverage of cultural background, aesthetic elements, diffusion studies, particularly of the historical period. 2nd, 1913 edition. 242 illustrations. lii + 439pp. of text.

20364-6, 20365-4 Two volumes, Paperbound $6.00

THE GENTLE ART OF MAKING ENEMIES, James A. M. Whistler. Greatest wit of his day deflates Oscar Wilde, Ruskin, Swinburne; strikes back at inane critics, exhibitions, art journalism; aesthetics of impressionist revolution in most striking form. Highly readable classic by great painter. Reproduction of edition designed by Whistler. Introduction by Alfred Werner. xxxvi + 334pp.

21875-9 Paperbound $3.00

A CATALOGUE OF SELECTED DOVER BOOKS
IN ALL FIELDS OF INTEREST

VISUAL ILLUSIONS: THEIR CAUSES, CHARACTERISTICS, AND APPLICATIONS, Matthew Luckiesh. Thorough description and discussion of optical illusion, geometric and perspective, particularly; size and shape distortions, illusions of color, of motion; natural illusions; use of illusion in art and magic, industry, etc. Most useful today with op art, also for classical art. Scores of effects illustrated. Introduction by William H. Ittleson. 100 illustrations. xxi + 252pp.
21530-X Paperbound $2.00

A HANDBOOK OF ANATOMY FOR ART STUDENTS, Arthur Thomson. Thorough, virtually exhaustive coverage of skeletal structure, musculature, etc. Full text, supplemented by anatomical diagrams and drawings and by photographs of undraped figures. Unique in its comparison of male and female forms, pointing out differences of contour, texture, form. 211 figures, 40 drawings, 86 photographs. xx + 459pp. 5⅜ x 8⅜.
21163-0 Paperbound $3.50

150 MASTERPIECES OF DRAWING, Selected by Anthony Toney. Full page reproductions of drawings from the early 16th to the end of the 18th century, all beautifully reproduced: Rembrandt, Michelangelo, Dürer, Fragonard, Urs, Graf, Wouwerman, many others. First-rate browsing book, model book for artists. xviii + 150pp. 8⅜ x 11¼.
21032-4 Paperbound $3.50

THE LATER WORK OF AUBREY BEARDSLEY, Aubrey Beardsley. Exotic, erotic, ironic masterpieces in full maturity: Comedy Ballet, Venus and Tannhauser, Pierrot, Lysistrata, Rape of the Lock, Savoy material, Ali Baba, Volpone, etc. This material revolutionized the art world, and is still powerful, fresh, brilliant. With The Early Work, all Beardsley's finest work. 174 plates, 2 in color. xiv + 176pp. 8⅛ x 11.
21817-1 Paperbound $3.75

DRAWINGS OF REMBRANDT, Rembrandt van Rijn. Complete reproduction of fabulously rare edition by Lippmann and Hofstede de Groot, completely reedited, updated, improved by Prof. Seymour Slive, Fogg Museum. Portraits, Biblical sketches, landscapes, Oriental types, nudes, episodes from classical mythology—All Rembrandt's fertile genius. Also selection of drawings by his pupils and followers. "Stunning volumes," Saturday Review. 550 illustrations. lxxviii + 552pp. 9⅛ x 12¼.
21485-0, 21486-9 Two volumes, Paperbound $10.00

THE DISASTERS OF WAR, Francisco Goya. One of the masterpieces of Western civilization—83 etchings that record Goya's shattering, bitter reaction to the Napoleonic war that swept through Spain after the insurrection of 1808 and to war in general. Reprint of the first edition, with three additional plates from Boston's Museum of Fine Arts. All plates facsimile size. Introduction by Philip Hofer, Fogg Museum. v + 97pp. 9⅜ x 8¼.
21872-4 Paperbound $2.50

GRAPHIC WORKS OF ODILON REDON. Largest collection of Redon's graphic works ever assembled: 172 lithographs, 28 etchings and engravings, 9 drawings. These include some of his most famous works. All the plates from Odilon Redon: oeuvre graphique complet, plus additional plates. New introduction and caption translations by Alfred Werner. 209 illustrations. xxvii + 209pp. 9⅛ x 12¼.
21966-8 Paperbound $5.00

DESIGN BY ACCIDENT; A BOOK OF "ACCIDENTAL EFFECTS" FOR ARTISTS AND DESIGNERS, James F. O'Brien. Create your own unique, striking, imaginative effects by "controlled accident" interaction of materials: paints and lacquers, oil and water based paints, splatter, crackling materials, shatter, similar items. Everything you do will be different; first book on this limitless art, so useful to both fine artist and commercial artist. Full instructions. 192 plates showing "accidents," 8 in color. viii + 215pp. 8⅜ x 11¼.   21942-9 Paperbound $3.75

THE BOOK OF SIGNS, Rudolf Koch. Famed German type designer draws 493 beautiful symbols: religious, mystical, alchemical, imperial, property marks, runes, etc. Remarkable fusion of traditional and modern. Good for suggestions of timelessness, smartness, modernity. Text. vi + 104pp. 6⅛ x 9¼.
                                                     20162-7 Paperbound $1.25

HISTORY OF INDIAN AND INDONESIAN ART, Ananda K. Coomaraswamy. An unabridged republication of one of the finest books by a great scholar in Eastern art. Rich in descriptive material, history, social backgrounds; Sunga reliefs, Rajput paintings, Gupta temples, Burmese frescoes, textiles, jewelry, sculpture, etc. 400 photos. viii + 423pp. 6⅜ x 9¾.   21436-2 Paperbound $5.00

PRIMITIVE ART, Franz Boas. America's foremost anthropologist surveys textiles, ceramics, woodcarving, basketry, metalwork, etc.; patterns, technology, creation of symbols, style origins. All areas of world, but very full on Northwest Coast Indians. More than 350 illustrations of baskets, boxes, totem poles, weapons, etc. 378 pp.
                                                     20025-6 Paperbound $3.00

THE GENTLEMAN AND CABINET MAKER'S DIRECTOR, Thomas Chippendale. Full reprint (third edition, 1762) of most influential furniture book of all time, by master cabinetmaker. 200 plates, illustrating chairs, sofas, mirrors, tables, cabinets, plus 24 photographs of surviving pieces. Biographical introduction by N. Bienenstock. vi + 249pp. 9⅞ x 12¾.   21601-2 Paperbound $4.00

AMERICAN ANTIQUE FURNITURE, Edgar G. Miller, Jr. The basic coverage of all American furniture before 1840. Individual chapters cover type of furniture—clocks, tables, sideboards, etc.—chronologically, with inexhaustible wealth of early American collectors. Introduction by H. E. Keyes. vi + 1106pp. 7⅞ x 10¾.
                  21599-7, 21600-4 Two volumes, Paperbound $11.00

PENNSYLVANIA DUTCH AMERICAN FOLK ART, Henry J. Kauffman. 279 photos, 28 drawings of tulipware, Fraktur script, painted tinware, toys, flowered furniture, quilts, samplers, hex signs, house interiors, etc. Full descriptive text. Excellent for tourist, rewarding for designer, collector. Map. 146pp. 7⅞ x 10¾.
                                                     21205-X Paperbound $2.50

EARLY NEW ENGLAND GRAVESTONE RUBBINGS, Edmund V. Gillon, Jr. 43 photographs, 226 carefully reproduced rubbings show heavily symbolic, sometimes macabre early gravestones, up to early 19th century. Remarkable early American primitive art, occasionally strikingly beautiful; always powerful. Text. xxvi + 207pp. 8⅜ x 11¼.   21380-3 Paperbound $3.50

ALPHABETS AND ORNAMENTS, Ernst Lehner. Well-known pictorial source for decorative alphabets, script examples, cartouches, frames, decorative title pages, calligraphic initials, borders, similar material. 14th to 19th century, mostly European. Useful in almost any graphic arts designing, varied styles. 750 illustrations. 256pp. 7 x 10. 21905-4 Paperbound $4.00

PAINTING: A CREATIVE APPROACH, Norman Colquhoun. For the beginner simple guide provides an instructive approach to painting: major stumbling blocks for beginner; overcoming them, technical points; paints and pigments; oil painting; watercolor and other media and color. New section on "plastic" paints. Glossary. Formerly *Paint Your Own Pictures.* 221pp. 22000-1 Paperbound $1.75

THE ENJOYMENT AND USE OF COLOR, Walter Sargent. Explanation of the relations between colors themselves and between colors in nature and art, including hundreds of little-known facts about color values, intensities, effects of high and low illumination, complementary colors. Many practical hints for painters, references to great masters. 7 color plates, 29 illustrations. x + 274pp. 20944-X Paperbound $2.75

THE NOTEBOOKS OF LEONARDO DA VINCI, compiled and edited by Jean Paul Richter. 1566 extracts from original manuscripts reveal the full range of Leonardo's versatile genius: all his writings on painting, sculpture, architecture, anatomy, astronomy, geography, topography, physiology, mining, music, etc., in both Italian and English, with 186 plates of manuscript pages and more than 500 additional drawings. Includes studies for the Last Supper, the lost Sforza monument, and other works. Total of xlvii + 866pp. 7⅞ x 10¾. 22572-0, 22573-9 Two volumes, Paperbound $11.00

MONTGOMERY WARD CATALOGUE OF 1895. Tea gowns, yards of flannel and pillow-case lace, stereoscopes, books of gospel hymns, the New Improved Singer Sewing Machine, side saddles, milk skimmers, straight-edged razors, high-button shoes, spittoons, and on and on . . . listing some 25,000 items, practically all illustrated. Essential to the shoppers of the 1890's, it is our truest record of the spirit of the period. Unaltered reprint of Issue No. 57, Spring and Summer 1895. Introduction by Boris Emmet. Innumerable illustrations. xiii + 624pp. 8½ x 11⅝. 22377-9 Paperbound $6.95

THE CRYSTAL PALACE EXHIBITION ILLUSTRATED CATALOGUE (LONDON, 1851). One of the wonders of the modern world—the Crystal Palace Exhibition in which all the nations of the civilized world exhibited their achievements in the arts and sciences—presented in an equally important illustrated catalogue. More than 1700 items pictured with accompanying text—ceramics, textiles, cast-iron work, carpets, pianos, sleds, razors, wall-papers, billiard tables, beehives, silverware and hundreds of other artifacts—represent the focal point of Victorian culture in the Western World. Probably the largest collection of Victorian decorative art ever assembled—indispensable for antiquarians and designers. Unabridged republication of the Art-Journal Catalogue of the Great Exhibition of 1851, with all terminal essays. New introduction by John Gloag, F.S.A. xxxiv + 426pp. 9 x 12. 22503-8 Paperbound $5.00

A HISTORY OF COSTUME, Carl Köhler. Definitive history, based on surviving pieces of clothing primarily, and paintings, statues, etc. secondarily. Highly readable text, supplemented by 594 illustrations of costumes of the ancient Mediterranean peoples, Greece and Rome, the Teutonic prehistoric period; costumes of the Middle Ages, Renaissance, Baroque, 18th and 19th centuries. Clear, measured patterns are provided for many clothing articles. Approach is practical throughout. Enlarged by Emma von Sichart. 464pp. 21030-8 Paperbound $3.50.

ORIENTAL RUGS, ANTIQUE AND MODERN, Walter A. Hawley. A complete and authoritative treatise on the Oriental rug—where they are made, by whom and how, designs and symbols, characteristics in detail of the six major groups, how to distinguish them and how to buy them. Detailed technical data is provided on periods, weaves, warps, wefts, textures, sides, ends and knots, although no technical background is required for an understanding. 11 color plates, 80 halftones, 4 maps. vi + 320pp. 6⅛ x 9⅛. 22366-3 Paperbound $5.00

TEN BOOKS ON ARCHITECTURE, Vitruvius. By any standards the most important book on architecture ever written. Early Roman discussion of aesthetics of building, construction methods, orders, sites, and every other aspect of architecture has inspired, instructed architecture for about 2,000 years. Stands behind Palladio, Michelangelo, Bramante, Wren, countless others. Definitive Morris H. Morgan translation. 68 illustrations. xii + 331pp. 20645-9 Paperbound $3.00

THE FOUR BOOKS OF ARCHITECTURE, Andrea Palladio. Translated into every major Western European language in the two centuries following its publication in 1570, this has been one of the most influential books in the history of architecture. Complete reprint of the 1738 Isaac Ware edition. New introduction by Adolf Placzek, Columbia Univ. 216 plates. xxii + 110pp. of text. 9½ x 12¾. 21308-0 Clothbound $12.50

STICKS AND STONES: A STUDY OF AMERICAN ARCHITECTURE AND CIVILIZATION, Lewis Mumford.One of the great classics of American cultural history. American architecture from the medieval-inspired earliest forms to the early 20th century; evolution of structure and style, and reciprocal influences on environment. 21 photographic illustrations. 238pp. 20202-X Paperbound $2.00

THE AMERICAN BUILDER'S COMPANION, Asher Benjamin. The most widely used early 19th century architectural style and source book, for colonial up into Greek Revival periods. Extensive development of geometry of carpentering, construction of sashes, frames, doors, stairs; plans and elevations of domestic and other buildings. Hundreds of thousands of houses were built according to this book, now invaluable to historians, architects, restorers, etc. 1827 edition. 59 plates. 114pp. 7⅞ x 10¾. 22236-5 Paperbound $3.50

DUTCH HOUSES IN THE HUDSON VALLEY BEFORE 1776, Helen Wilkinson Reynolds. The standard survey of the Dutch colonial house and outbuildings, with constructional features, decoration, and local history associated with individual homesteads. Introduction by Franklin D. Roosevelt. Map. 150 illustrations. 469pp. 6⅝ x 9¼. 21469-9 Paperbound $5.00

THE ARCHITECTURE OF COUNTRY HOUSES, Andrew J. Downing. Together with Vaux's *Villas and Cottages* this is the basic book for Hudson River Gothic architecture of the middle Victorian period. Full, sound discussions of general aspects of housing, architecture, style, decoration, furnishing, together with scores of detailed house plans, illustrations of specific buildings, accompanied by full text. Perhaps the most influential single American architectural book. 1850 edition. Introduction by J. Stewart Johnson. 321 figures, 34 architectural designs. xvi + 560pp.

22003-6 Paperbound $4.00

LOST EXAMPLES OF COLONIAL ARCHITECTURE, John Mead Howells. Full-page photographs of buildings that have disappeared or been so altered as to be denatured, including many designed by major early American architects. 245 plates. xvii + 248pp. 7⅞ x 10¾.

21143-6 Paperbound $3.50

DOMESTIC ARCHITECTURE OF THE AMERICAN COLONIES AND OF THE EARLY REPUBLIC, Fiske Kimball. Foremost architect and restorer of Williamsburg and Monticello covers nearly 200 homes between 1620-1825. Architectural details, construction, style features, special fixtures, floor plans, etc. Generally considered finest work in its area. 219 illustrations of houses, doorways, windows, capital mantels. xx + 314pp. 7⅞ x 10¾.

21743-4 Paperbound $4.00

EARLY AMERICAN ROOMS: 1650-1858, edited by Russell Hawes Kettell. Tour of 12 rooms, each representative of a different era in American history and each furnished, decorated, designed and occupied in the style of the era. 72 plans and elevations, 8-page color section, etc., show fabrics, wall papers, arrangements, etc. Full descriptive text. xvii + 200pp. of text. 8⅜ x 11¼.

21633-0 Paperbound $5.00

THE FITZWILLIAM VIRGINAL BOOK, edited by J. Fuller Maitland and W. B. Squire. Full modern printing of famous early 17th-century ms. volume of 300 works by Morley, Byrd, Bull, Gibbons, etc. For piano or other modern keyboard instrument; easy to read format. xxxvi + 938pp. 8⅜ x 11.

21068-5, 21069-3 Two volumes, Paperbound $10.00

KEYBOARD MUSIC, Johann Sebastian Bach. Bach Gesellschaft edition. A rich selection of Bach's masterpieces for the harpsichord: the six English Suites, six French Suites, the six Partitas (Clavierübung part I), the Goldberg Variations (Clavierübung part IV), the fifteen Two-Part Inventions and the fifteen Three-Part Sinfonias. Clearly reproduced on large sheets with ample margins; eminently playable. vi + 312pp. 8⅛ x 11.

22360-4 Paperbound $5.00

THE MUSIC OF BACH: AN INTRODUCTION, Charles Sanford Terry. A fine, nontechnical introduction to Bach's music, both instrumental and vocal. Covers organ music, chamber music, passion music, other types. Analyzes themes, developments, innovations. x + 114pp.

21075-8 Paperbound $1.50

BEETHOVEN AND HIS NINE SYMPHONIES, Sir George Grove. Noted British musicologist provides best history, analysis, commentary on symphonies. Very thorough, rigorously accurate; necessary to both advanced student and amateur music lover. 436 musical passages. vii + 407 pp.

20334-4 Paperbound $2.75

JOHANN SEBASTIAN BACH, Philipp Spitta. One of the great classics of musicology, this definitive analysis of Bach's music (and life) has never been surpassed. Lucid, nontechnical analyses of hundreds of pieces (30 pages devoted to St. Matthew Passion, 26 to B Minor Mass). Also includes major analysis of 18th-century music. 450 musical examples. 40-page musical supplement. Total of xx + 1799pp.
(EUK) 22278-0, 22279-9 Two volumes, Clothbound $17.50

MOZART AND HIS PIANO CONCERTOS, Cuthbert Girdlestone. The only full-length study of an important area of Mozart's creativity. Provides detailed analyses of all 23 concertos, traces inspirational sources. 417 musical examples. Second edition. 509pp.
21271-8 Paperbound $3.50

THE PERFECT WAGNERITE: A COMMENTARY ON THE NIBLUNG'S RING, George Bernard Shaw. Brilliant and still relevant criticism in remarkable essays on Wagner's Ring cycle, Shaw's ideas on political and social ideology behind the plots, role of Leitmotifs, vocal requisites, etc. Prefaces. xxi + 136pp.
(USO) 21707-8 Paperbound $1.75

DON GIOVANNI, W. A. Mozart. Complete libretto, modern English translation; biographies of composer and librettist; accounts of early performances and critical reaction. Lavishly illustrated. All the material you need to understand and appreciate this great work. Dover Opera Guide and Libretto Series; translated and introduced by Ellen Bleiler. 92 illustrations. 209pp.
21134-7 Paperbound $2.00

BASIC ELECTRICITY, U. S. Bureau of Naval Personel. Originally a training course, best non-technical coverage of basic theory of electricity and its applications. Fundamental concepts, batteries, circuits, conductors and wiring techniques, AC and DC, inductance and capacitance, generators, motors, transformers, magnetic amplifiers, synchros, servomechanisms, etc. Also covers blue-prints, electrical diagrams, etc. Many questions, with answers. 349 illustrations. x + 448pp. 6½ x 9¼.
20973-3 Paperbound $3.50

REPRODUCTION OF SOUND, Edgar Villchur. Thorough coverage for laymen of high fidelity systems, reproducing systems in general, needles, amplifiers, preamps, loudspeakers, feedback, explaining physical background. "A rare talent for making technicalities vividly comprehensible," R. Darrell, High Fidelity. 69 figures. iv + 92pp.
21515-6 Paperbound $1.35

HEAR ME TALKIN' TO YA: THE STORY OF JAZZ AS TOLD BY THE MEN WHO MADE IT, Nat Shapiro and Nat Hentoff. Louis Armstrong, Fats Waller, Jo Jones, Clarence Williams, Billy Holiday, Duke Ellington, Jelly Roll Morton and dozens of other jazz greats tell how it was in Chicago's South Side, New Orleans, depression Harlem and the modern West Coast as jazz was born and grew. xvi + 429pp.
21726-4 Paperbound $3.00

FABLES OF AESOP, translated by Sir Roger L'Estrange. A reproduction of the very rare 1931 Paris edition; a selection of the most interesting fables, together with 50 imaginative drawings by Alexander Calder. v + 128pp. 6½x9¼.
21780-9 Paperbound $1.50

AGAINST THE GRAIN (A REBOURS), Joris K. Huysmans. Filled with weird images, evidences of a bizarre imagination, exotic experiments with hallucinatory drugs, rich tastes and smells and the diversions of its sybarite hero Duc Jean des Esseintes, this classic novel pushed 19th-century literary decadence to its limits. Full un-abridged edition. Do not confuse this with abridged editions generally sold. Intro-duction by Havelock Ellis. xlix + 206pp. 22190-3 Paperbound $2.50

VARIORUM SHAKESPEARE: HAMLET. Edited by Horace H. Furness; a landmark of American scholarship. Exhaustive footnotes and appendices treat all doubtful words and phrases, as well as suggested critical emendations throughout the play's history. First volume contains editor's own text, collated with all Quartos and Folios. Second volume contains full first Quarto, translations of Shakespeare's sources (Belleforest, and Saxo Grammaticus), Der Bestrafte Brudermord, and many essays on critical and historical points of interest by major authorities of past and present. Includes details of staging and costuming over the years. By far the best edition available for serious students of Shakespeare. Total of xx + 905pp. 21004-9, 21005-7, 2 volumes, Paperbound $7.00

A LIFE OF WILLIAM SHAKESPEARE, Sir Sidney Lee. This is the standard life of Shakespeare, summarizing everything known about Shakespeare and his plays. Incredibly rich in material, broad in coverage, clear and judicious, it has served thousands as the best introduction to Shakespeare. 1931 edition. 9 plates. xxix + 792pp. 21967-4 Paperbound $4.50

MASTERS OF THE DRAMA, John Gassner. Most comprehensive history of the drama in print, covering every tradition from Greeks to modern Europe and America, including India, Far East, etc. Covers more than 800 dramatists, 2000 plays, with biographical material, plot summaries, theatre history, criticism, etc. "Best of its kind in English," New Republic. 77 illustrations. xxii + 890pp. 20100-7 Clothbound $10.00

THE EVOLUTION OF THE ENGLISH LANGUAGE, George McKnight. The growth of English, from the 14th century to the present. Unusual, non-technical account presents basic information in very interesting form: sound shifts, change in grammar and syntax, vocabulary growth, similar topics. Abundantly illustrated with quota-tions. Formerly Modern English in the Making. xii + 590pp. 21932-1 Paperbound $4.00

AN ETYMOLOGICAL DICTIONARY OF MODERN ENGLISH, Ernest Weekley. Fullest, richest work of its sort, by foremost British lexicographer. Detailed word histories, including many colloquial and archaic words; extensive quotations. Do not con-fuse this with the Concise Etymological Dictionary, which is much abridged. Total of xxvii + 830pp. 6½ x 9¼. 21873-2, 21874-0 Two volumes, Paperbound $7.90

FLATLAND: A ROMANCE OF MANY DIMENSIONS, E. A. Abbott. Classic of science-fiction explores ramifications of life in a two-dimensional world, and what happens when a three-dimensional being intrudes. Amusing reading, but also use-ful as introduction to thought about hyperspace. Introduction by Banesh Hoffmann. 16 illustrations. xx + 103pp. 20001-9 Paperbound $1.25

POEMS OF ANNE BRADSTREET, edited with an introduction by Robert Hutchinson. A new selection of poems by America's first poet and perhaps the first significant woman poet in the English language. 48 poems display her development in works of considerable variety—love poems, domestic poems, religious meditations, formal elegies, "quaternions," etc. Notes, bibliography. viii + 222pp.
22160-1 Paperbound $2.50

THREE GOTHIC NOVELS: THE CASTLE OF OTRANTO BY HORACE WALPOLE; VATHEK BY WILLIAM BECKFORD; THE VAMPYRE BY JOHN POLIDORI, WITH FRAGMENT OF A NOVEL BY LORD BYRON, edited by E. F. Bleiler. The first Gothic novel, by Walpole; the finest Oriental tale in English, by Beckford; powerful Romantic supernatural story in versions by Polidori and Byron. All extremely important in history of literature; all still exciting, packed with supernatural thrills, ghosts, haunted castles, magic, etc. xl + 291pp.
21232-7 Paperbound $2.50

THE BEST TALES OF HOFFMANN, E. T. A. Hoffmann. 10 of Hoffmann's most important stories, in modern re-editings of standard translations: Nutcracker and the King of Mice, Signor Formica, Automata, The Sandman, Rath Krespel, The Golden Flowerpot, Master Martin the Cooper, The Mines of Falun, The King's Betrothed, A New Year's Eve Adventure. 7 illustrations by Hoffmann. Edited by E. F. Bleiler. xxxix + 419pp.
21793-0 Paperbound $3.00

GHOST AND HORROR STORIES OF AMBROSE BIERCE, Ambrose Bierce. 23 strikingly modern stories of the horrors latent in the human mind: The Eyes of the Panther, The Damned Thing, An Occurrence at Owl Creek Bridge, An Inhabitant of Carcosa, etc., plus the dream-essay, Visions of the Night. Edited by E. F. Bleiler. xxii + 199pp.
20767-6 Paperbound $1.50

BEST GHOST STORIES OF J. S. LEFANU, J. Sheridan LeFanu. Finest stories by Victorian master often considered greatest supernatural writer of all. Carmilla, Green Tea, The Haunted Baronet, The Familiar, and 12 others. Most never before available in the U. S. A. Edited by E. F. Bleiler. 8 illustrations from Victorian publications. xvii + 467pp.
20415-4 Paperbound $3.00

MATHEMATICAL FOUNDATIONS OF INFORMATION THEORY, A. I. Khinchin. Comprehensive introduction to work of Shannon, McMillan, Feinstein and Khinchin, placing these investigations on a rigorous mathematical basis. Covers entropy concept in probability theory, uniqueness theorem, Shannon's inequality, ergodic sources, the E property, martingale concept, noise, Feinstein's fundamental lemma, Shanon's first and second theorems. Translated by R. A. Silverman and M. D. Friedman. iii + 120pp.
60434-9 Paperbound $2.00

SEVEN SCIENCE FICTION NOVELS, H. G. Wells. The standard collection of the great novels. Complete, unabridged. *First Men in the Moon, Island of Dr. Moreau, War of the Worlds, Food of the Gods, Invisible Man, Time Machine, In the Days of the Comet.* Not only science fiction fans, but every educated person owes it to himself to read these novels. 1015pp. (USO) 20264-X Clothbound $6.00

LAST AND FIRST MEN AND STAR MAKER, TWO SCIENCE FICTION NOVELS, Olaf Stapledon. Greatest future histories in science fiction. In the first, human intelligence is the "hero," through strange paths of evolution, interplanetary invasions, incredible technologies, near extinctions and reemergences. Star Maker describes the quest of a band of star rovers for intelligence itself, through time and space: weird inhuman civilizations, crustacean minds, symbiotic worlds, etc. Complete, unabridged. v + 438pp.   (USO) 21962-3 Paperbound $2.50

THREE PROPHETIC NOVELS, H. G. WELLS. Stages of a consistently planned future for mankind. *When the Sleeper Wakes,* and *A Story of the Days to Come,* anticipate *Brave New World* and *1984,* in the 21st Century; *The Time Machine,* only complete version in print, shows farther future and the end of mankind. All show Wells's greatest gifts as storyteller and novelist. Edited by E. F. Bleiler. x + 335pp.   (USO) 20605-X Paperbound $2.50

THE DEVIL'S DICTIONARY, Ambrose Bierce. America's own Oscar Wilde— Ambrose Bierce—offers his barbed iconoclastic wisdom in over 1,000 definitions hailed by H. L. Mencken as "some of the most gorgeous witticisms in the English language." 145pp.   20487-1 Paperbound $1.25

MAX AND MORITZ, Wilhelm Busch. Great children's classic, father of comic strip, of two bad boys, Max and Moritz. Also Ker and Plunk (Plisch und Plumm), Cat and Mouse, Deceitful Henry, Ice-Peter, The Boy and the Pipe, and five other pieces. Original German, with English translation. Edited by H. Arthur Klein; translations by various hands and H. Arthur Klein. vi + 216pp.
20181-3 Paperbound $2.00

PIGS IS PIGS AND OTHER FAVORITES, Ellis Parker Butler. The title story is one of the best humor short stories, as Mike Flannery obfuscates biology and English. Also included, That Pup of Murchison's, The Great American Pie Company, and Perkins of Portland. 14 illustrations. v + 109pp.   21532-6 Paperbound $1.25

THE PETERKIN PAPERS, Lucretia P. Hale. It takes genius to be as stupidly mad as the Peterkins, as they decide to become wise, celebrate the "Fourth," keep a cow, and otherwise strain the resources of the Lady from Philadelphia. Basic book of American humor. 153 illustrations. 219pp.   20794-3 Paperbound $2.00

PERRAULT'S FAIRY TALES, translated by A. E. Johnson and S. R. Littlewood, with 34 full-page illustrations by Gustave Doré. All the original Perrault stories— Cinderella, Sleeping Beauty, Bluebeard, Little Red Riding Hood, Puss in Boots, Tom Thumb, etc.—with their witty verse morals and the magnificent illustrations of Doré. One of the five or six great books of European fairy tales. viii + 117pp. 8⅛ x 11.   22311-6 Paperbound $2.00

OLD HUNGARIAN FAIRY TALES, Baroness Orczy. Favorites translated and adapted by author of the *Scarlet Pimpernel.* Eight fairy tales include "The Suitors of Princess Fire-Fly," "The Twin Hunchbacks," "Mr. Cuttlefish's Love Story," and "The Enchanted Cat." This little volume of magic and adventure will captivate children as it has for generations. 90 drawings by Montagu Barstow. 96pp.
(USO) 22293-4 Paperbound $1.95

THE RED FAIRY BOOK, Andrew Lang. Lang's color fairy books have long been children's favorites. This volume includes Rapunzel, Jack and the Bean-stalk and 35 other stories, familiar and unfamiliar. 4 plates, 93 illustrations x + 367pp.
21673-X Paperbound $2.50

THE BLUE FAIRY BOOK, Andrew Lang. Lang's tales come from all countries and all times. Here are 37 tales from Grimm, the Arabian Nights, Greek Mythology, and other fascinating sources. 8 plates, 130 illustrations. xi + 390pp.
21437-0 Paperbound $2.75

HOUSEHOLD STORIES BY THE BROTHERS GRIMM. Classic English-language edition of the well-known tales — Rumpelstiltskin, Snow White, Hansel and Gretel, The Twelve Brothers, Faithful John, Rapunzel, Tom Thumb (52 stories in all). Translated into simple, straightforward English by Lucy Crane. Ornamented with headpieces, vignettes, elaborate decorative initials and a dozen full-page illustrations by Walter Crane. x + 269pp.
21080-4 Paperbound **$2.00**

THE MERRY ADVENTURES OF ROBIN HOOD, Howard Pyle. The finest modern versions of the traditional ballads and tales about the great English outlaw. Howard Pyle's complete prose version, with every word, every illustration of the first edition. Do not confuse this facsimile of the original (1883) with modern editions that change text or illustrations. 23 plates plus many page decorations. xxii + 296pp.
22043-5 Paperbound $2.75

THE STORY OF KING ARTHUR AND HIS KNIGHTS, Howard Pyle. The finest children's version of the life of King Arthur; brilliantly retold by Pyle, with 48 of his most imaginative illustrations. xviii + 313pp. 6⅛ x 9¼.
21445-1 Paperbound $2.50

THE WONDERFUL WIZARD OF OZ, L. Frank Baum. America's finest children's book in facsimile of first edition with all Denslow illustrations in full color. The edition a child should have. Introduction by Martin Gardner. 23 color plates, scores of drawings. iv + 267pp.
20691-2 Paperbound $2.50

THE MARVELOUS LAND OF OZ, L. Frank Baum. The second Oz book, every bit as imaginative as the Wizard. The hero is a boy named Tip, but the Scarecrow and the Tin Woodman are back, as is the Oz magic. 16 color plates, 120 drawings by John R. Neill. 287pp.
20692-0 Paperbound $2.50

THE MAGICAL MONARCH OF MO, L. Frank Baum. Remarkable adventures in a land even stranger than Oz. The best of Baum's books not in the Oz series. 15 color plates and dozens of drawings by Frank Verbeck. xviii + 237pp.
21892-9 Paperbound $2.25

THE BAD CHILD'S BOOK OF BEASTS, MORE BEASTS FOR WORSE CHILDREN, A MORAL ALPHABET, Hilaire Belloc. Three complete humor classics in one volume. Be kind to the frog, and do not call him names . . . and 28 other whimsical animals. Familiar favorites and some not so well known. Illustrated by Basil Blackwell. 156pp.
(USO) 20749-8 Paperbound $1.50

EAST O' THE SUN AND WEST O' THE MOON, George W. Dasent. Considered the best of all translations of these Norwegian folk tales, this collection has been enjoyed by generations of children (and folklorists too). Includes True and Untrue, Why the Sea is Salt, East O' the Sun and West O' the Moon, Why the Bear is Stumpy-Tailed, Boots and the Troll, The Cock and the Hen, Rich Peter the Pedlar, and 52 more. The only edition with all 59 tales. 77 illustrations by Erik Werenskiold and Theodor Kittelsen. xv + 418pp. 22521-6 Paperbound $3.50

GOOPS AND HOW TO BE THEM, Gelett Burgess. Classic of tongue-in-cheek humor, masquerading as etiquette book. 87 verses, twice as many cartoons, show mischievous Goops as they demonstrate to children virtues of table manners, neatness, courtesy, etc. Favorite for generations. viii + 88pp. $6\frac{1}{2}$ x $9\frac{1}{4}$. 22233-0 Paperbound $1.50

ALICE'S ADVENTURES UNDER GROUND, Lewis Carroll. The first version, quite different from the final Alice in Wonderland, printed out by Carroll himself with his own illustrations. Complete facsimile of the "million dollar" manuscript Carroll gave to Alice Liddell in 1864. Introduction by Martin Gardner. viii + 96pp. Title and dedication pages in color. 21482-6 Paperbound $1.25

THE BROWNIES, THEIR BOOK, Palmer Cox. Small as mice, cunning as foxes, exuberant and full of mischief, the Brownies go to the zoo, toy shop, seashore, circus, etc., in 24 verse adventures and 266 illustrations. Long a favorite, since their first appearance in St. Nicholas Magazine. xi + 144pp. $6\frac{5}{8}$ x $9\frac{1}{4}$. 21265-3 Paperbound $1.75

SONGS OF CHILDHOOD, Walter De La Mare. Published (under the pseudonym Walter Ramal) when De La Mare was only 29, this charming collection has long been a favorite children's book. A facsimile of the first edition in paper, the 47 poems capture the simplicity of the nursery rhyme and the ballad, including such lyrics as I Met Eve, Tartary, The Silver Penny. vii + 106pp. (USO) 21972-0 Paperbound $2.00

THE COMPLETE NONSENSE OF EDWARD LEAR, Edward Lear. The finest 19th-century humorist-cartoonist in full: all nonsense limericks, zany alphabets, Owl and Pussycat, songs, nonsense botany, and more than 500 illustrations by Lear himself. Edited by Holbrook Jackson. xxix + 287pp. (USO) 20167-8 Paperbound $2.00

BILLY WHISKERS: THE AUTOBIOGRAPHY OF A GOAT, Frances Trego Montgomery. A favorite of children since the early 20th century, here are the escapades of that rambunctious, irresistible and mischievous goat— Billy Whiskers. Much in the spirit of Peck's Bad Boy, this is a book that children never tire of reading or hearing. All the original familiar illustrations by W. H. Fry are included: 6 color plates, 18 black and white drawings. 159pp. 22345-0 Paperbound $2.00

MOTHER GOOSE MELODIES. Faithful republication of the fabulously rare Munroe and Francis "copyright 1833" Boston edition—the most important Mother Goose collection, usually referred to as the "original." Familiar rhymes plus many rare ones, with wonderful old woodcut illustrations. Edited by E. F. Bleiler. 128pp. $4\frac{1}{2}$ x $6\frac{3}{8}$. 22577-1 Paperbound $1.00

TWO LITTLE SAVAGES; BEING THE ADVENTURES OF TWO BOYS WHO LIVED AS INDIANS AND WHAT THEY LEARNED, Ernest Thompson Seton. Great classic of nature and boyhood provides a vast range of woodlore in most palatable form, a genuinely entertaining story. Two farm boys build a teepee in woods and live in it for a month, working out Indian solutions to living problems, star lore, birds and animals, plants, etc. 293 illustrations. vii + 286pp.

20985-7 Paperbound $2.50

PETER PIPER'S PRACTICAL PRINCIPLES OF PLAIN & PERFECT PRONUNCIATION. Alliterative jingles and tongue-twisters of surprising charm, that made their first appearance in America about 1830. Republished in full with the spirited woodcut illustrations from this earliest American edition. 32pp. $4\frac{1}{2}$ x $6\frac{3}{8}$.

22560-7 Paperbound $1.00

SCIENCE EXPERIMENTS AND AMUSEMENTS FOR CHILDREN, Charles Vivian. 73 easy experiments, requiring only materials found at home or easily available, such as candles, coins, steel wool, etc.; illustrate basic phenomena like vacuum, simple chemical reaction, etc. All safe. Modern, well-planned. Formerly *Science Games for Children*. 102 photos, numerous drawings. 96pp. $6\frac{1}{8}$ x $9\frac{1}{4}$.

21856-2 Paperbound $1.25

AN INTRODUCTION TO CHESS MOVES AND TACTICS SIMPLY EXPLAINED, Leonard Barden. Informal intermediate introduction, quite strong in explaining reasons for moves. Covers basic material, tactics, important openings, traps, positional play in middle game, end game. Attempts to isolate patterns and recurrent configurations. Formerly *Chess*. 58 figures. 102pp. (USO) 21210-6 Paperbound $1.25

LASKER'S MANUAL OF CHESS, Dr. Emanuel Lasker. Lasker was not only one of the five great World Champions, he was also one of the ablest expositors, theorists, and analysts. In many ways, his Manual, permeated with his philosophy of battle, filled with keen insights, is one of the greatest works ever written on chess. Filled with analyzed games by the great players. A single-volume library that will profit almost any chess player, beginner or master. 308 diagrams. xli x 349pp.

20640-8 Paperbound $2.75

THE MASTER BOOK OF MATHEMATICAL RECREATIONS, Fred Schuh. In opinion of many the finest work ever prepared on mathematical puzzles, stunts, recreations; exhaustively thorough explanations of mathematics involved, analysis of effects, citation of puzzles and games. Mathematics involved is elementary. Translated bv F. Göbel. 194 figures. xxiv + 430pp. 22134-2 Paperbound $3.50

MATHEMATICS, MAGIC AND MYSTERY, Martin Gardner. Puzzle editor for Scientific American explains mathematics behind various mystifying tricks: card tricks, stage "mind reading," coin and match tricks, counting out games, geometric dissections, etc. Probability sets, theory of numbers clearly explained. Also provides more than 400 tricks, guaranteed to work, that you can do. 135 illustrations. xii + 176pp.

20335-2 Paperbound $1.75

MATHEMATICAL PUZZLES FOR BEGINNERS AND ENTHUSIASTS, Geoffrey Mott-Smith. 189 puzzles from easy to difficult—involving arithmetic, logic, algebra, properties of digits, probability, etc.—for enjoyment and mental stimulus. Explanation of mathematical principles behind the puzzles. 135 illustrations. viii + 248pp.
20198-8 Paperbound $1.75

PAPER FOLDING FOR BEGINNERS, William D. Murray and Francis J. Rigney. Easiest book on the market, clearest instructions on making interesting, beautiful origami. Sail boats, cups, roosters, frogs that move legs, bonbon boxes, standing birds, etc. 40 projects; more than 275 diagrams and photographs. 94pp.
20713-7 Paperbound $1.00

TRICKS AND GAMES ON THE POOL TABLE, Fred Herrmann. 79 tricks and games—some solitaires, some for two or more players, some competitive games—to entertain you between formal games. Mystifying shots and throws, unusual caroms, tricks involving such props as cork, coins, a hat, etc. Formerly *Fun on the Pool Table*. 77 figures. 95pp.
21814-7 Paperbound $1.25

HAND SHADOWS TO BE THROWN UPON THE WALL: A SERIES OF NOVEL AND AMUSING FIGURES FORMED BY THE HAND, Henry Bursill. Delightful picturebook from great-grandfather's day shows how to make 18 different hand shadows: a bird that flies, duck that quacks, dog that wags his tail, camel, goose, deer, boy, turtle, etc. Only book of its sort. vi + 33pp. 6½ x 9¼. 21779-5 Paperbound $1.00

WHITTLING AND WOODCARVING, E. J. Tangerman. 18th printing of best book on market. "If you can cut a potato you can carve" toys and puzzles, chains, chessmen, caricatures, masks, frames, woodcut blocks, surface patterns, much more. Information on tools, woods, techniques. Also goes into serious wood sculpture from Middle Ages to present, East and West. 464 photos, figures. x + 293pp.
20965-2 Paperbound $2.00

HISTORY OF PHILOSOPHY, Julián Marías. Possibly the clearest, most easily followed, best planned, most useful one-volume history of philosophy on the market; neither skimpy nor overfull. Full details on system of every major philosopher and dozens of less important thinkers from pre-Socratics up to Existentialism and later. Strong on many European figures usually omitted. Has gone through dozens of editions in Europe. 1966 edition, translated by Stanley Appelbaum and Clarence Strowbridge. xviii + 505pp.
21739-6 Paperbound $3.50

YOGA: A SCIENTIFIC EVALUATION, Kovoor T. Behanan. Scientific but non-technical study of physiological results of yoga exercises; done under auspices of Yale U. Relations to Indian thought, to psychoanalysis, etc. 16 photos. xxiii + 270pp.
20505-3 Paperbound $2.50